Omni

Dead Giveaway

and

What Bloody Man Is That?

Simon Brett

Back-In-Print Books Ltd

Copyright © Simon Brett 1985, 1987, 2004

The right of Simon Brett to be identified as the Author of the Work has been asserted by Simon Brett in accordance with the Copyright, Designs and Patents Act 1988.

Published by Back-In-Print Books Ltd 2004
ISBN 1 903552 48 6
Previously published in Great Britain by
Victor Gollancz under ISBN 0 575 03719 9 and 0 575 04003 3

All rights reserved. No part of this publication may be reproduced, stored in a retrieval system or transmitted, in any form or by any means without the prior written permission of the publisher, nor be otherwise circulated in any form of binding or cover other than that in which it is published and without a similar condition being imposed on the subsequent purchaser.

A CIP catalogue record is available from the British Library.

Printed and bound on demand by
Lightning Source.

Back-In-Print Books Ltd
PO Box 47057
London SW18 1YW
020 8637 0975

www.backinprint.co.uk
info@backinprint.co.uk

When Simon Brett studied at Oxford he became President of the OUDS, appeared in cabarets and directed the Oxford Theatre Group at the Edinburgh Festival Fringe in 1967.

Later he worked as a light entertainment producer for BBC radio and TV before taking up writing full time in 1979.

Simon created the Charles Paris and Mrs Pargeter detective series and, to his fans' relief, he is still writing more. He also made a name as the author of the radio and TV series *After Henry*. The radio series *No Commitments*, the best-selling *How to be a Little Sod* and the novel *Shock to the System* filmed starring Michael Caine are other fruits of his imaginative mind. He is married, has three children and lives in a village on the South Downs.

This is a Back-In-Print Book.

• This title was out of print for some time but Back-In-Print Books has brought it back in to print because of demand from Simon Brett fans.

• This re-print was produced on demand using digital printing technology.

• Paper and print quality are higher than most conventionally printed paperback novels.

• Digital printing may cost somewhat more but ensures that book titles need not go out of print as long as there are readers who want them.

What other titles are available from BiP?

Check out our web site at www.backinprint.co.uk for other titles released by Back-In-Print Books Ltd and news about forthcoming titles.

Do you want any other titles?

If you know of a title which is out of print and you think there might be a reasonable demand please contact us.

Back-In-Print Books Ltd
PO Box 47057
London SW18 1YW
020 8637 0975

www.backinprint.co.uk
info@backinprint.co.uk

DEAD GIVEAWAY

To Wendy and Chris

BY THE SAME AUTHOR:

CAST, IN ORDER OF DISAPPEARANCE
&
SO MUCH BLOOD

STAR TRAP
&
AN AMATEUR CORPSE

A COMEDIAN DIES
&
THE DEAD SIDE OF THE MIKE

SITUATION TRAGEDY
&
MURDER UNPROMPTED

MURDER IN THE TITLE
&
NOT DEAD, ONLY RESTING

A SERIES OF MURDERS
&
CORPORATE BODIES

A RECONSTRUCTED CORPSE
&
SICKEN AND SO DIE
&
DEAD ROOM FARCE

Chapter One

'MR...PARIS DID you say?'

'Yes.'

The girl on the desk at West End Television's main Reception looked dubiously down at a list. Charles Paris's name didn't seem to leap out of the page at her.

'For what show did you say?'

'*If The Cap Fits*.'

This title did not dispel her scepticism. 'No show of that name down on my list.'

'It's a pilot of a new game show. Something to do with hats.'

'Hats. Ah.' Comprehension dawned slowly. 'That might be what I've got down here as *Hats Off!*'

'It could be. Maybe the title's been changed. As I say, it is only a pilot. Studio A,' Charles added helpfully.

'Yes, that's where *Hats Off!*'s booked in.' The girl was forced, regretfully, to accept his *bona fides*. 'All right. If you like to sit down over there, someone will be down shortly.'

'Thank you.'

Charles started towards the low upholstered sofa she had indicated, when the girl's voice stopped him. 'That is, unless you're one of the celebrities. If you are, they'll send someone down specially.'

He turned to look at her.

'No,' she said. 'No, of course not. You go and sit and wait over there.'

He had to confess it hurt. Charles Paris was not an actor with an excessive amount of pride, but to have his non-celebrity status identified so immediately was a little galling. It rubbed in the humiliation of his very presence at West End Television that afternoon. As his agent, Maurice Skellern, had told him with considerable glee, the booking had only been made late the previous day.

'Just had a call from W.E.T.,' Maurice had announced over the phone.

'Oh yes?' Charles had replied eagerly. The shock of his agent's actually ringing him had given way to exciting fantasies of leading parts in long-running television series.

'They're doing this new game show.'

'Really?' The fantasies shifted to produce a new, suave Charles Paris on a panel of celebrities, quipping away with the best of them.

'Yes. Thing is, one of the rounds they have people from different professions and the contestants have to guess what they do from what they look like.'

'Oh?'

'For reasons best known to themselves, they want one of the people to be an actor.'

'Ah.'

'Obviously, though, they can't run the risk of having a face the punters are going to recognise.'

'No.'

'So they rang me to see if I'd got any actors on my books who the public were very unlikely to have seen.'

'Oh.'

'I thought of you immediately, Charles.'

Some actors might have reacted to this backhanded insult, some put the phone down, some bawled out their agent, many turned down the job. But Charles had been in the business too long, and been out of work too long, to afford such luxuries as pride. A job was a job. He'd agreed to participate.

The sofa on which he sat was extravagantly low, in keeping with the glamour of television. It was also extravagantly uncomfortable. It might have been all right for someone lying flat on his back, but any normal-sized adult trying to sit on it had to fold like a bank-note. Charles looked at the other people waiting in similar discomfort on similar sofas, and wondered whether any of them was involved in *If The Cap Fits*. Maybe they too were representatives of professions which had to be identified from their appearance. He tried to play the game, and came up with a bank cashier, an estate agent, a professional footballer, a dental nurse and a test pilot. But he didn't feel confident that he had scored very highly.

One of the lifts swished open and a girl emerged. She wore a khaki flying-suit, the television uniform of that autumn, and carried that symbol of television authority, a clipboard. Her hair was cut in the rigid shape of a crash-helmet and dyed the colour of copper beech. Her poise was daunting.

The pale-blue eyes went straight to the girl at the Reception desk, who nodded with something not far removed from contempt towards the sofas. The pale-blue eyes flickered upwards in a gesture of mock-prayer before joining her mouth in a professional smile as the girl moved towards her quarries.

'Good afternoon. Which ones of you are for *If The Cap Fits*?'

Charles, two other men and one girl rose with difficulty from their sofas. He'd been wrong about the estate agent and the test pilot, who did not stir.

'Hello. Welcome to West End Television. My name's Sydnee Danson.'

Why, thought Charles, not for the first time, why do girls in television always have silly names?

'I'm one of the researchers on *If The Cap Fits*. The producer and everyone else is delighted that you've all agreed to take part in the show, and we think you're really going to have a fun day. If you like to follow me, we'll go down to the studio and then you'll see what you have to do.'

A certain amount of mutual introduction and feeble joking ensued as the four followed the unnerving Sydnee to the lift doors. She pressed the button to go down, then looked back for another covert (but not quite covert enough to be unseen by Charles) grimace of mock-despair to her friend on Reception.

Her expression changed sharply as she saw someone coming through the main doors. 'Quick,' she hissed, like a demented sheepdog, hustling her charges towards a door marked EMERGENCY STAIRS. 'In here!'

They scrambled through in confusion and found themselves on a small concrete landing. Sydnee leant panting against the door after she had closed it.

'Sorry,' she replied to the four quizzical expressions. 'That was one of the contestants coming in. They mustn't see you till the show or the game's ruined.'

'What, so you've got to keep us apart all afternoon?'

'Yes,' said Sydnee, and then added without great enthusiasm, 'that's my job.'

The set for *If The Cap Fits* was a geometric confusion of red, blue and silver. Against the backdrop tall triangles of blue provided an Alpine horizon, in front of which was mounted a wheel of red, around whose perimeter the title *If The Cap Fits* was picked out in large letters of silver. Another blue triangle, this time tapering downwards, provided a lectern in the centre of the area, and to one side a long rectangular blue desk was set in front of four red chairs. On the desk were four red-and-blue-striped drinking glasses; another stood on the lectern beside a red-and-blue-striped carafe. Across the front of the desk and of the lectern the show's name was again printed in silver, lest the viewing public should at any time forget which programme they were watching (a very real danger in the world of game shows).

As Sydnee ushered her four 'professions' into the studio, a young man with a raven-black Mohican haircut and black leather bondage-suit was anxiously checking the spin of the red wheel. Over the studio loudspeakers a jingle was playing. Falsetto voices at high speed sang the deathless lyric,

If the cap fits,
If the cap fits,
If the cap FITS!

The noise was, to Charles's mind, nauseating. But the jingle, and the set, raised interesting questions about the show's title. 'It is called *If The Cap Fits* then?' he asked Sydnee, who was standing at his side.

She turned her incurious pale-blue eyes at him. 'What?'

'The show is called *If The Cap Fits*?'

'Yes. Of course it is.'

'At Reception they said something about *Hats Off!*.'

'Ah, that's the title of the American version. There was some thought of keeping that for here...until quite recently.'

'Not very recently.'

'What do you mean?' For the first time there was a glint of mild interest in her eye.

'Well, it must have taken time to get the set built and the music recorded.'

'Yes.' She nodded slowly, recognizing with a degree of surprise that she was talking to someone who knew a little about television. For a second Charles saw in her eyes that there might be a real person somewhere behind her professional exterior.

The moment passed as she raised her voice to address her charges.

'This is the set where you'll be performing. Shortly you'll be meeting the show's host.

'Oh, who is it?' asked the one female in the party.

'Barrett Doran.'

'Ooh,' she intoned with a wide-eyed giggle. 'My lucky day. I think he's dead sexy.'

To Charles, who was not a student of television game shows, the name meant nothing.

Sydnee continued her routine. 'You'll actually be standing over here when you do your bit, which is incidentally in the First Round...' She led the little group across the floor towards a blue-and-silver-striped flat. The black-leather Mohican turned as they passed. His face was white and anxious.

'This is Sylvian, who's designed the set.'

'Ooh, well done, Sylvian,' said the one female in the party. 'It's really lovely.'

The designer gave a twitchy nod in reaction to the compliment and turned back to his red wheel.

Before Sydnee could give more instructions, her attention was caught by the entry of a dumpy woman with blonded hair, on whose contours a khaki flying-suit hung less flatteringly. The new arrival carried not only a clipboard, but also a stopwatch, suggesting that her authority was that of a Producer's Assistant. She gave an imperious gesture and Sydnee scuttled across towards her.

A whispered conference ensued, and the researcher returned with her professional smile screwed back in place. 'I'm sorry. I'm afraid Barrett won't actually be able to come down to the studio for the moment, but the Executive Producer, John Mantle, should be along shortly and....'

She stopped on another gesture from the dumpy woman and crossed over for another quick whisper. 'No, I'm sorry,' Sydnee apologised as she returned, 'John Mantle's still tied up in...er, an important meeting, but the Producer, Jim Trace-Smith, will be here in a minute and he'll be able to brief you. Meanwhile, perhaps we ought to sort out the actual hats that you'll be wearing for the show.' Pitching her voice up, she called to the studio in general, 'Is there anyone from Wardrobe around?'

Her plea produced a tired-looking girl in a silver flying-suit and a limp-looking bald man in a pink flying-suit.

'I wondered if you'd sorted out the hats for the First Round...?' asked

Sydnee with diplomatic diffidence.

'More or less,' the girl replied, and then revealed the reason for the researcher's tentative approach. 'But we're still not happy about it. I mean, Wardrobe is about costumes that people *wear*. Hats for a game show I'd still have said come under Props.'

'Yes, I see your point, but the hats are actually going to be *worn*,' Sydnee cajoled. 'These people here are going to wear them.'

The girl's sniff showed that she remained unconvinced. 'Well, I've talked to Head of Wardrobe and she says we should do it for today – under protest, mind – but if the show goes to a series, alternative arrangements may well have to be made.'

'Yes, yes,' the researcher agreed readily. 'Let's cross that bridge when we come to it. But can we see what you've got for us today?'

The bald man in the pink flying-suit was grudgingly despatched, and soon came back with a selection of hat-boxes. 'But we would like to make it clear that we're still not happy about it,' he insisted.

'Yes, I understand.' Sydnee reached eagerly towards the boxes.

'Do you mind?' said the girl shirtily. 'You're not Wardrobe, are you?'

'No.'

'Well, handling hats is a Wardrobe job.'

'Yes, of course.' Sydnee withdrew, her poise momentarily threatened, while the girl from Wardrobe demanded, 'Right, who wants what?'

Sydnee stepped forward again. 'Now you see, each one of them has to wear a hat which symbolises his or her profession. Did you get the list of professions?'

'No,' the girl replied stonily.

'Well, Charles Paris here, for instance, is an actor…'

'Oh yes?' The girl in silver battle-dress reached into a box, pulled out a floppy Tudor bonnet and thrust it at Charles. 'Try that.'

He put it on. It was too big. 'I'm not sure that this actually says "actor"…' he began.

'That,' the girl hissed in a voice that brooked no disagreement, 'is what actors wear. That is your hat. That is what you will wear. You are now responsible for it. You will look after it. You will see that no one else wears it.'

'Ah,' said Charles. 'Right.'

'Erm…' Sydnee interposed. 'I'm afraid that won't quite work. You see, the point of the game is that they don't wear their right hats.'

The girl from Wardrobe looked at her pityingly.

'No, you see, they have to wear the wrong hats, and it's up to the punters – er, the contestants to change them round and get them wearing the right ones. That's why the game's called what it's called. *If The Cap Fits*,' Sydnee concluded lamely.

'Look, you wanted hats to fit four people. Now you tell me you don't want them to fit those four people – they've got to fit four other people. What is going on?'

'No, they're not meant to fit four other specific people. The contestants may move them around. They're meant to fit any of them, all four of them.'

The girl from Wardrobe folded her arms over her silver flying-suit. Her tired mouth took on an even harder line. 'I am not in Wardrobe to supply hats that don't fit. I am trained to supply costumes that do fit.'

Sydnee looked fazed. It was not clear how she was going to get out of this one. But, before she could attempt any solution, her eye caught movement at the side of the studio and was once again lit up by sudden panic. 'Quick, quick!' she cried. 'Someone's bringing the contestants in! Come on – this way!'

And again she did her sheepdog routine, bundling the four 'professions' out of Studio A.

Sydnee's party came through double doors out of Studio A and started up the corridor which led towards the lifts. As they approached, the lift doors opened and their leader saw something which made her reverse promptly, shepherding her flock back the way they had come.

'What was it?'

'Just getting out of the lift. Nick Jeffries.'

'Ooh,' squealed the one female in the party. 'You mean Nick Jeffries, the boxer?'

'Yes. He's on the panel for the show.'

'Ooh, you've got all the sexy ones on, haven't you? Did you select them. EH?'

This last was accompanied by a huge nudge to Sydnee, who offered hardly even a pretence of a smile in return. Then she looked behind her and saw, to her horror, a bulky man in a plush sheepskin jacket following them down the corridor. 'It's Nick Jeffries,' she gasped. 'Quick, in here!'

She thrust open the nearest door, over which a sign read, STUDIO B. AUTHORISED PERSONNEL ONLY.

They found themselves in darkness, cramped between a wall and a loose hanging curtain. 'Follow me,' urged Sydnee. They followed. Rounding the corner of the curtain, the five of them were momentarily blinded by the sudden glare of studio lights.

The set in Studio B was considerably smaller than that in Studio A. (Indeed, the whole studio was smaller.) It represented a study-like room, a cross between a barrister's chambers and an amateur laboratory. Shelves of leather-bound books encased the walls, while the surfaces were littered with a variety of phials and retorts. Firearms, daggers and the occasional skull had been scattered in calculated disorder. The set could have been designed for an updated remake of Sherlock Holmes.

And, though the man at the centre of this space could not have been mistaken for the great detective, he was, as it happened, speaking of crime. 'And here we have it –' he was saying, in an exaggerated French accent, indicating a small elegantly-shaped bottle with a glass stopper which he held between thumb and forefinger, 'perhaps the quickest-acting of all poisons. Cyanide. Beloved of detective-story writers, though significantly less popular with real murderers. Cyanide can kill in as little as ten seconds. Well, though I said it is not popular with murderers, there have still been one or two juicy cases where it was the favoured method. In 1907 Richard Brinkley...'

'Ooh, it's Melvyn Gasc,' hissed the one female in the party, peering at the speaker beyond the cameras. 'He did that series on torture, didn't he?'

'This is the follow-up,' Sydnee hissed back. 'It's called *Method In Their Murders*. Being made for Channel Four.'

'What are you doing here?' a third female voice hissed. Charles could make out a shapely outline in a flying-suit of indeterminate colour which had stepped in between his group and the light.

'Chippy. It's me, Sydnee. I'm trying to keep this lot out of the way. Mustn't be seen by the others in this game show.'

'Barrett's thing?'

'Yes.'

'Has the Great Shit himself put in an appearance yet?'

'He's around.'

'Maybe I should go and have a word with him…'

'No, Chippy. This show's going to be hectic enough without that kind of complication.'

'I don't know. I'd just be interested to see how the bastard reacted if I walked in. I bet he'd –'

But the girl called Chippy was cut short by another hissing voice, male this time, as a Floor Manager, complete with headphones, came up and asked what the hell was going on and what the hell they thought they were doing bursting into a studio while there was a rehearsal in progress and whether they would piss off out again double-quick or whether he'd have to bloody kick them out.

Sydnee peered out into the corridor as they beat their hasty retreat from Studio B, but all seemed to be clear. 'We'd better go back on to our set,' she said, and then, with a note almost of desperation in her voice, went on, 'Barrett may be there, or John, or Jim. Then we can get your bit of rehearsal sorted out. Or the hats sorted out. Or something…'

She got them to wait in the corridor while she slipped to check that Studio A was clear of contestants and celebrities. She took her duties seriously.

Within a minute they were ushered back on to the red, blue and silver set. Sylvian the Mohican was still fiddling, unhappy with the alignment of the lectern in the centre of the floor. Three cameramen were slumped lethargically over their cameras. There were more people around than there had been earlier in the afternoon.

One of them was Jim Trace-Smith, the Producer. Since there was no sign of Barrett Doran, and the Executive Producer, John Mantle, had yet to return from his, er, important meeting, it had fallen to Jim Trace-Smith to brief the 'professions' as to what they had to do.

The Producer was tall with dark-brown hair which stuck out on his crown as if cut by a school barber. There was something boyish about his whole appearance. Even his pale-blue flying-suit looked as if it had come from Mothercare. His face would have been astonishingly youthful, but for the almost comical creases of anxiety which were etched in between the eyebrows. He had the air of someone who took life *very seriously indeed*.

Nor was this impression dispelled when he began to speak. His voice had a slight Midlands flatness which, even when his words expressed great enthusiasm, seemed impervious to animation.

'Good afternoon, one and all.' He made what was perhaps intended to be an expansive gesture. 'And may I say how delighted I am that you have agreed to join us in the fun of *Hats Off!*'

'*If The Cap Fits*,' murmured Sydnee.

'Oh yes, *If The Cap Fits*. It's a really terrific game and I think there's no question that you're all going to have a ball. Now, as you've probably gathered, the show that we're recording tonight is what we call a "pilot". That means that we've all got to be our brilliant best, because, according to how we do this show, the "powers-that-be" will decide whether or not they're going to make a series of this terrific game. And we all want to make sure that there is a series of *If The Cap Fits* – don't we?'

This proposal was heartily endorsed by three of the 'professions'. Charles thought he'd reserve judgement until he'd found out what the game involved.

'Does it mean,' asked the one female in the party, 'being a pilot, that what we record will actually go out on the box?'

'Oh, almost certainly, yes,' the Producer lied. 'As I say, it's a terrific game. I'm sure we've got the casting right, and I'm sure that what we record tonight will be the first show in a series that will run and run!'

He made this rallying-cry with all the bravura of a librarian turning down the central heating.

'Now I hope you're all beginning to understand what you'll have to do. You are involved only in Round One of our terrific game, but I'm sure you're going to get the show off to a great start. Now you've all been carefully selected by our highly-trained research team...' He winked with awkward flirtatiousness at Sydnee, who ignored him.

'...because you all represent some kind of profession. This profession will in each case be symbolised by a hat, but, just to confuse the contestants, you'll all be wearing the wrong hats. They have to guess who are the rightful owners of the various forms of headgear.'

He then proceeded to explain that this was the reason for the game's name, a point which by now had penetrated the skull of even the dullest of the four 'professions'.

'Well,' Jim Trace-Smith continued with limp heartiness, 'have you all got your hats sorted out?'

'Erm, I'm afraid we're having a bit of a problem with Wardrobe about the hats...' Sydnee drew him to one side and a whispered discussion ensued.

When the Producer turned back to his audience, the furrows on his forehead were longer. 'Well now, just got to actually sort out the hats, but can I just check what your professions are...'

He drew a list out of his flying-suit pocket. Charles had been one hundred per cent wrong. There was no bank cashier, no professional footballer and no dental nurse. Instead, his colleagues proved to be a hamburger chef, a surgeon and a stockbroker. Incredibly, the one female in the party turned out to be the stockbroker.

'We've got the actor's hat sorted out,' Sydnee whispered, 'but I don't know where Wardrobe have gone now, so I'm not sure about the others.'

'I'll go and have a word with them,' said Jim Trace-Smith. 'Now we'll need a tall white chef's hat for the chef...'

'Actually that's not what I wear,' the chef objected. 'I have this little paper cap which –'

'*So far as the public's concerned*,' Jim Trace-Smith overruled, 'chefs wear tall white hats. Now for the surgeon we need one of those green mob-cap things...'

'Actually I very rarely wear one of those. I...' But the surgeon thought better of it and stopped.

'Now we've got the actor's hat sorted out.'

'Well –' was as far as Charles was allowed to get.

'And for the stockbroker, obviously, a bowler hat.'

'But I never wear a bowler hat.'

'So far as the public is concerned, stockbrokers wear bowler hats!'

'But I'm a woman, for God's sake! You can't expect me to –'

How this argument would have resolved itself can only be matter for speculation, because at that moment Sydnee's restless eye caught sight of a man and a woman entering the far side of the studio. 'Oh, my God, it's Bob Garston and Fiona Wakeford! Jim, the celebs are arriving! Quick, you lot, follow me!'

She started off, with her obedient foursome in tow, towards the exit that led to Studio B, but was stopped short in her tracks by the entry from it of a familiar bulky figure, followed by a dainty little woman in a fur coat and a short, balding, pale man.

'Oh God, it's Nick again! And Joanie Bruton! Quick! This way!'

The hamburger chef, the surgeon, the stockbroker and the actor, now as obsessed as their guardian with keeping their identities secret, dived after her through the door that led to the Control Gallery of Studio A, and left the set to the celebrities who were to be the stars of *If The Cap Fits*.

Chapter Two

JOHN MANTLE, EXECUTIVE Producer of *If The Cap Fits*, reckoned that he was doing well. As the third round of Armagnacs was served in Langan's Brasserie, he sneaked a covert look at his watch. Nearly half-past three. Even if they left within a quarter of an hour and got a taxi straight away, it would be well after four before they got back to W.E.T. House. And the longer they kept out of Studio A that afternoon, the better.

This thought was not prompted by laziness or an unwillingness to face his responsibilities. John Mantle was a deeply conscientious producer. He had been conscientious during the eight years he had spent learning his craft in the Light Entertainment Department of B.B.C. Television, and equally conscientious since, three years previously, he had moved to West End Television to do the same job for three times the money. But producing, he knew, did not only involve monitoring what went on in studios. That could frequently be left to an obedient underling, and he had the most biddable of lieutenants in Jim Trace-Smith, also from the B.B.C., whose invaluable attributes of diligence, even temper and total lack of imagination, John Mantle had quickly recognised, made him an ideal producer of Light Entertainment. The young man had been easily seduced into commercial television, again by the simple device of tripling his salary, thus becoming the first recruit to the entertainment empire John Mantle was slowly but surely annexing from his former employers.

The presence of Jim Trace-Smith in Studio A that afternoon at least ensured that the preparations for the pilot were proceeding, and freed the Executive Producer for more important duties, which in this case involved keeping his lunch guests out of Studio A as long as possible. The explosion when they finally got there was inevitable, but the later that happened, the less chance there would be of implementing the changes they were bound to demand.

There were two of them – Aaron Greenberg, podgy, grizzle-bearded, voluble, an untidy eater and drinker who allowed no word to go unsupported by an expansive gesture of his short arms; and Dirk van Henke, tall, blond, silent, drinking only Perrier water and constantly dabbing at his mouth with a corner of his table napkin. They represented the American copyright-holders of *Hats Off!*, the game show which had been successfully networked for three years in the States and the rights to whose format West End Television had bought for an almost unbelievable amount of money. They had followed the piloting and development of the show in the States and were thus the honoured bearers of the

'Bible', that partly written but mostly unwritten stock of information and advice which would save any new developer of the show from falling into the format's most obvious pitfalls. They were extremely protective of their property, regarding any proposed change in the show as a direct personal assault.

Since their arrival in London two days previously, John Mantle had spent every waking hour justifying to Greenberg and van Henke the inevitable alterations which transatlantic relocation of the show demanded. They had fought everything; he had had to explain and re-explain each tiny kink and quibble of the revised format; but, by sheer, relentless, debilitating tact and the granting of a few minor concessions, the Executive Producer had managed to satisfy them that their baby, the property that, as Greenberg kept asserting, meant 'somebody's gonna make a pot', was being treated with the care and respect that was its due. They now knew about every change and, grudgingly, they had accepted them all.

Except the title.

John Mantle had first broached the subject in the hire-car back from Heathrow, where he had personally met their Concorde flight. He had explained that *Hats Off!* did not have the right sound for a British game show, and that, after careful assessment of many possible alternatives, West End Television had decided on *If The Cap Fits*.

'What the shit does that mean?' Aaron Greenberg had asked.

'Well, it's a kind of saying. A proverb, if you like. "If the cap fits, put it on." It means, if something applies to you, then it applies to you...' John Mantle had continued feebly. 'It's a very common expression. Very right for the show. Don't you have that proverb in the States?'

Aaron Greenberg snorted. 'I never heard of it.'

'I think,' said Dirk van Henke in his quiet, precise voice, 'our equivalent would be: "If the shoe fits, wear it".'

'Yes. That sounds as if it has the same meaning.' John Mantle smiled enthusiastically at this point of contact.

'Shit,' objected Aaron Greenberg. 'You're not suggesting we call the show *If The Shoe Fits*? I mean, hell, it's about hats, not shoes.'

'Yes, I know that. Of course I'm not suggesting we call it *If The Shoe Fits*.'

'Thank Christ for that. Otherwise you would have screwed yourself out of a deal that's gonna make a pot for somebody.'

'No, I'm suggesting we call it *If The Cap Fits*.'

'No way. Forget it.'

'But –'

'*Hats Off!*' Dirk van Henke insisted softly. '*Hats Off!*

That is the name of the show. Call it anything else and we don't have a deal.'

The Executive Producer had left it there for the time being. Much of his work consisted of confronting people with unpalatable facts, and he knew that the most important element in any such presentation was always its timing. After he had deposited his guests at the Savoy, where they were going to 'shower and sleep off the Concorde-lag', he had returned to W.E.T. House and got on to the Legal Department, who had negotiated the long, wrangling purchase of the rights to develop the *Hats Off!* format. He wanted to know where he stood legally on changing the title.

Like everything to do with the law, the situation turned out to be ambiguous. The relevant clause was:*The licensees agree not to adapt, rearrange or alter the format in any way without the approval of the owner, such approval not to be unreasonably withheld*.

The crux of the issue was, of course, the last phrase, in particular its penultimate word. What was unreasonable? This, as the Legal Department advised him unhelpfully, was a matter of interpretation. They would investigate and get back to him.

The Executive Producer assessed the position. The set had been designed and built with the changed title all over it. The music links had been recorded. Even if there had been time to reverse the decision, alterations at this late stage would represent considerable expense. And John Mantle always prided himself on keeping within his budgets.

He decided to sit it out. He'd wait and hear what the Legal Department advised when they came back to him, but, unless that was really bad, he would stick by his original decision. It would inevitably lead to tantrums from Greenberg and van Henke, but, if they only found out about the new title on the afternoon of the recording, he judged they would have little opportunity to do anything about it. And, once the show had gone down well in front of the audience, he felt confident that they would be less worried about the change.

He kept his nerve pretty well for the next couple of days. Once he almost lost it, and that moment of uncertainty had led to the confusion of the title at Reception which Charles Paris had encountered. But basically the Executive Producer reckoned he'd get away with it. The Legal Department, when they finally came back to him, had little to add. Everything still depended on the interpretation of the word 'unreasonably', and they couldn't really say how that decision would go in a court of law unless the issue actually *went* to a court of law. In other words, the lawyers proved as helpful as ever.

John Mantle offered more drinks, but even Aaron Greenberg refused this time. As he settled the bill with his American Express Gold Card, the Executive Producer stole another look at his watch. Nearly four. The show started recording at seven-thirty. Only a few hours to survive the Americans' wrath.

On the way out of the Brasserie, he greeted West End Television's Head of Drama who was coming to the end of lunch with a moderately famous actress. As a further delaying tactic, he introduced the couple to his guests. Since the actress had recently been seen in a *Masterpiece Theatre* in the States, conversation developed satisfactorily.

John Mantle was discussing a vicious point of W.E.T. politics with his colleague, when he overheard Greenberg saying, 'Yeah, and do you know what they wanted to call it? Only *If The Cap Fits*!'

'Really?' The moderately famous actress chuckled throatily. 'Why – is it a show about contraception?'

Aaron Greenberg looked puzzled. 'What's that supposed to mean?'

'Cap, darling. Cap. Dutch cap. A form of female contraception.'

The American shook his shaggy head, still bewildered.

'It's a thing you put...' The moderately famous actress gave another throaty chuckle. 'I'm afraid we're liable to get a bit technical here. It's a...what would you call it? A diaphragm!'

'A diaphragm?' Aaron Greenberg echoed. 'You hear that, Dirk? You know that dumb title they wanted to use? *If The Cap Fits*. You know what a "cap" means over here? A diaphragm! A diaphragm, for Christ's sakes!'

John Mantle ushered his guests grimly out of the restaurant. He was not looking forward to the next couple of hours.

Sydnee's game of hide-and-seek with the hamburger chef, the surgeon, the stockbroker and the actor had continued through the afternoon. They had finally had their inappropriate hats grudgingly fitted in Wardrobe, been shown where to stand on the red, blue and silver set, and been conducted up five floors of W.E.T. House to the Conference Room where they were to await their call. Unfortunately, when Sydnee opened the door, she found the four non-celebrity contestants who were to play *If The Cap Fits* already ensconced, and had to beat another hasty retreat.

She led her four charges into an empty office, found a phone and immediately punched four digits. 'Hello. Mandy? Listen, how many Conference Rooms got booked for this pilot today? Well, no, there should have been three. Yes, I know on *Funny Money* it's one for the celebs and one for the punt-...for the members of the public, but in this game we've got two different sets of members of the public and they mustn't meet. Yes, well...what? No, we couldn't put the contestants in with them. Mixing with members of the public?...the celebs'd never wear it. No. Well, is there another Conference Room free? Oh, shit. No, no, okay, not your fault. Don't worry. I'll sort something out. Yes, after this little holocaust, fine. 'Bye.'

She turned to face the hamburger chef, the surgeon, the stockbroker and the actor. 'Sorry. Cock-up on booking. I'm afraid you're going to have to wait here in the Production Office.' She gestured round the room. 'Welcome to where I work. I'll organise some drinks and things for you later.'

'What's that?' The one female in the party pointed up at a wall which was covered with small head-and-shoulders snapshots pinned up in rows.

'Oh, that's our "Ugly Wall",' Sydnee replied. Then she seemed to wish she hadn't said it and try to cover up. 'I mean, it's a very ugly wall, so we just try to stick as many things as possible on it.'

The stockbroker looked more closely at the snapshots. 'These look like the sort of pictures we had to send in when we got your form about taking part in game shows.'

'Oh, do they?' asked Sydnee innocently. 'Now, can I get you all a tea or coffee?

I'm afraid you're going to have rather a long wait. You must understand, with a pilot it's always a bit difficult to work out quite how long all the rehearsal's going to take. I'm sure we'd get it sorted out better if the show ever went to a series.'

'I thought,' the stockbroker objected, 'the producer said it definitely would go to a series.'

'Oh yes. Yes, of course,' said Sydnee.

The office door opened and a tall man with steel-grey hair and thickly-lashed blue eyes entered. Ignoring the other four, he walked straight up to Sydnee. 'Where the bloody hell have you been? Have you got that list of "hat" lines?' he demanded brusquely.

'Oh yes.' She reached into a drawer and produced a few typewritten sheets. 'I went through all the dictionaries and books of quotations. I should think you ought to be able to work out some links from that lot.'

'I'll see. Other thing, check my glass on the set after rehearsal.'

'Your glass?'

'Its contents.'

'Oh. Oh yes,' said Sydnee, understanding.

The four 'professions' remained mystified by this exchange, but the stockbroker, bolder than the others, addressed the grey-haired man. 'It's Barrett Doran, isn't it?'

He turned on her the kind of look rose-growers reserve for greenfly. 'What?'

Sydnee stepped into the breach. 'Barrett, these four are the "professions" for the First Round.'

'Oh,' said Barrett Doran without interest, and turned to leave the room. But, as he reached it, the door opened and he was confronted by a pale youth with ginger hair and an apologetic expression.

'Ah, Barrett. I was looking for you. I have worked out a few one-liners on the "hat" theme. If you want to cast your eye over them, I'll be happy to –'

'I do my own links,' said Barrett Doran. 'I don't need any of your bloody crap.' And he walked out of the office.

The pale youth let the door close behind him and looked at the five who stood there. His face was vulnerable, almost tearful. 'Hello, Sydnee. If there's anything I can...you know, for this lot...'

She introduced him to the hamburger chef, the surgeon, the stockbroker and the actor. 'Jeremy Fowler's our Script Associate on the show. He's got an endless supply of funny lines for all the contestants and everyone. You know, so if you want to have a few witty ripostes, and you can't think of any yourself, ask Jeremy.'

The youth smiled weakly. 'I have got a few lines. I mean, I only got the list of your professions late yesterday, but I have worked out a few things you might say.'

'When?' asked the hamburger chef.

'When?'

'When might we want to say them?'

'Oh. Well, for example, when you've got the wrong hat on. I mean, say someone puts the surgeon's hat on you and you're asked if you are a surgeon, you could say, 'I don't think I'd be cut out for the job.'

'Why?'

'What do you mean – why?'

'Well, why should I say that?'

'It's a joke.'

'Is it?'

'Well, a sort of joke. Not a marvellous one, I agree,' Jeremy Fowler conceded, 'but it's the sort of thing that might get a laugh if you pong it enough.'

'*Pong* it?'

'Yes.'

'I don't understand it.'

'Well, it's a sort of pun. "Cut out for the job"…surgeon…*cut* out…'

'Oh,' said the hamburger chef seriously. 'Oh, I see. I don't think I probably will say that, actually.'

'Ah, well. Never mind. I've got a few lines for the rest of you…you know, if you think you might need them…They will get an opportunity to say something, won't they, Sydnee?'

'A bit, I should think. It really depends how Barrett plays it.'

'Yes. Well, as I say, I have got a few lines about, you know, being a hamburger chef…or a stockbroker...or an actor…or not being them. You know, these games always sound better if you get a bit of repartee going with the host. I mean…Anyone fancy any lines? I could write them down on cards for you or – Well, if you do want any, you only have to ask…as I say…It's up to you, really.'

He ran aground on silence.

'Right,' asked Sydnee brightly. 'How many teas, how many coffees?'

There was a marked contrast in moods in the two Conference Rooms that had been properly booked. One contained the four contestants who were actually going to play *If The Cap Fits*, the other the celebrities whose role was to add a little glamour to the show. In the first there was an atmosphere of obsessive nervousness; in the second, of equally obsessive insouciance.

For the four contestants, the day was the culmination of a long process. They had all originally written in to West End Television, saying how suitable they thought they would be as contestants in the company's major, long-running giveaway show, *Funny Money*. In reply to their letters they had been sent a yellow questionnaire, asking information about age, marital status, work, hobbies and 'any amusing incidents that may have happened in your life'. They had been requested to return the completed form, together with a recent photograph. It was these snapshots which ruled out most of the candidates. Television game shows are constructed on the premise that everyone is attractive, and those whose looks did not meet the researchers' approval had their participation in the world of television restricted to an appearance on Sydnee's 'Ugly Wall'.

Those who survived the scrutiny were requested to appear for interview at a large hotel in their locality on a given date. This date was not negotiable; those who couldn't make it lost their chances of participating in the show. At the interview (which for most of the candidates involved taking a day off work) they were chatted to for up to an hour by Sydnee or another of the researchers, who then decided which contenders attained that level of cheery triviality which game shows demanded.

The four in the Conference Room, having overcome all these hurdles, had been not a little disappointed when their magic phone-calls finally came through. Yes, they had been very impressive in their interviews. They were just the sort of people who would be ideal game show contestants. Unfortunately, W.E.T. had got all the participants required for the current series of *Funny Money*. But the company was about to launch a new game show, bound to be quite as successful as the other – would they like to be in on the start of a milestone in television history?

This was not what most of them had had in mind, but they all (in one case only after checking the value of the prizes that were to be given away) agreed to participate. The initial call had been followed by a letter, outlining the format of *If The Cap Fits*, and then further phone-calls making detailed arrangements about transport and, where necessary, overnight accommodation.

And there they were, actually in a Conference Room in W.E.T. House, guarded by one of Sydnee's fellow-researchers (with the equally silly name of Chita), and about to go down to Studio A to run through the game with the host, the notoriously good-looking and popular Barrett Doran. It was enough to make anyone a bit nervous.

But their nervousness took different forms, because for each of them the prospect of appearing on television had a different significance. For Trish Osborne, who, though she bitterly resented the description, would be introduced on the show as 'a housewife from Billericay', it was a symbolic act, a new start to her fifth decade, a decade in which she intended to assert her own individuality, to be herself rather than somebody's wife or somebody's mother. She had a momentary doubt, wondering whether the silk blouse and skimpy brassiere eventually selected for her appearance in front of the cameras was quite suitable, but she bit it back. This was her, Trish Osborne. She was going to prove that she had as much to offer as all those professional television people. She was going to make an impression. This was going to be the start of something.

For Tim Dyer, participating in *If The Cap Fits* signified something else entirely. For him it was a chance to win, and he was determined that that was what he was going to do. He had studied many game shows from his armchair, making notes on the techniques used by successful contestants. He had spent a long time checking through the format of the new game, and had boned up on General Knowledge and recent international news. He, needless to say, had been the one who had asked about the value of the prizes, and he felt confident that he could finish the evening at least £800 richer, with a video-recorder and camera, the prospect of a champagne weekend for two in Amsterdam and, if all went well, as the owner of a brand-new Austin Metro.

He had prepared himself as far as he could; now all he needed was a little luck. And that luck hinged mainly on which celebrity he was paired with. Joanie Bruton he reckoned was the most intelligent, though Bob Garston was also pretty bright. Either of them would do. Just so long as he didn't get lined up with that thick boxer, Nick Jeffries. Or even worse that dumb actress, Fiona Wakeford. Tim Dyer sat in the Conference Room, praying to that very specialised deity, the God of Game Shows.

In the other Conference Room the objects of his speculation lounged around, studiously laid-back.

None admitted to having read the format of *If The Cap Fits*, which had been sent to them, because this had overtones of swotting, taking the show more seriously than was fitting for someone of celebrity status. Nor had they shown much apparent interest when, first the researcher who was in charge of them, and then Jim Trace-Smith himself, had taken them through the mechanics of the game. It didn't do to look as if it mattered. There were two acceptable attitudes for the celebrities. The first was bonhomous condescension, as if one were helping West End Television out of a spot by taking part, just because one was that sort of person. The second was mercenary bewilderment…'The agent rang about it, I said how much, he said three hundred quid…well, I thought, I was only going to watch the box tonight otherwise, so what the hell, why not do it?'

They were a contrasted quartet, who might have prompted a philosophical observer to speculate on the nature of celebrity. However, the only observer present was a researcher called Quentin, so armoured with cynicism and so unsurprised by anything that television or fame could bombard him with, that such philosophical speculations did not arise.

Nick Jeffries' boxing career had ended three years previously. Its start, his winning of an Olympic bronze medal in the Middleweight division, had prompted the customary excesses of the British sporting press, who promised him a professional career of pure gold and saluted a future World Champion. He had held domestic and European titles for a while, but, when projected on to the world stage, had been so comprehensively defeated by the Number Eight contender that his boxing career virtually ended with that fight. However, his face was familiar to the British public through his many endorsements of sportswear, and since, unlike many in his chosen profession, he was capable of speech, he was taken up by a shrewd personal management and marketed as a celebrity. His long-term aim (which he would not achieve) was to attain that level of lovability which the British public had accorded to Henry Cooper. His short-term aim that afternoon (which would be achieved much more easily) was to chat up Fiona Wakeford.

She was an actress who had risen to public notice in a popular W.E.T. sit com, *Who's Your Friend?*, in which she played a pretty but totally brainless actress. Since this did not involve the slightest effort of acting on her part, her career looked set fair to be very successful. She didn't mind Nick Jeffries chatting her up. In fact, she was so used to everyone chatting her up that she was hardly aware of it. She wasn't aware of much, actually.

The other woman panellist was a very different proposition. Joanie Bruton had started life as a journalist on local newspapers and then moved towards women's magazines. The illness of the regular contributor on one of these had forced her one week to write the agony column, and she discovered such an aptitude for this line of work that within three years she had become a nationally-recognised guru, whose advice was solicited and respected on every embarrassing topic. Her petite good looks, forthright manner and boundless energy had quickly established her as a popular television personality. She made no secret of her appetite for hard work, and, when interviewed (which she was quite frequently) constantly paid tribute to the support of her husband, Roger, who had given up his own Civil Service job in the Department of Health and Social Security to manage the business side of her burgeoning career. He was there in the Conference Room that afternoon, a pale, rather breathlessly fat figure, checking through a pile of correspondence with his untiring spouse.

The fourth celebrity also appeared to be working, though the restlessness in his eyes suggested that he was motivated more by keeping up with the Joneses (or, in this case, the Brutons) than from a genuine desire to read the television script in front of him (which of course had nothing to do with *If The Cap Fits*; it was for a B.B.C. series called *Joe Soap*).

Bob Garston was a television journalist of the 'New Hearty' school. He had risen through those programmes of the late Seventies which had taken up serious causes like consumerism and treated them with such unremitting facetiousness that they produced a television equivalent of the tabloid press. He was the sort of presenter for whom no word was allowed out unsupported by a picture and no opinion unsupported by a pun. He worked assiduously on his image as a man of the people, and prided himself on the fact that the audience identified with him. In his heart of hearts he felt superior to everyone, but that afternoon, as he neglectfully scanned the script in front of him, he looked disgruntled.

The door to the Conference Room opened. Quentin, the guardian researcher, glanced up protectively, but then relaxed as Jeremy Fowler sidled in with his customary air of apology.

'Er, good afternoon. I'm the Script Associate on this show...I've worked out a few lines, you know, that some of you might want to use.'

'What sort of lines?' asked Joanie Bruton.

'Well, you know, er, funny lines...I mean, there may be a moment when you want to make a joke and, er, well, I've worked out a few jokes that might be suitable.'

'Oh, I'm hopeless when I try to do that,' confessed Fiona Wakeford. 'Honestly, I can never remember the line, and I get the joke all wrong and it's worse than if I hadn't said anything. I'm terribly stupid.'

No one contradicted her. Joanie Bruton and Bob Garston returned to their work, but Nick Jeffries looked interested. He recognised his limitations in the field of repartee. 'What sort of lines you got?'

'Well, erm, a lot of hat jokes. I mean, the show being about hats...you know.'

'Like...'

'Well, erm, there's this one about the man whose neighbour's dog eats his hat.'

'Who – the neighbour's hat?'

'No, no, the man's hat. And the man goes to complain, and the neighbour gets belligerent.'

'Gets what?'

'Gets angry...And the man says, "I don't like your attitude", and the neighbour says, "It wasn't my attitude, it was your attitude!"'

'Eh?'

'It's a pun. Attitude. 'At...'e...chewed. Hat. You see, the dog had chewed the hat. Get it?'

'Not really. I mean, this bloke didn't like the other bloke's attitude, I get that. But what I don't see is...'

The explanation of the joke might have gone on for some time, had the door not opened at that moment to admit John Mantle, still with his two Americans in tow. He was still playing his delaying game and keeping them out of Studio A. The detour up to the Fifth Floor Conference Room, ostensibly just to introduce the copyright-holders to the panellists, was, he reckoned, worth at least ten minutes. But he knew he couldn't keep them in ignorance much longer.

While introductions were taking place, the telephone rang and was answered by the researcher. 'All wanted down in studio,' he announced, 'to meet the contestants.'

'Oh Jesus! I didn't think we'd have to see that lot till the actual recording,' complained Bob Garston, the man of the people.

'Sorry. We've got to just run through a bit of rehearsal on the bits you do with them.'

'Shit,' said Bob Garston, with bad grace.

John Mantle decided that they'd all go down to Studio A together. He knew that he could no longer put off the crisis, but he hoped his American guests' reactions might be a little inhibited by the presence of the celebrities.

It was a vain hope. The minute the party walked on to the set, Aaron Greenberg looked up at the red wheel with its silver lettering and screamed, 'Christ Almighty! What the shit is that supposed to be?'

'John,' Dirk van Henke hissed in the Executive Producer's ear, 'you have just lost the rights in *Hats Off!*'

Chapter Three

JOHN MANTLE WAS no fool. He had been prepared for this reaction, and he had planned how to deal with it. For the time being, he led the two furious Americans up to his office and let the wave of anger wash over him.

'I mean, for Christ's sakes!' Aaron Greenberg was spluttering. 'What kind of a show do you think this is? We can't have that kind of talk on a show like this. Diaphragms? No way. I mean, this is meant to be wholesome family entertainment. This show will be going out to Middle America.'

'Actually, it won't be. You forget that –'

'Okay, Middle Europe. Who's counting?'

'Not actually Europe. This is England and –'

'England – Europe – what's the difference? The point is that, wherever it is, there are gonna be little old ladies out there who know what they want and who aren't gonna to want to turn on a show about diaphragms.'

'That isn't the first meaning most people will think of when they hear the title.'

'No? Well, listen, smartass, I've only mentioned it to one person and that's what she thought.'

'I'm not sure that actresses are typical of –'

'Don't you try telling me what's typical or not typical! All I know is that you're calling this show by the wrong name! And that's going to lose you your audience and lose you the chance of making a pot. I mean, for Christ's sakes, we're talking about the Golden Goose here and you're trying to wring its neck before it's laid a single goddamned egg!'

'What is more,' Dirk van Henke insinuated, 'you are in breach of contract.'

John Mantle let them go on. In a little while, he would summon his adviser from the Legal Department. Then maybe the Americans would produce a London-based lawyer to fight their side. All that would take time and, even if eventually they could take out some sort of injunction to stop W.E.T. from proceeding with the show (which, on balance, John Mantle thought was unlikely), there was a strong chance that by then the pilot would be recorded.

So he rode out the storm, confident all the while that downstairs in Studio A rehearsals for *If The Cap Fits* were still going on.

Barrett Doran was no keener to meet the contestants than Bob Garston had been, but Jim Trace-Smith insisted that they must rehearse the basic sequence of the show or the whole thing would be a shambles when they came to record it. Barrett Doran grudgingly agreed to this, though he was not going to put himself out by being polite to anybody.

His first action, on coming into the studio, was to look at the red, blue and silver set in horror. 'Jesus,' he said, 'what the hell's this? I didn't know the show was meant to be set in a bloody fast food restaurant. Is it no longer possible to get professional designers? What's the problem – money? Is that why we have to put up with this crap?'

Sylvian de Beaune, who had been slumped in the front row of the audience seating, rose as if to protest, but thought better of it, turned on his heel and flounced out of the studio. Jim Trace-Smith's eyes followed him out, then realised that the rehearsal must be moved along to cover this awkwardness.

'Now, for the First Round,' he said, with his customary limp élan, 'each of the contestants has to be paired up with one of the celebrities. This is where they have to change round the hats on the four "professions", and they're allowed to consult on this.'

'Seems to make it unnecessarily complicated.'

'I'm afraid that's how the format works, Barrett. Anyway, the viewing audience likes it. We've done some research on this and we've found out that people at home enjoy seeing the contestants and celebrities being all pals together.'

'Do they really?' growled the lovable Barrett Doran. 'All right, you lot!' He gestured imperiously to the four contestants. 'Come over here. Each of you's got to pair up with one of the panel for the First Round.' He turned to where the four celebrities sat at their long blue desk, sipping from their red-and-blue-striped glasses and discussing their tax problems. 'Now we'll do it so's we get a man and a woman in each line-up, so you, lady, go with Bob, you with Nick, you with Joanie and you with Fiona. Got that?'

'Erm,' Tim Dyer objected. 'Can we change it round? I'd rather be paired with Joanie.'

'Would you?' snapped Barrett Doran. 'Well, I don't give a wet fart what you'd rather do. The pairings will be as I said.'

Tim Dyer wasn't going to stand for that. He'd just been round the back of the set and seen the gleaming, brand-new Metro waiting for the moment when it would be driven on to awe-struck "Aaah"s from the studio audience. 'But I don't want to be with Fiona,' he insisted.

'Why, isn't she pretty enough for you? You think yourself damned lucky. It's the nearest a little shit like you's ever going to get to a bit of crumpet like that.' The host turned to his producer. 'What do you want them to do – stand behind the panellist they're paired with?'

'Yes, behind, slightly to the right. Then we can get them in a nice close two-shot.'

'Okay. Get to those positions.' Barrett Doran looked petulantly back at Jim Trace-Smith. 'Do you really want us to go right through the whole bloody thing?'

'We have to make sure everyone knows what they've got to do, where they've got to stand, that kind of number...'

'Okay, okay.' Barrett Doran went across to his lectern and stood there, drumming his fingers on its top.

Various researchers and stage managers were recruited to stand in the positions later to be occupied by the hamburger chef, the surgeon, the stockbroker and the actor. Some unrepresentative hats had been procured for them (though not from Wardrobe, who said they were still not convinced that they should be providing hats for the actual recording, but were damned sure they weren't going to provide any for rehearsal). The researchers and stage managers then invented professions for themselves and the contestants, with celebrity help, tried to say who should be wearing which hat. Since the hats were wrong anyway, all this took a long time. Barrett Doran conducted the proceedings without even a pretence of geniality.

At the end of the round, Jim Trace-Smith reminded the contestants that they would be awarded money prizes at this point, but that the one with least points would be eliminated. Tim Dyer objected volubly that he would be working under an unfair handicap because Fiona Wakeford was so stupid. The actress proved not quite stupid enough not to realise that this was an insult, and burst out crying. Nick Jeffries threatened to punch Tim Dyer's teeth out through his arse. Jim Trace-Smith managed to reimpose a kind of calm.

In the next round each of the celebrities was supplied with a hat-box by 'the lovely Nikki and the lovely Linzi', two terminally bored-looking models who were part of the set-decoration. The remaining three contestants were then given the names of four types of hat and had in turn to guess whose hat-box contained which hat, helped or misled by clues from the celebrities.

Trish Osborne was the first to play in this round. She had found that, once on the set, her nerves had given way to a mood of almost manic confidence. It was going to be all right. She would manage. Better than that, she would do very well. She would really make an impression.

As she stood beside Barrett Doran at the lectern, he flashed her a big smile. Looking at her for the first time, he had realised that she was rather attractive and thought it might be worth beaming a little of his charm in her direction. Nice short dark hair, full lips, nice trim little figure. Maybe he might invite her to his dressing room for a drink before the recording...He gave her the practice list of four hats – fedora, fire-helmet, beret and baseball cap. Trish started chatting with the celebrities, moving round to her decision. She felt in control. She was doing well.

'Oh God!' Barrett Doran suddenly exclaimed.

Trish Osborne turned curiously towards him.

'Look at her. We can't have this. I mean, God, this is peak viewing, a family show. We can't have her looking like that.'

Trish unwillingly followed the line of his accusing finger, which pointed straight at her bust. In the excitement of the occasion, she saw that both of her nipples had hardened, a fact which the thin blouse and brassiere did nothing to disguise.

Jim Trace-Smith came forward, nonplussed. It was not a situation he had had to deal with before, and he wasn't quite sure of the correct procedure.

'Well, come on,' shouted Barrett Doran. 'Do something. Get her off to Wardrobe. We can't have her looking as if she's panting for it like that. This isn't a bloody tit show, is it?'

At this point, Trish Osborne, utterly deserted by her new confidence, started to cry. She was led off with meaningless words of comfort by the researcher, Chita. In Wardrobe, after an unsuccessful experiment with Sellotape, her nipples were contained by two sticking plasters.

The rehearsal had to stop at six, so that everyone involved in Studio A could get their statutory hour's meal-break and the cameras could be lined up, before the audience was admitted at seven, ready for the seven-thirty recording. When the rehearsal ended, the celebrities and contestants had a variety of options as to where they could go. They could eat in the canteen, they could go and titivate, prepare or relax in their dressing rooms, or they could return to their separate Conference Rooms, now converted by the introduction of alcohol into Hospitality Rooms.

For the hamburger chef, the surgeon, the stockbroker and the actor, who had been stuck in the Production Office all afternoon, there were fewer options. Sydnee, still desperate to keep them apart from the other participants in *If The Cap Fits*, had ruled out their visiting the canteen, and arranged for sandwiches to be brought up to the office. There was, of course, no question of their sharing the largesse of Hospitality in the two Conference Rooms, but, after considerable thought and a few exploratory phone-calls, she decided that it might be safe for them to go downstairs to the W.E.T. bar, 'if any of them wanted to'.

Charles Paris was the first to state that he did want to. It had been a boring afternoon, it promised to be a boring evening, and he had long since discovered the beneficial properties of alcohol in the treatment of boredom. Since his only responsibilities in the show were standing up and putting on different hats, he did not have any anxiety about drink blunting his performing edge. He just knew that he would feel considerably more human with two or three large Bell's inside him.

Sydnee led the four of them conspiratorially down the back-stairs to the bar, which was very crowded. As well as the flood of after-work drinkers from the offices above, there were also many of the Studio A technicians and a lot of the team from Studio B, whose recording schedule for *Method In Their Murders* incorporated the same meal-break.

'I'll dive in and get you some drinks,' said Sydnee bravely. 'Then I must sort out your Make-up calls. That's going to be the most difficult bit of all. There's only one Make-up room and we've got to ensure that you don't meet any of the others in there. Anyway, what will you all drink?'

She took their orders, and thrust her way into the make round the bar. The four 'professions' stood around awkwardly. There was nowhere to sit and the afternoon upstairs had long since exhausted their limited stock of mutual conversation.

Charles saw a little knot of people gathered round Melvyn Gasc, the presenter of *Method In Their Murders*. Gasc had risen to prominence in the previous few years as a pop scientist and, like most who do well on television in that role, was more valued for his eccentricity than his academic qualifications. His plumpness, his broken French accent and his windmilling gestures all made him a readily identifiable persona, which coincided easily with the general public's view of scientists as mad professors. They also made him popular fodder for television impressionists, and Charles thought he could detect an element of self-parody in the vigorous way Gasc was addressing his circle of sycophants.

One of this circle was the girl, Chippy, whom the 'professions' had met on their hurried excursion into Studio B. In better lighting she proved to be strikingly pretty, with wispy blond hair and deep-set dark-blue eyes which gave her an air of melancholy, or even tragedy. As Charles watched, she detached herself from the group and moved towards the door, through which Barrett Doran had just entered.

But she had no opportunity to speak to the host of *If The Cap Fits*. He was immediately swept up by an earnest-looking man in a suit, accompanied by a short, dark, bearded man and a tall, thin, blond one. They were close enough for Charles to hear their conversation.

'Barrett,' said the man in the suit, who was John Mantle. 'Aaron and Dirk were watching a bit of the rehearsal, and they've got a few points.'

'Have they?' growled Barrett Doran. 'Get me a large gin.'

The Executive Producer, apparently cowed by the directness of this order (though in fact shrewdly deciding to leave his game-show host and copyright-holders alone to discuss their differences), made for the bar.

'Now what the hell is this?'

Aaron Greenberg looked Doran full in the eye. 'Just that with you the show is dying.'

'Oh yes?'

'Yes. You aren't getting anything out of these contestants. Okay, they're a bunch of loxes – God knows why your researchers couldn't come up with some with a bit more "pazazz" – but it's still up to you to get a bit of life out of them. The show's coming across like a pile of old dog-shit, and that's because you're such a bummer. If you stay on as host, it's not going to work and the company's going to lose the chance of making a pot. I mean, Eddie, who fronts the show in the States, would never allow anyone to –'

'I don't give a shit what Eddie would or wouldn't allow. I am doing this show – got that? I know my public, I know what they want, and, come the recording, that is what I will give them. So just keep your big nose out of this

– Okay? I've been in this business too long to take advice from some jumped-up little Yid!'

For a second it looked as if Greenberg would hit him, but Dirk van Henke laid a restraining hand on his associate's arm and it didn't happen. Barrett Doran turned away from them and met John Mantle returning from the bar with a large straight gin. He snatched it and hissed at the Executive Producer, 'I'll be in my dressing room. Keep this shit off my back – all right? Or you find yourself another presenter.'

He moved towards the exit, then caught sight of Sydnee, moving, laden with drinks, from the bar. 'You sorted out that glass for me?' he demanded.

She nodded. 'It's done.'

As he made for the door, Chippy moved forward as if to speak to him. Barrett Doran looked right through her.

She recoiled, her face even more tragic, and came disconsolately over towards the group to whom Sydnee was dispensing drinks.

'Now, there we are...a pint, lager and lime, dry white wine, and...yours was the gin and tonic, Charles? Right?'

'Oh. I asked for a whisky, actually.'

'Ah.' Sydnee looked back hopelessly at the increasing crowd around the bar.

'Never mind. That's fine,' said Charles, taking the drink, prepared to change the habits of a lifetime. He didn't like the taste of gin much, but alcohol was alcohol.

Chippy looked as if she wanted to speak to her friend, but she was interrupted by the arrival of a young man, whose earphones and transmitter identified him as a Floor Manager. 'Chippy, Clayton wants to go and have something to eat. Can you go and cover in the studio while he's off?'

'I suppose so.' Chippy didn't sound keen on the idea.

'He's waiting till you come.'

'Okay.' She turned to Sydnee. 'Listen, we'll talk later. Okay?'

'Sure. What have you got to do?'

'Keep an eye on the props in Studio B. We've got some rather valuable – not to say dangerous – stuff down there.'

'Sure. See you.'

Chippy wandered sadly off, and Sydnee went to phone Make-up and try and sort out a schedule for getting the 'professions' made up without meeting anyone they shouldn't. Make-up was proving to be a headache. Already the girls were having to work through their meal-break, which was going to put them on time-and-a-half. At least. Which was going to bump up the budget. Which would not please John Mantle.

The hamburger chef, the surgeon, the stockbroker and the actor stood, sipping their drinks, avoiding each other's eyes, unable to dredge up even the most fatuous scrap of conversation.

Charles Paris downed his gin and tonic, grimacing at the unfamiliar taste. He needed another drink. He hadn't bothered to bring a bottle with him, relying on television's usual plethora of Hospitality Rooms. But it looked as if on this occasion he might have come unstuck. He was going to have to stock up for the evening.

He didn't offer to buy drinks for the others. For one thing, none of them had finished their first round; for another, spending the whole afternoon with them had induced in Charles a kind of selfish misanthropy.

But his path to the bar was obstructed by Sydnee.

'I've sorted it out with Make-up. You're to go down first.'

'When?'

'Now. Straight away.'

'Oh, but I was just going to get another drink.'

'Isn't time. Sorry. They're just finishing with Joanie Bruton at the moment. Then one of the contestants is going in at quarter to seven. They want you at half-past six. Can you go straight there?'

'Well, I –'

'Thanks. And can you be sure you go down the backstairs, through Studio B and then through Studio A? That way there's no risk of you meeting anyone you shouldn't. You know where Make-up is when you come out of Studio A?'

Charles nodded, and left the bar with bad grace. He really needed another drink. It was bad enough to be given a gin instead of a whisky, but then to only have one...It had only been a single, anyway...He felt hard-done-by.

He stomped down the back-stairs, then into Studio B. There was no one about. The cameras were set facing their test-cards, ready for the half-hour's statutory line-up before the recording. The set looked unchanged, with its random scatterings of weapons and phials of chemicals. If Chippy was there guarding the exhibits from Melvyn Gasc's Black Museum, there was no sign of her.

He pushed through the double doors out of Studio B into the corridor, where he encountered the black-leather-clad designer, Sylvian de Beaune, who was pacing anxiously up and down.

'Set looks really terrific,' said Charles encouragingly.

'I hope so.' The designer did not seem to be convinced. 'I hope so,' he repeated, and walked off towards the lifts. Charles pushed through the double doors into Studio A, and found himself alone in the huge, dimly-lit space.

He was halfway across the set when he had the thought. Still feeling self-pityingly disgruntled about only having had one drink, he suddenly remembered Barrett Doran's words to Sydnee about his glass.

It was worth trying. With a look round to check that he was not observed, Charles went across to the blue, triangular lectern. On it stood a red-and-blue-striped carafe and a red-and-blue-striped glass. Both were full of colourless fluid.

The contents of the carafe had no smell.

But the contents of the glass smelt reassuringly of gin.

So that was how Barrett Doran fuelled his bonhomie in front of the cameras.

Charles looked at his watch. Nearly half-past six. He'd have to hurry to Make-up.

Still, that sod Barrett Doran could spare it.

Charles took a long swig from the glass.

Then, opting for a sheep-as-lamb philosophy, he took another.

The alcohol burned comfortingly inside him.

He topped up the glass with water from the carafe, and, feeling more cheerful, went out of the studio to Make-up.

Chapter Four

THE AUDIENCE WHO came to Studio A that evening had, to some extent, been victims of the same disillusionment as the contestants. All of them, applying either as individuals or on behalf of such organizations as Townswomen's Guilds, insurance company social clubs and amateur dramatic societies, had written in asking for tickets to attend a recording of that very popular, long-established game show, *Funny Money*. They had all, instead, been offered tickets for a brand-new game show entitled (as far as they were concerned – indeed, as far as everyone except two irate Americans was concerned) *If The Cap Fits*. There had been few rejections of the offer. After all, television was television, and the show didn't really matter so much as the fact of actually being there.

For many of them, it was their first visit to a television studio, and they gazed around with fascination at the suspended monitors above their heads and the Dalek-like cameras which patrolled the No Man's Land between them and the distant red, blue and silver set.

After a while an inexorably cheerful man, who introduced himself as Charlie Hook, bounced on to the set and welcomed them. It was lovely to see so many smiling faces on such a cold night, he asserted. He could see, just by looking at them, that they were going to be a lovely audience, and W.E.T. had got a really lovely show lined up for them that evening. There were a few lovely parties he'd like to say hello to. Was there a party from the Braintree Afternoon Club? Oh yes, there they were! Well, a really big hello to them. Didn't they look lovely? And were they all set to have a lovely time? Good, yes, that was the spirit. Now, as he said, it was going to be a really lovely show, and to make the show really go with a swing, he wanted to hear lots of lovely laughter and applause from the lovely audience. Would they be lovely enough to oblige him? Good, yes, that was lovely. Now, of course, at W.E.T., they didn't have little men holding up signs saying 'LAUGH' and 'APPLAUD'. What they were after was spontaneous reactions. On the other hand, there could be one or two moments when the audience might need to be told when these spontaneous reactions were required, her, her. So, if they saw him, Charlie, or one of the Floor Managers...Ooh, they'd like to meet the Floor Managers, wouldn't they? Yes, of course they would. Lovely fellows they were, the Floor Managers, lovely fellows. And here they were. Say a lovely big hello. Lovely. So, anyway, if he, Charlie, or one of the Floor

Managers raised their arms *like this*, would they please regard it as a cue to applaud and not a signal that they should leave the room, her, her. Lovely, right, good. Well, it would just be a few minutes before they got on with the show, so perhaps he could tell them a rather lovely story he'd heard a few days before about an Irishman who went into a cafe and ordered a hot dog...

Eventually, Charlie Hook introduced their lovely host for the evening's proceedings, someone they all knew very well from countless other shows, one of the loveliest, most genuine people and one of the most popular faces on British Television – Mr – Barrett – Doran!

As soon as he came on to the set, Barrett switched his charm on like a light-bulb. He chatted with members of the audience, told them he felt terribly nervous, reiterated how important their contribution to the success of the evening would be, explained a little about the mechanics of the game and then introduced 'our four celebrity guests, who will be playing *If The Cap Fits* with us tonight!'

The celebrities came on, with varying degrees of ostentation, and sat down behind their long blue desk. Barrett Doran told the audience that, once the show started, they would be meeting some delightful (and very plucky!) contestants who had also agreed to take part in *If The Cap Fits*. He then asked the Floor Manager how ready everyone was to start the recording. Had to check with 'the boffins in the box', he explained to the audience. Terrific production team they'd got on the show. Great Executive Producer, John Mantle. Really talented Producer, Jim Trace-Smith. Really great back-up team, as well. All great chums, one big happy family. How about a nice round of applause for all those people out of sight whose contribution was so important in making the evening the success it was absolutely bound to be?

The audience duly applauded.

There were a few more delays, but finally the recording was ready to commence. Members of the audience were advised to watch the monitors rather than the set, because the opening credits were on film. The audience duly gawped up at their monitors. They saw the clock which was used to identify the programme. It was started and ticked away for sixty seconds. For the last three of these the screen went blank.

Animated credits of cartoon figures changing hats appeared. High-pitched jingle voices sang out the words as the title, *If The Cap Fits*, appeared in silver letters on the screen. A deep, unseen voice intoned portentously, 'And tonight, on *If The Cap Fits*, our star prizes include...a portable video-recorder and lightweight camera...'

A shot of this hardware, carried by a grinning, bikini-clad Nikki, was shown on the screen. 'Ooh,' went the audience, and applauded.

'...a champagne weekend for two in Amsterdam...'

An inappropriate clip of a Dutch windmill appeared. 'Ooh,' went the audience, and applauded.

'...and tonight's super-duper star prize – a brand-new Austin Metro with all the extras, plus a full year's tax, insurance and petrol!'

The Austin Metro appeared on screen. Through its open window a grinning, bikini-clad Linzi waved awkwardly. 'Aaaaah,' went the audience, and applauded frantically.

More cartoon figures changed hats. 'All these could be won tonight by some lucky contestant,' the voice continued, 'if the cap fits! And here's the man who wears a variety of hats with equal success...Barrett Doran!'

The show's host bounced, smiling, up to his lectern. The audience gave him an ovation which might have been warranted if he had just invented an antidote to radiation sickness.

'Hello, hello, and thank you very much. Welcome to *If The Cap Fits*. And if it doesn't, well...keep it under your hat! Thank you, thank you. And without more ado – nice girl, Moira Do, pity she couldn't be with us tonight...thank you – without Moira Do, let's meet our panel of celebrities who are going to find out for themselves tonight...*if the cap fits!*

'First, it's a great pleasure to welcome that lovely actress, who you all know as Lizzie Parsons from that very funny series, *Who's Your Friend?* – Fiona Wakeford!'

The actress simpered prettily in response to the applause.

'Tell me, Fiona,' asked Barrett, 'are you really as dumb as you appear?'

'Well, no,' she replied, bewildered. 'I can talk.'

The audience screamed at this Wildean riposte.

'Next we have a gentleman who really packs a punch – Nick Jeffries!'

The audience saluted their faded Great White Hope.

''Ere!' The boxer made a fist. 'I don't like your attitude.'

The audience hailed another shaft of wit.

'Actually, Barrett,' Nick went on as the noise subsided, 'that reminds me of a joke about a man with a dog. This bloke –'

'I make the jokes around here,' said the host with a smile on his lips and a deterrent steeliness in his eyes. 'Next, we have a lady who's brought happiness to millions – and without taking her clothes off, which has to be a novelty – the country's favourite Agony Aunt – Joanie Bruton!'

The audience roared as she smiled in a brisk, no-nonsense manner.

'Tell me, Joanie – or may I call you Auntie? – could you help me with a little personal problem that I have?'

'Perhaps, Barrett.'

'Well, my trouble is that I keep thinking I'm a pair of curtains. What do you think I should do about it?'

'Pull yourself together, love.' Joanie completed the old joke with commendable promptness and the audience howled their appreciation for this devastating sally.

'Finally, we have a gentleman who never seems to be off your television screen these days, investigating frauds, righting wrongs, standing up for the little man...you may know him as Joe Soap – Bob Garston!'

The last panellist gave his gritty, proletarian smile as the audience clapped.

'Tell me, Bob, have you ever come across a major fraud that involved hats?'

'No, you're the first one, Barrett.'

The audience bayed with delight, honoured to be participants in this rare feast of wit. 'Eat your heart out, Congreve,' they seemed to say.

Barrett Doran's smile stayed in place, but the reaction of his eyes to Bob Garston's crack was less genial. 'And now, as well as this splendid line-up of celebrities, we also have four brave – or should I say foolish? – members of the public who have agreed to be with us tonight to play *If The Cap Fits*!'

On this cue, one of the high-pitched jingles was played and, under cover of the music, the four contestants, propelled by the invisible Chita, moved awkwardly on to the set. Barrett Doran, scooping up a little pile of printed cards from his lectern, moved across to greet them effusively.

'Now first we have a very charming lady who's come all the way from Billericay. Patricia Osborne is her name, but she's known to her friends as Trish.' He beamed the full force of his charm straight at her, and putting on a babyish voice, asked, 'Can I be one of your friends and call you Trish?'

'Of course, Barrett.'

'Terrific. Now I gather, Trish, that you're not the world's greatest decorator…'

'Not really, Barrett, no.'

'In fact…' He consulted the card, on which the researchers had summarised the answers to the 'any amusing incidents that may have happened in your life' part of their questionnaire. '…I gather you once papered your bedroom with vinyl wallpaper and woke up next morning to find it had all fallen off the walls on top of your bed!'

'That's right, Barrett,' Trish agreed over the audience's hoots of delight.

'And I bet your husband said, 'Trish, that's the vinyl straw!'

'No, he didn't actually.' But Trish Osborne's response was lost in the audience's acclamation of their favourite epigrammatist.

The other three contestants were introduced with comparable wit, and then the rules for the First Round were explained. The four contestants were paired with their celebrity helpers. (A last ditch attempt by Tim Dyer not to be landed with Fiona Wakeford was brutally thwarted.) Then, to the sound of another jingle, the hamburger chef, the surgeon, the stockbroker and the actor moved into their pre-arranged positions. The hamburger chef was wearing the Tudor bonnet, the surgeon the bowler, the stockbroker the chef's hat, and the actor the green hygienic cap. The camera moved slowly from one to the other, while the participants and audience tried to estimate which face went with which profession.

In turn, each contestant and celebrity team rearranged the hats to their satisfaction. Graphics superimposed over the picture recorded their guesses. It was all very riotous. Two out of the four contestants unhesitatingly identified Charles Paris as the hamburger chef.

To much oohing and aahing, Barrett Doran then gave the correct solutions.

Contestants and celebrities responded with extravagant hand-over-face reactions to their errors. The four 'professions' smiled fixedly as their true identities were revealed. The stockbroker was asked if she really was a stockbroker, the hamburger chef was asked to go easy on the onions, and the surgeon was asked if the first cut really was the deepest. The actor wasn't asked anything. The four were then fulsomely thanked for their participation and, as soon as the camera was off them, hustled unceremoniously off the set by a Floor Manager. At least one of them went straight to the bar and spent the rest of the evening there, risking topping up the earlier gins with Bell's whisky.

Which meant that Charles Paris didn't see the rest of that evening's rather unusual recording.

Points and money prizes were then awarded to the contestants. They got £50 for each correct hat. Two had scored a maximum of £200. One of these was Tim Dyer, who congratulated himself on his tactic of having ignored everything Fiona Wakeford said. The other was Trish Osborne. A third contestant scored £100. The fourth, who had managed to get them all wrong, was thanked by Barrett Doran for being a really good sport and asked if she had had a good evening. She assured him it had been the best of her life, before she was consigned to the outer limbo off the set. But, the audience was told, she would not be going away empty-handed. No, she would take with her a special *If The Cap Fits* cap, hand-made in red and blue velvet with a silver tassel. A shot of this artefact appeared on the audience's monitors and was greeted by the statutory 'Ooh'.

The three survivors were then detached from their celebrity assistants for Round Two. The lovely Nikki and the lovely Linzi, still (for the most basic of audience-pulling reasons) dressed in bikinis, brought on four red-and-blue-striped hat-boxes which they placed on the long blue desk beside each panellist. Barrett Doran read out a list of five types of hat (one was a red herring), and asked the four celebrities in turn to read out a clue of mind-bending ambiguity about the contents of their box. The contestants then had to hazard guesses as to which box contained which hat. The celebrities responded to these guesses with much elaborate bluffing, double-bluffing, tactical drinking from their water-glasses and heavy gesturing. Again, graphics recorded the contestants' final decisions and, at the end, Barrett Doran made his startling revelation of the truth. It was all very riotous.

Once again, £50 depended on each hat. With the red herring, that meant a possible total of £250, which Tim Dyer, much to his satisfaction, achieved. This win also earned him the portable video-recorder and camera. Trish Osborne had got two hats the wrong way round, so only won another £150. But she was still in contention. The third contestant, having identified only one hat correctly, departed from the show with £150 in winnings from his two rounds and, of course, with his *If The Cap Fits* cap.

'So,' Barrett Doran asserted, 'everything to play for after the break! See you in a couple of minutes, when once again it'll be time to see...if the cap fits!'

Barrett Doran left the set immediately the END OF PART ONE caption came up. Charlie Hook came forward to tell the audience what a lovely time they were having and what lovely people they were and how lovely the second part of the show was going to be. And weren't the panellists lovely? And the contestants. Lovely, really, lovely.

Then Jim Trace-Smith came on to the set. The Producer, Charlie Hook explained to the audience, needed some 'cutaway shots'. These were just reactions from some of the participants, which might have to be cut in later and would make editing the show a lot easier. Jim Trace-Smith only needed to do reaction shots with the two eliminated contestants; he'd do any others he needed at the end of the recording of Part Two. So the two failed candidates were hauled back on to the set, made to stand in fixed positions and asked to go through a variety of facial reactions – delight, annoyance, excitement, frustration, despair. Neither of them had much aptitude for it; they lacked the professional performer's ability to switch expressions at will; so the recording process took longer than it should have done.

But at last all was set for the restart. A Make-up girl flashed in with a final puff of powder for the face of Tim Dyer, on whom the pressure was showing in the form of sweat. The designer, Sylvian de Beaune, leapt on to the set for one last check of the position of the blue lectern. A Floor Manager escorted Barrett Doran back from his dressing room or wherever he had been. Charlie Hook gave the audience one last reminder that they were lovely, the clock was again started and the jingle and caption for PART TWO appeared.

Round Three was a simple General Knowledge round, though it was dressed up in a way that conformed with the hat theme of the rest of the show. The lovely Nikki and the lovely Linzi, still in their inevitable bikinis, entered carrying a large red-and-blue-striped box with a small opening at the top. Each of the surviving contestants had to reach into this box and pull out a hat. The hat dictated the subject on which they would be questioned. Once they knew the subject they were entitled to choose the celebrity guest who they thought best qualified to help them answer questions on that subject. They had five questions each. An incorrect answer gave the other player a chance at the question. Each question was worth £40, offering £200 for five correct answers (or, in the unlikely event of one contestant getting all five wrong and the other getting them all right, £400 for ten correct answers).

Trish Osborne pulled out a nurse's hat. This meant her questions would be on Medicine. Which of the celebrities, Barrett Doran asked, did she think would be best qualified to help her on that subject? Nick Jeffries volunteered his services, saying that he had always fancied nurses. Bob Garston said he'd got a badge for First Aid when he'd been in the Boy Scouts. It was all very riotous. Trish Osborne shrewdly chose to be helped by Joanie Bruton.

Tim Dyer's lengthy scrabbling in the box produced an opera hat. Nobody knew instinctively what subject this suggested, and Barrett Doran had to explain that it was the sort of hat worn by a first-nighter, so it meant Tim would be answering questions on the Theatre. So who was he going to have helping him? Well, it didn't seem too difficult to come up with an answer to that, did it...*when they actually had an actress on the panel*? Tim Dyer chose to be helped by Bob Garston.

'Right, so, Trish and Joanie, we start with you. And here's your first question: Which part of your body would be affected if you were suffering from galucoma? Glaucoma.'

Joanie whispered to Trish.

'Your eye.'

'Yes, that's right. Glaucoma is a disease of the eye. Well done. Forty pounds to add to your growing total, Trish. Over to Tim and Bob, and your questions, remember, are on the Theatre. Here's your first one: Who was the first actor ever to be knighted? The first actor ever to be knighted?'

A hurried consultation was followed by the answer, 'Henry Irving'.

'Henry Irving, good. Yes, that is the correct answer. Henry Irving became *Sir* Henry Irving in 1895. Well done. Back to the lovely ladies...'

It was nip and tuck all the way. Joanie and Trish missed out on their third question: How do you spell psittacosis?, but Bob and Tim couldn't do it either, so the scores remained level. The men couldn't get the answer to their third either. They didn't know which actress once played Hamlet with a wooden leg. Trish, prompted by Joanie, identified Sarah Bernhardt. One ahead.

The 'lovely ladies' couldn't answer their fourth; nor could the men. But the men got their own fourth answer right, so, with one question each to go, the scores were once again level.

'Right, ladies. Your last question,' said Barrett portentously, 'who was the Roman God of Healing and Medicine?'

Trish Osborne looked totally blank. Joanie Bruton's pretty little brow wrinkled as she tried to dredge up some distant memory.

'Have to hurry you. Who was the Roman God of Healing and Medicine?'

Joanie whispered to her partner.

'Was it Hippocrates?' asked Trish tentatively.

'No, I'm sorry, it wasn't. The correct answer was Aesculapius. Aesculapius was the Roman God of Healing and Medicine.'

A spasm of annoyance crossed Joanie Bruton's face. She recognised the right answer and felt cross with herself for not having said it.

'So it's over to the gentlemen, for a question which could win for you, Tim, not only a nice lot of money to add to what you've already collected, but also a champagne weekend in Amsterdam to add to your video-recorder and camera. Not only that, if you get this question right, you will also take part in our *Hats In The Ring!* finale, with a chance to win this evening's Super-Duper Star Prize – the Austin Metro!'

The audience exhaled a long sigh of gratified materialism.

'So here is your last question on the subject of Theatre:

From which of Shakespeare's plays does the following famous line come – "Once more unto the breach, dear friends, once more!"?'

Tim Dyer looked as if he knew, but, cautiously, he double-checked with Bob Garston. They both seemed to be in agreement.

'*Henry V.*'

'...is the right answer!' screamed Barrett Doran. The audience erupted into applause, through which another jingle played.

'Oh well done, Tim. Well done, Tim and Bob. But, ladies and gentlemen, a round of applause for our gallant loser. Thanks to Joanie Bruton, who nearly got her to the final, but not quite – and a big hand for Trish Osborne! Many thanks for playing the game, Trish. Have you had a good time?'

'Yes, thank you, Barrett, it's been really smashing.'

'That's great. That's what we like to hear. And, of course, Trish isn't going to go back to Billericay empty-handed. No, she takes with her £470 and don't let's forget....' He cued the audience to join in with him. '...her *If The Cap Fits* cap!'

Again the red, blue and silver creation appeared on the screen, as Trish Osborne was led off into the darkness.

Tim Dyer was looking very pleased with himself. All was going according to plan. He had won everything he intended so far. Only the Austin Metro remained. Quietly confident, he prayed again to his own specialised God.

'Now, for the big *Hats In The Ring* finale. Tim, will you come over here.' Barrett led the final contestant on to a little platform in the middle of the red spinning-wheel. 'Now on to this wheel, as you see, a variety of hats are fixed.' He pressed a button and the hats sprang into view. 'Let's see, what have we got – an admiral's hat, a fez, a busby, a bishop's mitre....Now each of these hats has a price marked on it, and that is the amount of extra money that Tim is going to win if that is the hat which, after the wheel has been spun, comes to rest above his head! So, you see, he gets £200 for the mitre, £500 for the busby, and so on...

'Now you'll notice, two of the hats haven't got any price marked on them. There they are – right next door to each other – the dunce's hat and the crown! Now if the dunce's hat comes to rest above your head, Tim, I'm very sorry, but you get absolutely nothing extra.'

'Ooh,' sighed the audience, contemplating a fate worse than death.

'If, on the other hand, it's the crown, you, Tim Dyer, will instantly become the proud owner of a brand-new Austin Metro!'

'Aah,' sighed the audience, reassured, and burst into spontaneous applause.

'Right, are you ready, Tim?'

The contestant, still praying and now glistening with sweat, nodded. All the lights faded except for those on the wheel and on Barrett's lectern.

'Here we go.' Barrett held the edge of the wheel and gave it a hefty pull. It span wildly.

The host returned to his lectern and watched. Tim Dyer didn't move a muscle. The audience was totally still.

'Nerve-racking stuff, this,' said Barrett Doran. 'Tense moment.'

He reached for the red-and-blue-striped glass in front of him.

The wheel showed little sign of slowing down. 'Goes on for ever,' said Barrett Doran jovially. 'Dear, oh dear, the excitement's too much for me. Need a drink of water to calm me down.'

He took a long swig from the glass.

The wheel was slowing. The audience started shouting at it, willing it to stop by the crown. Every eye was on a monitor, hypnotised by the decelerating ring of hats.

Suddenly they were all aware of a strange noise. It was a gasping, a desperate, inhuman wheezing.

A camera found Barrett Doran, from whom the sound came. The audience had time to register the face rigid with shock, before, pulling the lectern down with him, he crashed to the floor.

Full studio lights snapped up. Technicians rushed forward. The celebrities rose to their feet, overturning their long blue desk.

In the circle of hats Tim Dyer stood, pointing up at the still crown directly above his head. But no one looked at him. All eyes were drawn to the middle of the set, where Barrett Doran lay dead.

Chapter Five

CHARLES PARIS HEARD about Barrett Doran's death that evening. It was hard to escape it in the W.E.T. bar, where much less dramatic events were regularly inflated into Wagnerian productions. He heard that doctors and the police had been called, but had left W.E.T. House and was on his way back to his Bayswater bedsitter before anyone mentioned the word 'murder'.

The next morning the death was reported on radio and in Charles's *Times*, but it was not until the afternoon's edition of the *Standard* that it was suggested the incident might have been caused by anything other than natural causes. Two days later the press announced that a woman was helping the police with their enquiries into Barrett Doran's death, and the following day a 24-year-old employee of West End Television, Caroline Postgate, was charged with his murder. Then, as always with British crimes, all information on the case would cease until the trial.

The girl's name meant nothing to Charles, but, having been virtually on the spot when the murder happened, he felt intrigued by it and wanted to find out more. His first move was to contact his agent. Maurice Skellern, though completely deaf to vibrations of new productions coming up which might lead to jobs for his clients, had a very good ear for theatrical gossip, and was likely to know as much as anyone about a juicy theatrical murder.

Still, first things first. Charles asked the mandatory question about whether there was any work coming up.

Maurice Skellern laughed wheezily down the phone, as if this was the best joke he had heard for a long time. He did not answer the question; nor did Charles really expect him to. He knew that, on the rare occasions when something did come up, his agent would ring him.

Maurice was quickly on to the real subject of the conversation. 'Had a bit of excitement the other night at W.E.T., I gather.'

'You could say that.'

'You got any dirt on it to tell me?'

''Fraid not. I was ringing you in search of the same.'

'But come on, Charles. You were actually *there*.'

'Up in the bar.'

'So what else is new? So how much do you know?'

'Just that he died on the set at the end of the recording, and now some girl

I've never heard of has been charged with his murder.'

'Well, what can I tell you? For a start, he was poisoned. Did you know that?'

'No. With what?'

'Cyanide.'

'Ah.' One or two things began to fall into place. 'Cyanide which was being used for the programme in the studio next door?'

'You have it in one. Something that boring little poseur Melvyn Gasc was doing, apparently. Seems the cyanide got nicked from there and put into poor old Barrett's glass instead of water.'

'Gin.'

'What?'

'Instead of gin. Barrett's water-glass on the set was filled with gin.'

'Was it? How do you know that?'

Discretion dictated a slight editing of the next reply. 'One of the researchers was talking about it. So presumably this girl who's been arrested was the one who substituted the cyanide?'

'Yes.'

'Caroline Somebody-or-other. Know anything about her?'

'She was an Assistant Stage Manager on Melvyn Gasc's programme. She had been left in charge of all the props and that, so it was easy for her to lift the cyanide.'

'Ah.' Light began to dawn. 'Was this girl nicknamed Chippy?'

'That's right. Why, you know her?'

'I met her that night.'

The girl's beautiful, fragile face came into his mind. So, when he saw her, she had been contemplating murder. Perhaps that explained the tragedy in her deep, dark eyes.

'Needless to say, there was a background,' Maurice went on. 'She and Barrett had been having an affair. He had just broken it off. Classic situation. "Hell hath no fury...", all that.'

'Yes,' Charles agreed pensively.

'Not a lot more I can tell you,' his agent concluded. 'Though I gather, talking to people in the business, nobody's that sorry. Barrett Doran doesn't seem to have made many friends on his way to the top.'

'Having seen him in action, I'm not too surprised.'

'No. Presumably means they'll have to remake the pilot. Wonder if you'll get booked again...'

'Not if anyone's got any sense. It was a daft idea having an actor as one of the people in that round.'

'Ah, but nobody has got any sense in the game-show world.'

'You mean otherwise they'd be doing something else?'

'Stands to reason, doesn't it? Anyway, why do you say it's such a daft idea having an actor for the round?'

'Because the whole premise of that part of the game is based on people's anonymity, and actors, by definition, aren't anonymous. They're always in the public eye.'

'Are you saying somebody recognised you?'

Charles was forced to admit that this had not been the case.

'But, come the game, you mean subconsciously they all recognised you and all identified you as the actor?'

Charles was forced to admit that two out of the four contestants had thought he was a hamburger chef.

Maurice Skellern thought this very funny. His asthmatic laughter was still wheezing down the line when Charles said his goodbyes and put the phone down.

He stood for a moment on the landing of the house in Hereford Road. He was feeling shaken. Not by the news of the murder, but by the thought of his illicit sips of gin from Barrett Doran's glass. A little bit later and his thirst might have killed him. It was an unpleasant *frisson*.

He wondered whether he should ring his wife and tell her how close he had come to death. His relationship with Frances was once more in the doldrums. They had long ago separated, but ties remained and, like two pieces of wood floating down a river, they occasionally bounced back together again for brief periods. The love between them was too strong for either to form other permanent relationships, but soon after each reconciliation, the same old difficulties of living together reasserted themselves, and once again they would drift apart.

It had been a couple of months since their last such parting and, though he knew nothing would have changed, Charles needed to make contact again. Perhaps hearing that he had nearly swallowed a fatal dose of cyanide would make Frances forget their recent disagreements. It would be a good opening gambit, anyway.

He looked at his watch. No, of course not. It was a quarter to twelve in the morning. Frances was headmistress of a girls' school. She wouldn't mind his ringing her there in a real emergency, but just to mention casually that he'd nearly been poisoned...forget it.

On the other hand, at that time of day the pubs would be open. After his shock, Charles felt he deserved a little pampering. He went down to his local and had a few pints. By the third he had forgotten about the idea of ringing Frances. And, if he thought anything about Barrett Doran's death, it was only pity for the beautiful, sad girl who had been driven to such extremities by love.

And, but for a phone-call he received the next morning, he might have never thought any more about it.

The pampering of the previous lunchtime had escalated into evening pampering in various pubs and clubs where Charles always felt confident of meeting other actors. As a result, he was moving somewhat tentatively around his bedsitter, as if his exploding head was unattached and had to be balanced between his shoulders, when the telephone on the landing rang.

'Hello.' He hadn't intended it to come out as a growl, but that was the only sound of which his voice was capable under the circumstances.

'Could I speak to Charles Paris, please?'

'This is he...him.'

The caller then seemed to identify itself as 'Sidney Danson', which did not immediately ring bells. His fuddled mind was slowly registering that it was an unusually high voice for a man, when she mentioned West End Television and he knew where he was.

'What can I do for you, Sydnee?'

'It's about Barrett Doran's death.'

'Oh yes?'

'You know Chippy's been arrested and charged, don't you?'

'I had heard.'

'Well, I don't think she did it. I just can't imagine her...not killing him.'

'Ah.'

'Could we get together and talk about it?' She spoke very directly, with the confidence of someone who spent most of her working life on the telephone.

'We can meet if you like, but I don't think I'm going to be a lot of help to you. I didn't see anything. I was only in the studio for that first round.'

'I still think you could help.'

'Hmm. Have you any reason for thinking Chippy didn't do it?'

'Instinct.'

'Not always very reliable, I'm afraid, instinct. The police aren't fools. On the whole, they don't make an arrest until they've got a pretty good case worked out.'

Sydnee did not answer this objection. 'I'd like to talk about it,' she persisted.

'Okay. When do you want to meet?'

'Could you make it for a drink this evening after work?'

Charles was again reminded of how most people's lives were defined by the boundaries of work, while at times the only structure in his own seemed to be imposed by licensing hours, but he didn't comment. 'Sure.'

'Say...half-past six?'

'Fine. Where, down at W.E.T.?'

'No. Better off the premises. Too many people with their own theories down here. Do you know Harry Cockers?'

'I beg your pardon?'

'Cocktail bar. Covent Garden. Just off Floral Street.'

'I'm sure I could find it. What, there at six-thirty?'

'Yes.'

'One thing, Sydnee...'

'Yes?'

'Why did you get in touch with me?'

'One of the Stage Managers here mentioned you. Mort Verdon...you remember him?'

'Sure.'

'He said you'd sorted a few things out when those murders happened on the *Strutters* series.'

Charles felt childishly pleased as he put the phone down. He was amused by the idea that, while his acting career remained undistinguished, his reputation as an amateur detective was spreading.

The venue currently called Harry Cockers had been through many identities in the previous decade, as various kinds of bars and restaurants became fashionable. Its latest manifestation was very Thirties, with bright jagged lines along every surface, and wall-panels showing geometrically-stylised silhouettes of dancing figures in evening-dress. Overhead large fans swished.

It was full at that hour, and as he gazed at the clientele crowding the long bar, Charles felt infinitely old. The variegated flying-suits, the strident colours of fabrics and hair, the lurid make-up which would have been condemned at Drama School as 'horribly over the top', all seemed to point up the incongruity of his crumpled figure in its loyal sports jacket.

He needn't have worried. The bright young things at the bar were far too involved in themselves and each other to notice him as he peered from flying-suit to flying-suit, trying to identify Sydnee.

She wasn't there. At least, she wasn't there unless she had dyed her hair another colour (which was of course not impossible). He sat at an empty table on the outskirts of the action. If she was there, she could find him. He knew his own appearance hadn't changed in the last few days (or probably the last few decades).

He was gratified to discover that his invisibility did not extend to the staff. He had hardly sat down before a waiter, whose tail-coat and white tie seemed at odds with the yellow-and-green-striped hair and the Christmas Tree decoration dangling from the ear-lobe, materialised to take his order. He drew Charles's attention to the infinite list of highly-priced cocktails on the card in front of him.

'Er, just a large whisky, please.'

'On the rocks?'

'Please.'

The waiter vanished, very quickly to return with a tall glass so full of ice that the whisky had paled almost to invisibility, and a large bill.

Charles sipped his drink, while mortifying thoughts about how old and out of touch he was ran through his head.

Sydnee's hair was still the same copper-beech colour when she appeared a few minutes later. Her flying-suit this time was electric blue.

'Hi,' she said, offering no apology for her lateness. Television time, Charles remembered, except for the unshakable rigidity of studio schedules, is always approximate.

'Can I, er…?' He looked round for the waiter.

But she had already snapped her fingers to summon one, ordered herself a Screwdriver and 'another of the same' for him. Charles wasn't used to being with these thoroughly emancipated women.

Sydnee didn't bother with small talk, but went straight to the point. 'I'm convinced Chippy didn't kill Barrett, but I want you to prove that she didn't.'

'Is she a close friend of yours?'

'Fairly close, yes. We've worked on a lot of shows together. Been off on a few long locations. You get to know people pretty well stuck for a wet six weeks in a hotel in Scotland.'

Charles nodded. There were people he had got to know pretty well in similar circumstances.

'And, from what you know of her character, you don't see her as a murderer?'

'No way.'

'What is she like?'

'Well, she's dramatic and she's neurotic. Started as an actress before she went into stage management, so she tends to make a big production of everything. Also, looking like she does, she always has plenty of men after her...

'But she's one of those girls who always ends up falling for the ones who are complete shits.'

'Right.' Sydnee looked at him appraisingly, but with approval, respecting his judgement. As he had on the day of the recording, Charles caught a momentary glimpse of the real person beneath the surface efficiency.

'And Barrett Doran was the latest in this long line of shits?'

Sydnee nodded.

'How long had it been going on?'

'Maybe six months on and off. They met on another W.E.T. series. Another game show, actually. Chippy was A.S.M. on that.'

'They didn't move in together?'

'No. He'd just turn up at her flat every now and then. Usually not when he said he would. She spent a lot of those evenings sitting waiting with the dinner slowly drying up in the cooker. Then another night he'd turn up at one in the morning with no warning at all.'

'How to win friends and influence people.'

'Oh, Chippy lapped it up. There was always a kamikaze element in her relationships. She asked for it.'

'And she got it.'

'Yes.'

'Barrett presumably had other fish to fry?'

'You bet. He was the worst sort of celebrity. Reckoned, because he was a famous face, he could get off with anyone. And usually he could.'

'Did Chippy mind that?'

'At first I think she did. Then she realised that either she would have to accept all the others or forget it, so she stopped complaining. I think it kind of fuelled her masochism.'

'Was Barrett married?'

'Not significantly. I think there probably was a wife somewhere in the background, but it didn't inhibit his activities.'

'And, if Chippy was prepared to put up with all that, why was she suddenly reckoned to be capable of murdering him?'

'Because he broke it off. Didn't just stop turning up at her flat, didn't just stop ringing her...he actually told her: Forget it, it's all over.'

'Any idea why?'

'I think he was probably just bored with her. The sex, from her account, was pretty good, but then he could get plenty of sex elsewhere. I think also Chippy was a bit ordinary for him.'

'What do you mean?'

'Just an Assistant Stage Manager. Little bit of fluff, little bit of nothing. Barrett was getting to that stage of celebrity where he no longer just wanted to screw everything in sight, he only wanted to screw other celebs. You know, he wanted to be seen around with people, wanted to make it to the gossip columns.'

'And Chippy didn't match up?'

'No. Not famous enough.'

'Hmm. Sounds as if she was well shot of him.'

'Yes, of course she was. I told her it'd be a disaster from the start. Trouble was, Chippy reckoned she had fallen in love with him – no, let's be fair to her, she *had* fallen in love with him. I mean, I know she always dramatised things, but this time it was a bit different. I'd seen her in the throes of other affairs, but she had never been like she was with Barrett. She was just totally obsessed with him. She used to tape all his shows and sit at home on her own watching them.'

'What, game shows?'

'Yes.'

'She'd sit and watch game shows for pleasure? My God, it must have been love.'

Charles stopped short. He remembered that he was talking to someone whose work was game shows. He mustn't assume that she shared his cynicism on the subject, and be careful that he didn't offend her.

Sydnee's pale-blue eyes stared at him for a long, uncomfortable moment. Then, slowly, a childlike smile broke across her face.

'It's all right, Charles. I'm fully aware of the real quality of what I work on. But the work is nothing to do with the end-product. As you know, you can still be satisfied with your own professional contribution to a project that is utter rubbish.'

He nodded. He had frequently had that experience. There was now more of a bond between them.

His glass was empty. He looked around vaguely, but again a peremptory gesture from Sydnee produced the waiter and repeated their order.

'Presumably,' he said, picking up the threads, 'Chippy's obsession with Barrett is one of the reasons why the police reckon she killed him?'

'Yes. Oh, she was certainly doing all the classic things a murder suspect should...going round saying what a bastard he was, how much she hated him, how much she wished he'd never existed. I mean, none of us could deny that she had issued plenty of threats against him.'

'You were questioned by the police?'

'Oh yes. Everyone who was on the set at the time of the murder.'

'I'm surprised they haven't been on to me.'

'They've got your address and phone number. I just don't think they needed to spread the net any wider. They reckon they've got enough to convict Chippy already.'

'Hmm. Like what?'

'Well, let's say we've sorted out Motive. As I recall from my teenage reading of detective stories, the next point to be checked was always Opportunity.'

'That's right.'

'So far as Opportunity was concerned, Chippy was uniquely placed. She was working on *Method In Their Murders*, she knew Melvyn Gasc had insisted on the realism of having all the correct props for the series, so she knew that the bottle of cyanide was around.'

'And she went off to look after Studio B soon after six. I remember.'

'Exactly. So she had a unique opportunity to doctor Barrett's glass.'

'Which contained gin originally, am I right?'

'Yes. How did you know?'

Again Charles fudged the truth a little. 'I worked it out from things Barrett said to you.'

'He always insisted on his glass of gin. Don't blame him, actually. You need something to keep up that relentless good humour in front of the camera.'

'Hmm. One strange thing that struck me,' Charles mused, going off at a tangent, 'was why he didn't die earlier.'

'Sorry? I'm not with you.'

'Well, if he was that dependent on the gin, why didn't he take a big swig earlier on in the recording? Why did he wait till the end?'

'Yes, I wondered about that. The only reason I could think was that, under all that brashness, Barrett Doran was very nervous. He was concentrating so hard on getting the new show right that he forgot about the booze.'

'I suppose that's possible.'

'He did nip off to his dressing room for a big one at the end of Part One.'

'Ah.'

'Also, he played it well. I mean, in terms of drama. He only used the drink when the wheel was spinning, claiming that he couldn't stand the tension. He was a good showman, Barrett.

'Hmm.' Charles took a long, pensive swallow of whisky. 'Did you get a chance to talk to Chippy after the recording?'

'Yes, I did. We went out for a few drinks after the first round of police questioning.'

'What sort of state was she in?'

'Pretty terrible. Kind of numb and totally fatalistic. Like part of her was dead. With Barrett gone, she didn't reckon she had anything to live for. That's what worries me. If she's in that sort of state, she's not going to fight. I know her. She'll just accept being accused of the murder. She'll see it as a kind of punishment, yet another proof that it's a rotten world and she never had a chance.'

'But she can't just have been charged on circumstantial evidence. The police must have got a bit more on her.'

'Yes, I suppose they have. You see, she did fiddle around with Barrett's glass.'

'Did she?'

'Oh yes. She made no bones about it. She told me that evening. And presumably she told the police too.'

'What did she say she did?'

'While she was meant to be looking after Studio B in the meal-break, she was feeling really vindictive towards Barrett – you know, particularly after he'd cut her dead in the bar – and she decided she'd have a small revenge on him. She knew about the gin, knew he always had a glass on the set, so she just thought she'd deprive him of that comfort.

She said all she was going to do was to change his glass round with one of the others on the celebs' desk.'

'Did she say whose?'

'No. Anyway, she says she didn't do it. When she got into the studio, she picked up the glass, then realised how petty she was being and didn't bother.'

'She just left things as they were?'

'So she said. Well, the police ran fingerprint checks. Needless to say, hers were all over the cyanide bottle – she'd been handling the Studio B props all day. They were also all over Barrett's glass and decanter – along with a lot of other prints.'

'Oh really?' said Charles innocently.

'So, given that evidence, and her motive, and the fact that she and Barrett had a shouting match just before the recording...'

'Did they?'

'Yes. She went to his dressing room, silly girl. Shouted all kinds of things that a lot of people heard. Said how he wouldn't get away with the way he'd treated her, how she had planned how to get even with him...'

'Direct threats?'

'That's it, I'm afraid.'

Charles looked down at the melting ice of his drink. His conclusion was inescapable, but he wanted to phrase it as gently as possible.

'Listen, Sydnee, I know Chippy's a friend of yours and I can see exactly why you're doing what you're doing, why you're involving me, but I'm afraid it does sound pretty hopeless. I mean, Chippy had every reason to want Barrett dead, and she had the opportunity to kill him. From what you say of her mental state, she sounds to have been quite hysterical enough to have done it. I'm sorry, Sydnee, but I think the police are right. They've got their murderer.'

The pale blue eyes were full of pain. To his surprise, he saw tears gathering at their corners.

'As I say, I'm sorry, but that's how it must have happened. She went to Barrett's dressing room, hoping for the final reconciliation. He was as unpleasant to her as ever. She thought, all right, sod the bastard, I'll get him. She went back to Studio B, got the bottle of cyanide...into Studio A and filled his glass. Wouldn't have taken her more than a minute. And that was it.'

Sydnee was silent for a moment. Then, softly, she said, 'Except it wasn't.'

'What do you mean?'

'I heard about the argument going on in Barrett's dressing room, and I went down to get Chippy out of it. I then took her back to the bar and bought her a large drink. So she's got an alibi from the time she went into Barrett's dressing room.'

'Okay, so she must have doctored the drink before she went to see him. It doesn't make a lot of difference to the main outline of the crime. She told him she was going to get him.'

'Yes.'

Sydnee's reply was so listless, and she looked so dejected, that Charles felt he must summon up a little more interest.

'Let's look at the time-scale. When did she say she went into Studio A to switch the glasses?'

'First thing she did when she went down from the bar. And that's when the police say she put the cyanide in the glass. It was the only chance she had. She was seen going into Barrett's dressing room at twenty-five-past six, and I got her out of there about twenty to seven.'

Charles did the sums in his head. Then, slowly he said, 'Ah. You know, Sydnee, I think you may have a point, after all.'

Because, as he knew well (and with a degree of gratitude), at six-thirty the contents of the glass on Barrett Doran's lectern had been not cyanide, but gin.

Chapter Six

IT WAS THE first time Charles had had the privilege of his own research team in investigating a murder. Sydnee had mustered all of the researchers who had worked on *If The Cap Fits* to go through the events of the day Barrett Doran died. In an unguarded moment, when they had been trying to think of somewhere private to meet, Charles had suggested his bedsitter. He had not taken into account the fact that he had only two chairs. Nor had he thought through the reaction of these television sophisticates to his somewhat approximate view of tidiness.

None of them was impolite enough to say anything, but he sensed a sniff of disapproval in the air. Their standards were probably different from his. In domestic arrangements, Charles always made a distinction between hygiene and tidiness. And, though he knew he offended against the strict canons of the second, he felt confident that he did not transgress with regard to the first.

Assuming, of course, that one didn't regard dust as unhygienic.

There was a generous cover of dust over every surface. And, since none of these surfaces were flat, but tended to be piles of books, clothes, stationery and scripts, the general effect could be, to the uncharitable eye, seen as a mess.

This view seemed to be reflected in his visitors' expressions. Sydnee sat on a chair. The other girl, Chita, who had been responsible for the contestants on the studio day, had the other one. Charles shared the edge of the bed with the rather exquisite young man called Quentin, who had been in charge of the celebrities. Charles had offered whisky and wine; they had all chosen white wine. He had some chilling (a little belatedly – he'd only thought about it ten minutes before they arrived) in his small fridge, and had soon assembled a whisky tumbler, a half-pint tankard and a chipped glass that had been given away with soap powder for his guests. He was left with a pink plastic tooth-mug for his whisky.

The atmosphere was not unfriendly, though the three researchers seemed to be suffering mild disbelief at the idea of people actually living in such surroundings. Charles thought it might be only a matter of time before they started making a documentary about him.

Sydnee opened the meeting. 'Chita and Quentin are fully up-to-date with everything. They're as concerned as I am to get charges against Chippy dropped.'

'Have you mentioned to them the idea of going to the police?' Charles asked formally.

'Yes. We're all agreed that we shouldn't do that until we can point the finger at the person who really killed Barrett.'

'But surely…if all you want is to get Chippy free, all I have to do is go and tell the police that Barrett's glass still contained gin at half-past six and – '

'No.' Sydnee was implacable. 'Apart from anything else, that's then going to start the police being suspicious of you. We need your help; we don't want you shut up in a cell "helping the police with their enquiries".'

Charles agreed. It was an aspect of the situation he hadn't considered. So…he was committed to the case now. He'd better accept it with good grace.

'Right, so let's see where we are. We know that Barrett Doran's glass contained gin at six-thirty. What time would everyone start coming back from their meal-break? Sharp at seven?'

'Most people would, yes,' said Sydnee. 'Cameras have to line up for half an hour between seven and seven-thirty, so the cameramen would drift back at around five to.'

'But the P.A. would probably have been in the Gallery before that,' Quentin contributed. And there might be other people drifting back a bit earlier…stage managers, people checking props.

Chita agreed. 'Yes. It'd be quite a risk to try to do anything criminal after about ten to. Likely to be someone around then.'

'So we've narrowed down the time when the cyanide was put in the glass to the twenty minutes between six-thirty and ten to seven,' Charles summed up. 'Now, assuming that the murderer was someone connected with the show, which of your charges were out of your sight during that period?'

'I'll start,' said Sydnee, 'because my bit's probably the simplest. After I sent you down to Make-up, Charles, I was intending to send the other "professions" down at five-minute intervals, but then I had a call in the bar from one of the Make-up girls saying they were getting behind and could I hold it. So your three fellow-performers didn't leave the bar till after seven.'

'Are you sure? Because you went down to Barrett's dressing room at twenty to.'

'I'm sure. I left them in the charge of a friend up in the bar. He confirmed none of them left. He was a bit pissed off, actually…found he had to buy them all a round of drinks.'

So that ruled out the hamburger chef, the surgeon and the stockbroker.

'What about the contestants?' Charles asked Chita.

'Most of them stayed up in the Conference Room right through the meal-break. There were sandwiches and drink up there.'

'When did they go to Make-up?'

'Not till about ten to seven. They didn't need much. Just a quick slap of foundation and powder.'

'You said "most of them"…'

'Yes, a couple went out about quarter past six, but they were both back by twenty to seven.'

'Which ones?'

'The two who got through to the second half. The one who won...'

'Tim Dyer,' said Sydnee.

'And the housewife, Trish Osborne…'

'Madame Nipple,' murmured Quentin.

Charles ignored this. 'Where did they go to, Chita?'

'Well, they *said* they both fancied a steak and went down to the canteen…'

'But we've talked to Rose on the Grill Counter,' Sydnee picked up the story, 'who's got about the beadiest eyes in the business, and she's certain they didn't go in there.'

'Ah. Well, there's two who might be worth investigating. But you're sure the others stayed put?'

'I was with them all the time,' Chita confirmed.

'Right,' said Charles. 'On to the celebrities.'

Quentin let out a languorous sigh. 'Well, now, what can I tell you? We too were all cosy in our little Conference Room with lavish supplies of W.E.T. booze and W.E.T. sandwiches. There was a bit of toing and froing to dressing rooms…'

'Can you be more specific about this toing and froing?'

'Well…Fiona Wakeford "toed" into her dressing room at about six-fifteen, and Nick Jeffries "toed" into it at about six-sixteen. And she "froed" him out at about six-seventeen.' Quentin giggled at his little joke. 'Then she stayed in her dressing room until seven putting her hair in the Carmen rollers.'

'Are you sure about that?'

'Pozz. One of my friends is a dresser, and she called him in to help her just after Nick left. For protection, too, I think.'

'Nick?'

Quentin nodded. 'He'd been chatting her up quite shamelessly all afternoon. I think when he went into her dressing room and actually put his hand on something, even dear Fiona realised he was after a bit. So she… "froed" him out.' He repeated the joke, maybe hoping for more reaction the second time. He didn't get it.

'So, although Fiona's out of the running, Nick was on the loose from six-twenty-two until…when?'

'Only about six-thirty, I'm afraid. He was back up in the Conference Room by then, downing a large Scotch to soothe his wounded ego. He certainly wasn't in the studio area for the vital twenty minutes.'

'Sure?'

'Pozz.'

'What about the other two panellists?'

'Well now…' Another dramatic sigh was emitted. 'Joanie went down to Make-up at about ten-past six.'

'With her husband?'

'Oh yes, the faithful Roger was in tow.'

'Did he go into Make-up with her?'

'Apparently not. Perhaps even he thought that would have been taking devotion too far.'

'So he was on the loose down near the studios. Perhaps he should go on the list...'

'Uh-uh.' Quentin shook his head. 'Sorry, like Nick, they were back up in the Conference Room by half-past.'

'Ah. So that rules both out.'

''Fraid so. I had my beady little eyes on the pair of them for every second of the vital twenty minutes. Not a sight I relished, I must confess,' Quentin admitted with slight petulance. 'I can only take so much connubial bliss, you know.'

'What about Bob Garston?'

'Now he is much more interesting. Or, at least, his movements are much less well-documented. He was out of the Conference Room from about five-past six until twenty to seven. And no sightings, I'm afraid. Except that he was seen going down in the lift towards the basement, where the studios are. So he should certainly go on your little list.'

'Right. Three names, then. Three who had the opportunity.' Charles mused. 'Of course, we've limited it enormously. We've only dealt with the ones directly concerned with the show. I mean, there are so many people around a television studio. It could have been any of them. Even someone working on a different programme...'

'Like Chippy was...' said Chita.

But Sydnee wasn't going to let them get depressed by logistics. 'We've got to start somewhere,' she pronounced. 'Now, next thing we ought to think about motives.'

'I'll tell you who had the biggest motive,' said Quentin. 'Those two Americans. You know, the one who kept talking about "making a pot" and his tall, quiet friend. They were convinced that Barrett was ruining their precious show.'

'Did they have the opportunity?'

Quentin shook his head wistfully. 'Sorry, Charles. They spent the whole of the meal-break bending John Mantle's ear in the bar. Lots of witnesses for that.'

'What about the other three then, the ones on the list? How're we doing for motive there?'

Sydnee took over. 'Well, no one liked Barrett much. We know that. But who disliked him enough to murder him? ...that's a different question. What does drive someone to murder? Presumably it varies from person to person. I mean, Barrett really humiliated Trish.'

'You mean that business about her...her blouse?'

'Yes. He reduced her to tears in front of everyone. And she didn't seem to me to be the sort who cries easily.'

'A lot of women would take that pretty hard. Whether hard enough to commit murder...I don't know.'

'Won't dismiss it out of hand. What about the other contestant?'

'Tim Dyer's different. He was just totally obsessed by winning. And I mean *obsessed*. He's been on the phone every day since the recording.'

'About what?'

'About the car. What he describes as *his* bloody car. He maintains that the crown had definitely stopped over his head at the end of the *Hats In The Ring* finale, and that, regardless of the fact that Barrett Doran was at that moment dying, the Austin Metro should be his. W.E.T., in the person of John Mantle, takes a different view.'

'I'm not surprised. But do you reckon he had any motive against Barrett?'

'He was certainly extremely angry when Barrett paired him with Fiona Wakeford for Round One. He didn't reckon she would be much help to him.'

'One can see his point,' Quentin murmured.

'But whether you'd murder someone for that...'

Charles shrugged. 'As you say, he was obsessed. Depends on the depth of his obsession, I suppose. What about Bob Garston?'

'I don't think he *liked* Barrett,' Sydnee replied, 'but then who did? There was also, I suppose, a professional rivalry.'

'Oh?'

'Bob was considered for the job.'

'Hosting the show?'

'Yes.'

'And he knew that?'

''Fraid so. He shouldn't have done, but he did. Casting Director was a little indiscreet with his agent when checking availability.'

'And would he have wanted it?'

'I think so.'

'Course he would, Sydnee,' said Quentin. 'Just the sort of break he needs. Lose the "reporter" tag. Become a "personality". A future of infinite chat-shows. He'd love it.'

'And, of course, he may yet get it,' said Chita.

'How do you mean?'

'There's a reasonable chance he'll be booked as host on the second pilot.'

'Is there going to be a second pilot?'

'You bet,' Sydnee replied. 'W.E.T. shelled out a lot for the rights in that show. They're not going to let something minor like a murder stop them from capitalising on it.'

Charles bit back the actor's instinctive question ('If there is a second pilot, am I likely to be booked again?'), and said, 'So he stood to gain very directly from Barrett's death. We should definitely investigate Bob Garston.'

'Him first?'

'I'm not sure. I think we should try and see all three of them. Who's going to be the easiest to get in touch with?'

Sydnee laughed. 'Tim Dyer. He's desperate for someone to go and talk to him about his bloody car.'

Charles Paris grinned round at his research team. 'Then maybe we should start with Tim Dyer.'

Chapter Seven

SYDNEE DROVE AN old red MG Midget, fast. The hood was up, against the autumn weather, and she and Charles travelled in their noisy cocoon out along the A3 towards Petersfield, where their first suspect lived.

'Are you sure he's not going to think it odd, me coming along with you?' asked Charles.

'I don't think he'll give it a second thought. The only thing on his mind is that bloody Austin Metro.'

'Is that what you said you wanted to talk about when you rang?'

'No, I didn't say it, but I think that's the way he took it. Wouldn't occur to him that there was anything else to talk about.'

'Could be the second pilot.'

'Could be, I suppose. Though, if the truth were known, he's very unlikely to be involved in that.'

'Oh?'

'It's a matter of research time. It's difficult getting contestants, but it was more difficult setting up the rest of the programme. Probably be better to leave all that intact and just slot in four new contestants.'

'What, leave the rest of the show just as it was?' asked Charles, scenting another booking.

'Yes. Assuming the powers-that-be don't want major changes in the format.'

'Are they likely to?'

'Who can say? John Mantle and the American copyright holders are watching the tape through today.'

Charles grimaced. 'Fairly grisly experience.'

'Only the end. Up to there the show ran as it should. Very few recording breaks, it was fine. John Mantle won't waste the recording. I mean, for him it'll be great, having the luxury of a second pilot. Another bite of the cherry, a chance to make sure it's all dead right.'

Charles winced. '*Dead* right.'

'Sorry.'

'Has it been decided yet whether Bob Garston will host it second time around?'

'Not definitely, no. I think it's a strong possibility.'

'Hmm.' Charles fell silent, his mind circling round the murder, round the possible motives and opportunities of its perpetrator.

They reached the outskirts of Petersfield. 'Could you reach into my handbag? There's a sheet of W.E.T. notepaper where I wrote down the directions he gave me on the phone.'

Charles complied and guided Sydnee towards their quarry. 'What does he do?' he asked, as they turned into the road where Tim Dyer lived.

'He said on his form that he was a computer programmer.'

'You sound sceptical.'

'Yes. Just something about him sounds warning bells. Also, he said he'd be at home any time I cared to call.'

'You mean you don't think he has a job?'

'Wouldn't surprise me.'

'One of the unemployment figures? Made redundant, and too proud to admit it?'

'Possible.' She didn't sound convinced. 'Except that computers are one of our few boom industries. Wouldn't imagine there are that many redundant programmers.'

'So what do you think?'

'I think he may have slipped through our net. I think he claimed to have a job just to put us off the scent.'

'I'm still not with you.'

'I rather suspect that Tim Dyer is one of those characters who all researchers try to spot and weed out. If I'm right, I'll kick myself for not having recognised it earlier.'

Charles was mystified. 'What sort of character?'

Sydnee stopped the car outside a neat, Thirties semi. In the drive stood a brand-new, gleaming Vauxhall Cavalier. She looked at Charles with a little grin as she pulled on the handbrake and replied, 'A professional contestant.'

It was clear as soon as they got inside the small front room that Sydnee had been right. Tim Dyer made no attempt to disguise what he did for a living. Indeed, he exulted in it. Perhaps, having played his part in *If The Cap Fits* and having, to his mind, won an Austin Metro from W.E.T., he saw no further necessity for secrecy.

He indicated a table, on which papers and open reference books lay between piles of cardboard coupons. 'Doing another of the soap powder ones,' he announced airily. 'Pretty simple General Knowledge. Difficult bit's always the tie-breaker.'

'Tie-breaker?'

'Bit at the end. Always a variation on the old "I LIKE THIS PRODUCT BECAUSE...in not more than ten words". Mind you, there is a knack to them,' he added smugly.

'You've won in the past?' asked Charles. As Sydnee had predicted, Tim had registered no surprise, or indeed interest, at his presence.

'Just a few times.' Tim Dyer smiled indulgently at the understatement. 'Out of these I've won fifty pounds a week for life, three music centres, a food processor, a sailing dinghy and a fortnight's holiday for two in Benidorm.'

'Good God. What do you do with all that lot?'

'Keep some. Sell a few. Though selling's always a pity, because you drop a lot on the price, even when it's brand-new. I prefer barter. I've got a good barter deal going with my local electrical shop.'

'What did you do about the fortnight's holiday for two in Benidorm?'

'Oh, I went on that.'

'Nice break for you and the wife.'

'I'm divorced,' said Tim Dyer. 'No, I went, and sold the other half of the holiday to someone I used to work with. Had to drop the price a bit, but did all right. Trouble is, very few of the companies who put up these prizes are ready to give cash equivalent.'

'Do you enter for everything?' asked Charles, bemused.

'Everything I hear about. And everything where there's a bit of skill involved. Like I say, there's a knack to it. The ones where it's pure lottery, it's not worth bothering, I've got no advantage over anyone else. Don't do any of those...well, except the *Sun* Bingo and *Times* Portfolio. Check them first thing every morning before I start on the rest.'

'And you really find there are enough of them to keep you going?'

'You bet. In fact, I don't have time to do them all. I work weekends too, you know,' Tim Dyer concluded piously.

'So you just sit here and –'

'Have to spend a lot of time in the supermarkets, checking the new promotions that are coming up, seeing what the competitions are, getting entry forms, coupons, buying up relevant stock.'

'Relevant stock?'

'Come and have a look.'

He led them through into what had presumably been intended as a dining room. But it contained no table and chairs. Instead, it was crammed full like a supermarket warehouse.

Tim Dyer gave them a conducted tour. He pointed to a ceiling-high pile of Cook-in-a-Bag Curry boxes, from each of which a side panel had been neatly cut. 'Did all right out of that. Won a three-week holiday for two to India.'

'Did you go on it?'

'No, sold it through the local paper.' He indicated a wall of food cans, none of which had any labels. 'Four different competitions, those were. Canned mange-touts, new instant custard launch, lychees in syrup and chilli con carne. Got a yoghourt-maker, cut-glass decanter set, tennis racket and two hair-dryers. Sold them all.'

'Why no labels?'

He looked at Charles as if he were dealing with a moron. 'They've got the coupons on. You have to get them off.'

'Well, how can you tell whether it's instant custard or chilli con carne?'

'You can't. I just open one and hope for the best.'

'You do eat them?'

'I'm working through,' said Tim Dyer, and pointed to a pile of washing-up powder boxes. These had also had coupons removed and powder spilled through the rectangular holes to make little peaks on the carpet. 'Working through this lot, too. Good, though. Won a BMX bicycle on that. Sold it.'

'How did you win the Vauxhall Cavalier?' asked Sydnee, who had been silent for a long time.

Tim Dyer looked at her sharply, realizing that the conversation had come round to something important. 'Let's go into the front room.'

When they were sitting, Sydnee persisted, 'Where did you win the Cavalier?'

'Doesn't matter.'

'I see. Another television show.'

For a moment he looked as if he were about to deny it, but a slow, smug smile crept across his face. 'Yes. Right. *Something For Nothing* I won that on.'

'You've done a lot of other tellies.'

He nodded slyly. 'Oh yes. I've done most of them.'

'Just a minute,' said Sydnee, remembering something. 'How did you get on *Something For Nothing*? That's a show for married couples.'

'Yes.'

'But you said you're divorced.'

'I persuaded the wife to come back just for the show.'

'And *you* got the car.'

'Oh, come on. She got the fridge-freezer, the home computer with full range of software, the exercise bicycle plus His and Hers track-suits, the cordless telephone and the crate of vintage champagne.'

'You still got the best of the deal.'

'Well, I did the research, didn't I? And I answered all the questions.'

'Erm...' Charles asked out of pure curiosity, 'did appearing on the show together bring you and your wife back together at all?'

'Good God, no.' Tim Dyer dismissed that idea and moved on to a subject that interested him more. 'Now, about this Austin Metro...'

'Yes,' said Sydnee, mentally girding up her loins for battle.

'I've taken legal advice on this, and my solicitor says it depends on whether the crown was definitely over my head when it stopped. Now I know it was, and that would be visible on the recording of the show that you have. If W.E.T. tries to withhold that tape, my solicitor says he would be able to –'

'We have also taken legal advice,' Sydnee quelled him.

'Our Legal Department has no precedent for this situation, but their view is that the rules of the game constitute a kind of verbal contract. In other words, W.E.T. has agreed to give away certain goods to contestants who fulfil the requirements demanded by the game.'

'Exactly.' Tim Dyer grinned hungrily. 'Which I had done.'

'However,' Sydnee continued, 'it is their view that this situation only lasts as long as the game continues, and they feel that the game cannot be said to continue after the death of the host.'

'What!' He was furious. 'But that's just cheating. Anyway, the crown had stopped over my head before he died.'

She shook her head. 'We've checked the tape. Barrett Doran definitely stopped moving before the wheel of hats did.'

'I don't believe it. I demand to see the tape!'

'You're welcome to do so. Your solicitor is also welcome to do so. It won't change anything. The Austin Metro remains the property of West End Television.'

Tim Dyer let out a terrible howl of frustrated materialism. 'Cheats! You're just all cheats! I won that fair and square, and now you're saying I didn't! I'll fight it! I'll sue you! I'll get that car!'

'Try, by all means,' said Sydnee equably, 'but let me warn you, you're going into a very vague area of the law, and, as a general rule, the vaguer the area, the more expensive the law becomes.'

Tim Dyer was silent, his mouth ugly with disappointment. He looked as if he had been winded by a blow to some vital part of his anatomy. And that was not far from the truth. He had just received a serious blow to his greed.

Charles judged it a good moment to move on to the real subject of their visit. 'You didn't like Barrett Doran, did you?'

Tim Dyer looked surprised at this change of direction, but was still too much in shock to do anything but tell the truth. 'No, I didn't. So?'

'Why did you dislike him? You'd only met him that afternoon, hadn't you?'

'Oh yes. But it doesn't take long to get the measure of someone like that.' A glint of paranoia came into Dyer's eye, as he said, 'He was out to stop me winning.'

'What?'

'Oh yes. That bastard was out to nobble me from the moment we were introduced. He saw that I was the most likely contestant to win, and he was out to stop me.'

'I don't think he was bothered with –'

'Oh, come on. Didn't you see the way he paired me off with that subnormal actress? It was quite deliberate. He was out to sabotage my chances.' The paranoia gave way to satisfaction. 'But I showed the bastard. I still won, didn't I?' The paranoia quickly reasserted itself. 'Or I would have won if I hadn't been cheated of my car!'

'Listen...' Sydnee began, but, on a signal from Charles, she stopped.

'What did you do during the meal-break?' the actor asked suddenly.

Again he had judged it right. Tim was too surprised by the sudden demand to question why it should be asked. 'Well, I...er...what do you mean?'

'You were in the Conference Room with Chita and the other contestants. You and Trish Osborne left there about quarter past six, and didn't get back till twenty to seven. You said you were going down to the canteen, but neither of you did. What were you doing?'

'Well, I wasn't with her, if that's what you were thinking,' Tim replied truculently. 'If she was getting off with anyone, it wasn't me. We only left the room together. We got in different lifts.'

'Both going down?'

'I think so. Mine was, certainly.'

'Which floor did you get off at?'

'I....Look, what is this? Why are you giving me the third degree in my own home? Who the hell do you think you are?'

'Someone's been murdered,' Charles announced with all the chilling authority he had used in *Witness For The Prosecution* ('Profoundly unmoving' – *Plays and Players*).

'And someone's been charged with the murder.'

'Yes. We happen to believe that the police have got the wrong culprit. Which is why we are checking what everyone was doing during the meal-break.' By now he had slipped into the voice he had used as a Detective-Inspector (shortly to be killed) in a *Softly, Softly* ('A rather routine episode in this generally excellent series' – *New Statesman*). 'So tell me exactly what you did when you left the Conference Room.'

The Detective-Inspector manner had its effect. Tim Dyer spoke unwillingly, but at least he spoke. 'I went down to the floor where the studios are. I just wanted to have a look round. I was nervous, you know, wanted to get on the set, get the feel of it. I thought it'd calm me down.'

'And, once in the studio, what did you do?'

'I...well, I just looked round. You know, round the back.'

'You looked at the displays of prizes?'

'All right. So what if I did? I needed to psych myself up for the show. I needed to sort of get the adrenaline going.'

'So you went and gazed at the Austin Metro?'

'Yes,' the contestant admitted sheepishly.

'And that's all you did?'

'Yes.' But Tim Dyer would not look into his interrogator's eyes as he spoke.

'You were out of the Conference Room for twenty-five minutes. Sounds like a long time to look at a car.'

'Well, I didn't go into the studio straight away.'

'What, not immediately after you left the lift?'

'No. I was going in there, but I saw one of the celebrities coming along the corridor and I didn't feel like chatting, so I turned into one of the phone booths along there till he'd gone past.'

'Who was it?'

'Bob Garston.'

'And he was coming from Studio A?'

'From that direction, certainly.'

'This was straight after you came out of the lift?'

'Yes.'

'So, say, twenty-past six?'

'Round then.'

'Was Bob Garston on his own?'

'No, he was with Joanie Bruton's husband.'

'Roger Bruton, eh?' Charles looked at Sydnee. 'Who'd presumably just escorted his wife into Make-up.' She nodded. 'So, Tim, you just stayed in the phone booth as they walked past?'

'That's what I meant to do, but they stopped just outside and talked for a bit.'

'Did you hear what they said?'

'Yes. It was strange. Bob Garston was saying, "I didn't think anyone knew about it. Still, since you obviously do, you'll understand that I'm finding it pretty difficult to work in the same studio as the bastard." And Roger Bruton said, "Joanie's done a lot of counselling on infidelity in marriage. You ought to talk to her about it. She's very understanding." And Bob said, yes, perhaps he would.'

'And that was it?'

'Yes. Then they walked on.'

'And you came out of the phone booth and went into Studio A?'

'Yes.'

'To look at your car.' Tim Dyer did not deem this worthy of comment, so Charles went on. 'Did you see anyone in the studio?'

A twisted smile came to the contestant's lips. 'Only you.'

'Oh.'

'I saw you swigging from his glass.'

Charles blushed, but pressed on. 'So you knew that it didn't contain cyanide at that point.'

'Never occurred to me that it would. Why should I think that?'

'Somebody put cyanide in it between six-thirty and seven.'

'Well, don't look at me. What do you take me for? I wouldn't do anything like that.'

'No, I don't think you probably would.' A new thought struck Charles. 'Just a minute. You say you saw me drinking from Barrett's glass...'

'Yes.'

'I didn't see you.'

'So?' Tim Dyer looked uncomfortable.

'If you'd been behind the curtain round the back of the set, you wouldn't have been able to see me. If you'd been in the audience seating, I'd have seen you. That means you must have been out of sight, actually on the set.'

'Well...' Tim Dyer began wretchedly.

'And the only thing on the set big enough to hide you would have been the spinning wheel.' Suddenly Charles knew he was right. 'You were behind that wheel...tampering with it.'

'No, I wasn't.' But the denial carried no conviction.

'Wouldn't take much, would it? All you needed to do was fix a counterweight on the wheel, directly opposite the crown, and that would guarantee it would always come to rest with the crown overhead. Simple.'

Charles knew from the man's expression that he had inadvertently hit on the truth. Confidently, he asked one final question. 'You didn't see anyone else in the studio after I left?'

Tim Dyer shook his head miserably and whispered, 'I went out straight after you. Didn't see anyone else.'

There was a long silence. Then Sydnee rose to her feet. 'Better be going, I suppose.'

Charles got up too, and they moved towards the hall. Just before they left the room, Sydnee looked back and said, 'And, if you want to take up that point about cheating over the car, I suggest you get in touch with our Legal Department.'

Tim Dyer did not respond. He stayed crumpled in his chair, looking as comically guilty as a schoolboy with stolen jam on his face.

Chapter Eight

SYDNEE RANG CHARLES the next morning. 'You were right,' she said.

'About what in particular?'

'Tim Dyer trying to fix the wheel. I spoke to Sylvian this morning.'

'Who?'

'Sylvian de Beaune, the designer. I mentioned what we thought might have happened, and he went to check. The set's in store, you see, waiting for the definite go-ahead on the second pilot. Anyway, there it was – small polythene bag filled with sand, stuck on the back of the wheel with sticky tape, just opposite the crown. As you said.'

'Quite a feat of improvisation, to sort that out in the studio.'

'I think Mr Dyer went prepared.'

'Took the sandbag with him, you mean?'

'Wouldn't surprise me. As we know, he's a *very dedicated* competitor. He knew the format of the show. He knew about the wheel. I think he planned it in advance.'

'Bloody nerve. Where's the traditional British spirit of fair play?'

'That was invented before game shows.'

'Yes. I suppose no one could have predicted the day when ritual humiliation would become a participant sport.' Charles chuckled. 'God, Tim would have been furious if he'd doctored the wheel and then someone else had got to the final.'

'He was pretty confident it was going to be him. As he kept saying, there's a knack to these things. He knew what he was doing.'

'Hmm. Presumably, if the show had run its course, he would have won his Austin Metro with no questions asked.'

'Yes. Until you found out about his cheating, there was a possibility that he would have got it, anyway.'

'Really?'

'Yes. All that guff I quoted from our Legal Department was sheer improvisation. I did consult them, but they were going to look for precedents and come back to me. So, you see, Charles, your quick thinking has saved W.E.T. a few thousand quid.'

'Good. Not that I think W.E.T. needs the money, but I would really resent the idea of that little wimp Dyer getting it.'

'I agree. Sylvian, incidentally, was furious.'

'About what?'

'The idea of someone tampering with his set. It was his first big one, you see. He'd been assistant on a good few, but this was the first on which he was going to get a sole credit.'

'I thought he looked rather nervous all day.'

'He certainly did. Kept fiddling about and rearranging things. Anyway, he really blew his top when he saw what Tim had done. Said it ruined the game. He's got a strangely puritanical streak, Sylvian. He was particularly annoyed, because he'd already resisted one attempt to fix the result.'

'What – another of the contestants tried it on?'

'No, no. It was John Mantle. He asked Sylvian to arrange that the wheel *didn't* end up with the crown on top.'

'Good Lord.'

'Well, it's an Executive Producer's job to keep his costs down. And it *was* only a pilot. Anyway, as I say, Sylvian refused to do it.'

Charles was not given time to reflect on the perfidy of television producers as Sydnee went on, 'So, where do we go next?'

'Which suspect, you mean?'

'Yes. We've still got Trish Osborne and Bob Garston – that is, assuming we've found out the full extent of Tim Dyer's evil-doing.'

'I'm fairly confident we have. Well, of the other two suspects, Bob Garston at the moment seems much the more suspicious. Trish Osborne had very little opportunity to put the cyanide in the glass during the vital twenty minutes, whereas Bob was certainly around the studio area. He also stood to gain directly from Barrett's death...'

'*Has* gained from it already. Heard this morning he's been definitely booked to host the second pilot.'

'Has he? There was also that strange conversation Tim Dyer overheard...'

'About infidelity...'

'Yes, *marital* infidelity...Could have meant that Bob's wife had been unfaithful. Has got a wife, has he?'

'Oh yes. She's an I.T.N. newscaster. I wonder who she was supposed to have been unfaithful with...?

'Be wonderfully neat if it turned out to be Barrett Doran. Which would also tie in with Bob's line about "finding it difficult to work with the bastard under the circumstances".'

'Yes,' Sydnee agreed excitedly. 'And that would give Bob another reason for getting rid of his rival.'

'All interesting speculation. Well, the person he was talking to, and who obviously knew what he was on about, was Joanie Bruton's husband. I think we should put Trish Osborne in cold storage for a while, and try and find out more from Roger Bruton.'

'Probably mean talking to Joanie too. It's not often they're seen apart.'

'That's fine. She may know even more about it. The question is: How do we make the approach? Do you claim you want to talk about the second pilot? And, if so, how do you explain me away? Tim Dyer was too obsessed about his car to take much notice, but Joanie Bruton's no fool. I'm afraid she's likely to be rather more observant.'

'Yes.' There was a silence from the other end of the phone, while Sydnee made up her mind. 'I think the best thing is to tell them the truth.'

'Tell them that we don't think Chippy killed Barrett and we're trying to find out who did?' Charles asked, amazed.

'Yes. Why not? After all, they've both got rock-solid alibis for the relevant twenty minutes, so there's no way either of them could have been involved in the crime. Also, as you say, Joanie's a shrewd lady. I think she'd respect us more for telling her the truth. And we needn't worry about her discretion. By the nature of her work, she's used to keeping secrets.'

'What about Roger?'

'He does what she does. No, the more I think about it, the more I'm convinced we should tell them everything. Joanie' s a bright lady, and very understanding. I think she could help us a lot.'

'Okay. If you're sure.'

'I am. Leave it to me, Charles. I'll set it up.'

The house in Dulwich Village, outside which the MG drew up, was large, probably Edwardian. Its exterior had been recently decorated. A new Volvo was parked on the paved semicircle at the front.

The porch in which they stood as Sydnee pressed the bell-push was wooden-framed with the original windows of coloured glass. The red and white diamond tiles underfoot had been cleaned that morning.

Roger Bruton opened the door. Charles was again struck by his pallor which, combined with the wispy hair around his bald patch, gave him a slightly effete appearance. His voice, soft and precise, did nothing to dispel this impression.

'Good morning. You're right on time. I'm afraid Joanie hasn't quite finished her correspondence, but she'll be with us very shortly. Come through.'

He led them across the tiled hallway and opened a stripped pine door into a large front room, which could be doubled in size when the folding partition doors were opened. A dumpy sofa and two dumpy armchairs gave a feeling of expensively casual comfort. A window-seat in the bay at the front was littered with apparently random cushions. Books were stacked with careful asymmetry on the shelves either side of the fireplace, in whose grate a Coalite fire glowed scarlet. Invitations and jocular cards were stuck into the frame of the high mirror above the mantelpiece. Everything demonstrated that perfection of cleanliness only to be found in a house without children.

'Do sit down, please.' Roger gestured to the armchairs. Charles and Sydnee appropriated one each. They were both aware of a woman's voice talking rapidly and incisively on the other side of the partition.

Roger explained it immediately. 'Joanie dictates her letters into a tape-recorder. Then her secretary comes in in the afternoon and types them up. It's the only way we can keep ahead. I'm afraid, what with the magazine and the radio spot and now the television show, the mail-bag just gets bigger every day.'

'Actually,' said Charles, 'it was you we wanted to talk to, at least initially.'

Roger Bruton looked startled at the suggestion. 'I think it'd be better if you talked to both of us together. After all, I wasn't involved in the show at W.E.T., that was Joanie's bit. I was just sort of hanging around.'

'Which must have given you an ideal chance to see what was going on.'

'Oh, no. I'm not observant,' said Roger Bruton, with a self-depreciating shrug, and then firmly changed the subject. He indicated a low table, on which stood a tray with a china coffee-set on it. Four cups and saucers were neatly laid out. 'I'll just fill the pot. Coffee all right for both of you?'

They confirmed that it was, and he hurried out of the room with evident relief. 'What did I tell you?' whispered Sydnee.

Charles might have responded to this, but the voice next door stopped, and they heard movement from behind the partition. The central door opened, and Joanie Bruton appeared. Charles rose to his feet.

'Good morning. Sorry to have kept you.'

Seen close up, and in her own surroundings, she was strikingly pretty, tiny but perfectly proportioned. Her short hair was the kind of ash blond that melts almost imperceptibly into grey, she had a smooth, clear skin with only a tracery of lines around the eyes, and it was impossible to say what age she was. Anything from thirty to fifty. She was one of those fortunate women on whom time leaves little mark.

She briskly clattered the partition doors back, revealing a tidy office area at the other end of the room. On a red desk stood a word processor and two telephones. Colour-coded files filled one wall of shelves. It was all neatly expensive, like a home office design from a colour supplement.

She came and shook their hands. 'Sorry, there wasn't a great deal of opportunity to get to know either of you on the studio day.' She flopped gracefully on to the dumpy sofa and gestured Charles to sit, too. Turning her shrewd blue eyes on Sydnee, she said, 'So you think the police have got the wrong murderer, love?'

'Yes. I'm convinced that Chippy didn't do it.'

'Hmm. Is she a friend of yours?'

'Yes.'

'It's quite natural that you should disbelieve it. We all get shocked when we hear unwelcome things about our friends. Apart from anything else, it seems to cast doubt on the quality of our own judgement. Pretending the unpalatable news is not true is quite a common reaction. Are you sure you're not just doing that, love?'

'Quite sure. We've almost got proof Chippy didn't do it.'

Quickly, Charles explained about his drinking from Barrett Doran's glass at six-thirty. He slightly edited the truth, saying that he had just wanted to check the rumour going around that the host always had gin on the set, but Joanie's appraising eyes seemed to see through the subterfuge.

She looked pensive when he'd finished. 'It never occurred to me to look for any other explanation of the death...I mean, once I'd heard the girl had been arrested. I suppose we can rule out the possibility of accident...'

'The cyanide had to be taken from Studio B, the gin had to be emptied out of the glass and the cyanide put in.'

'No, you're right. It could hardly have been accidental. So that means you're looking for another murderer?'

At that moment Roger Bruton came into the room with the filled coffee-pot, and there was a pause while he filled the four cups and passed them round. When he was seated beside his wife on the sofa, she put her hand on his knee and said, 'As I told you after the phone-call yesterday, Sydnee and Charles are convinced that the girl who's been arrested did not kill Barrett Doran.'

'In that case,' he asked almost without intonation, 'what do they think happened?'

'Perhaps we should ask them,' said Joanie. 'Do you have any theories about what really went on?'

'Only vague theories,' Charles replied. 'I mean, obviously someone else murdered Barrett...'

The couple on the sofa seemed to relax slightly now this statement of the situation had been made.

'...and we've been checking out the movements of people involved in the show during the relevant time.'

'During the meal-break, you mean?' asked Roger.

'Well, only during a very specific part of it. The cyanide must have been put in the glass after six-thirty.'

'After six-thirty?' Roger echoed in surprise.

'Yes, because I drank from Barrett's glass at six-thirty and it contained gin.'

'Gin?' Another surprised echo.

'He always had gin when he was doing a show.'

'Oh. And after you'd drunk from the glass, did you swap it round with one of the others?'

'No, of course he didn't,' Joanie almost interrupted her husband. Then, more gently, she repeated, 'No, of course he didn't, love.' Turning to the others, she asked, 'So *who* are your suspects?'

Charles smiled. 'Well, you'll be glad to hear that you two are off the list. You weren't down in the studio area at the pivotal time, so you're in the clear.'

Joanie clutched at her throat in mock-panic. 'What a relief.'

'Just concentrating on the people who actually appeared on the show, we've ruled out all of the four "professions" – that's except for me, assuming that I would be devious enough deliberately to stir up an investigation into my own guilt...'

'I think we'll give you the benefit of the doubt.'

'Very gracious. Of the four contestants, the only one who hasn't got an alibi for the relevant time – or perhaps I should say the only one whose alibi we haven't heard about – is the lady from Billericay, Trish Osborne. Of the panellists, you're all in the clear...except for Bob Garston.'

'Ah.' Joanie Bruton did not sound surprised, rather as if the mention of the name confirmed a suspicion.

'Now, at the moment we are concentrating our investigations on Bob Garston. As I say, he had the opportunity, and he had at least some motive.'

'Oh?' Charles got the impression that Joanie knew something, but was biding her time, waiting to see how much of it they knew already.

'He was considered for the job of hosting *If The Cap Fits*,' Sydnee explained. 'In fact, he's going to do it on the second pilot.'

'So you reckon that was the reason he would want Barrett out of the way?'

Again Charles felt Joanie was holding back, unwilling to volunteer more than she had to.

'That's one reason. We've a feeling there may also have been something more personal.'

She raised a quizzical eyebrow at him. 'Like what?'

'That's why we've come to see you. We thought you might know something about his private life.'

She chuckled. 'I know a great deal about a great many people's private lives, love. But one of the reasons why people tell me things, and the reason why I keep my job, is because I respect the confidentiality of such secrets.'

'Of course.'

While Charles tried to think of the next move, Sydnee came in, typically direct. 'You were overheard, Roger, talking to Bob. There was a suggestion that Bob Garston's wife had been having an affair with someone.'

This shook Roger Bruton. 'Who overheard me? Who was spying on me? Where were they? What did they see?'

Again his wife's calming hand went on to his knee. 'It's all right, love, all right.' She turned her eyes on Charles. 'Since you seem to know already, I can't do any harm by confirming it. Yes. Bob's wife did have an affair.'

'With Barrett Doran?'

She nodded. 'I knew about it, because I was there when they met. On some Thames Television chat-show. I saw them go off together. It was obvious to me what was happening. I do know a bit about the mechanics of sexual attraction.'

'Was Bob around at the time?'

'No. He heard about it, though. His wife must have told him herself, because nobody else knew. I gather he took it pretty badly. I talked to him about it when we next met, told him that these things happen, that often a little fling like that needn't affect the basic stability of the marriage.' She had dropped into the no-nonsense counselling manner she used to telephone callers on her weekly radio programme.

'And it wasn't in the gossip columns or anything? I had understood Barrett liked to make his conquests public.'

'Not this one. I think she must've insisted on keeping it quiet. I never heard it even hinted at by anyone.'

'Was the affair still going on when Barrett died?'

'No. Only lasted about a month, I think. Bob and she didn't split up or anything. I gather they'd more or less got over it, but Bob must have found it difficult suddenly having to be in the same studio as the man who'd cuckolded him.'

'How difficult, I wonder?'

'What you mean is, did it make Bob angry enough to decide to kill his rival? Who can say? People react differently to things. With some the trigger to violence is very delicately balanced; others will put up with almost anything.'

'And what would your professional judgement be of Bob Garston in that respect?'

'Do I see him as a potential murderer?'

'Yes.'

'On balance, no. I can see him getting very angry, and I can see him contemplating violence against someone who he reckoned had wronged him. But I think that violence would be expressed much more openly. I can see him going up to Barrett and punching him on the nose, but this devious business with the cyanide...no, doesn't sound his style.'

'I think you're probably barking up the wrong tree,' said Roger Bruton abruptly. 'The police aren't fools. They don't arrest people without good reason. I'm sure the girl they've got is the right one.'

'Yes, Roger,' his wife agreed soothingly, 'but you can see why Charles and Sydnee want to try and prove otherwise. It would be terrible if the wrong person did get sentenced for the crime.'

Roger Bruton did not look as if he agreed, but he didn't pursue the argument further.

'I know we're just feeling our way at the moment,' Charles admitted, 'but we do definitely think that we're on to something.'

'Of course.' Joanie's voice was very nearly patronizing as she said the line that had become her catch-phrase. 'I fully understand, love.'

'Tell me, as someone who was in the studio all through the show, did you notice anything strange at any point?'

'Strange?'

'Did anyone appear to be behaving oddly, anyone on the panel, any of the contestants...?'

'Well, no one was behaving very naturally, but then it's hardly a very natural situation. Everyone was tense, of course, concentrating on their performance. Is that what you mean?'

'No, I meant more than that. Did you notice anyone doing anything that you thought at the time was out of character?'

'I don't think so, love, no.'

'And, when Barrett drank the poison, did you notice anyone reacting in an unusual way?'

'Good heavens.' She chuckled. 'You ask a lot. It was a moment of terrible shock when he started gasping. We were none of us in any state to start checking each other's reactions. We just all leapt up to see if we could do anything to help him.'

A new thought came into Charles's mind. 'The desk got knocked over when you all stood up.'

'Yes. That big oaf, Nick Jeffries. There's a lot of him, you know. The original bull in the china shop.'

'Hmm. Yes.' Charles looked across at Sydnee. 'I think that really covers everything we were going to ask, doesn't it?'

The researcher nodded.

'We're very grateful to you both for giving up your time. As I say, we are still just feeling around. And I know we've voiced suspicions which are almost certainly scandalous...'

'My mind,' said Joanie, 'is the repository of so much scandal that the odd bit more's not going to hurt. It's as safe as a numbered Swiss bank account. Lots and lots of secrets locked away in there, aren't there, love?'

She grinned at her husband, who gave a nervous grin back.

'So where do you go from here?' he asked Charles.

'With our investigations?'

'Yes. If you persist in thinking there's anything to investigate,' he added sceptically.

'Well, I suppose we try and find out more about Bob Garston's movements during the meal-break. You saw him. Were you with him for long?'

'No. I'd just left Joanie in Make-up and I met him outside. We walked along the corridor and parted at the lifts.'

'Did he get into a lift?'

'Yes, he did.'

'Didn't say where he was going?'

'No.'

'And you stayed down waiting for Joanie?'

'Yes. There's a sort of Reception area there with chairs. I sat and waited.'

'I don't suppose you saw anything odd going on round the studios?'

'I wondered when you were going to ask me that,' Roger Bruton announced primly. 'Yes, I did see something rather odd going on.'

'What?' asked Charles.

Joanie Bruton said nothing, but she looked hard at her husband. Her expression was one of surprise mixed with something that could have been alarm.

Roger Bruton relished his moment centre stage. 'I saw the Trish Osborne person. Looking most unhappy. Crying, in fact.'

'What was she doing?'

He smiled smugly. 'Coming out of Barrett Doran's dressing room.'

Chapter Nine

'FRANCES. IT'S ME, Charles.'

'Keeping rather earlier hours than usual.' Her voice was unruffled, warm without being positively welcoming. If she was surprised to hear from him after three months, she didn't show it.

'I wanted to catch you before you went to school.'

'Well, you have. Just. I have to be in the car in three minutes.'

He visualised her yellow Renault 5 parked outside the house, then remembered he was projecting the wrong image. She had moved out of the Muswell Hill home they had shared and now lived in a flat in Highgate. He had not been there often enough to visualise the Renault outside it.

'Listen, I wondered if we could meet up...'

'Another reconciliation?' Her voice was wary.

'Just to see you. I just want to see you.'

'Well...'

'Couldn't we meet for dinner tonight? Not at the flat. That Italian place in Hampstead. What do you say?'

'Well...'

'Come on. I'll behave myself. No romantic red roses. No unwelcome attentions...that is, if they really are unwelcome...'

'Watch it. You're on the verge of the "women always mean yes when they say no" heresy.'

'No, I didn't mean that. I'd just like to see you, talk about things...' Then with inspiration he added, '...talk about Juliet, talk about our grandchildren...'

'Charles, I had just reconciled myself to the idea that I wasn't going to hear from you again for a long time.'

'Well, unreconcile yourself.'

'I'm not sure. You've no idea, once the initial hurt and emptiness had worn off, just how restful the thought of not seeing you for a while has become.'

'Oh.'

She responded to the disappointment in his monosyllable by asking cautiously, 'You don't just want to see me because you're depressed, do you? Because I'm pretty ragged by this stage in the term, and I don't think I've much spare capacity for the old hand-holding "I understand, I understand" routine.'

'I'm not depressed. Not more than usual.'

'Great,' she said with resignation. 'Have you just come to the end of one of your little affairs?'

'No. Honestly. There hasn't been anyone on the scene for months...nearly a year.'

'Hmm.'

'Oh, come on, Frances, do have dinner with me. After all, I am your husband.'

As soon as he'd said it, he knew that this might not be the best argument to put forward, and it received a well-deserved slap-down. 'Depends very much, I would have said, on your definition of "husband"...whether the word is a once-and-for-all title bestowed at marriage or whether it implies a continuing active role, like, say, the word "lover".'

'I don't quite see what you're getting at,' he said evasively.

'Yes, you do. The word "lover" suggests something's happening. When the affair's over, people become "ex-lovers". It's not the same with "husband". Even if the marriage is over, you don't become an "ex-husband" without getting divorced.'

'Oh, you're not on about that again. I thought we agreed that there was no point in our getting divorced.'

'*You* agreed that. I don't recall my opinion being canvassed.'

'Frances...'

'I have to be in the car in twenty seconds.'

'Frances, will you please meet me for dinner in the Italian place at eight o'clock this evening?'

'All right. But, Charles Paris...'

'Yes?'

'Don't you dare be late.'

'I won't be, love. You know me.'

'Yes. I do.'

Sydnee had said she'd ring him once she'd fixed up for them to see Trish Osborne, and she came through about half-past ten.

'She's set up. Happy to talk. I said we'd be over early afternoon.'

'Did you say what we wanted to talk about?'

'No. Mind you, she didn't ask. Presumably, like Tim Dyer, she just assumes it's something to do with the show.'

'Good. Well, look, can you pick me up at the bedsitter? Or will it be easier if I make my way to somewhere more central...?'

'Charles, I've got problems here. Just after I'd spoken to Trish, John Mantle came in. I'm afraid I've got to start out on the contestant trail again.'

'For the second pilot?'

'Yes. They've got a studio date now. The schedule's been rejigged so that the pilot goes into Studio A next Thursday. Which means we've got to get a move on getting the contestants.'

'I thought you always had some spares lined up.'

'Yes, but I don't think they'd be good enough for John. The American copyright-holders have been bending his ear. They say the contestants we had on the first pilot showed about as much life as General Custer after Little Big Horn. They say we've got to get a new lot with more "pazazz".'

'Where do you start looking for "pazazz"?'

'Same places as I looked when 'pazazz' wasn't on the shopping-list. The trouble is, what these Americans don't realise is that people over here haven't yet lost their inhibitions about game shows. It's going to take a few years before the British reserve cracks and you see the kind of hysterical commitment you get in the States. Still, from John Mantle's point of view, I must be seen to be busy. Four brand-new contestants with "pazazz" must be found.'

'Are the contestants the only changes you'll make in casting?'

'Well, obviously we'll need one new celeb now Bob's moved up to host. Lots of names have been mentioned, but I don't think it's been offered to anyone yet. And we'll have to set up four more "professions".'

'Oh.' Charles saw a potential booking disappearing over the horizon.

'Come on, Charles, we couldn't book you lot again. With three of the same celebs on the panel, they're going to remember what your real professions were.'

'I doubt it. They didn't take any notice of us, didn't see us as people at all. I bet, if I was back on, two of them'd still think I was the hamburger chef.'

'You're probably right. But we can't take the risk. People get very uptight about these game shows. Any hint of rigging or cheating or someone being "in the know", and you can get some very nasty reactions.'

'I suppose so.'

'Anyway, Chita's busy setting up four new "professions" – "professions", of course, who might just conceivably wear hats, which let me tell you, is not as easy as it sounds – and I have got to shoot off to Manchester to interview some punters in the fruitless search for "pazazz".'

'Oh.'

'What I'm saying, Charles, is can you go and interview Trish Osborne on your own?'

'But what ever excuse can I give for being there? At least, with you, I'd have some sort of W. E .T. credibility, but on my own…'

'I'm sure you'll think of something, Charles.'

It took Charles longer than he had expected to get to Billericay, and it was after four when he finally reached the neat dark-red-brick three-bedroomed house where Trish Osborne lived.

He got a whiff of perfume as she opened the door, and saw that she was wearing a pale-blue flying-suit. She had dressed up for her continuing contact with the media world.

Though he had had plenty of travelling time during which to work out his excuse for appearing on her doorstep, he hadn't come up with much. 'I'm afraid Sydnee suddenly had to go to Manchester,' he said lamely, 'so there's just me.'

'Never mind.' She ushered him into her living-room. The carpet had a yellow and green zigzag design, whose colours were picked up on the open curtains. White patterned net against the double glazing shut out the darkening world. The mahogany veneer surface of the dining table gleamed, as did the yellow-upholstered chairs marshalled around it. Light refracted through the spotless glass ornaments above the matt silver music centre on the room divider. On the walls, in yellow velvet tasselled frames, were photographs of three children at different ages. In pride of place, on the mantelpiece over the 'log-effect' gas fire, lay her red, blue and silver *If The Cap Fits* cap.

She gestured to a lime-green three-piece suite with dark wood arm-rests and rigidly plumped yellow cushions. 'Do sit down. What can I get you? Tea? Coffee? Something stronger?'

This last was offered with a kind of insouciant daring, Trish demonstrating her freedom from the conventional restraints which might have inhibited someone not accustomed to media circles.

Charles resisted the temptation. 'Tea'd be lovely.'

She must have had the kettle boiling when he arrived, because she appeared in only a couple of minutes with a loaded tray. Charles still hadn't worked out his line of approach, so, while she poured, he played for time by indicating the photographs. 'Nice-looking kids.'

'Yes. Taken some time ago. They're all grown-up now.'

'Really?'

'Youngest's twenty.'

He looked at her. He knew it was going to be a corny line, but it was still true. 'You don't look old enough to have children of that age.'

She coloured very slightly in acknowledgement of the compliment. Her dark hair was even shorter, must have been cut since the recording. It came down to little peaks in front of her small ears. 'If you start breeding at seventeen, it's quite possible to have them all off your hands by the time you're forty.' She hesitated. 'And then look around to see if there's anything left of your life.'

'Lots, I'm sure.' Charles smiled in meaningless reassurance. 'Even at my age, one still hopes there are more good bits to come.'

She didn't look convinced. Nor did she look at ease, perched on the edge of her lime-green armchair. Charles took a long swallow of tea. He still hadn't decided how to explain his presence. True, she hadn't questioned it yet, but the moment must come.

He made a kind of start. 'Terrible business at the recording, wasn't it?'

'Yes. The poor girl. I mean, I know men can be bastards, but to be driven to that...to kill someone...'

'Yes. Poor Chippy.'

'I thought the name was Caroline something.'

'Chippy was her nickname, the name she used at work.'

'I wonder what she'll get. Surely not life for something like that...? I mean it was a crime of passion, wasn't it?'

'I suppose so. Though that's not always a category the British Law recognises. She could still get a hefty sentence.'

'But I'd have thought when something's spur-of-the-moment like that...'

'Not completely spur-of-the-moment. Taking the cyanide from one studio to the other must have involved a degree of premeditation.'

'As I said, poor girl…'

Charles decided to take a risk. 'There has been talk around W.E.T. that maybe she wasn't the one who did it…'

'What do you mean?'

'There have been suggestions that someone else killed Barrett Doran.'

'What!' She turned her wide brown eyes on him in amazement. Either the idea was a total shock to her, or she was putting up a very skilful front. Charles, who knew a bit about the subject, didn't think she was a good enough actress to be shamming. He decided it was worth taking another risk. The truth, he had often found, could be a useful surprise tactic.

'In fact, that's why I'm here. As I say, various people at W.E.T. have had doubts about Chippy's guilt and I'm just sort of investigating, on their behalf, to see if there's any other possible explanation for what happened.'

'I see.' The eyes went down quickly, but not quickly enough to hide their disappointment. 'And, if Sydnee had been able to come today, is that what she would have been coming about?'

'Yes.'

'Ah.' The hurt was still there.

'Why, what did you imagine she might –?'

'Nothing, nothing.'

Charles looked at the bowed dark head in its neat suburban living-room, and suddenly he saw everything. It was just another manifestation of the power of television. Trish Osborne thought she had done well on *If The Cap Fits*. And indeed she had. She had been a good lively contestant (in spite of what Aaron Greenberg and Dirk van Henke felt). But that was all she had been. She, with that ignorance of scale that always afflicts amateurs, had not recognised the limits of her performance. She had seen it as the start of something. With time on her hands at home for ideas to grow like ginger-beer plants, she had fantasised of directors hailing her as a 'natural' for television, of offers of work, of a new impetus to dig her out of her domestic rut, of a career to fill the void left by her departed children. She had thought that Sydnee's wish to see her would be about the next step on that ladder. It was all very commonplace, very predictable and very sad.

He knew he was right, but he passed no comment on his findings. 'So I'm here, really, to ask you to think back over that studio day, think if there was anything suspicious, anything you noticed that seemed out of the ordinary.'

She laughed, jogging herself out of self-pity. 'The whole day seemed pretty out of the ordinary to me. I'd never been in a television studio before. It may seem pretty ordinary to you, but let me tell you, being on television is the answer to many a Billericay housewife's dreams.' Her face clouded. 'I suppose, after what happened, I'm not even going to *be* on television. I mean, there's no way they can put out that recording, is there?'

'No.'

She clutched at a straw. 'They couldn't sort of edit on another ending…?'

Charles shook his head. 'Sorry, love.' (For a moment he wondered, 'Do I normally say 'love' as much as this, or have I picked it up from the infinitely understanding Joanie Bruton?') 'Think about it – with a show of that sort, you can't suddenly change hosts in the middle. You couldn't even if there had been no publicity about Barrett's death. As it is…'

'Yes, I'm sorry. I was just being silly. Not thinking. Of course they couldn't use it.'

Moved again by the disappointment in her eyes, Charles searched for another reassurance. 'It probably hasn't made that much difference, actually, love.' (Doing it again.) 'With a show like this, they'd be very unlikely to put out the pilot. They'd be almost bound to want to make some changes in the casting or the format before they got into a series.'

This was not at all the right thing to say. The brown eyes blazed. 'What, you mean we went through all that for nothing? We were just being used as guinea pigs with no chance of the show actually being on the television? The producer swore it would go out unless there was something terribly wrong.'

'Well,' said Charles, redirecting the conversation off this sticky patch, 'there was something terribly wrong, wasn't there?'

This brought her up short. 'Yes,' she replied softly.

'Barrett Doran's death. Can we talk about that?'

'If you like.' She remained subdued, still inwardly boiling at the perfidy of a television company that could put her under such strain on what she regarded as false pretences.

'Starting from the idea that Chippy didn't kill her former lover…'

'Was he? I didn't know that.'

'Yes. That was presumed to be her motive. 'Hell hath no fury…'

'Sorry?'

'…like a woman scorned.'

She gave a small shake of her head. The quotation didn't mean anything to her.

'Anyway, if Chippy didn't, somebody else did. And the murderer put cyanide in Barrett Doran's drink at a very specific time. During the meal-break, between six-thirty and ten to seven. Sydnee and I have been going round, checking up on the movements of people connected with the show at that time.'

'Oh yes?' There was a new reticence in her manner; she didn't volunteer anything.

'I wondered what you were doing then, Trish...'

She coloured. 'Oh, you know. This and that. I can't really remember.'

'You left Chita in the Conference Room at a quarter past six. You were back in there at twenty to seven. You left the room with Tim Dyer. You both said you fancied a steak. Neither of you had one.'

'You *have* been doing your research.'

'Outside the Conference Room you both got into separate lifts. I want to know what you did for the next twenty-five minutes.

She now looked very flustered. 'I said. I can't really remember. I was very nervous. I just walked about to calm me down.'

'This is important, Trish. I'm talking about the time that the cyanide was put into the glass.'

The brown eyes widened. 'But surely you don't think that *I* had anything to do with it?'

'I'm just trying to eliminate as many people as possible from suspicion,' Charles replied stolidly, in a voice he'd used as a Detective-Inspector in an Agatha Christie play ('About as lively as a Yorkshire pudding that's still wet in the middle' – *West Sussex Gazette*).

'Well, there wasn't anything suspicious about what I was doing.'

'Trish,' he said with a little more force, 'nothing was seen of you from the moment you got into the lift...until you came out of Barrett Doran's dressing room at about twenty-five past six. At which time you were crying.'

She looked for a second as if she might be about to cry again, but then regained control of herself and appeared to make the decision to tell the truth. 'All right. I did go to his dressing room.'

'Straight after you came out of the lift in the basement?'

'Yes.'

'Why did you go there?'

'He'd invited me for a drink.' The words were dragged out truculently.

'And you agreed to have a drink with him? Even after the way he had humiliated you in the afternoon?'

Her blush spread down her neck. Charles's eyes, unwillingly following it, were uncomfortably aware, through the thin material of the flying-suit, of the unmentioned subject of their conversation.

'Yes, I suppose he had humiliated me. But I overreacted. I shouldn't have burst into tears on the set. I know you've got to be tough if you're going to get anywhere in television.' She repeated this last line devoutly, like an article of faith.

'Presumably, when you agreed to go and have a drink with him, you were aware of Barrett Doran's reputation as a womaniser?'

'That's why I agreed,' she almost snapped at him. Charles gaped. 'God, have you any idea how boring life is in Billericay? I want my life to *start*, I want to catch up on all the things I missed while I was having babies and polishing furniture. No, I didn't like Barrett Doran, he'd upset me a lot during the rehearsal, but I knew that he fancied me. I wasn't going to miss a chance. I know you have to sleep around if you're going to get anywhere in television.'

This again was spoken like part of a creed, received wisdom which she had picked up and was determined to believe. Charles found himself shocked by her strange mixture of outrageousness and naiveté, and a little frightened by the desperation that accompanied it.

'So can I enquire what happened when you got into his dressing room?'

'Don't see why not.' Her attempt at brazen insouciance was not coming off. There was something engagingly pathetic about it, like a teenager adding a couple of years to her age at a party. 'Fairly predictable, really. He poured me a drink, then he put his arms round me and started to kiss me. That was what I had expected, so it wasn't such a big deal...'

'But...' Charles voiced the unspoken conjunction.

'*But* he was a bit too...He rushed me. I wasn't quite ready for...I hadn't expected him to...' All the skin above her neckline was now deep red. '...to want to do it so quickly,' she pronounced finally.

'He hadn't got long. Only time for a quickie,' said Charles without much emphasis.

'Anyway, he was scrabbling at my clothes, trying to undress me – not all of me, just the bits he needed, and I was sort of holding him back, but not quite holding him back and...and then the door opened.'

She sat back in her chair, relieved, as if the worst part of the narrative was over.

'It was a girl. Blonde girl. Pretty, I suppose. I didn't recognise her.'

'Had she got on a light-grey sort of all-in-one suit...cut like the one you're wearing?' Trish nodded. 'That was Chippy, the one who's been charged with his murder.'

'Good heavens. Was it? I didn't really look at her. You know, I was flustered, pulling my clothes around me. It was...well, it was embarrassing.'

'And was that what made you cry?'

'No. It was what Barrett said to me.' She looked once again tearful at the recollection.

'Can I ask...?'

'I won't tell you exactly what he said, but he dismissed me, as if I were...I don't know, a waiter, a taxi-driver...no one...as if I wasn't a person at all.'

'I'm rather afraid that's how he treated most people.'

'Yes.' She seemed listless, tired out by her account.

'So you left the dressing room and went out into the corridor?'

'Yes.'

'Where you met Roger Bruton.'

'I saw him. I turned away. I didn't want him to see I was crying.'

'Any particular reason, or wouldn't you have wanted anyone to see you crying?'

'I wouldn't want anyone to, but...' She let out a little cough of laughter. '...I particularly didn't want him to. I was afraid he'd get Joanie to come along and ask what the matter was. I couldn't have faced her *understanding* me. God knows how he's stuck it all these years. What hell it must be for a man whose wife really *understands* him.'

'Most men complain of the opposite.

'Do you?' Her brown eyes found his.

'Complain that my wife doesn't understand me? No, I'm rather afraid she does. But, since we've been separated for fifteen years or so, the point's really academic.' He needed to break the link between their eyes, so he looked away and moved briskly on. 'You left Barrett's dressing room at about twenty-five past six. You weren't back up in the Conference Room till twenty to seven.'

'No.'

'What did you do? Can you account for that quarter of an hour?'

'I went to the Ladies, the one near Make-up. I was crying. I didn't want people to see me crying. I went to sort of pull myself together.'

It was a fairly shaky alibi, but she said it so ingenuously Charles felt inclined to believe her. 'Did you see anyone apart from Roger Bruton before you got back to the Conference Room?'

'I saw Bob Garston.'

'Oh?'

'After I'd come out of the Ladies. While I was waiting for the lift. It took ages to come. Bob came and waited too.'

'Did he say anything?'

'Commented on how inefficient the lifts were, that sort of thing. I was still trying to hide the fact that I'd been crying, so I didn't want to make conversation.'

'No. And this'd be...what? Round twenty to seven?'

'Must've been by then, yes.'

'And when the lift finally came, did you both travel up to the fifth floor together?'

She nodded.

'I don't suppose you saw where Bob came from? Did he walk all the way along the corridor to the lifts?'

'Oh no. He came out of one of the doors half-way along.'

'Do you remember which one?'

'Yes, certainly. The door from Studio A.'

'Ah,' said Charles, as non-committally as he could, smothering the surge of excitement inside him.

Trish Osborne did not seem aware of the portent of her words. She stretched her arms behind her neck and yawned.

The movement emphasised what Barrett Doran had thought unsuitable for family viewing. 'That's really tired me out, going through all that again. Let's have a real drink now.'

Charles didn't refuse, and was soon equipped with a large glass of Chivas Regal. Trish had a schooner of sherry. She sat down on the sofa beside him and looked at her watch. 'That's not bad. Kept off the booze till half-past five today.'

This remark, like some of her earlier ones, seemed designed only to shock.

Charles did not react. He reckoned he had got what he came for. Bob Garston had been seen coming out of Studio A at exactly the right time. The investigation was proceeding.

'Nothing else you can remember struck you as odd during the studio day? Nothing that happened just before his actual death or...?'

'I wouldn't have seen it if there had been anything. I was eliminated, remember.'

'Oh yes, of course. Well, did your husband see anything from the audience?'

She let out a short, bitter laugh. 'He wasn't there. He's not interested in any of my activities.'

'Oh.'

'The only thing that interests him is his work. That's why he gets home at ten every night. "Working late at the office." Classic cover-up for an affair. I sometimes think I wouldn't mind if it was an affair. At least that'd give another dimension to him, he wouldn't be one hundred per cent boring. But I'm afraid, in his case, no, it really is work.'

'Oh,' said Charles. Trish seemed closer to him now on the sofa, her shoulder brushing against his. He sat forward. 'Really should be off. I'm very grateful to you for...'

'There's no hurry. Have another drink.'

'Oh no, I shouldn't, well, just a small one.'

It wasn't a small one. Trish's refill wasn't small, either. She suddenly giggled as she bounced down on to the sofa beside him. 'Awfully embarrassing, wasn't it, in the studio, that business about my blouse? I bet you didn't know where to look.'

'Oh, it was...all right. I'm sure you were more embarrassed than anyone else was. I've seen that sort of thing happen a lot before.'

'Oh?' She arched an eyebrow.

'Well, I mean, I've been to lots of costume calls and photo calls where that kind of thing arises – I mean, happens.' He didn't think he was doing this very well. 'There are always problems like that. Men have to be told to put jock-straps under their tights and ladies...well...' He found his eyes were ineluctably drawn to the objects of discussion. 'Happens all the time in the theatre,' he babbled. 'Always has. Dr Johnson told David Garrick he'd have to stop going backstage because the actresses' breasts unsettled him.'

Trish Osborne did not seem over-interested in this snippet of literary anecdote. Instead, she looked down at her cleavage. 'Barrett Doran was wrong, actually.'

'Oh. What about?'

'Well, he said they'd gone like that because I was panting for it.'

'Oh yes, so he did. I remember vaguely.'

'That wasn't the reason. It was just nerves, you know, being in the studio and all that.'

'Oh. Well, there you go.'

'I mean, the effect is the same, but it *was* nerves.'

'Ah.'

'It's not nerves now,' she said.

Charles felt bad as he entered the restaurant in Hampstead. In spite of her apparent sophistication, it turned out that he was the first man with whom Trish had cheated on her husband, and that had led to a few tears. Also the brazenness of her approach, and the fact that he was clearly not an individual but some rite of passage into her fifth decade, left him feeling soiled.

And he was late. Twenty to nine.

There was no softness in Frances's face as she demanded, 'Where the hell have you been?'

'Oh,' he said. 'Billericay.'

Chapter Ten

BOB GARSTON'S CAREER was on an upward spiral. His early success as an on-screen researcher for a pop consumer programme had given him public recognition. People stopped him in the streets, turned their heads as he passed, pointed to him in restaurants. He loved all the attention.

And he got more of it when he started his own series. A shrewd producer, recognizing how readily people identified with Bob Garston, had devised a format which used his populist qualities to the full. The show was called *Joe Soap* and its piously avowed intention was to explain the workings of bureaucracy to the general public. Each week Bob Garston in his *faux-naïf* role as Joe Soap would attempt some enterprise – to have a house extension built, to take the Gas Board to court, to set up his own minicab business – and go through the necessary bureaucratic hoops to realise that ambition.

His interviews with the various officials were filmed, and these film inserts linked in the studio by Bob, whose wry commentary was interspersed with recollections and horror stories from 'ordinary people' who had been through the same processes. As ever in television programmes dealing with members of the public, their contribution was edited with professional cunning to extract the maximum humour and, almost always, to leave them looking stupid.

The series was an instant success. Its format skilfully provided the audience with a justification for laughing at their fellow human beings. Like an investigative television sex programme, and with the same degree of calculation on the part of its makers, *Joe Soap* was watched by most of its viewers for the wrong reasons.

The series, like the earlier consumer programme, was made by the B.B.C.. Bob Garston's only work for I.T.V. had hitherto been a few guest appearances on quiz show panels. His assumption of Barrett Doran's mantle on *If The Cap Fits* would be an important stepping-stone towards the big money and wider audience of commercial television.

These thoughts went through Charles Paris's head as he sat with Sydnee watching the recording of the latest *Joe Soap*. She had had a legitimate excuse for contacting Bob Garston, since John Mantle had delegated her to check through the format of *If The Cap Fits* with its new host. Long circular harangues from Aaron Greenberg and Dirk van Henke had led the Executive Producer to make a few revisions in the proposed presentation of the show. Patience and his customary diplomacy had ensured that these changes were minimal and cosmetic, but he had given straight-faced assurances to the copyright-holders that every detail would be communicated to the new host.

(The Americans had not been convinced that Bob Garston was the right man for the job. They saw little evidence that he possessed the 'pazazz' which, to their minds, Barrett Doran had lacked. Once again, John Mantle had had to spend many hours of cajoling and apparent concession over expensive food before he got his own way. At least one good thing had emerged out of the first pilot, however; the Americans had been so concerned about other details that they put up no further objections to the English title for the show. On that point, John Mantle's slow, wait-and-see diplomacy had paid off, and he felt confident that, given time and patience, it would pay off on the other details too.)

Though Sydnee had a perfectly legitimate reason for going to see Bob Garston, explaining Charles's presence at the recording was going to be more difficult. Bob had suggested a meal after the show to Sydnee, secure in the glamour of his television persona (and not realizing that her long exposure to the medium had left her a little more cynical than most women about that glamour). Charles had, needless to say, not been included in the invitation, and he had a feeling his being there would cast him in the unwelcome role of gooseberry. Whether or not Bob Garston had sexual designs on Sydnee, he was the kind of man whose ego would be massaged by dining alone with any attractive girl.

On the other hand, the way their investigation into Barrett Doran's death was pointing made both determined that they should confront their suspect together.

Sydnee reckoned their best approach would be an edited version of the truth. They should voice their suspicions that Chippy had not killed Barrett and say that they were trying desperately to clear her. For that reason, they were talking to all those who had been involved in the show, trying to find out if anyone had seen anything that might help their case. They would not make any direct accusation to Bob, but hope that something he said might confirm their suspicions.

Charles thought this was pretty risky. If Bob Garston were guilty, it would only alert him to his danger and lead him into evasion. But, try as he could, Charles couldn't come up with another, safer approach, so he had been forced to accept Sydnee's suggestion, unsatisfactory though it was.

He sat back and watched the show. Bob Garston, with the mock-innocence of Joe Soap, was on film, applying to a Local Council Planner for permission to build a greenhouse in his back garden. 'But suppose I just put the thing up, I'm sure you wouldn't really mind...You'd turn a blind eye. Don't you think?'

'Oh, I couldn't do that.'

Charles, who knew a lot about vocal inflections, could recognise that the Planner had been going to say more, but had been cut short by the edit. The effect was exactly as the programme-makers intended. The man sounded as if the thing he 'couldn't do' was 'to think'. The audience duly roared their approval of this ambiguity.

Cut back to Bob Garston in the studio. 'Well,' he said with a wolfish grin,

rubbing in the joke for those too slow to understand first time round, 'he said it!'
The audience around Charles again roared sycophantically.

Getting 'a television person' on his own is never easy. Programme-making always involves a lot of people and those who work in the medium tend to hunt in packs. To see a single person, or even just a couple, in a television bar is a rarity; instead there are clusters, large groups representing different production teams.

There was a large *Joe Soap* group round Bob Garston in the B.B.C. Television Centre bar that evening after the recording. Sydnee and Charles were the exception, just two people, drinking respectively white wine and Bell's whisky. Bob had waved recognition at Sydnee through the crowd in his dressing room, led her up with the crowd to the bar, and joined the crowd at the entrance to sign her in. Charles had taken advantage of the crowd to sidle in without benefit of signature. Bob had shown no sign of recognizing him. The problem of explaining his presence remained.

Beyond buying her a drink, Bob Garston had made no attempt to include Sydnee in his group. As a television person, she understood this completely. She knew the wild laughter and gesticulation around him was part of that mutual release of tension that came at the end of a long studio day. She knew that all the conversation would be of late cues, shadows from microphone booms, recalcitrant interviewees, references and in-jokes that could have no meaning for those who had not lived through the same day.

Charles had no expectation of being included. His dominant worry remained how to explain himself, how to make sure that he and Sydnee got a chance to talk to Bob alone. He looked around the bar, and saw a couple of actors he knew buying drinks for Light Entertainment producers. He felt the recurrent wave of despair that came over him whenever he thought about his career. He knew actors should keep a high profile, be seen by the people who mattered, the people who controlled that arcane magic of employment. On the rare occasions when his agent ceased to think of him as a lost cause and proffered advice, Maurice Skellern always said, 'Put yourself about, Charles, get yourself seen. Got to be up front as an actor, you know. Remind people you exist. Actors got to let their light be seen, shine upon producers, dazzle them. Whereas all you seem to do is find thicker and thicker bushels to hide yours under.'

He knew partly it was true. Some of his failure in his chosen career could be attributed to the eternal problem of too many actors chasing too few parts, some perhaps to only an average talent, but within him there was also the fatal flaw of diffidence, a kind of laziness that kept him from hustling as hard as he knew he should.

Sounds of an argument at the bar shook him out of this orbit of self-pity. Time had been called, but one of the Light Entertainment producers was vigorously asserting that he needed another drink. People were starting to look around for abandoned handbags and briefcases. The party was breaking up.

With many good-humoured waves and shoulder-slappings, Bob Garston detached himself from the *Joe Soap* group and came across towards them. 'Sydnee, hi. You set?'

'Sure.' She indicated her companion. 'This is Charles Paris.'

'Oh yes?' There was no interest and no recognition in his glance.

'You remember, he was one of the "professions" in the first *If The Cap Fits* pilot.'

Bob gave a nod which recognised this fact without giving it any importance. With a perfunctory grin at Charles, he reached out an arm to Sydnee. 'Shall we be off then?'

She looked at Charles with an expression that told him he had to get out of this one. 'Bob,' he said. 'We want to talk to you.'

'Sydnee and I are just going off to talk. I don't see where you fit in.'

'We want to talk about Barrett Doran's murder.'

Bob Garston's eyes narrowed. The hearty public face slipped away, to be replaced by something more furtive.

'You'd better come along then,' he said.

Bob Garston's car was directly in front of Television Centre, where only the highly privileged were allowed to park. It was a new Jaguar. Bob and Charles sat in the front, Sydnee in the back.

'Right, what is this?' The voice was unrecognisable from the confident, insinuating tones of Joe Soap. It was breathier, tighter; and the note of tension could have been fear.

Charles explained evenly, without specifying their reasons, that they didn't think Chippy had killed Barrett.

'Are you going to make your suspicions public? Are you going to the police?'

'We will eventually, yes. We'd rather go with the name of the person who did kill him and some evidence to prove it. But if we can't get that fairly soon, we'll just have to go and tell them why we know Chippy's innocent.'

'Why is that?'

'We have our reasons,' Charles replied infuriatingly.

Bob Garston was silent for a moment. Then he said, 'You realise that, if the girl's eliminated, I become the obvious suspect?'

This was too easy. 'Yes,' said Charles. 'That's the conclusion we were coming to.'

'I wanted the host job from the start. I never made much secret of the fact. I don't believe in disguising ambition. I think if you say what you want, you stand a damned sight better chance of getting it.' The forthright Joe Soap quality came back briefly into his voice. 'So I suppose that could look like a motive...'

'Not the only one,' said Charles gently.

A light that had not been switched off in an office above them filtered through the windscreen, illuminating one side of Bob Garston's face. Charles saw bewilderment, then understanding, quickly followed by fury. 'How the hell did you hear about that?'

Charles protected his source. 'Let's just say I heard.'

'Did my wife tell you?'

'No. I've never met your wife.'

'Look, if this gets out to the gossip columns I'll bloody murder you.' Realisation of what he had said came into Bob Garston's face. It was followed by a twisted smile. 'Unfortunate remark perhaps, in the circumstances. So...you think I killed Barrett. May I ask how I'm supposed to have done it?'

'Anyone who was round the studio area between six-thirty and six-fifty could have done it. They only needed to take the cyanide from Studio B into Studio A and put it in the glass. Would have taken two minutes, maximum.'

Bob Garston nodded grimly.

'You were seen at about twenty-five to seven – coming out of Studio A.'

'Yes.' He lost his temper. 'Dammit! Why the hell did I go in there?'

'You tell me,' said Charles.

Bob Garston let out a long sigh. 'I didn't do it, you know. I didn't kill Barrett.'

'No?'

'No, I bloody didn't!'

'Then why are you getting so upset?'

'Because, as I said, I'm the obvious suspect. The same day you tell the police Chippy didn't do it, they're going to be round knocking on my door, asking questions. It'll be down the station, "helping with enquiries"...they might even bloody arrest me.'

'But if you can prove you're innocent –'

'Doesn't make a blind bit of difference. Look, my career's at an important stage, could take off quite dramatically in the next couple of months. The last thing I need now is my name over the papers.'

'But, as I said, if you can prove you're innocent –'

'Listen. If there's one thing doing my sort of programme has taught me, it's that mud sticks. I make some allegation on the show, however oblique it is, about some official, and that bloke never lives it down. He's lost credibility...his colleagues don't trust him any more. I know, I've got plenty of letters to prove it. I've even been sued a few times. Once the allegation's been made, no amount of public denial can make it go away completely. Look at the newspapers – thousands read the scandalous headline – how many read the little printed apology for getting the facts wrong that comes out the next week?'

Under other circumstances, Charles might have questioned the assurance with which Joe Soap admitted destroying the credibility of his victims, but it wasn't the moment for moral debate. 'Well, I'm glad you're aware of the stakes,' he said. 'So now perhaps you realise that the only way for you to keep the police off your doorstep is to prove to our satisfaction that you are innocent.'

'Oh, I am.'

'Good. Tell us why, and then perhaps you can help us find out who did kill Barrett Doran.'

'Right.' Bob Garston was clearly ill at ease as the subject of interrogation, and made a bid to take over the interview himself. In his best hectoring manner, he demanded, 'You want to know what I was doing between six-thirty and six-thirty-five that evening?'

'Yes. We know you went into Studio A.'

'All right, all right. I did. I'm not denying it.'

'Why?'

'Don't rush me. I'm about to bloody tell you, aren't I?' He paused, as if composing his next sentence into the most palatable form. 'The fact is, I wanted to get on to that set. I wanted to stand by Barrett's lectern. I just wanted to get the feel of it...to know what it felt like to be in charge of that kind of show. You know, just like a little lad trying on his Dad's overalls...'

This winsome simile would have gone down well with the *Joe Soap* audience, but it failed to charm Charles. 'That doesn't sound very convincing to me. And I'm not sure that the police would be that convinced either.'

'Well, it happens to be the bloody truth!' Bob Garston snapped petulantly. 'I can't help it if the truth isn't convincing, can I?'

'I'm only thinking of you, Bob,' said Charles with needling magnanimity. 'You're the one who wants to keep the police off your doorstep. Of course, they may be convinced by this story of whimsical role-playing, but I doubt –'

'Look!' Bob Garston pointed an angry finger in his antagonist's face. 'You just asked me why I went in. I told you. What happened when I got there is a different question. There was no way that I could have fiddled around with Barrett's glass. I'd have been seen.'

'There was someone else in there?'

'Of course there bloody was!'

'Who? The contestant, Tim Dyer? Hadn't he left?'

'No. Not him. It was the designer, wasn't it? Him with the bloody stupid haircut. He was there, fiddling with his precious set.'

'Sylvian,' murmured Sydnee, breaking her long silence.

'So what did you do?' asked Charles.

'Well, I wasn't going to start prancing round, pretending to be the host, was I? Not with him there. I turned straight round and walked out again.'

Charles's mind was racing as he voiced a formal thanks.

'Don't think I told you because I wanted to. But just bloody see that when you do go to the police, you tell them I'm out of the bloody reckoning. I haven't worked this hard on my career to have it shot to pieces by some half-baked rumour.' Without waiting for any response, he turned round to Sydnee. 'Right, with that out of the way, perhaps we'd better go and talk about this bloody game show.' He leant across Charles and clicked open the passenger door. 'You can get out and walk.'

Charles got out. And, as he walked the three miles back to Hereford Road, he thought again and again of what Barrett Doran had said about Sylvian de Beaune's first television set design.

Chapter Eleven

SYLVIAN DE BEAUNE'S flat was at the top of an old converted warehouse in what used to be London's Dockland. It was up four flights of stairs and there was no Entryphone, so a long gap ensued between their ring on the bell and his appearance at the front door.

He looked surprised to see them, recognizing Sydnee, but apparently never having seen Charles before in his life. He had put in further work on his appearance. The black Mohican strip on his head now had orange tufts at the front, and clusters of orange feathers depended from his ears. His face was covered with white make-up, relieved only by a dab of orange on lips and eyelids. He was out of the leather gear now, and dressed in a kind of pyjamas of off-white sackcloth, joined at the seams by beige leather thongs. The effect was, to Charles, reminiscent of a line-drawing of medieval underwear from a school textbook with a title like *Social Life in the Middle Ages*. He was coming to the conclusion that, amongst other things, Sylvian de Beaune designed his own clothes.

It was clear, when they got upstairs, that he was his own interior designer as well. The flat was really one long room, whose exposed rafters under a pitched roof should have given it the appearance of a Saxon mead-hall. And would have given it the appearance of a Saxon mead-hall if every surface had not been painted silver. The floor had been painted the same colour, and what must have been lovely views over the Thames were excluded by silver paint over the panes of the high windows. The area was lit by theatrical spotlights, the harshness of whose glare was subdued by gels of red and blue. Their beams were trained on to matt-black rectangular boxes, which, by a process of elimination, Charles deduced to be furniture (though which was a table and which a chair he would not like to have had to specify).

Sydnee showed no surprise at the surroundings, which must mean either that she had been there before, or that all her colleagues lived in similar environments. (If the second were the case, it was not surprising that the three researchers had found the Hereford Road bedsitter a little unusual.)

On one of the matt-black shapes a sheet of paper was pinned, and the selection of pens, templates and rulers nearby suggested that Sylvian had been working on his latest design when interrupted by the doorbell. Charles did not dare to contemplate what it might be.

As they entered, music, which could either have been South American flutes or a team of asthmatics competitively blowing blockages out of hose-pipes, sounded loudly. Sylvian de Beaune went across to a matt-black box with an array of matt-black buttons on the front, and moderated the volume. He gestured to them to sit. Charles had almost fully descended when he heard the words, 'No. That's a table', and moved accordingly to a smaller matt-black box.

Sylvian remained standing. 'What is it, Sydnee?'

'*If The Cap Fits*.'

'Don't tell me – John Mantle wants more bloody changes?'

'No. It's harking back to the first pilot.'

'Oh yes?'

'Barrett Doran's death.'

Had there been any natural colour in Sylvian de Beaune's face, that would have bleached it out. He gaped, stupefied.

'Chippy didn't kill him,' Sydnee continued. Because he still seemed incapable of speech, she persisted, 'Charles here drank from Barrett's glass at about six-thirty. At that point it definitely contained gin.'

'Oh, my God.' The words were hardly audible.

Charles picked up the initiative. 'So the cyanide was put in the glass after that time. You were seen m the studio just after six-thirty by Bob Garston.'

The orange lips moved, but this time no sound came out.

'It was your first major set, isn't that right, Sylvian? You were very proud of it, very worried about it. We know what Barrett Doran said when he saw it for the first time. Not very appreciative of your efforts, was he?'

Still no words came, but the designer shook his head, as if in disbelief. Slowly, he subsided on to one of the matt-black rectangular boxes. It was the one he had said was a table, but Charles didn't think it was the moment to say anything. He and Sydnee maintained the silence.

Finally, Sylvian de Beaune spoke. His voice was dull, as if he were repeating something learned by rote. 'I hoped it hadn't happened. I went into a terrible state of panic when he died and I heard it was cyanide. But then when Chippy was arrested, and I heard about how she had a motive to kill him and the opportunity to get the poison, I thought it was all right. I thought he'd got the right glass.'

'The right glass? Did you put the cyanide in it?'

The black and orange tufted head shook. 'No. Why on earth should I do that? No, that's not what I did.'

'Then what did you do?'

The voice retained its monotone as he told them. 'As you say, it was my first major set. As you say, I was worried about it. I kept looking at it from different angles, kept trying to see things that didn't work. That's why I went back into the studio during the meal-break. I was worried that something had looked wrong, so I went in to check.'

'What were you worried about – the wheel?' asked Charles, remembering what Tim Dyer had done to that part of the set.

'No. There was just something in the colours that had looked wrong. Something wrong with the balance between the lectern and the celebrities' desk. I'd looked and looked at it, and eventually the only thing I could think of was the glasses – the four on the desk and the one on the lectern.'

'But they were all the same – surely?'

'They were all nearly the same, yes. But they had been specially made to match the set. Hand-painted. I thought maybe they were slightly different, maybe there was more red on one, more blue on another. It was only likely to be a tiny difference –something definitely looked wrong. I couldn't think of anything else.'

'So what did you do?' asked Charles, with a sick feeling he knew the answer.

His worst fears were confirmed. 'I started changing them round.'

'Oh, my God.'

'Just to see if it made the colour balance better.'

'So which one did you change with Barrett's?' asked Charles, resigned.

'I can't remember.'

'Oh, come on. You must remember,' Charles snapped. 'You realise how important this is, don't you?'

'Yes. I do. Now. But, honestly, I can't remember. I tried them every way. I moved first one and then the other. I really couldn't say at the end which one was where. That's why I felt so awful when I heard about the cyanide. Then, when Chippy was arrested, I thought, thank God, at least he got the right one back.'

'Except that his right one contained gin at six-thirty.'

'Yes.' The tufted head drooped.

'But surely,' said Sydnee excitedly, 'the police would have checked the glasses afterwards. If we go to them and say what happened, and find out who had the one containing gin –'

Charles shook his head. 'The desk got knocked over. The glasses were scattered all over the place.'

Sylvian raised his head. 'Yes, I don't understand that. I designed it to be very stable. I mean, the centre of gravity was –'

But Sydnee didn't think it was the moment for a discussion of the intricacies of furniture design. 'Surely, Charles, the celeb who had gin in his or her glass would have noticed?'

'Must've done, yes. But nobody's said anything, have they? Otherwise Chippy wouldn't have been arrested. Which must mean the intended victim knew the poison was meant for him –'

'Or for her.'

'Yes...and is deliberately keeping quiet about it.'

'And all the while letting Chippy suffer,' said Sydnee, boiling with resentment.

'You realise something else...'

Sydnee looked at him curiously.

'If the cyanide wasn't put into Barrett's glass but into someone else's, it could have been done at any time during the meal-break.'

'Oh no. And all our checking of people's movements has been quite worthless.'

Charles nodded, then let out a long sigh. 'I think we're going to have to get our little research team together again, Sydnee.'

Chapter Twelve

NO ONE EVEN suggested that the second meeting of Charles's research team should take place in his bedsitter. They met instead at Harry Cockers, where Sydnee, Chita and Quentin obviously felt much more at ease.

'Isn't it a bit of a risk,' Charles had said when the idea was mentioned, 'talking about this sort of thing in such a public place?'

'Good God, no,' Sydnee had replied airily. 'It's ideal. Perfect security. Nobody at Harry Cockers goes to listen to anyone else. They just go to listen to themselves.'

And, as he once again sat watching the screeching variegated flying-suits at the bar, Charles had to admit she was right.

He had asked Sydnee to view the tape of the ill-fated pilot, concentrating on two specific moments, and the first business of their meeting was her report on this.

'I'm afraid it didn't help, Charles. The trouble is, television's such a selective medium. You only see the shots that the director chooses and that the vision-mixer punches up. What you were hoping to see probably happened off-camera.'

'There must have been shots of the celebrities drinking.'

'Oh yes. There are. But in none of them are they showing any unusual reaction.'

'But come on, if you pick up a glass you think contains water and take a swig from it and find it contains gin, you *must* react. There's no way you can help yourself.'

'You're probably right. And I expect someone did react like that, but the fact remains that the camera wasn't on them while they did it.'

'Damn.' Another hope bubbled up in his mind. 'Did any of them not drink at all? That might be as much of a pointer as a reaction to the first swig. Once they'd identified the gin – '

The copper-beech hair swished as Sydnee shook her head apologetically. 'No. All four of them take a drink from their glass at least once while they're in shot.'

'One of them must have been covering up,' Quentin drawled.

'Covering up what?' asked Charles.

'As soon as the person in question smelt the gin, he or she must have realised what had happened, realised that the cyanide glass had been switched and that someone else was going to cop it. So they'd want to hide the fact that they knew anything about it.'

Charles grimaced. 'Sorry, Quentin, that doesn't work. The only person who knew there was a glass with cyanide in it was the person who put it there. Unless we're talking about an elaborate suicide plot, the discovery by that person that he or she had gin would not automatically mean that the proposed murder victim's glass had been switched. They'd just think, funny, why have I got gin in here?'

'But why wouldn't they have mentioned it when questioned by the police? Surely then the police would have realised there was something odd and –'

'No. You see, by then the proposed murder victim would know what had happened. As soon as Barrett Doran reacted to the poison, they must have understood, and realised why they had gin in their glass. But, for some reason of their own, they didn't want the police to know that someone was out to kill them. Which was why they upset the table – to send all the glasses over the floor and confuse the evidence.'

He looked across at Sydnee, who shook her head lugubriously. 'Camera wasn't on it. There's a shot of the celebs before Barrett takes his fatal swig, then the camera stays with him as he starts choking. Next time we see the celebs, they're running forward and the desk's already tipped over.'

'So we've no idea who pushed it?'

'No.'

'Because that person, I'll lay any money, was the intended victim.' Charles looked at Chita and Quentin. 'You two were on the set. You didn't by any chance see...?'

His words trickled to a stop as they shook their heads. 'Sorry. There was so much confusion and chaos that we didn't really see anything.'

Sydnee spoke. 'Joanie Bruton said it was Nick Jeffries who pushed the desk over.'

'Yes.'

'Any reason to disbelieve her?'

Charles shrugged. 'Not really, but I'm now getting so paranoid about this case that I'm suspicious of everyone.'

'On the new time-scale, of course,' Quentin announced slowly, 'Nick Jeffries would have had time to put the cyanide in a glass himself.'

'Yes, but I think the person who pushed the desk over was the intended victim rather than the murderer.'

Sydnee corrected him. 'Not necessarily, Charles. As soon as Barrett Doran had started choking, the murderer would have realised that something had gone wrong and have exactly the same reason to confuse the evidence as the intended victim.'

Charles was forced to admit the truth of this.

'In fact, a much more straightforward reason than the intended victim.'

He was forced to admit the truth of that too. He looked round at his researchers. 'Right, so Nick Jeffries is now in the running. Who else? Back we go to the tedious business of retracing everyone's footsteps.'

'We've done it,' said Chita, and handed him a blue folder.

Charles looked at her in surprise.

'Well, we knew you'd want to know, so we got together and went through everyone. We are professional researchers, you know.'

'Yes. Of course.' He opened the folder and looked at the list inside. It read as follows:

SUSPECTS WITH OPPORTUNITY

1. BOB GARSTON – Left Conference Room at 6.05. Not seen again until 6.20 when he was observed by Tim Dyer walking along the corridor with Roger Bruton.

2. JOANIE BRUTON – Left Conference Room at 6.10 with Roger to go to Make-up, where he left her. According to Make-up, left them at 6.20. Roger Bruton claims she met him by the lifts a little before 6.30. By that time both of them were back up in the celebrity Conference Room.

3. ROGER BRUTON – See above. On his own after depositing his wife in Make-up. Seen with Bob Garston by Tim Dyer at 6.20. Again presumably on his own until meeting his wife again just before 6.30.

4. NICK JEFFRIES – Left celebrity Conference Room, following Fiona Wakeford, just after 6.15. Seen entering her dressing room at about 6.20, and seen leaving it again about a minute later. Not back in the Conference Room until just after 6.30.

NOTE: These are the facts as accurately as they can be ascertained. They do not, however, take into account the possibility of any of the witnesses lying, nor of a conspiracy amongst any of the above to poison the water glass.

'But just a minute,' said Charles, as he finished reading the document. 'Surely there are a couple more we should be considering. The two contestants, Tim Dyer and Trish Osborne. They both left their Conference Room at six-fifteen. She went to Barrett Doran's dressing room, but was out of there by twenty-five past and...'

Chita shook her head. 'She's in the clear. She went straight to the Ladies. One of the Assistant Stage Managers was in there and saw her, trying to repair her make-up. She'd been crying, apparently. She was there till after half-past.'

Charles felt obscurely relieved that Trish had been telling the truth. 'But what about Tim Dyer?'

Quentin shook his head. 'No. We've found another witness there too. One of the dressers saw him hanging around the corridor, looking suspicious. There've been quite a lot of costumes going missing recently, so the dresser watched what he was up to. Tim Dyer went into Studio A just before half-past, but he quite definitely did not go into Studio B.'

'So he couldn't have got the cyanide. Oh well, at least thank God that's two of them eliminated.' Charles looked down at their list. 'Thanks for this. Good bit of work.' He sighed ruefully. 'I don't know. Bloody marvellous, isn't it? Four murder suspects and I don't even know who they were trying to kill.'

'I'm sorry,' he said to Sydnee later that evening. 'I'm not proving to be much use to you. I'm afraid my reputation as a detective has been a little over-inflated.'

She did not deny this, but told him that at least she had been glad of someone to talk to about the case. They were sitting over coffee after dinner in a Covent Garden Italian restaurant. Charles felt very low. The first snagging self-doubts of depression threatened. When the depression came, it could be a long one.

He sighed. 'So I suppose now we do what we should have done in the first place – go to the police about it. I tell them that Barrett Doran's glass contained gin at six-thirty. At least that'll let Chippy off the hook.'

'And then the police will get on to Sylvian,' Sydnee said listlessly. 'And he won't be able to tell them which glass he changed for which, because he fiddled about with all of them...'

'But at least sorting out all these bloody suspects then becomes the police's problem. It is their job, after all. That's what they're trained for.'

Sydnee nodded and was silent for a moment. 'Of course, the police aren't going to be terribly pleased with you.'

'What do you mean?'

'Withholding evidence. Why didn't you go and tell them what you knew earlier?'

Charles shrugged. 'That's a risk I'll have to take.' But he didn't warm to the idea.

'I just feel we've got so close to it,' said Sydnee doggedly.

'Oh yes. I thought we were getting close with Bob, but after finding out about the glasses being switched, I don't know, the whole case is so wide open that everything we've done seems to have been wasted.'

'Not everything.'

'What do you mean?'

'We now know our suspects pretty well. We know what makes them tick, what their priorities are.'

'Yes.' In spite of himself, Charles felt a flicker of interest. 'So where does that lead us?'

'Well, it enables us to think of reasons why they might want to murder each other.'

'Go on.'

'All right, let's start with Bob Garston. We worked out a lot of reasons why he might want to murder Barrett. In doing that, we should have found out enough about his character to see reasons why he might want to murder someone else.'

'His character seems very simple to me. Totally selfish. He's motivated solely by considerations of his career. Anyone who threatened that might be expendable. But Barrett was the only one on the show who represented any kind of threat.'

'Maybe. Bob was also desperately worried about adverse publicity.'

'That's just another facet of the same thing. It threatened his career.' Charles mused in silence for a moment. 'The thing that really seemed to get him uptight was that we knew about Barrett and his wife…'

'Yes, he didn't want the gossip columns to get hold of that, did he?'

'No.' Charles found his mind wasn't as exhausted as he'd thought. It was waking up again, starting to make connections. 'And before the show, the only person he thought knew about the affair was Joanie Bruton...'

'And Roger. Remember, Tim overheard Roger talking about it.'

'Yes. My God, do you suppose that what Roger was actually saying was a blackmail demand? You do something for us or we'll tell the press about Barrett and your wife.'

'It's possible.'

'Far-fetched, though. Why should someone as successful as Joanie Bruton want to resort to blackmail?'

'People are greedy. Even the rich – particularly those who've just become rich – always want that little bit more. And Joanie's success may not be that secure. Okay, she's Flavour of the Month at the moment, but we both know how quickly television faces go out of fashion. Then she'd be just back to the journalism. It's not as if she writes books or has got any other nice little earner going for her.'

'No.' Charles thought about it. 'And Joanie is of course ideally placed as a blackmailer. As she said, she's a repository for a great many secrets.'

'Exactly.'

There was a new excitement in Sydnee's pale-blue eyes. Charles gave her a wry smile. 'I can see what you're doing. You're just trying to get me interested in the case again, aren't you?'

'So what's wrong with that?'

'What's wrong with that is that I have so far spent a fortnight getting precisely nowhere, while what I should have done was to go to the police straight away.'

'Don't you like a challenge, Charles?'

'I have been challenged and I have shown myself unequal to the challenge.'

'Doesn't that frustrate you?'

'Of course it bloody does!' he snapped.

'It certainly frustrates me.' This was a new Sydnee, her surface poise giving way to a girlish stubbornness. 'I'm a researcher, and the aim of research is to get to the bottom of things, to get to the truth. Nothing pisses me off more than failing in that quest. Go on, you must feel the same. If you don't find out who the murderer is, you're going to be really pissed off, aren't you?'

Charles couldn't deny it.

'Then let's bloody find out who it is. Look, we've already got a motive for Bob to want to kill Joanie. Let's see if we can get any motivations for the rest of them.'

Charles was thoroughly hooked again by now.

'Well, the new entrant into the suspect stakes is of course Nick Jeffries. He didn't seem to have a particularly benevolent nature, but I'm not sure I see him as a murderer. Still, let's try and think who he might want to murder.'

'Fiona, for refusing his advances?'

'Seems extreme.'

'Very sensitive plant, the male ego.'

'You don't have to tell me,' said Charles ruefully. 'On the other hand, I don't really see poison as Nick Jeffries' style. I can see him thumping someone, but…Still, I suppose it's possible.' He shook his head in frustration. 'Oh, I'd just like to see them all together again. I'm sure I'd get some feeling of what they felt for each other if I did.'

'You'll have the chance tomorrow.'

'What do you mean?'

'It's the second pilot. You may see something.'

'Yes, I suppose I may. I must say I'd rather see the first one again. I don't mean the tape. I mean the whole thing. I'm sure if I could see their reactions to the drink or who knocked the desk over, I'd be able to…'

He stopped. Sydnee looked at him curiously. She was even more curious when she saw the beatific smile which had spread across his features.

'What on earth is it?'

'Sydnee,' he said with a new, calm confidence, 'I have had an idea.'

Chapter Thirteen

THE DAY OF preparation for the second pilot of *If The Cap Fits* closely followed the pattern of the first, though generally everything was more efficient. John Mantle had gathered an experienced game-show team around him and they had learned from the shortcomings of the previous pilot.

As a result, three Conference Rooms had been booked, so that the 'professions' did not have to spend the afternoon pondering Sydnee's 'Ugly Wall'. (On this occasion the researchers had assembled a shepherd, a metallurgist, a coach-driver and a vicar, the last of whom thought, mistakenly, that his appearance on the programme would help to make the Church seem more accessible to ordinary people.) The hide-and-seek game of keeping the various participant groups apart was better orchestrated, so that there were fewer sudden rushes for cover.

An acrimonious confrontation between John Mantle and the Head of Wardrobe had resulted in the hats being ready when required (though the sullen expressions on the faces of the staff who produced them suggested that they still did not think it was their job). However, arguments could not be avoided on the subject of what sort of hats metallurgists wore and whether a Church of England vicar could really be properly identified by a biretta.

Sydnee had had a long session with Make-up and finally organised a schedule that would get everyone done without transgressing the sacred and expensive lines of the meal break.

The new contestants spent the afternoon in the same state of nervous tension as their predecessors. The extrovert personalities for which they had been selected seemed to desert them once on the set, leading Aaron Greenberg and Dirk van Henke, who had just returned from a long lunch at Inigo Jones with John Mantle, to turn on him and object that this bunch had even less 'pazazz' than the last lot.

They were also suspicious of Bob Garston's 'pazazz'-rating. His gritty Northern approach to the job of host contrasted unfavourably with the more flamboyant style of 'Eddie back in the States', and John Mantle had to endure a further barrage of talk about killing Golden Geese stone-dead and screwing up something which could mean 'someone making a pot'. As ever, he trimmed and shifted, full of magnanimous concessions which gave away nothing. He could see the end in sight. The next day, come what might, the Americans would be on Concorde on their way back home. The massive accumulations of their bill at the Savoy and the charges on his Gold Card would be at an end, and John Mantle would at last have some time to himself.

He felt confident that, by the time that magic moment arrived, he would also have the makings of a very successful game-show series which would run for years. As Sydnee had suggested, for him, having to do a second pilot had been like a gift from heaven. It had given him the opportunity to adjust the format, to regulate the pace of the show and give the whole package an additional gloss. Good housekeeper to the end, he was even confident that his budget would not suffer too much. Whereas there had been almost no possibility (even without Barrett Doran's murder) of the first pilot being transmitted, there was a good chance that the second could be, probably not as the first of the series, but safely tucked away four or five into the run. All in all, John Mantle was very pleased with the way things had turned out. Barrett Doran's death couldn't have come at a better time for him.

It was a subject that was not mentioned in the celebrity Conference Room. The foursome reverted to the required laid-back approach to the proceedings. The three who had played the game before had good reason to take it lightly; they now knew the format so well there was no need even to pretend to be doing any homework on it. Joanie and Roger Bruton muttered their way through a file of correspondence. Fiona Wakeford painted her fingernails with studious concentration. Nick Jeffries, whom this studious concentration was intended to exclude, sat around restlessly looking at a newspaper and resorting too often to the hip-flask in his pocket.

The newcomer, brought in to fill the gap on the panel left by Bob Garston's promotion, was George Birkitt. He was an actor with whom Charles Paris had worked on numerous occasions. Of moderate talent, he had been elevated by appearances in various television series to celebrity status. Since he was devoid of personality, he had no inner star quality, but was content to assume the mannerisms and behaviour of authentic stars he had met. The act was successful, in that the television audience seemed unable to distinguish him from the genuine article.

George Birkitt joined in the occasional, insouciant banter of the Conference Room, saying things like, 'Never sure about these damned game shows myself. Still, the agent says they're good, keep the old face in front of the public, show there's a man behind the actor. So I suppose I should take his advice. After all, that's what I pay the old sod such a large chunk of my income for…'

He did, however, refer to his copy of the show's format rather more often than was strictly proper for someone of his celebrity status.

Between the Conference Rooms Jeremy Fowler flitted, a lost soul trying to shed his burden of wacky one-liners about shepherds, metallurgists, coach-drivers, vicars and hats. He found few takers, though George Birkitt, who recognised that he had the imaginative faculty of a bar of soap, did scribble down an old joke about a rock-star's school cap being discovered when he had a haircut.

And all the while Bob Garston dashed about the place, expending enormous energy and charm. He was determined to show not only that he could host the show a damned sight better than Barrett Doran, but also that he could be lovable with it. The effort he put into his affability was almost physically painful.

In Studio A rehearsal wound on its dilatory way. Jim Trace-Smith exhorted the participants to bravura performances with all the damp aplomb of fruit juice soaking through a paper bag.

And Sylvian de Beaune, dressed for the occasion in a leopard-skin T-shirt and gold lame trousers, fussed around his set and wondered why Sydnee had asked him to meet Charles Paris for a chat in the bar at half-past six.

For Charles it was a day of nerves. Not terrified, panicky nerves, but nerves of anticipation, that jumpy surging twitchiness which precedes a first night, the feeling that a great many different strands are coming together and that if one can only keep going a little longer, everything will be all right.

This state covered the whole spectrum of emotion and included moments of great confidence. In one of these, he rang Maurice Skellern, assertively demanding what there was coming up on the work front.

The fact that his agent gave the predictable reply, 'Nothing. Very quiet at the moment, Charles', did not instantly deflate his mood, so he made another audacious phone-call. He rang the number of Frances's school and asked to speak to the headmistress.

'What on earth is it?' Her voice was tight with anxiety. 'Something to do with Juliet or the boys?'

It was predictable that her first thought should be for their daughter and grandchildren, though why she should think he might know anything of Juliet's troubles Charles could not imagine. If there were anything wrong, Juliet would have got straight on to Frances. Experience had not encouraged her to rely on her father.

'No, Frances. It's just me ringing to say hello.'

'You know I'm at work.'

'I told you never to ring me at the office,' hissed Charles in the voice he'd used as a panicked adulterer in a tired bedroom farce at Blackpool ('If it's laughter you're after, stay at home and watch television.' – *Liverpool Daily Post*).

'I've got someone with me,' she said in the frosty voice of reprimand which was much imitated by her fourth-formers.

'I want to see you.'

'We met a couple of weeks ago.'

'I know. It's habit-forming. I want to see you again. Another dinner?'

'Well...'

'Name a date. Any evening you like. Except tonight.'

'Next Wednesday. The Italian place.'

'I'll book.'

'You certainly will. Eight-thirty. On the dot. Or forget it.'

The headmistress put the phone down on him, but that didn't extinguish the little spark of excitement inside. If he and Frances really could get together again...He was in his fifties, too old for self-dramatizing actresses, too old for desperate housewives in Billericay. Maybe this time it really would work again with Frances...Why not, after all? They were both mature human beings, both knew the score. The separation had enriched their relationship in some ways. If he was patient, if he was sensible, he was sure it could work...

He went from the payphone on the landing into his bedsitter. He made a pretence at reading and resisted the temptation to have a drink. No, need all his wits about him later.

There was nothing he could do until the evening. He just hoped that Sydnee had done her stuff.

Chapter Fourteen

SYDNEE HAD DONE the first bit of her stuff, anyway. When Charles arrived at the Reception of W.E.T. House and identified himself, the girl, the same one as on his previous visit, immediately handed him an envelope which contained a ticket to that night's recording of a brand-new big-prize game show, *If The Cap Fits*, together with a Visitor's Security Pass, stamped for that day only.

This latter document meant that, rather than joining the queue of Townswomen's Guild, insurance company social club and amateur dramatic society members round the back of the building, he could go inside to the bar.

It was a little before six-thirty. He bought himself a large Bell's and stood alone sipping it, a sore thumb amidst the tight fists of programme groups. Flying-suits giggled and gesticulated, disparaging rival productions, reliving location disasters, calculating overtime payments, repeating the day's insults.

Sylvian arrived promptly. He was not wearing make-up for the day in the studio, so the shiny pallor of his face was his own. His eyes flickered about the bar. He refused the offer of a drink.

Charles reminded the designer of something he had said in his silver Dockland flat. Sylvian, expecting a completely different line of questioning, readily answered Charles's query about the celebrities' blue desk on the set of *If The Cap Fits*.

Their conversation lasted less than two minutes. The ice in Charles's glass had not had time to melt before he drained the whisky and went down to Studio A.

It was about quarter to seven. The studio was empty and still. No one yet had come back from their meal-break. The red, blue and silver set gleamed under working lights. The cameras were pointed at cards on caption-stands, ready for the half-hour's line-up time, due to start at seven. Air-conditioning hummed slightly, and gave the atmosphere a surprising chill, before the full lighting and crowds of people would warm it up.

Charles walked on to the familiar set, but he did not go to the side where he had stood two weeks before with the hamburger chef, the surgeon and the stockbroker. He walked round the back of the long blue desk where the celebrities would sit, and looked under it. It was exactly as Sylvian had said.

Next he inspected the four blue-and-red-striped glasses, which stood on the desk in front of each red chair.

He also looked at the other glass and the carafe on the host's lectern.
All were empty.
Good. Sydnee was continuing to do her stuff.

She had advised him to watch from the area just to the right of the block of audience seating. This was where the stage managers, who shared their power on studio days with the floor managers, and the make-up girls, who were poised to leap on with saving puffs of powder, stood during recordings. The advantage of the position was that it commanded an uninterrupted view of the centre of the set. From any of the audience seats the outlook would be interrupted by cameras and their operators, sound men and floor managers.

The members of the audience entered at various speeds. A party later to be identified as the St Richard's Church Youth Club scuttered in on a cloud of giggles. A works rugby club, who had met for a few jars in the pub beforehand, thumped noisily down the stairs to their seats. A Senior Citizens' Day Group wheezed in arthritically with much clattering of sticks. Once seated, they all decided they needed to go to the lavatory before the recording started, and wheezed out again. Some of the rugby club members also went off to lose a few pints.

Charles was only partly aware of these commotions. He kept his eyes firmly on the set. At one point Sydnee flashed round the corner of it. She gave him a quick grin and a thumbs-up before going back to calm the nerves of her shepherd, metallurgist, coach-driver and vicar.

Sharp at half-past seven, when most of the audience were back from the lavatories (though some of the Senior Citizens' Day Group were still waiting in the queue that had built up in the Ladies), Charlie Hook bounced on stage, picked up a microphone and started to tell them all how lovely they were.

It was a lovely show they were going to see, too, he assured them. Indeed, everything was lovely. He welcomed a few lovely parties, exchanged a few lovely innuendoes with the rugby club and indulged in a little lovely banter with one lovely Senior Citizen making her way back from the Ladies.

Then, on a 'speed-it-up' signal from the Floor Manager, he moved on to the introductions. 'And our host for tonight's show is a really lovely feller – somebody you all know and love from your television screen as Mr Joe Soap – well, here he is tonight without the Joe – and without the soap either...ladies and gentlemen, give a lovely warm round of applause to...Mr – Bob – Garston!'

A lovely warm round of applause was duly given, as the show's new host strode on, oozing common touch from every pore. He grinned ruggedly at the audience and exchanged a few gritty pleasantries with them.

He gave a brief outline of what the game was about, but said it was basically very simple and they'd have no problem picking it up as they went along. Then he distributed accolades to the 'boffins in the back-room', without whom the show would not be possible. He praised the humour of Jim

Trace-Smith and the organizing skill of John Mantle, before moving on to introduce 'tonight's celebrity panel'.

Charles tensed as they came on and sat in their appointed seats. Nick Jeffries shadow-boxed at the audience, much to their delight. Fiona Wakeford simpered at them, which they found equally rewarding. Joanie Bruton marched on, looking sensible, bright, but nonetheless feminine (and many of the female Senior Citizens turned to each other to comment on how sensible, bright, but nonetheless feminine she was). George Birkitt came on grinning and gave a wave, secure in the familiarity of his television face.

Bob Garston then introduced 'the plucky foursome who, believe it or not, have actually volunteered to take part in this circus', and the contestants, propelled by the unseen hand of Chita, came blinking on to the set.

In the Gallery, Aaron Greenberg looked at Dirk van Henke, then, accusingly, at John Mantle. 'About as much "pazazz" as a wet noodle,' he grumbled.

John Mantle smiled evenly.

It was nearly seven forty-five. The lovely Nikki and the lovely Linzi, after final checks at the straps of their bikinis, took up their positions by the prizes. The Senior Floor Manager stepped forward to tell Bob Garston to wind it up and get ready to record. Charlie Hook instructed the audience to wait for an applause cue from him and to watch the opening credits on the monitors above their heads.

The clock for the beginning of Part One appeared in shot. The one-minute countdown began.

Twenty-five seconds in, Nick Jeffries started waving in distress.

He had gone to have a drink from his red-and-blue-striped glass and discovered it to be empty.

The Senior Floor Manager looked annoyed at the delay. Charlie Hook came forward to reassure the audience that they were still lovely. A hustled-looking Floor Manager came on to the set with a jug on a tray. He poured liquid into the four celebrities' glasses, then crossed to the lectern and filled Bob Garston's. The remains of his jugful went into the carafe.

He scurried off and the Senior Floor Manager bustled forward for the restart of the recording. They must get moving, he insisted, they were wasting time. No more breaks, please. Must get on with it.

He got the message that the video-recording was stable, and the clock once again appeared on the monitors. This time it ran the full minute, disappearing just before the animated credits and music began.

Charles Paris stared across at the celebrities' desk. The concentration made his eyes hurt.

Nick Jeffries, who had been the one who wanted a drink, took a swig from his glass. Charles noted his expression with satisfaction.

Good old Sydnee. She'd done her stuff, all right.

The prizes for the second pilot were a gas-fired barbecue, over which the lovely Nikki draped herself lasciviously, a week's holiday for two in Eilat, and the Austin Metro (which Tim Dyer reckoned should by rights be his), from which the lovely Linzi once again waved. The audience oohed and aahed and applauded appropriately.

While the credits were running, Joanie Bruton took a sip from her red-and-blue-striped glass. Charles Paris noted her reaction.

Bob Garston introduced the celebrities with suitable jocularity. George Birkitt tried to launch into his joke about a rock-star having a haircut, but was cut short by the smiling host. Disgruntled, the actor took a drink from his glass. Though it was not relevant to his enquiry, Charles Paris noted George Birkitt's expression.

The shepherd, the metallurgist, the coach-driver and the vicar all came on wearing inappropriate hats. With celebrity help (and, in Aaron Greenberg's view, with total lack of 'pazazz'), the contestants changed the hats round. Three of them identified the metallurgist as a vicar. It was all very riotous. At the end of Round One, one contestant was eliminated, but she didn't go away empty-handed – no, she took with her a lovely *If The Cap Fits* cap!

The lovely Nikki and the lovely Linzi brought on the hat-boxes for Round Two. The three survivors made their guesses, and another member of the public was put out of contention. But of course he had won himself some money – not to mention his *If The Cap Fits* cap!

It was the End of Part One. None of the celebrities left the set while Charlie Hook re-emphasised the loveliness of the audience and explained that the Director would have to take some cutaway shots of the eliminated contestants.

Two celebrities had still to touch their red-and-blue striped glasses.

In Round Three the remaining contestants picked out of the box respectively a Roman helmet and a baseball cap. This meant that they had to answer questions on History and Sport. The first, clearly a man of no judgement but with an eye for a pretty girl, chose Fiona Wakeford to help him on History. The second, slightly shrewder, selected Nick Jeffries as his adviser on Sport.

When her protégé had been eliminated and while he was being told about his *If The Cap Fits* cap, Fiona Wakeford returned to her seat. She sat down and took a drink from her glass. Charles Paris noted her reaction.

There was now only one contestant left and it was time for the Hats In The Ring finale, with a chance to win the Super-Duper prize – a brand-new Austin Metro, complete with tax, insurance and a year's supply of petrol!

'Ooh!' sighed the audience, barely able to contain themselves (in fact, completely unable to contain themselves in the case of two of the Senior Citizens, who once again set off noisily for the Ladies).

The surviving contestant stood in the middle of Sylvian de Beaune's red wheel, while Bob Garston explained to her what was to happen.

He gave the wheel an enormous pull to set it spinning, and withdrew to his lectern. Once there, while the audience vociferously willed the wheel to stop with the crown overhead, he copied Barrett Doran's timing and used his red-and-blue-striped glass as a prop to increase the tension of the moment.

He took a long swallow. Charles Paris noted the expression on his face.

The audience sighed in communal disappointment. Above the final contestant's head had come to rest a fez. It was worth another £200 to add to what she had already won – not forgetting, of course, her *If The Cap Fits* cap!

John Mantle was no fool. After the close call of the first pilot, he had summoned Sylvian de Beaune into his office and ordered the designer to fix the wheel so that any hat but the crown ended up on top.

Charles Paris was unaware of that trickery. Nor, at that moment, would he have been interested to hear about it. His mind was too full.

He knew who the intended victim had been on the previous pilot.

And he knew who the murderer was.

He went out into the corridor that led from the dressing rooms. By the lifts was a small Reception area, with a few uncomfortably low armchairs.

In one of them Roger Bruton was sitting.

He looked up at Charles with no particular pleasure.

'Oh. Hello. I'm just waiting for Joanie.' Charles sat down beside him.

'I think I'll wait for her too,' he said.

Chapter Fifteen

'I KNOW WHAT happened,' said Charles after a long pause.

'Sorry?' Roger Bruton seemed miles away. Charles looked at the weak face, whose baby-like roundness was belied, on close inspection, by an elaborate map of tiny lines. Roger was older than one might at first think. Well over fifty, anyway. And his exquisitely-preserved wife was probably about the same age.

'I know what happened on the last pilot.'

The faded brown eyes turned towards him, but still did not look very interested. 'Oh?'

'When Barrett Doran died.'

A minimal flicker of alarm came into the eyes, but the tone was still confident as Roger Bruton said, 'I'm sorry. I don't know what you're talking about. What happened?'

'Do you think he was killed by the girl, Chippy?'

'As I said when we last discussed it, that is what the police seem to think.'

Charles shook his head. 'It doesn't work that way. You know, at the end, after Barrett had fallen down, all the celebrities got up and tipped over their desk.'

'Yes.'

'Hard thing to do, overturn that desk.'

'Oh?'

'Yes. I've talked to its designer. It's got a low centre of gravity.'

'Nick Jeffries is a strong man.'

'Hmm. And Joanie quite definitely said that Nick Jeffries was the one who overturned it. But, you see, it's not strength that matters with that desk. It's simple physics...levers...a matter of applying force at the right point.'

'I'm not with you.'

'There's a bar along the back. A good upward pull on that would tip the desk over. And it wouldn't take a lot of strength. But you'd have to be the right height to do it unobtrusively. Anyone tall – anyone, say, Nick Jeffries' height – would have to bend right down to the bar.'

Roger Bruton did not react, so Charles spelled it out. 'Nick Jeffries couldn't have done it. Even in all that confusion someone would have noticed. The only person who could have done it was Joanie.'

Roger Bruton attempted bluster. 'So? So Joanie knocked the desk over. So what?'

'So she had a reason to do it. She wanted to break all the glasses, create confusion, do anything that would disguise the fact that hers contained gin.'

The tired eyes stared hauntedly at Charles, but there were no words.

'I've confirmed that this evening,' Charles continued. 'By a simple trick. I arranged that all the water-glasses tonight should contain gin. That's why they were empty when the recording started. I didn't want anyone to draw attention to it earlier. Once the show was under way – particularly under way late – I knew that no one would dare stop the recording. They'd all just press on. But I also knew that they'd react. It's a shock when you pick up a glass which you believe to contain water and find it's full of gin. No one, however professional a performer, could disguise that initial split-second of shock. No one, that is, who hadn't been warned...no one to whom it hadn't happened before.'

Roger Bruton remained as still as a corpse.

'The only person who gave no reaction when she discovered the glass contained gin was your wife.'

'So...' The man's lips hardly moved as he spoke. 'What do you reckon that means?'

'Joanie's very quick-witted, isn't she? Her mind moves fast. Quite fast enough on the first pilot to link the fact that Barrett had been poisoned with the fact that her glass contained gin. She knew he always had gin on the set, so it was a fair assumption that the two glasses had been changed round. She also knew that someone hated her enough to want to murder her. But because that person was someone very close to her, she tried to confuse the evidence, so that the truth would never come out.'

A long silence hung between them.

'I'm right. Aren't I, Roger?'

Slowly the tension drained out of him. Muscle by muscle, Roger Bruton's body relaxed, till he lay slumped back on the low armchair.

With something that sounded like a little laugh, eventually he said, 'Yes. You're right.'

'Why?'

The murderer looked at Charles and slowly, wryly, shook his head. 'You wouldn't understand.'

'No? But Joanie did. Joanie always understood, didn't she? And that was why you hated her.'

The faded eyes looked at Charles with a new respect. 'Yes,' Roger said softly, 'that's why.'

He paused, gathering his thoughts, before continuing. 'No one who hasn't been through it can know what it's like, how smothering, how emasculating it is, always to be understood. Oh, if the understanding is warm, if it's sympathetic, that's different. But when it's clinical, when it treats you like a specimen, a case-history, that's when the hatred builds up.

'It was never a good marriage. The sex side was never...Joanie just wasn't interested. Oh, happy enough to give forthright, frank advice to others, but in our own bed...nothing. That's why we never had children. I wanted children, but if there's no sex, well...' He shrugged. 'At first I had a few affairs, but Joanie always understood. She was always so bloody understanding, welcomed me back, forgave me, patronised me, made me feel like a delinquent teenager. A couple of years of that, and it takes the fun out of extramarital sex.'

'Why didn't you leave her?'

Roger Bruton grimaced hopelessly. 'Because I'm weak. Because she's a stronger personality than I am. Maybe just because I'm a glutton for punishment. So I stayed with her, listening to her pontificating hour after hour, listening to her advise everyone and anyone about their lives, and feeling the hollowness within my own just growing and growing.'

'When did you first think of murdering her?'

He let out a sharp little laugh. 'On our honeymoon, I suppose. When it became clear that I could forget it as far as a sex-life was concerned. And it was always there, the idea of killing her, a pleasing fantasy, something I could retreat to when she became too intolerable. But I suppose it's got worse over the last few years. As her career's taken off, as she's more and more omnipresent, as I can't switch on a radio or television without hearing it, more and more bloody understanding.'

'But was there any particular reason why suddenly two weeks ago...'

Roger shrugged. 'I don't know. A feeling that I couldn't stand it any longer. I don't think the camel can say which is going to be the final straw, but he sure as hell recognises it when it's put on his back.'

'You hadn't had a row?'

'Not a major one. No more than usual. We don't really have rows. For a long time now I've suppressed all my real feelings.'

'I still don't understand why you should suddenly try to kill her.'

'No? Opportunity, I suppose. It was a spur of the moment thing. I'd just taken Joanie into Make-up and she'd said a very lovey-dovey farewell to me. It's moments like that I hate her most, when I see a public display of sexuality from someone I know to be totally without sex. I was angry. I walked through Studio B. There was no one about. I saw the bottle of cyanide. I took it, went through to Studio A, emptied the water from her glass into the carafe on the lectern and filled the glass up with poison. I felt very rational and happy. I just couldn't think why I hadn't done it before.'

'But you'd never have got away with it. If she had been killed.'

The murderer gave another little shrug. 'I don't honestly think I'd have cared that much. I'd have been shot of her, that's all that mattered to me. And I'd have been spared what happened afterwards.'

'After Barrett's death?'

'Yes.'

'Joanie knew what you'd done?'

'Oh yes. Instantly. She worked it out. And guess what...'

'She was very understanding about it.'

Roger Bruton grinned bitterly as he nodded.

There was another silence.

'So what do I do now?'

'The police have to be told the truth. Chippy's got to be released.'

'Yes.' Roger looked pensive.

'It might only be manslaughter,' said Charles encouragingly. 'I don't know the law well enough, but maybe when you try to kill one person and ending up killing someone else...I don't know, but...'

The murderer shook his head. 'Doesn't matter a lot. I don't see myself enjoying prison, somehow.'

'What, losing your freedom, you mean?'

'God, no.' This he seemed to find really funny. 'You can't talk to me about losing my freedom. I lost that the minute I got married. No, what I couldn't face about prison is the visiting.'

'Joanie?'

'Understanding me again. No, thank you.' He shuddered. Then, in a new, calm voice, he said, 'I'll write to the police and tell them exactly what happened. They'll get the letter tomorrow.'

'Roger.'

They both looked up towards the sound. Joanie, tiny, beautiful, her fur-coat around her, was hurrying along the passage with arms outstretched. 'Roger, darling.'

He let her get close before he stood up. Then, after giving her a look of such paralysing contempt that it stopped her dead in her tracks, Roger Bruton walked away from his wife in silence, free of her at last.

Chapter Sixteen

ROGER BRUTON'S SUICIDE was announced on the radio two days later. He had cut his wrists in a hot bath in a hotel room. Neatly on the bedside table he had left a letter addressed to the police.

As a result of this, a day later, Caroline Postgate, known to her friends as Chippy, was released from custody and, although the news got little press coverage, the police closed their file of investigation into the murder of Barrett Doran. Few of the public ever noticed that the case did not come to trial. Barrett Doran's popularity at the time of his death had been enormous, but television reputations are as disposable as used tissues. The shows which had brought him to prominence were of the ephemeral sort which never get repeated, so he was quickly forgotten.

The press coverage of Joanie Bruton was considerably more extensive. The irony of an Agony Aunt's husband committing suicide was not lost on the tabloids, but they were quickly made to change their tune. Joanie mounted her own vigorous press campaign, being interviewed whenever possible, describing her reactions to her husband's death. She particularly stressed the tragedy of depressive illness, whose insidious attacks on the mind can be resistant to any amount of love and understanding. Within a week she was once again the darling of the public, her status enriched by suffering. In descriptions of her, to the words 'sensible', 'bright' and 'forthright', the word 'plucky' was quickly added.

Her career continued to blossom. She added depression, bereavement and suicide to the special subjects on which she so readily gave advice to anyone and everyone. She presented the pilot of a new television series on sexual problems, which quickly became a series. Its large viewing public explained away their prurient interest by saying it was 'good to get these things out in the open'. Everyone agreed that Joanie Bruton was the perfect presenter for such a series, 'because she was so understanding'.

Charles Paris signed on again at the Lisson Grove Unemployment Office the following Monday. As had become a ritual with him, he rang Maurice Skellern before setting out on this mission, just in case there was any prospect of an acting job coming up. There wasn't. His agent assured him that things were still 'very quiet', so Charles kept his appointment. He needed some cash. He was taking his wife out to dinner two days later. Must be careful not to drink it all away before then.

It was about half-past eleven on the Wednesday morning when Sydnee phoned, asking if she could buy him a drink 'to say thank you'. He said he was busy later in the evening, but it would fit in very well if he dropped by W.E.T. House for a drink about half-past six.

At first he couldn't see her in the bar, but then identified a new yellow flying-suit in the middle of a group in the corner. Tentatively, he went across and tapped her on the shoulder.

'Charles. Great. We're celebrating.'

'What's happened?'

'Just heard this afternoon. We've got a series!'

'Of *If The Cap Fits*?'

'Yes.'

'That was quick.'

'A gap in the schedule. John Mantle got it edited and shown to the powers-that-be as quickly as possible. We've got the go-ahead for a series of thirteen.'

'Well done.'

'First studio in four weeks, which means we've got to work like hell.'

'Getting all the contestants together?'

'Yes. That and a million other things. Finding fifty-two professions who can be identified by their hats is going to be a bit of a headache, for a start.'

'I can see that.'

'Let me get you a drink, anyway.'

'Oh, are you sure I can't –'

'No. My idea. My thank you. What is it?'

'Whisky'd be great. Bell's.'

'Chita and Quentin are here. And Sylvian.' She pointed into the crowd.

Sylvian heard his name and turned to give Charles a little nod of uninterested recognition. His Mohican strip was all orange now. Chita and Quentin also saw Charles and gave little waves. But they turned back quickly. They were deeply involved in the series, planning, thinking ahead with relish to all the crises which would inevitably arise.

Jim Trace-Smith was in the centre of the group, and Charles could hear him saying, 'What really excites me about this project is that it's so much more intelligent than the average game show. I mean, a lot of them are, quite frankly, mindless shit, but *If The Cap Fits* has got so many elements. There's an educational content…and a bit of lateral thinking…and that all-important factor of pure luck. And then there's the prize element, which ensures healthy competition. No, some of the other giveaway shows I'd quite honestly be ashamed to have my credit on, but this one I really think is going to break new ground in television…'

The group around him nodded their agreement.

'One large Bell's.'

'Bless you, Sydnee.'

'Well, thanks for all you've done. Really been great.' Somehow her words sounded formal. She was back to the professional researcher thanking a contestant for taking part in the show. The real Sydnee Charles had glimpsed from time to time seemed to have gone back into hiding.

'Has Chippy come back to work yet?'

'Sure. And because this series has got to get put together in such a hurry, she's going to be an Assistant Stage Manager on it. You see, they brought in someone else on Method in Their Murders while she was...away, and that girl's staying there, so it's all worked out very well.'

'Yes.'

'Actually, she was in the bar earlier. I'm sure she'd like to thank you personally for what you've done.'

The pale-blue eyes flickered round until they saw the familiar blond head. It was bent over a drink close to a darker head. The darker head belonged to Bob Garston, who seemed to be taking a very intense interest in his companion.

'Oh. Yes,' said Sydnee. 'John got Bob to come in this afternoon as soon as he heard about the series. Quite a few things to talk about...with the first studio coming up so soon.'

Charles looked across at the couple, and wondered if he was seeing Chippy's unerring instinct for unsuitable men coming into play once again.

'I'm sure you could go and interrupt them, Charles. I mean, as I said, she's dying to say a personal thank you.'

'Oh, there's no hurry...'

Sydnee didn't press it.

They talked in a desultory fashion, but there didn't seem that much to talk about. Charles recognised what was happening. He'd experienced it before at the end of television series. For three months, or longer, you work intensely closely with a group of people, their concerns become your concerns, you are bound together by the overriding imperative of the programme. You spend all your time with them. You work with them, eat with them, not uncommonly sleep with them.

Then suddenly the series ends, and you're back to being a selection of disparate individuals. Without the link of a mutual project, you realise that you never really had that much in common.

With the murder solved, that was what had happened to him and Sydnee.

He offered her another drink, but Jim Trace-Smith had just bought around, and a hand snaked out of the *If The Cap Fits* group to pass her one. She asked if Charles was going to have another, but he looked at his watch and said, no, he'd better be going. She kissed him on the lips without passion, thanked him again for everything, and with something like relief coalesced once again with her group.

It was not yet seven, but Charles moved purposefully towards the exit. Just as he got there, though, he encountered a fellow-actor who had just emerged from 'the most dreadful, but the most dreadful day in the studio on this bloody bomb disposal soap opera'. He was in desperate need of a transfusion of alcohol. Surely Charles had time for one little drink with him.

'Oh, all right,' said Charles, looking at his watch again. 'Just one.'

It was nearly ten to nine when he got to the Italian restaurant in Hampstead. There was no sign of Frances.

'Hasn't she arrived?' he asked the proprietor. 'She would have asked for a table in the name of Paris.'

'Oh yes, signor. The lady was here. She left about five minutes ago.'

'Did she leave any message?'

'No, signor. No message.'

WHAT BLOODY MAN IS THAT?

To Lucy again,
in case she feels neglected

Chapter One

CHARLES PARIS looked out from the bar of the Pinero Theatre, Warminster, over the gathering September twilight, and felt mildly guilty that he wasn't really listening to what Gavin Scholes was saying. The warmth of the third large Bell's and the glow of being in work cocooned him and he only caught the occasional word of the director's exposition of *Macbeth.*

'For me, Charles, it's the tragedy of an unimaginative man, whose imagination, which has for so long lain dormant, is suddenly awakened. And he doesn't know how to cope with this new dimension in his life.'

'Ah.'

'Don't you see it that way?'

'Well, er...'

'So, I mean, the Weird Sisters...well, they just knock him sideways. His mind's kind of invaded by these alien thoughts that he can't understand. You know, "there are more things in heaven and earth than are dreamt of in your philosophy"...'

'Surely that's Hamlet, isn't it?'

'Erm...yes, of course it is, but I always think that in approaching a Shakespeare, one has to think in terms of the Complete Works.'

'Ah.'

'Each play is just another facet of the sparkling diamond that was Shakespeare's Genius. Don't you agree, Charles?'

'Well, er...' The actor didn't feel up to pursuing this metaphor. He indicated the director's wine glass. 'Get you another of those, Gavin?'

'Thanks.'

Charles looked along the counter, but there was no sign of the barman. Everything was empty and unready, the Pinero Theatre gearing itself up slowly to the start of another season of creative endeavour.

'I think Norman's just putting on another beer barrel,' said Gavin. 'He'll be back in a min.'

But the break in their conversation did not deflect him from his theorising. 'You see, Charles, I think this is the only way that Macbeth's behaviour makes any kind of sense. He's not a particularly sensitive man – indeed, he's probably the least sensitive of all Shakespeare's tragic heroes – so when he suddenly develops an imagination, the shock is profound. Cataclysmic almost. Don't you agree?'

Charles nodded and, as he did so, remembered that Gavin had always been like this, always seeking agreement to bolster his vulnerable confidence. He remembered, too, that Gavin had always been a talker, and that he always selected one person in every production as his confidant, the honoured recipient of long anxieties over many drinks at the end of each day's rehearsals. Charles was rather afraid that he had got that particular short straw, that he had been cast in the role for the duration of Gavin's production of *Macbeth*.

As the director continued to impose his preconceptions on Shakespeare, Charles thought back to how he had got the job, how elated he had been to hear about it, how conveniently his mind had forgotten what a bore Gavin Scholes in full flood could be.

The call had come through from Charles's agent, Maurice Skellern. One afternoon in early August, the actor had been lying on the yellow candlewick bedspread of his Hereford Road bedsitter, trying to remember what being in work felt like, when he had heard the payphone on the landing ring. Assuming it was yet another call connected with the bemusingly complicated sex-lives of the Amazonian Swedish girls who occupied most of the other bedsitters, he had let it ring on until it became clear that he was alone in the house. Only then had he stirred himself to answer it.

'Charles, it's Maurice.'

For his agent to ring him was sufficiently unusual for Charles to do a quick mental checklist of what the call could possibly be about. A cheque for a fee due on the sale to Zambia of some long-forgotten television series had just come in? No, Maurice would never ring him to mention that; the agent's method was to sit on any money that came in until he was virtually prised off his chair.

The National Theatre had finally seen the error of its ways and was inviting him to give his Lear? No, no, Charles, don't be ridiculous, you're far too old and cynical even to give such fantasies mind-room (and yet he still did, he still did).

No, to be realistic, if Maurice was calling him, it was bound to be something riveting like a National Insurance enquiry.

So, without much optimism, he had replied, 'Hello, Maurice. What gives?'

'Charles, you know I've been saying for some time that you ought to be getting back to your roots, in the classical theatre...'

Charles didn't know this. So far as he could recall, Maurice had never said anything of the kind. On the rare occasions that the agent did proffer any advice on what the actor laughingly referred to as his career, the recommendation had always been, 'Get a good telly, Charles. That's where the money is.'

But there was never any point in taking issue with Maurice on minor points like the truth. Charles confined his response to a non-committal grunt.

'Well, I think,' Maurice went on, 'that my careful groundwork's beginning to pay off.'

Again, Charles could not be bothered to contest this. Maurice was congenitally incapable of careful groundwork. If any offer of work had come in for one of his clients, it had nothing to do with the agent's ministrations. Any groundwork that had been done had been done by the client himself. Or the offer had just come in out of the blue.

So it proved. But Maurice once again demonstrated that, whatever his shortcomings in other aspects of an agent's work, he was highly skilled at taking for himself any credit that might be available.

'Listen, I've just had a call from Gavin Scholes...'

'Oh yes? He's Artistic Director of some place out in the West Country now, isn't he?'

'The Pinero Theatre, Warminster.' There was a note of reproof in Maurice's voice implying that the least his client could do was to keep up to date with who was in charge of the various provincial theatres. Since Charles was confident that his agent had been unaware of Gavin's appointment until the moment of his telephone call, this too was mildly galling.

'Anyway, he's just starting a new season, doing *Macbeth*, and, thanks to all the ringing round and prodding I've been doing...' (Lies, lies, thought Charles) he's specifically asked for you to join the company.'

'Oh.' Any offer of work was gratifying. And, once again, despite the curbs his cynicism tried to impose on them, Charles's fantasies strained at the end of their leashes. He'd worked with Gavin Scholes a couple of times, and the director had always seemed pleased with what he'd done. So it should be a substantial part. Banquo, maybe...? That was all right, you got the nice haunting bit in the Banquet scene...unless you'd got one of those stupid directors who thought the ghost should be invisible...Hmm, trouble with Banquo was, he did tend to fade away a bit in the second half. Excellent part, though, for nipping off to the pub after the interval and just staggering back in time for the curtain call.

There are quite a few good Shakespearean parts like that, actually...Tybalt in *Romeo and Juliet*, that's terrific, killed off in Act Three Scene One...The one you want to avoid at all costs is bloody Fortinbras in *Hamlet*. One boring scene leading your soldiers, then you have to wait right till the very end of the play for your "Go, bid the soldiers shoot" routine...And *Hamlet*'s such a long play, it nearly always finishes after closing time, anyway...

Or what about Duncan in Macbeth ...? Charles wondered. He's certainly a good boozer's part...gets killed off good and early...Trouble is, though, he hasn't got many lines, and directors have a nasty habit of doubling him with the Scottish Doctor in the Sleepwalking Scene, which really wreaks havoc with your drinking...And, surely, Charles thought, I'm not old enough for Duncan, am I? I mean, that's a real old stager's part...not right for someone who's...well, let's say in their fifties...

Macduff, though...Not a bad part. True, he goes a bit quiet in the middle of the play, and he has got that turgid scene with Malcolm in England...But, on the other hand, he gets good chances of a bit of emoting when he hears his family's been killed...*And*, of course, he's got the sword fight at the end. Yes, quite a lot to be said for Macduff.

Or...was it possible...? Charles had been around for a long time...He'd certainly got the experience for therole...And Gavin did like his work...Hadn't the director said, when Charles had been giving his Lane the Manservant in *The Importance of Being Earnest* ('subtly insolent' – *Yorkshire Post*), that he'd like to work with him in a bigger part...? Yes, it was about time...After all, why not? Every director has to take a chance some time...And every actor has to get his big break some time...And, God knew, Charles had waited long enough.

Yes, why not Charles Paris as Macbeth?

All this flashed through his mind in actor's mental shorthand before he casually asked Maurice, 'What's the part?'

'Well, he definitely wants you to do the Bleeding Sergeant in Act One.'

'Ah,' said Charles. Thirty-six lines, if his memory served him correctly. Mind you, thirty-six lines of fairly long-winded poetry...a lot of directors cut a few of them.

'And he wants you to double the Drunken Porter.'

'Oh yes.' Thirty-three lines. And that worst of all fates, a Shakespearean character who's meant to be funny. Charles was prepared to believe that lines like "Have napkins enow about you; here you'll sweat for it" got belters from the groundlings at the Globe; but he knew that to a modern audience they were about as funny as a rise in the mortgage rate.

'Still,' Maurice went on, 'Gavin says there could be other good parts in the offing.'

'Oh.' Well, that was encouraging. Maybe not in *Macbeth*, but there might be leads in later productions. 'Is it a booking for the season?'

'Well, no, it's just *Macbeth* at the moment. Gavin's booking one production at a time...but he was optimistic that there could be some other good parts.'

'And what money are they offering?'

Maurice told him.

Charles winced. 'They've got to pay more than that. You're going to push for more, aren't you?'

'Oh, Charles...' Maurice sounded mortally offended. 'What do you take me for?'

Charles restrained himself from answering that one.

'I'll be as tough as nails. Got to earn my fifteen per cent, haven't I?'

'Yes. Maurice, I'm still not happy about this fifteen per cent business. Most agents only take ten. I mean, I know you call it Personal Management, but I haven't really seen much evidence that –'

'Charles, trust me.'

'Hmm.'

'I'll screw them for every penny they've got. And then a few. Come on,

Charles, you know me, don't you?'

'Yes,' Charles agreed gloomily.

He knew the sort of money he would get. Maurice might screw another five a week out of them, but it was still going to be an income most tea-ladies would reject with derision. A lot of actors, he knew, just said they couldn't afford to do rep. 'Love to do it, darling, super part, and I really want to get back to my roots in the live theatre, but I'm afraid, with the money they were offering, the sums just don't add up.'

But the people who said that were actors who had good chances of getting parts in television. The sums didn't add up for Charles either, but in his case there weren't at that moment any other options.

And even the pittance that the Pinero Theatre, Warminster, was offering was more than the dole. Just.

And it was work. He felt ridiculously elated when he put the phone down. Like most actors, he went into a sort of limbo, a suspended animation, when he wasn't working. Now at least he had a chance to do what he was supposed to do.

And the parts weren't really that bad. Already he was starting to think of the accents he would use for the two. Something contrasting. Yes, be nice to get a notice like he had when playing Pompey and the Clown in Antony and Cleopatra ('an acutely differentiated pair of cameos by Charles Paris' – *Western Evening News*).

Hmm, the Bleeding Sergeant and the Drunken Porter...Not at all bad.

And it could have been a lot worse. Charles recalled the opening stage direction for Macbeth Act One Scene Seven: "Enter a Sewer".'

At least he hadn't got that part.

'Now the question is, of course, how much imagination has Lady Macbeth got? That's the important thing, isn't it, Charles?'

'Er, sorry?' With an effort he dragged his concentration back to what Gavin was saying. 'Yes, yes,' he said, opting for a safe response.

'She's obviously not such a stranger to the imaginative dimension as Macbeth himself is. Is she?'

'No,' Charles agreed, continuing his safety play. So long as he got the Yesses, Noes and Ahs in the right places, he reckoned he'd be all right.

'I mean, clearly, when we first see her, reading Macbeth's letter, she has already imagined the possibility of her husband becoming King. Wouldn't you agree?'

'Oh yes.' He added the 'Oh' for simple variety.

'But just *how* imaginative is she? I mean, could Lady Macbeth cope with the Weird Sisters?'

'Ah.'

'And indeed does she get less imaginative as Macbeth gets more imaginative? Does she actually –?'

The US Cavalry, in the form of the barman, appeared at the end of the counter and Charles, whose ammunition against death by boredom was running dangerously low, hailed the lifesaver effusively.

'Could we have the same again, please?'

'Sure.' The barman took their glasses. He was a quiet man, whose face was permanently set in an expression of rueful apology. While their drinks were being served, Charles made a determined effort to shift the conversation away from Gavin Scholes' theory of hidden resonances in Shakespeare's text. There'd be time enough for all that once they started actual rehearsal. It was the Saturday evening; they'd got till Monday morning before they had to address themselves to the problems of interpretation and characterisation. And Charles didn't really think that finding the concealed behavioural triggers of the Bleeding Sergeant and the Drunken Porter was going to take him that long.

'Who else is in the company, Gavin?'

'Well, I told you George Birkitt is giving his Macbeth...You ever worked with him, Charles?'

'Yes.' Charles left it at that. No point in going into the details of his previous encounters with George, on a television sit com called *The Strutters*, in a play called *The Hooded Owl* which had transferred to the West End, most recently on the pilot of a ghastly television game-show entitled *If the Cap Fits*. Nor did Charles wish to be drawn on what he thought of George Birkitt's talent as an actor.

'Very lucky to get him,' said Gavin. 'Big telly name like that.'

'Yes.'

'He's got to have a couple of rehearsal days out for filming some new sit com he's doing, but basically we've got him right through.'

'Oh, good,' said Charles, permitting himself an edge of irony. Down at his level in the profession, you didn't get days off rehearsal for doing other jobs; it was only so-called stars who could get that kind of thing written into their contracts.

But Gavin seemed unaware of the intonation. 'Then I was terribly lucky to get Felicia Chatterton for Lady Macbeth. Ever come across her?'

Charles shook his head.

'No, well, you wouldn't have done unless you'd been with the Royal Shakespeare. She went straight out of Central to Stratford and hasn't worked anywhere else. Done some lovely stuff...super notices for her Perdita. And a smashing Celia. Anyway, like most of them do, she's now venturing out into the real commercial world.'

'How old is she?'

'Late twenties.'

'Bit young to be partnered by George, isn't she?'

'Oh, I don't know. She's very clever. And, anyway, I think a younger Lady Macbeth helps the sensuality in the relationship. Don't you?'

Charles tried another nod this time.

'The sexual dimension is so important. You know, that whole business of whether she's had children or not...She has the "I have given suck..." speech, but then Macduff says, 'He has no children.' Now, are we meant to assume –?'

'Yes.' Charles diverted the subject forcibly. 'Who else is there?'

'What, in the company?'

'Yes. Who's Duncan, for instance?'

'Oh.' Gavin smiled slyly. 'I got Warnock Belvedere for that.'

'Ah.'

'From your tone of voice, I gather you know him.'

'Only by reputation.'

Again Gavin Scholes read something in Charles's intonation. 'Oh, I think that's probably all bullshit. I mean, you know how easily someone gets a name for being difficult. One director they don't get on with, and suddenly all these stories start circulating round the business. I'm sure he'll be fine.'

'You haven't worked with him?'

'No. I've spoken to him on the phone, and he sounds absolutely charming. Anyway, when you book someone like that, one of those larger-than-life characters, in my experience you get so much in return. You know, those older actors really know how to fill the stage. Don't you agree?'

Charles did agree, and said 'Yes.' But he didn't say that, in his experience, actors who 'filled the stage' hadn't a lot of time for the other actors who tried to share it with them.

'Oh, I'm not worried,' Gavin went on breezily, though something in his expression belied the words. 'With most so-called difficult actors, I think it's all down to how the director handles them. Don't you agree?'

This time there was no mistaking the naked appeal in Gavin's eyes. It confirmed Charles's suspicion that he had been booked as much to give the director moral support as to give his Bleeding Sergeant and Drunken Porter.

'No, there'll be no problem,' Gavin continued protesting too much. 'Most actors who behave badly are just insecure. If you take a firm line from the start –'

But the director didn't get time to articulate his full theory of how to deal with difficult actors. Behind them the swing doors into the bar clattered dramatically open and a huge fruity voice boomed out, 'Who do you have to fuck to get a drink round here?'

Gavin Scholes and Charles Paris looked round. But they both knew what they would see before they saw it.

A mountainous man propped up on a silver-topped walking stick swayed near the door. He wore a shapeless suit of thick checked tweed over a bottle-green waistcoat across which a watch-chain hung pretentiously. His mane of white hair and beard seemed to have been modelled on the elderly Buffalo Bill. A monocle was screwed firmly into the veined purple face.

'Charles Paris,' said Gavin Scholes as he moved towards the door, 'I don't believe you've met Warnock Belvedere...?'

Chapter Two

THE OLD ACTOR'S presence was so commanding that it was only as Gavin and Charles drew near that they noticed he had not entered the bar alone. Slightly behind Warnock, eclipsed by his bulk, stood a thin boy, scarcely out of his teens, on whose face an eager-to-please smile hovered nervously.

'Oh, hello, Russ. Charles, I don't think you've met Russ Lavery either...?'

'No, I –'

'Never mind that,' boomed Warnock Belvedere. 'Time enough for pleasantries when you've got me that bloody drink. God, a man could die of dehydration in this place.'

'Yes, yes, of course,' said Gavin, scuttling back to the bar, and suggesting to Charles that the director's 'firm line' in dealing with the supposedly difficult actor would be based on abject subservience.

'What's it to be?' Gavin asked from the bar.

'Brandy. Large one,' Warnock Belvedere replied as he limped heavily across the room.

Charles reached out his hand to the young man who had been introduced as Russ Lavery. 'Charles Paris. Are you in the company?'

'Yes, it's my first job out of Webber Douglas.'

'Welcome to the business.'

'Thanks. Yes, I just finished my training this summer. I was very lucky. An agent liked what I did in one of the final term productions and signed me up.'

'Well done.'

'It was Robbie Patrick, actually.' The boy was demonstrably keen to get the name into the conversation. And with reason. Robbie Patrick was one of the most successful and fashionable agents on the scene. To be signed up by him was about the best start any aspiring actor could have.

'Anyway, Robbie put me up to audition for Gavin and it went okay, and I've got one of the Pinero's provisional cards.'

'Again, well done.' It was quite an achievement. The actors' union, Equity, paranoid about too many people entering a hopelessly overcrowded profession, restricted most theatres to admitting two new members a year. To have got one of the coveted union cards so quickly was what every drama student in the country prayed for.

'What are you playing?' asked Charles, with a grin.

The grin had the right effect, and the boy seemed more relaxed as he replied, 'Fleance and Young Siward.'

'Great.'

'Yes, I'm very excited about it. You know, the chance to play two contrasting roles. Using different voices.'

There was something puppyish about the boy's enthusiasm. Charles for a moment felt almost patronising, until he reflected that he himself had reacted in exactly the same way to the prospect of playing two minor roles.

'I'm sure you'll have lots of fun,' he said.

'Yes, I mean just the chance to work in a company with –'

'Come over here, boy!' Warnock Belvedere bellowed from the bar. 'Come and sit by me. Pretty boy's just bought me dinner. Least I can do is to get him a drink.'

Russ Lavery flushed and moved across to the bar. Charles followed more slowly. He didn't like the sound of what Warnock had just said. The old actor was a notorious sponger, but to sponge off someone like Russ seemed pretty shabby. Nearly all actors are poor, but the ones who've just finished drama school tend to be even poorer than the rest.

Nor did Charles like the 'pretty boy' reference. Warnock Belvedere's reputation encompassed fairly aggressive homosexuality, and Charles hoped that Russ wasn't going to find himself in an awkward situation with the old actor. There was an air of naïveté about the youngster, which was capable of misinterpreting Warnock's interest as something more altruistic, the simple desire of an old stager to help someone making his first tentative steps in the business.

Charles's misgivings were not dispelled when the old actor put his arm round the young one's shoulders and hoisted him on to a barstool. 'Now what's it to be, Russ? It's still Gavin's round, so ask for whatever you want.'

Russ Lavery coloured. 'Oh, after all that wine we had at dinner, I don't think I need anything else –'

'O! reason not the need!' Warnock quoted grandiloquently, prompting Charles to wonder whether the old actor had ever actually played Lear. If he ever did, Charles thought vindictively, I bet it was a really hammy Lear.

'Good heavens,' Warnock continued, 'you can't come into this business if you can't take your liquor. Christ, boy, what do you think keeps the theatre going? It's not talent, it's not arty-farty acting, it's not blooody Arts Council grants – it's alcohol, pure and simple. Wouldn't you agree?'

This last was flashed maliciously at Charles, who found the question a slightly uncomfortable one to answer. Much as he hated to side with Warnock Belvedere, he could not deny the considerable contribution that alcohol (in particular, Bell's whisky) had made to his own theatrical career.

'Come on, boy, have something.'

'Well, um, a small sherry.'

'Sherry! After dinner. Good God, have you just let go Mummy's apron-strings? Don't you know anything?'

Russ Lavery looked deeply humiliated. It was clear that the answer to both

Warnock's questions was affirmative. Charles observed how, as with the snipe at him about alcohol, the old actor had a knack of homing in on people's private anxieties. It made him a potentially difficult person to deal with.

'Get the boy a sherry,' Warnock ordered, and Gavin Scholes obediently reached for his wallet.

'Sweet, medium or dry?' Norman the barman asked impassively.

The old actor looked at Russ. 'Well, come on boy. You must give Mine Host an answer. I'm afraid I don't know the appropriate etiquette for after-dinner sherry drinking.'

The boy blushed as his humiliation was rubbed in. 'Dry, please,' he said in a small voice.

Still impassive, Norman poured the drink. Warnock, seeming for a moment to regret his cruelty, continued in a softer voice. 'Oh, I remember, when I was young, I once made a terrible cock-up over drink. It was when I was working with Ralph.'

'Ralph Richardson?' asked Russ Lavery, awe-struck.

'Yes,' Warnock Belvedere conceded casually, well aware of the impact his words were having. 'I was quite new to the business...maybe a little older than you – and not nearly as pretty, I'm afraid...'

Russ looked confused, confirming Charles's suspicion that the boy didn't know how to deal with this homosexual badinage. It's always difficult in the theatre. There's so much effusiveness, so much jokey campness that it's sometimes hard to spot an authentically gay approach. In this case, though, Charles could have told Russ that he was up against the real thing.

'Anyway, at the end of the rehearsal one day, Ralph said he'd buy us all a drink. I was about as clueless as you are, young Russ, so I thought, well, here we are in the big, glamorous theatrical world, and I asked him for a glass of champagne. Hadn't a clue what it cost. And in those days, it was going to be a question of opening a bottle – none of this wine-bar nonsense where they keep one open under the counter. Anyway, give the old darling his due, he bought it for me without demur. Handed me the glass, and, as he did so, he said – very straight-faced, 'You show good taste, young man. If you always insist on living life by champagne standards, there's no reason why you shouldn't succeed. No one ever lost out by aiming too high.

"Ah, but a man's reach should exceed his grasp,

Or what's a heaven for?"

Never forgotten that bit of advice, you know.'

Needless to say, for the reported lines, the old actor dropped into impersonation. Charles had yet to encounter an actor who didn't do an impression of the late Sir Ralph Richardson. The quality varied from reasonable verisimilitude to a kind of decrepit bleat, but every actor had one tucked away for the vast supply of stories, true and apocryphal, which had accreted round that larger-than-life figure.

Warnock Belvedere's impersonation was actually rather good, but whether or not Richardson had ever given him the advice claimed or had ever quoted Browning at him, Charles doubted.

Russ Lavery was, however, impressed and so Warnock Belvedere pressed home his advantage with one of the more familiar Richardson anecdotes.

'Actually, dear old Ralph...' (he pronounced it 'Rafe', needless to say) '...once did something rather wonderful at a first night of some turgid new play he was doing. Started the First Act and, you know, they were getting nothing from the audience, but nothing. Obviously the thing was a real turkey...flopperoonie wasn't in it...So suddenly Ralph stops in the middle of a speech, walks down to the footlights, and says to the audience, "Is there a doctor in the house?"'

'Little bloke stands up at the back of the stalls. "Yes, I'm a doctor".'

'Doctor,' says Ralph, 'isn't this a terrible play?'

Though familiar to Charles, the story was well told, and he joined in the laughter that greeted its punchline. Even the barman Norman allowed himself a flicker of a smile. But, as Charles laughed, he wondered why Warnock Belvedere had suddenly turned so affable. He had a nasty feeling that the old actor wanted to ingratiate himself back into favour with Russ Lavery; he realised he'd pushed too far about the sherry, and was now making up for that lapse. What Warnock's ulterior motive was, Charles didn't think would be too difficult to guess.

Before the old actor could plunge into another anecdote of the distinguished company he kept, the bar-room doors rattled again and they all turned to look at the new arrival.

It was a woman, mid to late forties. Her hair was probably naturally black, but had been assisted to a uniform blackness which did not quite look natural. The blue eyes were rimmed with heavy make-up and her slightly sulky mouth was outlined in a harsh red. She wore a tight black skirt, seamed black stockings and shiny cream blouse. Chunky jewellery clustered at her neck and on her wrists. She didn't quite look tarty, but damn nearly.

Gavin and Norman's reactions to the arrival showed that she was a familiar figure in the theatre. The barman seemed to look away with lack of interest, while the director gave a little wave and called out, 'Sandra, love. Get you a drink?'

'Please. A Tia Maria.'

Norman had the bottle in his hand and was pouring from it before she said the words.

'Oh, I've just finished sorting it all out,' the woman sighed, depositing herself with elaborate mock-exhaustion on the bar-stool.

'The postal bookings?' asked Gavin.

She nodded. 'Using credit cards is supposed to make the whole thing simpler, and I'm sure it does when everyone gets their details right. But when they ask for the wrong price, or the wrong night...huh. Some of them even get their credit card numbers wrong.'

Gavin moved the glass of dark brown fluid across the bar to her. 'Never mind, you'll feel better after this.'

'Thanks.' She took a long, grateful swallow.

'Sorry, should introduce you. Warnock Belvedere...Charles Paris...Russ Lavery...' The actors nodded acknowledgement. 'This is a most essential lady – our Box Office Manager – or should it be Manageress...'

'Manager. I do the job quite as well as a man would,' she insisted with perhaps unnecessary vehemence.

'You certainly do,' Gavin Scholes gave a sycophantic smile of agreement. 'Sandra Phipps.'

She smiled round at them, then said, 'Give us a packet of peanuts, Norman. I'm starving.'

The barman handed them over, asking for, and apparently expecting, no money in return. Sandra glared at him. 'Don't look so hangdog. We will get something to eat later.'

'I didn't say anything.'

'No, you just looked it. We'll pick up a Chinkie on the way home.'

'Fine.' The barman turned to straighten up the rows of fruit juice bottles.

Gavin Scholes stepped into the rather awkward silence that ensued. 'Should explain, Sandra and Norman are married.'

'Oy,' she said skittishly. 'Don't spoil my chances with all these lovely young actors.'

'Thank you for the "young", Madam.' Warnock Belvedere leant across and kissed her hand with mock-courtesy. 'Nicest thing anyone's said to me all evening.' Then, in an elaborate aside, he whispered, 'Fancy nipping down the car park for a quickie?'

Knowing the actor's sexual orientation, Charles found this remark unbearably arch, but it appealed to Sandra Phipps, who burst into a raucous ripple of giggles.

'All the same, you bloody men,' she accused (inaccurately, as it happened, in Warnock's case), 'only think about one thing.' Then, with a glance at Norman's back, added, 'With exceptions, of course.'

Clearly, this sexual sniping was part of the couple's relationship. It made Charles feel rather uncomfortable.

Gavin again stepped in as the peacemaker. 'I tell you, without Sandra and Norman, the Pinero would just literally fall apart. I mean, sod the actors and directors, if you don't sell the tickets, you're left with a marked lack of bums on seats. And, if the audience can't get a drink in the interval, well, it's the end of everything.'

'And, if the cast can't,' said Warnock, banging his glass on the counter to attract Norman's attention, 'it's the end of civilization as we know it.'

Silently, the barman refilled the brandy glass and looked around quizzically at the others. Russ Lavery shook his head, but the rest signalled acquiescence and had their glasses recharged.

'How's the advance?' Charles asked Sandra Phipps, feeling he should show an interest in her work.

'Pretty good. Considering we don't open for nearly a month. Fridays and Saturdays okay – though a lot of those are subscription seats – and the Schools' Matinées are virtually full.'

'Comes of doing a set text,' said Gavin smugly. 'All the kids have to come and see it or they're going to make a balls-up of their exams. Eminently satisfactory.'

'For the management, maybe,' said Charles. 'Not so hot for the actors.'

'What do you mean?' asked Warnock Belvedere.

'Well, maybe you've been lucky enough not to have had to do any Schools' Matinées, but –'

This was clearly the wrong thing to say. Warnock bridled. 'I'll have you know, I have performed in every kind of theatre that there is. I've done more bloody Schools' Matinées than you've had hot dinners.'

'All right. Sorry. But then you know what I'm talking about.'

'No.'

'I mean the kids' behaviour. None of them are there because they want to be. It's just a chore. Another boring old lesson – except with the advantage that the lights are out. As a result, they do all the things they'd like to do at school. If they're single sex schools, they fight and giggle. If they're mixed, you've pretty soon got a full-scale orgy.'

'That has not been my experience,' said Warnock loftily. 'I find that that sort of thing only happens when they've got nothing interesting to look at on stage. When they're looking at actors of stature...when they're seeing people who can properly *command* a stage, the problem does not arise.'

The inference was there – and it was a fairly insulting one – but Charles could not be bothered to pick it up. Warnock Belvedere was one of those people who thrives on reaction to their rudeness. Give them nothing back, and their attack is disarmed.

So it proved. After a few seconds of staring at Charles, the old actor gave up and turned pointedly towards Russ Lavery. 'Actually, dear boy, there's another story about Ralph I must tell you. It's a weeny bit smutty, but I'm sure you don't mind a bit of smut.'

At the same moment Gavin left, saying he just had to check something in the office, so Charles had to make conversation with Sandra Phipps. Under normal circumstances, this would not have been a chore. She was attractive enough, and could chatter along quite merrily at a level of harmless but covert innuendo.

However, with her husband so close, Charles felt a little awkward. Particularly as she was obviously keeping up the innuendo principally for Norman's benefit. Charles wasn't interested in how they brought excitement into their marriage. That was up to them. But he just wished they wouldn't involve him.

Sandra started in the way she intended to continue. 'So you know I'm married – in name, anyway – how about you? You tied up or are you available?'

'Well…' said Charles, very conscious of Norman's proximity.

'Go on, don't be coy. Are you married?'

'Yes. Technically.'

'What on earth does that mean?'

Charles wished he knew. He and Frances were not divorced, but he would have been hard put to define exactly how close their relationship was. At times, although they lived apart, it could still be very close. But this wasn't one of those times. In fact, they were probably further apart at that moment than they had been at any stage in their lives.

It was his fault. As usual. But admitting that didn't make it any easier to accept. Basically, he had blown it. He had stood Frances up. He had invited her out to dinner, then he had got delayed and when he arrived at the restaurant, there had been no sign of her.

All right, that wasn't such a big deal. That sort of thing had happened many times in the course of their switchback relationship. What was different this time was the way Frances had reacted to the affront. When they'd made the dinner arrangement, she'd instructed him to be there on time 'or forget it'. But then she'd often said things like that. What made this time different was that she clearly meant it.

She actually wouldn't speak to him on the phone. As soon as she recognised the voice, down went the receiver. Being an actor, of course, he could sometimes make it difficult for her to recognise his voice, but once he had engaged her in conversation in the spurious guise of a Glaswegian plumber or an Indian double-glazing salesman, there had to come the moment when he changed back to himself and tried to say what he wanted to. And each time he got to the point, she put the phone down.

Only once had she spoken directly to him since the broken dinner date. And her words then had been among the most hurtful he had ever heard.

'You're not good for me, Charles Paris.'

That was all she had said. Then, once again, the receiver had gone down.

Of course, he could have tried to go and see her. Arrive on the doorstep of her flat in Highgate, waylay her as she set out for the school of which she was headmistress. But always something stopped him. Basic inertia. The sudden need to have a drink, to go out and meet people, other actors, people he wasn't *close* to.

And maybe, after all, Frances was right. Maybe he was bad for her. Maybe they were better off apart. After all, he was the one who had walked out all those years before, walked out in the search of a freedom which he knew, even as he left, would prove illusory.

And, since Frances had made no attempt to make contact, perhaps she was better off with him erased from the map of her life.

He only wished he felt the same.

And now here he was, working miles away from her, and she probably didn't even know he was in Warminster. Somehow, he must re-establish contact. Send her a card, perhaps...? He'd have to have something to say on it, though.

'Come on, it wasn't that difficult a question. Not as if I'd asked you if you could remember how many times you done it or something like that.'

Sandra Phipps' words, and the suggestive giggle that followed them, brought him back to the Pinero Theatre, Warminster.

'Sorry, miles away.'

'You can say that again. Naughty fantasies, I dare say.'

'No, not in fact. I...' It didn't seem worth continuing. 'Have you been working here in the theatre long?' he asked, moving to a dull, uncontroversial subject that should offer few opportunities for double meanings.

'Getting on for fifteen years in all.'

'Really?' said Charles, sounding impressed, because she had said it in a way that demanded an impressed reaction.

'Yes. Well, there was a break in the middle when I went off to have my baby.'

'Ah.'

'Stewart. He's thirteen now.' She smoothed down her blouse over her waist. 'Do I really look old enough to have a great big son aged thirteen?'

Again, Charles gave the expected reaction, though in fact Stewart's age was no surprise to him. He wouldn't have fallen off his bar-stool if she'd said she had a son of twenty-five.

'Actually, you'll be seeing Stewart soon.'

'Oh, will I?' Charles was all in favour of keeping the conversation going about her son; it seemed to be the only subject which she didn't infuse with double meanings.

'Stewart's in the play.'

'In *Macbeth*?'

'Yes. He's playing Macduff's son.'

'That must be very exciting for you.'

'Ooh, and for him. He's really chuffed. Has to get licensed and everything.'

'Of course.'

'And he'll have to have some time off school. But, touch wood, they're being very good about it. Say it's fine, so long as his work doesn't suffer. But Stewart's a bright boy...not really academic, but bright.'

'Oh, good. So we'll see him at the read-through on Monday?'

'Well, no. School wants him to be off the minimum time, so he'll be coming for the first time when Gavin's blocking his scenes. Thursday afternoon, it should be.'

'I look forward to meeting him. Maybe the start of a great theatrical career.' Charles provided the platitudes automatically.

'We'll see. Maybe the start of a great career of me as a theatrical Mum.'

Sandra let out an appalled giggle at the prospect. 'Aren't they the ones who have to sleep with all the producers.

'No, I don't think so,' said Charles evenly, trying to crush that particular conversational opening at source.

'Last orders,' said Norman lugubriously.

'Is it really?' Charles looked at his watch. Yes, it was. 'How time flies when you're inebriating yourself. Look, this is my round.'

Another Tia Maria for Sandra. Large brandy for Warnock. Assume Gavin would want another large white wine. 'Russ...?'

'No. No, I really must go back to my digs.'

'Oh, come on, dear boy. It's not that late,' Warnock protested.

'Sorry. Really must go.'

Abruptly the young man left the bar. The abruptness suggested either that he was going to be sick from the unaccustomed alcohol, or that Warnock had made some unequivocal suggestion to him that he didn't like. The expression of frustrated annoyance on Warnock Belvedere's face made Charles favour the second interpretation.

'Bloody kids!' the old actor grumbled. 'Hardly out of nappies and they're trying to get on to the stage. Huh.' Then, in a cruelly accurate parody of Russ's earnestly breathless voice, he parroted, "I played Richard II at Webber Douglas. The local paper gave me a smashing notice. And I've got this wonderful agent, Robbie Patrick." Huh. What the hell does he think he knows about theatre?'

'Time,' said Norman quietly.

Warnock Belvedere drained his brandy glass in one and slammed it down on the table. 'Right, Mine Host, give me another one.'

'I'm sorry. I just called "time".'

'I don't give a wet fart what you called. I asked for another brandy.'

'I'm sorry, Mr Belvedere. I can't serve you. I am the licensee of this bar, and I'm afraid I can't risk trouble with the police.'

'Oh, come on, for Christ's sake!' Elaborately, Warnock looked around the empty bar. 'Look at all the police. Place is bloody swarming with them, isn't it? Don't be so pathetic. Give me a drink.'

'I'm sorry.'

'Norman, don't be so bloody pussy-footed!' Disloyally, but predictably, Sandra Phipps joined the attack.

'I've told you. I can't.'

'Give me a bloody drink!' This time Warnock slammed his glass down with such force that it broke.

'I'm afraid I'll have to charge you for that glass,' said Norman Phipps evenly.

'No, you bloody won't! You're not going to charge me for anything! Do you know who I am? I'm not just anyone, you know. I'm not some little teenage shit just out of drama school. I am Warnock Belvedere, and when I bloody ask you for a drink, I bloody get one!'

The barman shook his head. 'No.'

Warnock's voice had reached fever pitch. 'Look, am I going to have to –?'

He stopped at the sound of the bar doors, which heralded Gavin's return.

'Any trouble?' asked the director, with a coolness belied by the nervous glint in his eyes.

'Mr Belvedere wants a drink and I've called time.'

'Ah...Ah.' Gavin Scholes for a moment looked as if he might make a stand, but quickly caved in. 'Give him a drink, Norman.'

'But I can't –'

'I'll take the responsibility.'

'That's all very well, but it's not your responsibility. I am the licensee and –'

'Oh, shut up and give him the bloody drink, Norman,' snapped Sandra.

Wordlessly, Norman took a clean brandy balloon from the shelf and filled it with a large measure. He placed it in front of Warnock Belvedere, then picked up a small dustpan and brush, and cleared the debris of the other glass.

'Thank you. About bloody time, too.' The old actor raised the glass in the air. 'Cheers,' he said. 'Here's to the *Scottish Play*.'

He downed the drink in one. No one spoke as he moved to the bar-room door. He stopped and looked back ruminatively, as if selecting an appropriate exit line.

'*The Scottish Play*,' he repeated. 'Yes, *The Caledonian Tragedy...The Harry Lauder Show*...call it what you like, it really is bad luck, you know. Not just superstition. Something always goes wrong with a production of the *Scottish Play*. Accident...illness...death...murder even. He laughed abruptly and triumphantly. 'I wonder which it's going to be this time...?'

He turned on his heel, surprisingly agile for a man who walked always with a stick, and pushed through the doors.

They clattered closed behind him, unnaturally loud in the vacuum of silence he had left.

Chapter Three

FIRST READ-THROUGHS are always edgy occasions and the Monday morning one for *Macbeth* at the Pinero Theatre, Warminster, was no exception.

The edginess arises from insecurity. Everyone present is worried about the first impression they are creating. The director and resident staff of the theatre are in the position of hosts, anxious that their guests will be happy with the facilities offered. Some of the cast may be concerned about their parts and how they're going to play them, some still raw from their agents' unsuccessful battles to screw more money out of the administration. And all of the company are wary, stalking round each other, antennae acutely adjusted to get the feel of the people they will be working with for the next few weeks. In the theatre there are happy companies and unhappy companies. Every actor knows how miserable it is to spend a couple of months in an unhappy company, so at the first read-through they are all trying to gauge the feeling of the ensemble.

And whereas dogs express this kind of anxiety by sniffing at potential invaders, in actors the unease is translated into a kind of flamboyant jokiness. Voices are too loud, only moderately amusing anecdotes are greeted with excessive laughter, and a lot of extravagant hugging goes on.

In most companies everyone will already know someone, or at least have mutual friends. These relationships are quickly re-established, and so before the read-through starts, the actors and actresses form into little clusters of badinage. Even Russ Lavery, new to the business, by having come down to Warminster a few days before rehearsals started, had made enough contacts to have someone to talk to, as the terrifying moment of his first work as a professional actor began.

Charles Paris also had the advantage of having been there a few days, though, on reflection, he felt slightly resentful about that. Gavin had specifically requested that he come early 'so that we can have a few jars and *really talk* before we all get swept up in rehearsal', but Charles was increasingly sure that the director had only suggested it because he needed moral support. Certainly, there had been no opportunity to '*really talk*', and Charles felt he had been drafted in only as a buffer between Gavin and the potentially difficult Warnock Belvedere.

Still, he didn't feel that much resentment. His digs were comfortable, and he'd spent a peaceful Sunday exploring the pubs of Warminster, dozing with the papers between opening times and putting off further attempts to make contact with Frances.

So he felt remarkably cheerful on the Monday morning. He wasn't as tense as the rest of the company, many of whom had only driven down from London that morning. And, attractive though the double roles of Bleeding Sergeant and Drunken Porter were, he didn't actually feel too much anxiety about how he was going to play them. Home in on an accent, do the moves that Gavin gave him, and count a good performance as one in which he managed to wring a single laugh out of the Porter's dismally unfunny lines – that was how he intended to approach the job.

He was also delighted to see an unexpected, but welcomely familiar face at the read-through. It was a snub-nosed, freckled face, belonging to John B. Murgatroyd, an actor with whom Charles had worked on numerous occasions and whose career was almost exactly as successful as his own (i.e. not very).

John B., they quickly established, would also be offering a double of amazing versatility to the good burghers of Warminster. He was to give his Lennox and First Murderer. 'Not one of the most memorable Shakespearean roles, Lennox,' he admitted to Charles, 'but one I feel could be *profoundly rewarding*.' He slipped into a parody of thespian intensity. 'I feel that the part is really only as good as the actor, and I'm sure, given the right performance, Lennox could become a *deeply significant role*.'

'Yes.' Charles joined in the game, also adopting a manner of humourless earnestness. 'Rather like the Bleeding Sergeant in that respect.'

'Absolutely.' John B. nodded sagely.

'And, as for the First Murderer...'

'One of the great Shakespearean roles.'

'Exactly.'

'So much depth. So much poetry.'

'Oh yes.'

'Do you know, Charles love...' The mocking intensity was becoming greater with each word '...when Gavin rang me about the production, he said, "Look, old darling, I'll put my cards on the table. I'm doing *Macbeth* and I really want you to play the title role. But I know how you feel about the First Murderer, and if that's really what you decide, I'll have to bow to your decision. So what's it to be, old darling – Macbeth or First Murderer?" Well, of course, Charles, there was just no contest. I said to him straight away, "Sorry, love, you'll have to find some inferior telly starlet for Macbeth. I'm not going to throw up the chance of First Murderer for anything".'

The fantasy spluttered to an end in laughter. Charles felt encouraged. With John B. around, there was no danger that the next few weeks would be dull.

He looked across to the 'inferior telly starlet' referred to. He had waved to George Birkitt when he first saw him but now the star of *What'll The Neighbours Say*, the ill-fated *Strutters* and other sit coms too humorous to mention, was sitting in the front row of the auditorium, the centre of a little cluster of sycophants.

Charles, who had watched George Birkitt's growth to fame, observed how the actor's face had become permanently set in the expression of someone opening a church bazaar or a supermarket. But there was now a nobler, more serious wrinkle to the brow. This, after all, was a significant moment, the actor who had found success in the mushroom medium of television, returning to his roots, demonstrating the more profound aspect of his character, the versatility which now made him ready to tackle one of the classic Shakespearean roles.

Charles tried to curb the uncharitable thoughts that the sight of George Birkitt always prompted. He knew that to think the actor's success was the product of a very moderate talent and a great deal of luck was probably only a sour grapes reaction.

And yet, he could never quite believe in George. He had watched the man who was about to give his Macbeth gradually gather the trappings of stardom, but he could never see the inward spark of genius that should irradiate a star. To Charles Paris, George Birkitt remained a perfectly amiable but rather dull actor, who had had a few lucky breaks and who was now too famous for anyone actually to observe that he wasn't particularly talented. Certainly, Charles allowed himself the bitchy thought, if Gavin Scholes saw Macbeth as a man devoid of imagination, it had been type-casting.

The other figure who had gathered a little coterie around him was, it went without saying, Warnock Belvedere. Like most self-appointed 'characters', the old actor's reputation preceded him, and there was no one in the company who had not heard of him and was intrigued to meet the reality. There was a tendency in the theatre, which Charles disliked, for perfectly repellent people to be tolerated – and even lionised – simply on the basis of being 'a character'. Warnock fitted this role with relish, and was determined very deliberately to live up to his image. As Charles looked at him, he could hear the old actor once more name-dropping and pontificating. 'Well, of course, I knew Larry back in the days when he was still with Vivien. Goodness, the two of them together were...' Russ Lavery, Charles noticed with interest, was not in Warnock's circle of sycophants. He had joined the group around George Birkitt, exchanging the anecdotage of classical theatre for that of television Light Entertainment.

Only one member of the company sat alone, on an aisle seat halfway up the auditorium. She was strikingly pretty, small, with wispy blond hair scraped back into an artless knot. She wore a grey and purple designer jogging suit of the kind marketed to housewives who pretend to do aerobics. She was reading studiously, and the book was a copy of *Macbeth*.

By a process of elimination, Charles concluded that this must be the recent darling of the Royal Shakespeare Company, Felicia Chatterton, taking her first tentative step out of the womb of subsidised theatre into what Charles Paris thought of as the real world.

She looked intense, rather than tense. And she appeared to be reading the script, not as a pretence of having something to do, but because it interested her deeply.

Gavin Scholes appeared on stage and clapped his hands. The flamboyant chatter subsided raggedly, and over its end Warnock Belvedere's voice, in a well-judged stage whisper, was heard to say, 'Oh Christ, it's that prat of a director.'

Gavin joined in the little ripple of laughter which greeted this, but it clearly didn't make him any less nervous. He started in a voice of exaggerated bonhomie.

'Erm...yes, here I am, the prat of a director himself. Ha. First, I'd like to welcome you all to the Pinero Theatre, Warminster, for the first production of a new season, which is always exciting for all of us who work here. And also, it being the first production has a great practical advantage – namely, that we can rehearse from Day One on the stage, so we don't have all those hassles of suddenly discovering that the dimensions of the set as laid out in the rehearsal room are totally different from what we're faced with in the theatre. And let me tell you, with only three and a half weeks' rehearsal, we need all the advantages we can get!'

'Three and a half weeks?' echoed a thrillingly husky voice from the auditorium.

'Yes.'

'But you can't do a Shakespeare in three and a half weeks...'

'Of course you can,' said Gavin cheerfully. 'I once put on *The Merchant* in ten days.'

'Oh.' From her tone, Felicia Chatterton did not seem to find this a very admirable achievement.

'But surely, Felicia love, your agent told you the schedule...?'

'Well, yes he did,' she admitted, 'but I didn't believe him.'

'Oh, well, he got it right. Three and a half weeks. Don't worry, it's going to be a great production,' Gavin Scholes asserted with emphatic but diminishing confidence. 'Now, I'd like to introduce our Company Manager, who's going to tell you a few things about how we run the Pinero...'

The Company Manager was like all company managers, and his spiel was the same as that of all company managers – details of the allocation of dressing rooms, places to eat (inside the theatre and out), where his office was, when those whose money didn't go directly to their agents would get paid, etc., etc..

Charles switched off. He'd heard it many times before. But he was amused to see that Russ Lavery was drinking in every word. For the boy, just being there was magical, the consummation of all his dreams. He was a professional actor, embarking on his first professional job. The enthusiasm was almost embarrassing in its intensity.

Cynically, Charles Paris tried to remember if he had been so raw and callow when he had been in the same position at the end of the forties. Rather sheepishly, he concluded that he had been. Exactly the same, ecstatic with excitement just at the prospect of being paid to do what he'd always wanted to do. Oh dear, he wondered, how long did it take for my attitude to change...?

After the Company Manager, other members of the Pinero resident staff were introduced. The Stage Manager, dour in the manner of all stage managers. The Assistant Stage Managers, bright-eyed and bushy-tailed. The Lighting Director, introverted and technical. The Wardrobe Mistress, a symphony in hand-woven fabrics (which didn't fill Charles with confidence – if there was one thing he hated on stage, it was a costume that tickled).

Then the Catering Manager, Norman Phipps, and the Box Office Manager, Sandra, were introduced. She put in the customary plea that the cast give her as much notice as possible for any complimentary or first night tickets they wanted, and made the customary complaint that if they left it to the last minute it not only made her job very difficult, but also caused disappointment and bad feeling.

She had dressed up more for the occasion than for the previous Saturday, but her clothes were again just on the decent side of tarty. This time it was black leather trousers and a cotton loose-knit sleeveless sweater.

And again it wasn't just her dress that was sexy. She also peppered her talk with a few innuendoes, and reacted flirtatiously to questions from the actors. Again, as he had on the Saturday, Charles wondered how much of this was just talk and how much of it she might put into action. Of course, with a constant supply of actors through the theatre, most of whom were enduring long separations from wives and girlfriends, she was in a good position to have plenty of little flings if she wanted them. And, if her relationship with her husband was as bad as she implied, then she might be tempted to indulge herself.

And yet something in Charles doubted it. Her sexuality was so upfront, so aggressively emphatic, that he couldn't believe in it. He felt it was probably all talk, just part of her manner, her personal way of facing the world around her.

The next person to be introduced was the Designer, who spoke at great length about the totally new concept of theatre represented by his set, but whose description of it sounded to Charles exactly like 90 per cent of the sets on which he had strutted in doublet, hose, toga and armour, giving voice to the words of the immortal Bard.

When you cut through the exotic description, all there was going to be onstage was, as usual, a set of battlements at the back, and a pair of mobile towers which could be wheeled on and off for relevant scenes. The outlines of all the crenellations would be sufficiently vague, so that, with a few lighting changes, they could represent A Desert Heath, A Camp Near Forres, Inverness – A Court Within the Castle, The Same – Another Room in the Palace, A Cavern, Fife – Macduff's Castle, Dunsinane, Birnham Wood, The Same – Another Part of the Plain, and so on. Charles felt infinitely old, a Struldbrug of the theatre, who had seen everything and heard everything an infinite number of times before.

'But now,' said Gavin Scholes, once everyone down to the Stage Doorman had been introduced, 'the play itself...'

A little murmur of excitement went round the cast. It wasn't that they were necessarily excited; it was just that Gavin delivered his words in a manner that demanded a little murmur of excitement.

'Now, as I see it, *Macbeth* is the tragedy of a man without imagination, whose life is suddenly shaken to the core by the introduction of an imaginative dimension.'

'Ah,' said George Birkitt blankly. 'That sounds very interesting.'

Encouraged, Gavin went on, 'Lady Macbeth, of course, from the start, has had this imaginative dimension. She is the more intuitive of the pair. She reacts instinctively, whereas Macbeth's reactions are more intellectual...'

'But surely,' objected the deeply vibrant voice of Felicia Chatterton, 'hers is the intellectual approach. I mean, she has the detachment, the cold-bloodedness if you like, to take an overall view, while Macbeth only responds minute by minute.'

'Erm...' said the director.

'I mean, the first time we see Lady Macbeth, when she's reading the letter, she refers back to conversations about Macbeth's chances of becoming King...'

'Yes, yes...but –'

'So she is the one who's doing the long-term planning. She is the one who thinks things out intellectually. It's only when Macbeth becomes King that he starts doing things off his own bat.'

'Erm...'

'You know, the murder of Banquo, the massacre of the Macduff family...'

'Yah...but –'

'But he's still only reacting minute by minute. Like an animal, covering his tracks. He doesn't think the murder through. Each crime is just a cover-up for the previous one. I think there are very valid parallels with Watergate, you know.'

'Yes, yes, I'm sure. But if you could just let me spell out in a bit more detail the way I see the play...'

'But I do think it's important that we all see the play the same way. I mean, we really should find its intellectual pivot before we get into rehearsals.'

'Oh, I do agree, Felicia. I do agree. But I think what we've got to –'

'Oh, for Christ's sake,' boomed Warnock Belvedere. 'Let's just bloody get on with it. Acting's nothing to do with bloody talking about the words, it's just standing still, being audible and not bumping into the furniture.'

This paraphrase of another of the late Sir Ralph Richardson's dicta was greeted by relieved laughter, and Gavin Scholes took the opportunity to redirect the conversation. 'Look, actually, Felicia, I think you've raised some very valid points there, which we certainly must discuss...if we have time. But I think if I could start by giving you all my views on the play, and, you know, if you could hear me out, then we could make the discussion more general once I've finished. How do you feel about that?'

'Absolutely fine,' Felicia Chatterton agreed very reasonably. 'I hope you don't mind if I take notes...?'

'Erm, no, no.' Gavin cleared his throat. 'Well, er...Macbeth, as I say, is a play about imagination – or rather, perhaps I should say, it's a play about lack of imagination. Or perhaps both imagination and the lack of it...'

Mentally, Charles switched off again. In his experience, directors' theories of plays soon got abandoned in the face of the purely logistical problems of rehearsal. Getting the cast on and off stage quickly took priority over the overall concept of the piece.

He'd only been in one production in his life where a director had followed a single interpretation through from first read-through to first night, and that had been a disaster.

The director in question had seen *The Tempest* as a fantasy taking place inside Prospero's mind. There was nothing wrong with the idea itself; indeed many directors have moved towards that kind of interpretation. Nor was there anything inherently wrong with having a set in the shape of a hollowed-out cranium. Charles really only began to part company with the concept when he saw the costume designs, and realised that all the characters except for Prospero himself were to be dressed as brain-cells.

The director's ideas then got even more convoluted, and he started dividing the cast into different kinds of brain cells, according to which of Prospero's functions they controlled. Ariel was deemed to control the Visual Area, Caliban the Taste Area, Miranda the Sensory Speech Area, and so on. At the play's climax, the lines, 'But this rough magic I here abjure', Prospero was instructed by the director to have a stroke, thus killing off certain of the other characters (in their roles as brain-cells), and making the principal actor play the rest of the action with slurred speech and one side of his body paralysed.

It was grotesque, it ran counter to Shakespeare's text at almost every point, but at least the director stuck to his guns and saw it through.

And Charles Paris hadn't done too badly out of it. From press notices of universal condemnation, he, by the good fortune of having one of the smallest parts (that of the Shipmaster) had culled the following review:

'Charles Paris was easily the most effective performer on the stage, chiefly because we saw least of him.'

It was one of those notices which, if you snip off the second half of the sentence, looks very good in a scrap-book.

Gavin Scholes concluded his exposition of the way he saw Macbeth and announced, 'Well, now I think we'd better get straight on with the reading, don't you?'

'Surely we're going to discuss the interpretation first?' Needless to say, this bewildered objection came from Felicia Chatterton.

'No, no, I'd rather come to it fresh.'

'Oh.' This clearly didn't sound a very good idea to her, but she suppressed further objections.

'Erm...now, inevitably, with such a big cast we're going to be into a bit of doubling. Now I've cleared extra parts with some of you...'

Charles and John B. Murgatroyd chuckled knowingly.

'Some parts I'm cutting. For instance, I've divided Angus's lines up between Lennox, Ross and Mentieth...'

'Gosh,' whispered John B. to Charles in a voice that had overtones of Felicia Chatterton. 'That could be tricky. I mean, I'll have to *talk* Lennox and *think* Angus.'

'Then the Fourth Murderer,' Gavin went on, 'I've assimilated into the other three, and of course I've cut Hecate –'

'Have you?' asked Felicia Chatterton, shocked.

'Yes. Well, everyone cuts Hecate.'

'The recent R.S.C. production didn't.'

'No, well, I mean everyone in the real world –' He thought better of finishing his sentence and said hastily, 'Anyway, I've cut her.'

'But surely that removes any occult frame of reference for the Weird Sisters?'

'Well, yes, I suppose it...' Gavin looked totally nonplussed. 'Yes, well, I'm afraid we're just going to have to live with that,' he concluded firmly.

'Hmm. Well, if you don't feel you're short-changing the audience...'

'No, I don't. Now a few more doublings. Charles, I know you're already giving us your Bleeding Sergeant and your Drunken Porter...would you mind adding a couple more snippets...?'

'No problem. The more the merrier.'

'Right. Well, if you could do the Old Man who talks to Ross...?'

'Sure.'

'And the Third Murderer...'

'Fine.'

'Um, and the English Doctor...you know, the one who comes in and talks about Edward the Confessor...?'

'Okay.'

'Oh, aren't you going to cut that bit?' asked Felicia Chatterton.

'No.' Gavin looked uncertain. 'Why? Do you think I should?'

'No. No, goodness, no, it's terribly important in terms of the definition of Kingship.'

'Yes. Exactly,' Gavin agreed, thinking on his feet. 'That's why I'm keeping it in.'

'Good. Just a lot of directors do cut that bit.'

'Not me,' said Gavin Scholes smugly. 'Very important, the definition of Kingship. Then of course there's the other Doctor...' he went on hesitantly, '...the Scottish Doctor, the Doctor of Physick in the Sleepwalking Scene. It's a natural doubling with Duncan, actually. Often done. I was wondering, Warnock, whether you might possibly...?'

'No.' The word was loud and unambiguous.

'But it would be a great help if –'

'No. I am Warnock Belvedere and Warnock Belvedere does not double. I was engaged to play Duncan in this production of *Macbeth*, and that is the only part I intend to play.'

'Ah.' Gavin hesitated for a moment, as if contemplating remonstrance. But his nerve gave, and once again he turned to where he knew he would get a more accommodating response. 'Erm, in that case, Charles, I wonder if you'd mind...'

Eventually, the read-through started. Felicia Chatterton wanted to stop and discuss each line as it came up, but grudgingly conceded agreement that they'd do one straight read-through and then start talking.

The reading demonstrated a marked contrast in styles between the two principals. Felicia, in spite of wanting to discuss interpretation so much, had already done a great deal of homework. For a start, she knew the lines. And she spoke them with enormous skill and passion, utilising the full range of her magnificent voice.

George Birkitt, by contrast, gave an appalling reading. He appeared never to have seen or heard any of the lines before in his life and, from some of the readings he gave, certainly not to understand them. Even famous quotations were delivered with leaden incomprehension. George Birkitt's approach to intonation seemed to be based on the simple rule that all personal pronouns should be emphasised. '*I* have done the deed.' 'How now, you secret, black, and midnight hags! What ist *you* do?' Even '*She* should have died hereafter.'

There was also a problem of volume. Not only did George stumble, he also mumbled. He was used to the intimacy of television, where, with microphones continuously poised above the actors' heads, there was no need for projection. Obviously he was going to have to be reminded what it was like to work in the theatre.

But the actor himself did not seem worried by his bad reading. There was no embarrassment as he fluffed and floundered through some of the most famous lines in the English language. Charles was going to be very interested to see how that particular performance grew in the course of rehearsal.

The rest of the cast read predictably. Russ Lavery's Fleance was way over the top, clearly the product of much detailed agonizing in front of his mirror.

Warnock Belvedere was also over the top, but with a chilling authority. From his first line, 'What bloody man is that?', he dominated his scenes, and Charles the bloody man in question, looked forward with interest to sharing what was left of the stage with him.

The reading went through jerkily, but without major interruptions, until they broke for coffee at the end of Act Three. The only long silence in the second half occurred in the Apparition Scene. The first Witch cued the first manifestation (an Apparition of an Armed Head) with the line, 'He knows thy thought: Hear his speech, but say thou nought', and nothing happened.

'Erm...' said Gavin vaguely. 'Oh, sorry, haven't I cast this? I wonder, Charles, would you mind...?'

As he read the lines, Charles Paris reflected on the ambiguity of his agent's words about Gavin being 'optimistic that there could be some other good parts'.

Charles had blithely assumed that that had meant parts in future productions. From the way things were going, it looked as if they all would be in *Macbeth*.

Chapter Four

AFTER THE read-through they broke for lunch. The theatre was some way out of the town, so most of the company ate and drank in Norman's bar, where a pair of motherly ladies dispensed salads and one hot dish (Irish stew that Monday) from behind an angled glass counter.

Charles Paris joined John B. Murgatroyd and a group of other small-part actors for a good giggle about past theatrical disasters. Warnock Belvedere still held court to a circle of admirers, regaling them with further apocryphal anecdotes of theatrical giants, and drinking far more brandy than seemed suitable for an actor proposing to work in the afternoon.

Gavin Scholes, not surprisingly, found himself monopolised by Felicia Chatterton. But, recognizing that he was going to have to hear her views on the true meaning of *Macbeth* at some point, he shrewdly decided to give up his lunch hour and get them out of the way quickly.

When the company assembled in the auditorium at two, however, he made it clear that there was not time for further discussion.

During the break, the ASMs had marked out the stage, showing the proportions of the fixed sets, and had assembled a selection of tables and chairs to represent the moving parts. Gavin Scholes moved to the centre of a stage that looked like a furniture warehouse and clapped his hands for attention.

'Erm...Okay, everyone, now we're going to block the play through from the start. We'll get on as quickly as possible, so please I must ask none of you to leave the theatre premises, because I don't want any delays. Go to your dressing rooms, by all means. Or the Green Room. Out on the terrace, if you like. But, please, be somewhere where the ASMs can find you. Okay? Right.'

He reached round for a ring-file on a chair and opened it, revealing the text of Shakespeare's play, interleaved with blank pages. 'Okay. "Act One Scene One. A desert heath." Could I have the Three Witches up here, pronto? Come on love, leave your knitting, cut the cackle. We've got work to do.'

'But, Gavin...' came a predictable husky voice from the auditorium.

'Yes, Felicia love?' Already there was a hint of strain in his voice. He had listened to her right through lunchtime and he felt he'd done his duty by her. From now on he couldn't afford the time to be so accommodating.

'You aren't really going to start blocking now, are you, Gavin?'

'That's exactly what I'm going to do, yes.'

'But we haven't discussed the characters.'

'You and I spent all lunchtime discussing the characters.'

'But that's only scratched the surface. And we can't start making decisions about where the characters are going to move until we know who those characters are, can we?'

'So what do you suggest we do?'

'Well, I suggest...I'd assumed that we'd talk through the characters for a bit, try to sort out their interrelationships...'

'For how long?'

'Oh, only a week.'

'A week! Out of a three-and-a-half week rehearsal period? You've got to be joking. What, a whole week before we start blocking any of the moves?'

'But once we know who the characters are, then the moves will arise instinctively. We'll know where to go because we'll know who we are.'

'I'm sorry, Felicia.' Gavin tapped his ring-file. 'All the moves are in here.'

'What, you mean you've actually worked them out before we've started rehearsing?' she asked, appalled.

'Exactly. And I'm afraid, given the time-scale that we have, that is the only way we can possibly get the production ready for the opening.'

'But –'

'Sorry, Felicia. We're already ten minutes late starting.' And he turned his back on her. 'Erm, Witches. Okay...Right, I know the text says, "Enter Three Witches", but I want to have you discovered when the tabs go up. Okay? So let's have you centre stage and...'

Charles saw Felicia turn in bewilderment and ask, to no one in particular, 'Does he always work like this?'

'I should bloody well hope so,' snapped Warnock Belvedere, sprawled bad-temperedly across a seat beside her. 'About the one good thing so far you can say for him as a director is that he seems prepared to just get on with it.'

'But how can you make a move that doesn't feel right?' she asked in plaintive incomprehension.

'You can make any move you're told to, so long as you're visible to the audience.' Warnock fixed the flower of the R.S.C. with a bloodshot eye. 'And let me tell you, theatre was a damned sight healthier before everyone started bloody intellectualising about it. First, the directors began taking the text apart. Now we've got bloody pea-brained actresses turning academic on us.'

'But –'

'When I started in the theatre,' he continued inexorably, 'actresses knew their bloody place – which was either getting up there and saying the lines, or getting down there on their backs and giving the actors what they wanted. They didn't fart on about characterization and motivation.'

'So what you're saying is –'

'What I'm saying is just be thankful you're in work and keep your bloody mouth shut!'

There was no ambiguity about this rudeness, and the offence was compounded by the fact that some of Warnock's circle of sycophants sniggered at his words. The colour drained from Felicia Chatterton's face; she turned and moved with dignity to the back of the auditorium.

On stage, Gavin Scholes pretended he hadn't heard the altercation and continued studiously showing the Three Witches where to move. The blocking of the short scene was quickly completed, the Witches ran it a second time following the pencilled notes they had made in their scripts, and then the director was ready for the next scene.

'Okay. "Act One Scene Two. A Camp near Forres." Let's have you on stage, please, Duncan, Malcolm, Donalbain...oh, and this is Lennox, isn't it? Come on John B. and Charles. Bleeding Sergeant.'

The Bleeding Sergeant and Lennox rose to their feet and moved forward.

'No, loves, no. You stay there. I want you to make your entrance from the auditorium.'

Oh God, thought Charles. All the old tricks. Gavin Scholes really was a boringly traditional director. The predictable set, all the moves worked out in his interleaved script (moves which, Charles knew, would always end up, whenever there were more than three characters on stage, in the time-honoured theatrical semicircle). And entrances from the auditorium. How corny.

In a flash Charles saw exactly what the finished production would be like – a faithful telling of the story, no controversy, no excitement, ideal Schools Matinée fodder.

'Right, so, Duncan, you enter downstage left.'

'Downstage?' echoed Warnock Belvedere.

'Yes.'

'I think not.'

'But –'

'Duncan is a King. The natural place for a King to enter is through the upstage centre archway.'

'Erm, yes, except that that entrance is going to represent various castles in –'

'This is where I will enter,' announced Warnock Belvedere, stationing himself firmly upstage centre.

'Well, I suppose that'd be all right if –'

'I'll have some attendants, won't I?'

'Well, you'll have Malcolm and Donalbain...'

'What about Lennox?'

'No, I've got Lennox helping on the Bleeding Sergeant.'

'Surely the Bleeding Sergeant can come on on his own. He's not bleeding that much.'

'No, I'm sorry.'

Warnock Belvedere sniffed his disapproval. 'Oh well, I suppose these two will have to do. Right, we'll try the entrance.'

Duncan, followed by Malcolm and Donalbain, disappeared through a break in the curtains at the back of the stage. There was a long pause, during which a muttered confabulation could be heard, then the curtains parted to admit Malcolm and Donalbain, who took up positions either side of the entrance.

After another pause, Duncan swept in. His two sons bowed as he moved centre stage. He looked slowly round the auditorium, then demanded in a booming voice, 'What bloody man is that?'

'Erm…' Gavin Scholes' voice strayed tentatively up from the front row.

'What?'

'I think that's fine…I mean, as a move...'

'Of course it is.'

'But, er, Warnock, if you could say the line as you come in, rather than waiting till you've taken up your position…?'

'Why?'

'Well, you know, it's just pace, love, pace. I mean particularly at the beginning of the show, we do want it to move along. Can't have too long a pause.'

'Are you suggesting,' asked Warnock Belvedere, puffing himself up with affront, 'that I do not know how to judge the length of a pause?'

'No, no.'

'I tell you, Noel Coward himself – Noel Coward, no less – admitted that he couldn't hold a candle to me when it came to timing…'

'Yes, yes, of course, but –'

'And Tony Guthrie once said to me…'

'Heigh-ho. It's going to be like this all the time,' John B. Murgatroyd whispered to Charles, with a tremor of a giggle in his voice.

'Best spectator sport since Christians being thrown to the lions,' Charles murmured back.

On stage the diatribe continued, until Gavin once again crumbled and agreed to let Warnock do it his way. Then the director turned to the auditorium to direct the entrance of the Bleeding Sergeant.

Following instructions, Lennox supported the wounded man up the centre steps on to the stage.

'I think they'd bow now,' said Duncan.

'I'm not sure…'

'Duncan is a King, Kevin…'

'Gavin.'

'Kevin, Gavin, what the hell? They'd bow.'

'I don't know…Well, okay, try it, Charles and John B.'

They collapsed on to the floor, and Charles could feel the silent vibration of John B. Murgatroyd giggling beside him. Oh dear. He suddenly remembered that John B. was one of the worst corpsers in the business. They were going to be lucky to get through this scene every night without breaking up.

Malcolm then stepped forward and instructed the Bleeding Sergeant to 'say to the King the knowledge of the broil

As thou didst leave it.'

Charles began, 'Doubtful it stood:
As two spent swimmers, that do –'

'Erm, I think we'd better have you standing for this, Charles. Want the audience to see you a bit, don't we?'

'I don't see the necessity,' boomed Warnock Belvedere.

Well, sod you, thought Charles. See if I care. At least if I keep my back to them throughout the scene, it'll save another make-up change.

Rehearsals did progress through the week. They slipped behind a bit, but, considering the ridiculous schedule Gavin was trying to keep to, the slippage could have been a lot worse.

Warnock Belvedere, having imposed his personality on the company to his satisfaction, seemed to calm down a bit. Or perhaps it was just that he wasn't around so much. Duncan, as Charles had observed, gets killed satisfactorily early in the play and so, since they were working through from the beginning, Warnock was soon free while the rest of the blocking continued. He wasn't called for either the Wednesday or the Thursday's rehearsals. And, without his malevolent presence, the mood of the company improved.

Felicia, too, stopped making objections and buckled down to hard work. Accepting that she was not going to be allowed to discover movements that arose naturally from her discovery of her character, she began instead to devote her considerable powers of concentration to making Gavin's imposed moves fit into her developing concept of Lady Macbeth.

She also found a confidant in Russ Lavery, whose earnestness matched her own, and who was evidently more than happy to spend long hours agonizing with her over nuances of Shakespeare's text. This new friendship was a great blessing to Gavin Scholes, because it got Felicia off his back.

Her attitude towards the director changed. Whereas at first she had been trying to challenge his methods of production, now she seemed to feel only pity for his philistinism, sorrow that the fine workmanship of the Bard should have to suffer at the clumsy hands of such a botcher. But at least she didn't stop to argue every point, and the rehearsals were allowed to proceed.

George Birkitt also got better, but slowly. He still had a great many television habits to shake off. Apart from the problem of projection, he was also having considerable difficulty implanting Shakespeare' s immortal lines in his mind. Actors in television sit coms are notorious paraphrasers, who give rough approximations of their lines, only homing in with accuracy on the ones which are likely to get laughs. For someone used to that discipline, it was a considerable challenge to have to repeat lines which half the world knew off by heart (and which, at Schools Matinées, might even be being followed in the script by the light of pencil torches).

For a couple of days, George floundered hopelessly. The lines just would not stick. It was only when Charles Paris gently reminded him of a play called *The Hooded Owl* that a marked improvement was seen. They had both been in the first production of the piece, in which the star, Michael Banks, unable to remember his lines, had had to go through the ignominy of having them fed to him from the wings through a radio receiver disguised as a hearing aid. The threat of a repeat of this procedure soon bucked George up – apart from anything else, the presence of a hearing aid in eleventh century Scotland would be difficult to explain away.

Once the lines had started to come, the performance grew. George had a good stage presence and, when he bothered to use it, a strong voice. And in one respect his television training proved useful. Recognising (though not admitting) that he had no instinctive ear for a comic line, he had always been quite happy to parrot intonations given him by sit com directors. Once Gavin Scholes realised that George was not offended by being told how to say the lines – in fact, even welcomed it – the director took full advantage of the concession. Whatever George Birkitt's limitations as a creative actor may have been, he had a great ability for copying an intonation. So the director spoke the lines as he wanted them delivered, George reproduced the director's emphases, and slowly a performance emerged.

The pairing of this Macbeth and Lady Macbeth was unusual, the one a mere parrot of lines, the other unable to deliver a line that had not been dissected and re-assembled half a dozen times, but, though their routes to it could not have been more different, both arrived at a remarkably consistent style.

Another problem with George Birkitt, however, was that he, the member of the cast who needed most rehearsal, was going to have least. The filming days for his new sit com, so carefully negotiated into his contract, would take him out of *Macbeth* rehearsals for two full days.

And that was not all. On the Wednesday of the first week, Gavin Scholes for the first time outlined his longer-term rehearsal plan.

'What we're working towards,' he said, 'with all this manic blocking, is a full run-through of the play on Saturday.'

The shock of this proposal was so great to her that Felicia Chatterton could not help reacting. '*This* Saturday?'

'Yes.'

'A full run? After five days' rehearsal?'

'Yes. Just to fix the blocking in your minds. It won't really be a full run-through. More a stagger-through.'

'A drunken lurch-through for Warnock, no doubt,' John B. Murgatroyd whispered to Charles, with a giggle.

'Yes,' Gavin went on. 'We've got to try it. See how the play hangs together. Not too rushed, though. First half Saturday morning, second half in the afternoon.'

'Ah,' George Birkitt interposed.

'Some problem, George?'

'Yes. Saturday afternoon. No can do.'

'What?'

'Didn't the agent tell you?'

'No.'

'God, he's hopeless. The money I pay him and...No, I've got to fly to Paris for filming on Sunday. Flight late Saturday afternoon. Car picking me up here at one.'

'Oh.'

'I'm sure the agent must've mentioned it.'

'I don't think so.'

George Birkitt shrugged. 'Well, sorry, old chum. 'Fraid that's the way it is.'

'So it sounds as if we can't have a full run-through on Saturday.' Felicia Chatterton sighed with relief.

'Oh yes, we can,' Gavin Scholes countered. 'We'll do the whole play Saturday morning.'

Felicia Chatterton's mouth gaped in pained disbelief. It had never been like this at Stratford.

By the Thursday afternoon, rehearsals were starting to slip behind schedule again. They were doing the Apparition Scene which, since Gavin was not resorting to any stylisation but doggedly insisted on all the manifestations being seen by the audience, was very complicated.

Gavin's little drawings of movements in his interleaved script somehow didn't match the size of the stage for this scene, and the problems of getting the apparitions on and off unseen required a major rethink of his plans. He kept saying, 'There'll be lots of dry ice. And with proper lighting the audience won't notice a thing', but the cast weren't convinced. They'd all, at some time or other in their careers, been caught in some ungainly posture on an ill-conceived entrance or exit, and none of them wanted to get laughs of that kind again.

So, while the scene was rethought, time passed and they slipped further and further behind schedule.

'I'm sorry,' Gavin said after a while. 'I can't concentrate in here. Just give me a quarter of an hour – break for tea – and I'll go and work it out in the office.'

The cast all trooped up to the bar, where Norman's motherly ladies dispensed tea and rock cakes. Charles sat down at a table with John B. Murgatroyd, who suddenly asked, 'Have you ever played the Walnut Game?'

'I don't think so. What is it?'

'It's an old actor's game. Has to be in a play with a big cast. Shakespeare's ideal.'

'What happens?'

'It's a matinée game. Or late into a run. When the director's not monitoring the performances too closely.' John B. Murgatroyd winked.

'What do you have to do?'

'Somebody comes on stage with a walnut and secretly...you know, in a handshake or something, they pass it to another actor. Then he has to pass it on. The aim is to keep it on stage throughout the show.'

'Just passing it from one to the other?'

'That's it. You lose if you're the one who takes it offstage.'

Charles smiled mischievously. 'Sounds wicked.'

'Must try it one day.' John B. Murgatroyd looked innocently out of the window.

'If you're thinking what I think you're thinking,' said Charles, 'be advised. There are one or two people in this company who wouldn't see the joke at all.'

'Felicia...'

'To name but one.'

'She wouldn't see a joke if it knocked her over and raped her.'

'No. Sad, isn't it, really,' Charles mused, 'that someone so amazingly dishy should be utterly devoid of humour.'

'Tragic,' John B. agreed. 'I wonder what she does for sex...?'

'Talks about it, I'm sure. At length. At great, great length.'

'You don't think young Russ is getting anywhere there?'

'No.' Charles lengthened the vowel in disbelief.

But further speculation about Felicia's sex-life was interrupted by the arrival of Sandra Phipps, with a shy-looking schoolboy in tow.

'Charles, I wonder, do you mind? Could you just keep an eye on Stewart?'

'Sure. No problem.'

'I've been with him all afternoon, but I must go and check what's going on in the Box Office.'

'Fine.'

'You see, I'm meant to be chaperoning him...'

'Of course.'

'The law says kids have got to have chaperones. Good old Gavin, always ready to save a few bob, says, "Why book anyone else when we've got Mum on the premises?" so I'm doing it.'

'Don't worry. I'll see he doesn't get into any mischief. Do you want a drink, Stewart?'

The boy looked up at him through long lashes. He was still at a downy girlish stage of boyhood, just before his skin would coarsen and his beard start.

'I wouldn't mind a Coke, please, if that's all right, sir,' the boy replied politely.

'Sure. But please don't call me sir. Charles is fine.'

Sandra looked at her watch. 'I won't be long. How late do you go on?'

'Half-past five...six.'

'Stewart was called for two.'

'Running late. The murder of the Macduffs is the next scene, though.'

'Hmm. You think Gavin'll get to it today?'

'I know he's hoping to.' But Charles's optimistic prediction proved incorrect. They worked on the blocking of the Apparition Scene (which now involved much use of the stage trap-door) for the rest of the afternoon. When they broke, the director shouted out, 'Okay. Thanks for all your hard work.

Macduff murder scene prompt at ten in the morning – okay?'

'Is that okay for you?' Charles asked the boy sitting beside him in the auditorium. 'I mean, with school?'

'Oh, I'm sure it'll be all right.'

'Where are you at school?'

'St. Joseph's.'

The name didn't mean anything to Charles. But then the name of none of the local schools would have meant anything to him. Stupid question to ask, really.

'Hey, that's great,' said Stewart. 'It means I'll miss Double English.'

'From your tone of voice, that's pretty boring.'

'And how!' The boy grimaced. 'Boring.'

'Why? What are you doing?'

'*Macbeth*,' Stewart Phipps replied with a groan.

Chapter Five

THEY DID MANAGE to get the whole play blocked by the end of rehearsal on the Friday, but only by dint of going into overtime. Most of them worked through till just after eight, because virtually the entire cast was involved in the battle scenes at the end. (Charles, incidentally, had picked up a couple more parts here – one of the soldiers in Malcolm's army who grabs a bit of Birnham Wood, and then, with a change of allegiance which might have confused an actor of more Stanislavskian approach, one of Macbeth's army who runs away as the tide of battle turns.)

All the cast logged in their overtime with the theatre administration. To Charles this still seemed strange. Though he approved of much of what Equity had done to improve actors' working conditions, and though he always welcomed a little extra money, this unionised clock-watching seemed dangerously closer to the world of the Civil Service than the theatre. Charles felt wistfully nostalgic for the days of weekly rep. Then you worked ridiculous hours, you moaned and groaned and complained about it all the time, but the feeling of mutual exhaustion kept everyone on a permanent high, pumping adrenaline at a rate he had never since encountered.

Still, those days were gone. Now there were rules fixing the permissible hours of work, and those rules had to be obeyed.

Stewart Phipps' scene was blocked first thing on the Friday morning, as Gavin had intended. It didn't take long. Stewart spoke the rather prissy lines of Macduff's Son with commendable animation, and was clearly going to relish the moment of his death, when he was despatched by John B. Murgatroyd (as the First Murderer) with the immortal words,

'What! you egg, Young fry of treachery!'

But the boy didn't leave straight after his scene. The theatrical atmosphere patently excited him, and he gazed from the auditorium with sparkling eyes, taking in everything that was going on.

'Shouldn't you be getting back to school?' Charles asked just before they broke for lunch, but the boy said, 'No. They won't mind. They aren't to know how long I'm actually needed for rehearsal.'

Charles shrugged. It wasn't his business. And Sandra Phipps, whose business in her dual role of mother and chaperon it certainly was, spent most of the day in the Box Office and was either unaware of, or unworried by, her son's continuing presence.

So, by the end of the Friday, every move in the play had been gone through at least once. All was set for the Saturday morning run-through – though the less optimistic definitions of stagger-through, lurch-through, hobble-through, stumble-through or even tumble-through, became increasingly likely to be apt.

The advantage of doing a full run so prematurely was that at least everyone in the cast got an idea of what they were up against.

Felicia Chatterton, who had given up remonstrating about the folly of running the play so soon, approached the exercise with her customary seriousness, and was to be found at nine-thirty on the Saturday morning in the middle of the stage, working through a series of yoga postures and breathing exercises. She felt that proper preparation was always essential in acting, even just for a first run.

Beside her on the stage, shadowing her every movement, and with his face set in an expression of equal reverence, was her faithful dog – or perhaps puppy – Russ Lavery.

The other actors who trickled into the auditorium may have grinned covertly at what they saw on stage, but at least they restrained themselves from outright sniggering. Though they didn't all favour such intensity of approach for themselves, they were a tolerant lot. If that's how Felicia wanted to work, fair enough, it didn't cause any trouble.

'Oh, Christ love,' hissed John B. Murgatroyd to Charles in a voice of agonised campness, 'how can Gavin expect me to give a performance at this kind of notice? My body-clock's all set wrong for a start. And then, although I did all my Lennox exercises before I left the digs, I just haven't had time to do my First Murderer workout.'

'You think you've got problems, sweetie,' Charles murmured back in matching style. 'I tell you, I've been up half the night. First, I had to do my Bleeding Sergeant build-up, then my Drunken Porter build-up...'

'Must be hell getting yourself into that part.'

'Yes, character acting's always difficult. Then I had to do my Third Murderer exercises, then the English Doctor, then...'

They both subsided into stifled giggles.

But once the run started Charles was made aware of the problems that his multiplicity of parts caused. Not acting problems – he could come up with a sufficient variety of accents and postures with no effort at all – but purely logistical problems. The blocking rehearsals had taken the play scene by scene; it was only when the whole thing was linked together that the difficulties of so many entrances and exits became apparent.

It soon became clear that Charles Paris would spend almost the entire play running at full tilt round the back of the stage.

As the Bleeding Sergeant, he entered from the auditorium and exited downstage right (had to be downstage – in any scene featuring Duncan, only Warnock Belvedere got upstage exits). Then, in Act One Scene Seven, Charles had to enter upstage left and cross over to exit upstage right. (Yes, the worst had happened – he'd also been lumbered with the part of that bloody Sewer.) As the Drunken Porter, he entered and exited downstage left. As the Old Man who talked to Ross in Act Two Scene Four, he entered and exited upstage right. The Third Murderer, like the Bleeding Sergeant, entered through the auditorium and, after the despatch of Banquo, went off upstage left.

There was then a brief respite, which encompassed the interval (Gavin Scholes had predictably followed the traditional practice of placing this immediately after the Banquet Scene), until Charles had to give his Apparition of an Armed Head. For this, following Gavin's rethink, he made his entrance through a trap door under the stage, to emerge in a haze of dry ice through the Witches' cauldron (assuming that this particular bit of stage magic worked – an assumption which, at that point, only the director was making with any confidence). The Apparition vanished the same way he'd come.

The Third Murderer was once again enlisted to help massacre the Macduff family, and for this occasion he entered and exited downstage left. The English Doctor, whose four-and-a-half lines were so pertinent in the definition of Kingship, entered and exited upstage right. The Scottish Doctor, brought in as a consultant on the Lady Macbeth sleepwalking case, also entered and exited upstage right.

From there on, Charles was into acting soldiers on one side or the other in the final conflict, and for these the entrances and exits (sometimes with and sometimes without chunks of Birnham Wood) were respectively downstage left, upstage right, from the auditorium, upstage left, downstage left and upstage left.

Basically, it seemed to Charles that each performance would qualify as a heavy training session for a decathlete.

And that was before he started thinking about costume and make-up changes.

The Pinero Theatre, Warminster, was only about twenty years old, and of an attractive and intelligent design. Its one drawback was its location which, though it commanded beautiful views over towards Salisbury Plain, was too far out of town for economic health. It was not a theatre which shoppers would pass; anyone who wanted to go and see a play had to make a special expedition. This did not help in the crazy game of knife-edge juggling by which most theatres manage their financial affairs. Arts Council and local council grants come and go, lucrative transfers from the provinces to the West End are rare, and the basic survival of a theatre depends on the time-honoured resource, much cited by Gavin Scholes, of 'putting bums on seats'. In achieving this, the Pinero was always going to be hampered by its position.

But those who did make the effort to get to the theatre, found a welcoming environment. They entered a large, glass-fronted foyer, which housed Sandra Phipps' Box Office. Staircases on either side of this took the visitors up to Norman Phipps' bar, at either end of which were the two main entrances to the auditorium.

The bar was directly above the dressing room area, which was thus behind and under the auditorium rather than in the traditional backstage position. Passages led along the sides of the theatre to the wings, and there were pass-doors at the corners of the auditorium.

In the course of that first Saturday morning run-through, Charles Paris got to know this geography rather well.

It was a somewhat giggly occasion for those of the company prone to giggling (in other words, everyone except Gavin, who was too busy, and Felicia, who didn't know how to...oh, and Russ, whose devotion to Felicia would not allow him to).

Faced with the enormity of the whole play, George Birkitt's performance slipped down the few notches it had so laboriously climbed during the previous week. Apart from anything else, he was distracted; his mind was on the next day's filming in Paris, and he continually glanced at his watch or peered out into the auditorium for the outline of a hire-car chauffeur.

The interval break was brief, because of the pressure of time, and the company struggled into the Green Room to make themselves coffee from an inadequate number of electric kettles. Charles decided to avoid the crush; he'd wait till lunchtime and have a proper drink then. A good few proper drinks. After all, there'd be no more work till the Monday morning. He looked forward to the weekend. A few days before he had contemplated another attempt to make contact with Frances, but since then he'd discovered that John B. Murgatroyd had a car, and they had agreed to devote the break to an in-depth investigation of the pubs of Wiltshire.

As Charles came out of his dressing room, trying to remember what the hell character he had to play next, he encountered Norman Phipps and his son staggering along under the weight of a large metal beer keg. They were carrying it from the delivery door to a small storeroom where the bar supplies were kept.

'Can I give you a hand?'

Norman accepted the offer gratefully. 'There are three more outside. And a few crates. Why they have to deliver on a Saturday I don't know.'

The keg was heavy. Charles took over one end from Stewart and Norman backed into the store-room. 'Watch out, Charles. There's a little step down.'

They collected the other three. After his multi-character exertions in the first half of *Macbeth*, Charles found he was quite puffed as they wheeled the last keg clattering into position. He leant back against a padlocked cupboard in the storeroom.

'Thanks very much,' said Norman. Stewart had run off as soon as he saw his father had alternative assistance. The boy seemed to run everywhere. He was in the state of high stage-struck excitement, and, until the moment for his big scene came, just couldn't see enough of what was going on backstage. He seemed to have lost his initial shyness and now chattered away cheerfully to anyone and everyone in the company.

Charles looked around the store-room. There were gas cylinders beside the kegs and from the top of each keg thin translucent tubes ran up to holes in the ceiling.

'That's how the beer gets pumped up?'

Norman nodded, as he clamped the fixture at the end of one of the tubes on to a new barrel. There was a little hiss of escaping gas. 'Yes, for the ones who like their beer fizzy. The Real Ale specialists don't like the idea of CO_2 near their beer. Theirs is done by hand-pumps.'

'Do you get much call for Real Ale?'

The Bar Manager shrugged. 'Not as much as there was a few years ago. The campaign seems to have died down a bit.'

'What do you keep in here?' Charles indicated the padlocked cupboard.

'Spirits. Can't be too careful. Lots of people come in and out of a theatre.'

'Actors, you mean?'

The Bar Manager allowed himself a brief smile. 'Not just actors.'

At that moment Russ Lavery appeared in the doorway. 'Oh, I've often wondered what was in here.'

'My stock-room,' said Norman Phipps stolidly.

'Don't worry, I recognise it,' said Russ. 'I've been working as a barman the last couple of years to supplement my grant.' He turned to Charles. 'They've started the Apparition Scene.'

'Oh, I'd better shift. I wonder if they've got the trap working this morning...'

Norman Phipps followed him out of the store-room, switching the light off as he came. Then he closed the door, and bent to attach another padlock to the metal rings that fixed it.

'Don't you use the ordinary lock?' asked Charles, indicating a keyhole in the door.

'Broken. This room's been raided more than once.'

'Actors?' asked Charles again.

The suggestion got another small smile from Norman. 'I didn't say so.'

John B. Murgatroyd came bustling up to Charles. 'Come on, ready to give your Apparition of an Armed Head?'

'Do you know if the trap's working?'

'You bet. Come on.'

In the area under the stage stood a wooden framework which housed the trap-door mechanism. At the bottom of this was a platform, supported on ropes. It was counterweighted, so that it could be raised quite easily with the full weight of a human being on it. Assistant stage managers would pull down on the ropes on the given cue, and the actor on the platform would suddenly appear up on stage. The skill in working the trap lay in controlling the speed of the ascent.

There were no members of the stage management about when Charles and John B. Murgatroyd reached the apparatus. 'Are you sure we're meant to be using it for this run?' asked Charles.

'Yes. The ASMs are all tied up at the moment, but they asked me to operate it.'

'Oh well, if you say so.' Charles stepped gingerly on to the platform as John B. took hold of the rope with both hands.

'What's the cue, Charles?'

'Come high or low;
Thyself and office deftly show.'

'Okay.' John G. Murgatroyd braced himself. They were silent, listening to the heavy footfalls and muffled voices above their heads. They could hear the whine of the Witches and the booming tones of George Birkitt, but the precise words were difficult to distinguish.

'That's it,' said Charles, as he thought he recognised the cue.

'Bon voyage,' giggled John B. Murgatroyd, and he gave an almighty heave on the rope.

Charles felt himself shoot up in the air like a rocket. He was aware of the bemused expressions of George Birkitt and the Witches as he burst into view. Then he felt the jolt of the platform beneath him suddenly stopping, and then nothing beneath his feet as his own ascent continued.

Landing back on the platform with a spine-jarring thump, he could hear a wicked, muffled giggle from beneath the stage.

'Sod you, John B. Murgatroyd!' shouted the Apparition of an Armed Head.

The tone of the run had been fairly giggly before this incident, but after it the floodgates of laughter were released. Hardly any scene passed without a complete break up amongst the cast. Almost all actors are susceptible to corpsing and, if the director doesn't stamp on it firmly, it can quickly become an epidemic. Gavin Scholes did not have it in his nature to stamp on anything firmly, so the play just seemed to get funnier and funnier to the entire company.

The climax came in Macbeth's final scene. In his confrontation with Macduff, George Birkitt had regained a kind of stature and he was rather impressive as he began his last speech.

'I will not yield,
To kiss the ground before young Malcolm's feet,
And to be baited with the rabble's curse.
Though Birnham Wood be come to Dunsinane,
And thou oppos'd, being of no woman born,
Yet I will try the last: before my body
I will throw my warlike shield. Lay on, Macduff,
And damn'd be he that first cries...'

But at this vital juncture, Macbeth's attention wandered. He sighted something at the back of the auditorium and concluded the speech, 'Oh, sorry, loves, there's my car, must dash.'

This unintentional bathos brought the house down, and under cover of the laughter, George Birkitt made good his escape, ignoring Gavin Scholes' plaintive voice following him with 'Could you just hang on for a few notes, love...?'

It was the end of the run-through, stagger-through, stumble-through, tumble-through or fumble-through. The director had no hope of re-imposing control after that, and he bowed to the inevitable. 'Okay, we'd better leave it there. Notes first thing Monday morning. Do look at the lines over the weekend. Don't worry. There are still a few rough edges, but it's coming.'

This understatement prompted another round of laughter, and the company adjourned to the bar in a state of high hilarity. Needless to say, there was one person who did not see the joke.

Felicia Chatterton, a few minutes later, strode through the prattling throng in the bar towards the Director, who was just hoping to relax over a glass of wine. Russ Lavery was a rather nervous acolyte in her wake.

'Gavin...' she began in a steely voice.

'Yes, love?'

'I'm afraid we can't go on like this.'

'What do you mean?'

'This total lack of discipline.'

He smiled a smile which had in the past proved disarming. 'Yes, okay, I admit this morning was a complete shambles, but you're bound to get one rehearsal like that. Don't worry, everyone's got it out of their system now. We'll really buckle down to it on Monday.'

She was not reassured. 'I'm afraid I can't act with people who behave like that. I find it impossible to concentrate and build a performance.'

'So what are you suggesting?'

'I am suggesting that the disruptive elements are removed from the cast.'

'What?'

'Either they go, or I'll have to go.'

The director was struck dumb, but another voice took up the challenge.

'Who does she think she is – Sarah Bloody Bernhardt?' Warnock Belvedere sounded even more belligerent than usual. He looked angry and disappointed, and the brandy he clutched was not his first of the morning.

'I just want to work with people who are professional, that's all,' Felicia explained reasonably.

This really caught Warnock on the raw. To cast doubts on his professionalism is the worst insult to any actor. 'And who are you calling unprofessional, you jumped-up little tart?'

Felicia maintained her dignity. 'I am talking about any members of this company who aren't taking the play seriously.'

'Like me, for instance?' The old actor was now enjoying baiting her.

'Yes.'

'So you're saying that *I* should get out of the company?'

'Yes,' she replied evenly. She fixed him with her fierce blue eyes. 'One way or another, you've got to go.'

Chapter Six

THE SECOND MONDAY of rehearsals was a really bad day. In fact, in the long annals of theatrical disasters, there can have been few to match it.

For Charles Paris it started unfortunately, because he woke up with a grinding hangover. His in-depth investigation of the pubs of Wiltshire with John B. Murgatroyd had perhaps gone in too deep. When they met at the theatre on the Monday, Charles discovered that John B. was in exactly the same condition as he was. Their recollections of the final stages of the previous evening were equally vague.

What made it terrifying in retrospect was that John B. had actually driven them back to their digs.

But two hungover small-part actors did not pose a great threat to Gavin Scholes' rehearsal plans. Indeed, hungover actors at morning rehearsals are such a common occurrence that he hardly noticed their bleariness and slow reactions.

What did throw his schedule into disarray, though, was the phone message that came through at ten-fifteen. George Birkitt was fog-bound in Paris. There had been no flights out of the city the previous night and, unless the weather showed a very sudden improvement, there was no chance of his putting in an appearance at that day's rehearsals.

But troubles, as Shakespeare, that well known provider of platitudes for every occasion, observed in another of his plays, do not often come singly. Before Gavin had had time to digest his first gobbet of bad news, Sandra Phipps came into the theatre to announce that Stewart was no longer going to be allowed to take part in the production.

Apparently his blithe confidence that St. Joseph's School wouldn't mind about his taking the Friday off for rehearsal had been misplaced. Because he hadn't even taken the precaution of telling his form master he would not be present, there had been a heated phone-call to the Phipps' home on the Sunday evening, the upshot of which was that Stewart was forbidden to continue in the play.

So, not only had Gavin Scholes lost his principal actor for an unspecified length of time, he was also faced with the problem of finding another son for Macduff. And he knew how time-consuming booking and licensing juveniles could be.

'Don't you think there's a chance if I rang up St. Joseph's and spoke to the teacher myself, he might relent?' the director asked plaintively.

'No,' Sandra replied. 'Not in the mood he's in at the moment. In fact, I must ask you, please, not to do it. Stewart's in bad enough odour there already. I think a call from you could only make it worse for him. No, I'm sorry, he's definitely out. His form master only grudgingly allowed him to be in the show in the first place – on the understanding that his work didn't suffer, you know, with his exams coming up. And now...' She shrugged helplessly. 'He's Head of English, this master, you see, and he's Stewart's English master, and I'm afraid English isn't Stewart's strongest subject.'

So that was that. Two-and-a-half weeks to go, and another Macduff's Son needed in a hurry. Oh dear, Gavin thought, probably have to go to a stage school now. And I did specifically want to avoid that. Stage children are so self-consciously theatrical. He looked dejectedly round the auditorium.

When the director's eye lighted on Charles Paris, John B. Murgatroyd leant forward and whispered in his friend's ear. 'Watch it. I think he's about to say, "Charles, I wonder if you'd mind...?" Oh, come on, love, an actor of your wide versatility should have no problem adding the role of a ten-year-old boy to your portfolio...'

Charles giggled weakly. But giggling was a bad idea. It only made his head ache more.

To compound the director's problems, Warnock Belvedere arrived at rehearsal late, and in a fouler mood than usual. Something must have happened over the weekend to upset him. He looked mean and disgruntled, and no one escaped the lash of his tongue.

But he kept his most vicious lines for Gavin and Felicia. Once, when the director tried to suggest a change of intonation to him, the old actor snapped out, 'Come on, love, make a decision. Do you want me to do the line the way you tell me, or to do it *right*?'

As with most of Warnock's lines, it was not original. Charles had heard it attributed many times to various theatrical luminaries. He had even heard it used once or twice. But never with such belittling venom.

Felicia, too, suffered from Warnock's tongue. When she entered to welcome Duncan to her castle in Act One Scene Six, she stood for a moment locked in thought.

'Get on with it!' Warnock hissed.

'I'm having a lot of difficulty with the delivery,' Felicia said thoughtfully.

'Oh, Christ!' Warnock Belvedere swept downstage and boomed out over the stalls, 'Is there a bloody midwife in the house?'

Felicia recoiled as if struck in the face, and turned appealingly towards Gavin. The director seemed suddenly to have found something deeply riveting in his script.

The moment passed, but the bad feeling didn't.

From its bad start, the day deteriorated. After the debacle of the Saturday run-through, Gavin Scholes needed a really hard-working, concentrated rehearsal to re-establish his authority, but the absence of George Birkitt had made that impossible.

Instead, the concentration of the cast wavered. Silly mistakes were made, there was more giggling. But this time it was not a genial hilarity, just a kind of niggling, annoying fooling-around, a joke that had outlived its humour. It was difficult, under the circumstances, to get any constructive work done.

Charles Paris participated in this silliness, which did not improve his mood, but merely increased the self-distaste engendered by his hangover. Then, because it was the only thing likely to make him feel better, he overindulged in the bar at lunchtime. The new drink topped up the old drink of the night before, and he felt quite drunk when he returned for afternoon rehearsal.

It became clear, as the afternoon progressed, that he wasn't the only member of the company in that condition. The silly giggling continued through the rehearsal, until Gavin Scholes was driven to stage an ineffectual and embarrassing tantrum.

Charles felt despicable as the company spirit deteriorated. He could sense the burning resentment of Felicia Chatterton for what was going on, but seemed incapable of turning the tide of childishness in himself, let alone in anyone else.

He knew that actors very rarely behaved so badly. Most of the time they are diligent professionals. But, like anyone else, they need discipline and, in the face of uncertainty and indecision, they can get out of hand. The limpness of Gavin Scholes' manner was doing nothing to put them back on the right track, and Warnock Belvedere seemed to be taking malicious glee in exploiting the situation, constantly pointing up the director's weakness and, presumably by implication, his own strength.

When Gavin finally gave up the unequal struggle and ended the rehearsal soon after five, it was to reactions of universal relief.

But days which start that badly rarely demonstrate sudden improvements. And, true to form, this one got decidedly worse. Charles knew that the sensible thing to do at the end of rehearsal was to go out and have a brisk walk to clear his head; then go back to his digs for a plain supper and early night.

Equally, he knew that what he would do would be to make everything worse by hanging around the theatre until Norman's bar opened at six, and then stay there far too long.

Which was exactly what he did.

In fact, he stayed in the bar until closing time.

By then he really was woozy. He hadn't been on a continuous bender like that for some years.

But it had not been a joyous inebriation. It had been one that he knew he would regret, one that he regretted even as he nurtured it. With the looming of each new round, he knew he should stop, quit while he was...well, if not exactly ahead, at least not as far behind as he would be if he had another drink.

But each time he weakened and succumbed. A kamikaze recklessness took hold of him, and his own spirits sank as alcoholic spirits fuelled his self-disgust.

John B. Murgatroyd had been with him at the start of the evening, but he, showing better judgement than his friend, had left after a couple of pints.

Charles was not the only member of the company still in the bar when Norman called his impassive 'Time'. Warnock Belvedere had left only a moment before. Gavin Scholes was sharing his troubles and a bottle of Riesling with Lady Macduff and two of the Witches. And, surprisingly, in a corner booth over a glass of Perrier, Felicia Chatterton remained, vigorously dissecting her art to the unquestioning ear of Russ Lavery.

Alone, her back pointedly turned to the bar and her husband, Sandra Phipps sat, balefully nursing the last dregs of her Tia Maria.

As 'Time' was called, Charles, also by now sitting on his own, decided he must go down to his dressing room to fetch his coat and then, finally, get back to his digs. But, as he shifted his bulk off his bar-stool, the floor seemed suddenly and vindictively to have been moved. He sprawled in an ungainly heap, the bar-stool tumbling after him.

'Are you okay?'

The figure of Gavin loomed over him. Russ Lavery's anxious face was also just on the edge of his field of vision.

'Yes, yes, I'm fine.' Charles knew the words were coming out slurred, and hated himself for it. Without dignity, he pulled himself up against the bar and, in an unsuccessful attempt at insouciance, waved a furry 'Goodbye' to the assembled throng before making his ignominious exit.

The stairs to the foyer had taken on the quality of an escalator, and he moved down them gingerly, hand gripping what seemed to be a moving rail. He staggered through the pass-door and strode resolutely but elliptically along the passage.

This involved passing the open door of Warnock Belvedere's dressing room. The old actor's huge body was piled on top of a defenceless plastic chair. He was swigging from a full bottle of Courvoisier, but he cocked his monocled eye at Charles's erratic approach.

Finishing his swallow, he observed with relish, 'What a bloody shambles of a day.'

'Hear, hear.' Charles's hand found the support of the door-frame, which proved to be further away than it looked.

'Nothing you can do with a day like this but get well and truly plastered.'

'That,' Charles agreed, with a bizarre attempt at poise, 'has been my solution to the problem.'

'The ideal now, in fact, to complement this bottle...' He waved the Courvoisier. '...would be a nice juicy little bumboy.'

'Ah,' said Charles.

'Not your sort of thing, is it...? By any chance...?'

In his fuddled state, it took Charles a moment to realise that he was in fact being propositioned. The idea seemed incongruous. He didn't know whether to be flattered or insulted.

But he wasn't too drunk to know that he should refuse the offer. 'Sorry,' he mumbled apologetically. ''Fraid it's never appealed...'

'Ah well,' Warnock mused. 'Don't know what you've been missing.' He took another swig from the bottle. 'I'll have to content myself with just the booze.' He looked appreciatively at the Courvoisier. 'What it is to have a generous friend.'

Charles suddenly felt almost faint from weariness. 'Must go. Tired out. Just get my coat and...'

He eased off the door-frame and propelled himself towards his own dressing room. His eyelids were weighted with lead.

He pushed through the door. The light from the passage illuminated the chair in front of his mirror, and he made towards it without bothering to switch on the dressing room light.

At the third attempt, he slumped into the chair. By then the door, self-closing as the fire regulations demanded, had clicked shut and he was in the dark.

But he didn't mind. He lowered his head gratefully on to the table in front of the mirror, and, in a matter of seconds, Charles Paris was asleep.

Chapter Seven

HE WOKE WITH a head like a hornet's nest, a mouth like a blocked drain, and a desperate need to pee.

For a moment he didn't know where he was. The darkness was total. Then, remembering, he felt along the table towards a light switch.

The sudden blaze drove red-hot nails into his eyes. He blinked in agony. Not time to get to the Gents along the passage. He used the wash-basin noisily, comforting himself with the thought that some of the old actor-laddies reckoned that brought good luck.

He swayed erratically until he had overcome the apparently insuperable problem of doing up his zip. Then he looked at his watch.

Ten to three. Ugh. He must get back to his digs.

There was no light in the passage outside. Oh no, the Stage Doorman must have thought the theatre was empty, and locked up. God, he might be stuck in there till the morning. That'd give the rest of the company a good laugh, he thought ruefully.

He found a switch in the passage and deluged himself with more scalding light. He made his way gingerly towards the Stage Door, hoping against hope that it might just be secured on a latch that could be opened from the inside.

As he edged along, he noticed that the door to Norman's store-room was open. Curious, he moved closer.

The padlock had not been unlocked, but one of the rings to which it was attached had been wrenched away from the door-frame. The screws still stuck forlornly out of the metal plate.

There was no light in the store-room, so he found the switch and once again light seared his eyeballs.

When he had stopped blinking, he stepped down into the room and looked at the scene that greeted his aching eyes.

The padlock on the spirits cupboard had also been forced, and one or two bottles had crashed on to the floor. Also, a couple of the tubes which ran from the kegs to the ceiling had been pulled down.

And on the floor, in the middle of this chaos, face-down, lay Warnock Belvedere.

Beside him was his walking stick. Ragged scrapings on its shiny surface suggested that it had been used to force the padlocks.

In Warnock's hand the bottle of Courvoisier was still clasped. It was empty.

Beer from one of the broken plastic pipes bubbled fitfully over the thick tweed of his suit and into his stained beard.

God, the old soak must have been desperate. Finished the brandy bottle and still needed more. So he'd broken into the store-room, tried first to get some beer, and then attacked the spirits cupboard.

As Charles Paris looked down at the crumpled, sodden heap on the floor, and as his own head throbbed like an old dishwasher in its final cycle, he swore that he would never touch another drop.

Oh well, better wake the old bugger up, he thought. See if we're both going to be locked in here for the night.

He reached down to shake the prostrate actor's shoulder, but got no response.

He shook harder; then turned Warnock over on to his back.

The face revealed was grotesquely more purple and congested than usual.

Nobody was going to wake up Warnock Belvedere.

Ever again.

Chapter Eight

CHARLES TRIED the Stage Door and the main doors in the Foyer. He tried the delivery door through which he had helped Norman with the beer kegs and he even tried the big shutter door of the scenery dock. They were all firmly locked from the outside.

He was imprisoned in the theatre with the corpse of Warnock Belvedere.

It gave him an uncomfortable feeling. He was unwilling to go back and look at the body, for in his imagination it had become more grotesque, the colour more livid, the eyes more bulging. Charles shuddered at the image. He felt ghastly. Apart from anything else, his head still seemed to be full of disgruntled piranha fish, nibbling away at it.

He would have to summon help. He went up to the administration area. The Artistic Director's door was locked, but fortunately Gavin's secretary had an extension line in the outer office. Charles picked it up. The dialling tone prompted him to wonder whom he should ring.

Obviously the police. But maybe he should ring Gavin first. After all, the Pinero was Gavin's responsibility; he should be informed of the accident as soon as possible.

Yes, the director first, then the police.

Gavin lived alone. There had been a wife for some years, but because of his obsession with the theatre, she had rarely seen her husband. And when she finally walked out, Gavin had hardly noticed her absence.

The phone was answered on the third ring. Gavin sounded fully alert. Maybe he had been awake, agonizing over his production and how he was going to make up the lost rehearsal time. If that was the case, the news Charles was about to give wasn't going to ease his troubles.

'Gavin, it's Charles Paris. I'm calling from the theatre.'

'Why the hell are you there?'

'I got locked in by mistake.'

'And you want me to come and let you out?'

'Maybe, but in fact it's worse than that. Warnock Belvedere's here too.'

'You and Warnock staying behind...well, there's a turn-up. What were –?'

Charles cut through this untimely attempt at humour. 'Listen, Warnock's dead.'

There was a silence from the other end of the phone. Then, in an appalled whisper, Gavin Scholes' voice said, 'What, in my theatre?'

* * *

The police voice which answered the phone was impassive as it took down the details of what had happened. Or if the voice had any colouring at all, it was a tone of slight sceptical disbelief. Charles cursed all the alcohol he had had that night. He knew his speech was still slurred.

He explained that the theatre was locked, and gave them Gavin's address, so that the keys could be picked up. Yes, Mr Scholes would be awake; they had just spoken on the phone.

Right. The police would be along as soon as possible. Would Mr Paris please remain where he was until they arrived.

Fat bloody chance of doing anything else, he thought as he put the phone down.

The theatre was aggressively silent now, and it seemed full of the looming presence of Warnock Belvedere's body.

Charles shivered again. God, he felt terrible. Really needed a drink. As he walked down towards the foyer, he looked wistfully through the padlocked grille of Norman's bar.

For a moment, he thought of the open store-room downstairs All those bottles. Or easy enough to fill a glass from the dribbling beer tubes...

But no. He didn't want to confront that congested face again.

Besides, he was going to give up the booze. Wasn't he?

The police were there in ten minutes, but it was a long ten minutes for Charles Paris. They came in through the Stage Door and he met them in the passage which led to the dressing rooms. There were two uniformed officers, but he could hear the sounds of other cars drawing up outside.

Charles felt very weary and unsteady. His words, he knew, were still fuzzy with drink, and he did not miss the sceptical exchange of looks between the two policemen as he showed them where Warnock Belvedere lay.

They thanked him politely and asked where they could find a telephone. They asked if he would mind waiting in the theatre for a while. In his dressing room? Yes, that would be fine. They wouldn't keep him longer than was necessary.

In the dressing room, Charles's head once again found the cushion of his table, and once again he dropped into a dead, unhealing sleep.

'Excuse me, sir. Mr Paris.'

His shoulder was being shaken, and it took him a moment or two to realise where he was.

The policeman who was waking him was a new face. Not in uniform, this one.

There was another unfamiliar figure in the doorway, and, beyond, he could see the anxious face of Gavin Scholes.

'Sorry,' Charles mumbled through a mouthful of slimy cotton-wool. 'Middle of the night, you know. Very tired.'

'Yes, very tired, I'm sure, sir.' Was he being hypersensitive to hear a hint of reproof in the policeman's voice? Oh, why on earth had he drunk so much?

'We don't want to keep you here longer than necessary this evening. But we would be most grateful if you could just describe exactly what happened.'

'What, you mean when I found Warnock...the, er, body?'

'Well, yes, and before that. We've spoken to Mr Scholes about the earlier part of the evening. If you could take it from the moment that you left the bar at closing time...?'

Suddenly the two policemen were sitting and one had a pencil poised over a notebook to take down Charles's words.

There didn't seem much to tell. Charles had spent most of the time between leaving the bar and discovering the body in an alcohol-induced stupor. How much detail did they want, he wondered. Did he have to tell them about peeing in the wash-basin? He decided to edit that detail out of his account.

'Why didn't the Stage Doorman realise that you were still in the theatre?'

'My dressing room light was not switched on.'

'That seems rather strange. Why were you sitting in the dark?'

'Well, I just...I just didn't switch it on.'

'I see.' The words were delivered without emphasis, but their implication was apparent. The policeman turned to the door where Gavin still waited.

'Mr Scholes, would the Stage Doorman check that all the dressing rooms were empty?'

'He should do, yes.'

'So, if he didn't, you're saying he was failing in his duties?'

No, that wasn't at all what Gavin wanted to say. His Stage Doorman had been at the Pinero for eleven years, and Gavin was very loyal to his staff. Somehow, these policemen had a way of making everything sound suspicious.

'Let's just say that on an evening like this the Stage Doorman might be more casual than when we've got a show on.'

'I'm sorry. Could you explain that?'

'I mean that, while we're in rehearsal, there are fewer people around by the end of the evening. When there's a play actually in performance of course all the cast would be here till late, and there'd still be a lot of members of the public in the bar and so on.'

'Ah. I see. Thank you very much, Mr Scholes.' The unemotional tone was evenly maintained.

'Mr Paris, could you describe exactly what you saw when you went into the store-room? And, indeed, why you went in there in the first place?'

Charles explained about seeing the forced padlock, and described what he saw in the store-room. He knew he didn't do it very well. The words seemed too big for his mouth, and many of them got mixed up between his brain and his tongue.

At the end of his recitation the policeman thanked him politely and asked for the address where he was staying.

'I don't think we need keep you any longer this evening, Mr Paris. I'm sure the best thing for you to do will be to go back to your digs and...sleep.'

Again Charles wondered if he was unduly sensitive to that hesitation. Had the policeman really just stopped himself from saying, '...sleep it off'?

'Yes. Sure. Thank you.' He rose gracelessly to his feet.

The policeman also rose and turned to Gavin. 'I would like to talk to you a little more, Mr Scholes, about the late Mr Belvedere. If you don't mind...? I realise it is very late.'

'Oh, don't worry. I don't need much sleep. Anyway, once I've been woken up, that's it for the night. I never get back to sleep.'

'Thank you, Mr Scholes. Shall we go up to your office?'

'Fine. See you in the morning, Charles.'

'What, we'll be rehearsing as usual?'

'We must. Ten o'clock call, as ever. Somehow I've got to get this show on.'

'What show is it you're rehearsing on at the moment, Mr Scholes?' the policeman asked politely.

'*Macbeth*.'

'Oh. That's the play that's meant to be bad luck, isn't it?'

'Yes,' said Gavin wryly. '*The Scottish Play*.' Then the implication of Warnock's death struck him again. 'Oh Christ, I'll have to get another Duncan.' He looked hopefully at Charles who was walking past him with concentrated caution. 'Charles, I wonder if you'd mind...?

'Sorry.' A shake of the head. 'Not that I don't want to help out, but I am the Bleeding Sergeant, aren't I? I think I'm as versatile as the next actor, but even I can't envisage standing up on the stage and saying, "What bloody man is that?" to myself.'

'No. No,' said Gavin wistfully. 'Pity...'

The police kindly drove Charles back to his digs. When he got up to his room, and before he collapsed into the long-desired haven of bed, he looked through the curtains to the road outside.

The police car was still there.

A chill thought struck him.

Was the alcohol making him paranoid?

Or was he under surveillance?

Chapter Nine

THE NEXT morning the police car had gone, so Charles shrugged off his anxieties. Or at least he would have done, if shrugging hadn't been far too painful an activity for the delicately poised time-bomb which was now balanced on top of his neck. He had the worst hangover he could remember.

The gentle September light seemed to laser through his eyeballs into his brain. He took one look at his landlady's bacon, eggs and fried bread and had to leave the dining room, thus causing irremediable damage to their relationship – his landlady was one of those women whose emotional life is conducted solely through the medium of food and for whom every unconsumed crust or potato-skin is a mortal affront.

He couldn't face the claustrophobia of a bus, so he walked to the Pinero, arriving a little after ten. But the fresh air didn't help.

And what greeted him at the theatre did little to improve his mood. He was met at the Stage Door by the policeman of the night before who, courteous as ever, said, 'Mr Paris, good morning. As I mentioned last night, I would like to talk to you a little further. Mr Scholes has kindly said that we may use his office, so if you'd care to come up with me straight away...'

'Oh yes. Fine. But I am meant to be rehearsing. Perhaps I'd better have a word with Gavin to –'

'That's quite all right, Mr Paris. I have spoken to Mr Scholes. I won't keep you any longer than necessary.'

'Oh. All right.'

They didn't speak again until they were up in Gavin's office. It was a crowded room, its every surface high with copies of *Spotlight*, scripts, set designs and the other impedimenta of theatre production.

The policeman sat at Gavin's desk and indicated a low chair for Charles. 'Mr Scholes' secretary was kind enough to offer to make us coffee if we wanted any.'

'It would be very welcome. Black, please.'

'Of course.'

The policeman, like a good host, went to the door and arranged the order. Then he returned to the chair. He looked very alert, in good condition for someone who had presumably been up most of the night.

'Sorry,' said Charles. 'I didn't get your name in all the confusion.'

'Detective Inspector Dowling.'

'Ah.'

The Detective Inspector looked up as someone entered the room. It wasn't the coffee. Instead, Charles was aware of the other plain-clothes policeman of the night before moving silently to take a chair in the corner behind him. 'Detective Sergeant Halliwell will once again be taking notes. We have to have a record, obviously.'

'Of course.'

There was another pause while Gavin's secretary brought in the coffee. Charles gulped at his too avidly, burning his tongue.

When the door was safely closed behind the secretary, Detective Inspector Dowling, who had yet to touch his own coffee, looked directly at Charles. 'Mr Paris, how well did you know Mr Belvedere?'

'I only met him about ten days ago, when we started rehearsal. Before that I'd heard a certain amount about him, but we'd never actually met.'

'How had you heard about him?'

Charles shrugged. Incautiously. It still wasn't a good idea. His head felt as fragile as ever. 'The theatre's a fairly small profession. You hear about people. Particularly the so-called "characters". Stories tend to build up about people who're "larger than life".'

The Detective Inspector nodded. 'And what had you heard about Mr Belvedere?'

'That he was an actor of the old school...'

'Could you clarify what that means for...' A helpless gesture of the hands '...a mere layman?'

'I suppose that it means Warnock worked in a more flamboyant style than modern actors. More expansive...if you like, more hammy...' Charles caught the incomprehension on the Detective Inspector's face, '...likely to be a bit over-the-top...' That evidently wasn't much clearer, '...tended to overact a bit...'

'Ah. Thank you. I understand. And what else did you hear about him?'

'That he could be difficult.'

'Difficult for whom in particular?'

'For a director. Actors of that generation don't really think directors are necessary, just kind of jumped-up stage managers. They think all the important bits of theatre come from the actors themselves.'

'Thank you. This is fascinating, Mr Paris...you know, for me, coming into a place like this, knowing, I regret to say, very little about the theatre and theatrical people...' He paused, then changed his tone. This, Charles was beginning to recognise, was a technique with the Detective Inspector. First he would disarm with courtesy, then come in hard with the questions he really wanted to ask. 'Would you say Mr Belvedere was liked amongst the group?'

It sounded wrong, the word 'group'. 'Company' he should have said. But then, by his own admission, he knew nothing about the theatre.

Still, there was only one answer to the question. 'No. He wasn't liked. I mean, some people were amused by him – he could be very funny, though usually in a pretty vicious way – but I would be lying if I said he was liked.'

'Hmm.' The Detective Inspector paused again. 'Did you know that Mr Belvedere was homosexual?'

'Well, yes, obviously…' Charles shrugged again. Ooh, he must stop doing that. 'But I mean, in the theatre, so many people are, you don't really think about it.'

'No, I suppose not.' For the first time, Charles caught a whiff of prejudice in the Detective Inspector's voice. For all his politeness and ingenuous enquiries, the man seemed to be building up a personal case against the theatre and theatrical people. Perhaps he was one of those who had always thought of actors as drunken, effeminate layabouts. If that were the case, what he had seen during the previous six hours would have done little to dispel the impression.

'I gather from Mr Scholes that Mr Belvedere was also a heavy drinker.' The 'also' suggested the Detective-Inspector was compiling a catalogue of the dead man's moral shortcomings.

'Yes.'

'From the way he was found last night, one might assume that he had drunk a whole bottle of brandy.'

'Yes.'

'He also, I gather, had had a fair amount in the bar in the course of the day…?'

'Yes.'

'Surely that would be an excessive amount for him to drink?'

'Excessive, yes, but not out of character. I mean, he was notorious for going on benders.'

'I gather quite a few actors do that…'

'Some.' Charles found himself avoiding the Detective Inspector's eye.

'Do you think it possible that Mr Belvedere broke into that store-room in search of alcohol?'

'Well, one doesn't want to speak ill of the dead…'

'Much as I appreciate your delicacy, Mr Paris, I'm afraid we in the police sometimes have to ignore such niceties.'

'Of course. Well, yes, then I would say it is possible. When I spoke to him before going into my dressing room last night, he did express an intention to get very drunk.'

'Did he?' The Detective Inspector's head shook slightly in disbelief at the existence of people who behaved like that. 'Hmm, well, that would certainly conform with our findings so far. It'll have to be checked, but it seems fairly certain that Mr Belvedere's walking stick was the instrument used to force the padlocks on the door and cupboard.'

'Ah.'

There was another silence, before the next question was posed with studied casualness. 'What do you think Mr Belvedere died of, Mr Paris?'

'I'm sorry?'

'Seems a straightforward question. What do you think killed him?'

'Well, I hadn't really thought.' It was true. In the shock of discovering the body, and in the alcoholic haze in which he had discovered the body, Charles had not asked himself this basic question. 'I don't know. I suppose, a heart attack...? A stroke...? He was grotesquely overweight. Or maybe just alcoholic poisoning...?'

His interrogator shook his head. 'None of those. He died of asphyxiation.'

'You mean he was strangled?'

'No, no. We don't have to be so melodramatic, Mr Paris. Asphyxiation simply means the obstruction of the body's respiratory system. You don't have to strangle someone to achieve that. There are many other ways of cutting off the supply of air to the lungs.'

'So what do you think happened in this case?'

'Well, we'll have to get it confirmed by forensic tests, but the police doctor's made a few educated guesses. I'll tell you what we think, because it's possible you might have some evidence to support our theories...you know, having been on the spot when it happened...albeit dead to the world at the time.' This time there was no mistaking the edge of contempt in the Detective Inspector's look.

'Right, here's a scenario for what might have taken place. Mr Belvedere leaves the bar at closing time. He's had a lot to drink, but, being an alcoholic, he still wants more. He goes down to his dressing room and waits. You see him down there, but he presumably doesn't know that you stay in the building. He switches out the light in his dressing room, so that the Stage Doorman won't realise there's anyone there when he does his final rounds before locking up.

'When he's confident that the theatre's empty, Mr Belvedere, by now desperate for a drink, makes for the store-room. Using his walking-stick as a lever he forces open the door and then does the same to the lock of the cupboard. He steals a bottle of brandy and starts drinking it down, there on the spot. The brandy, on top of all the other alcohol he's had in the course of the day, makes him stagger around a bit, and that's when he pulls down the beer pipelines. Or maybe he just does that out of spite, or to make it look as though it's been an outside raid by kids...it's not really important which, the important thing is that the lines get broken.

'Then, finally, the alcohol gets to him, and he passes out, flat on the floor.

'Unfortunately, though, when the beer lines got broken, so too did the lines carrying gas to pump the beer. That gas, of course, is carbon dioxide, and an elementary knowledge of chemistry will tell you that it's heavier than air and so sinks to the ground. When it gets to the ground, it forces out the oxygen and so, for anyone who happens to be lying there, it's really rather bad news. Particularly in a room where there's a step up to the door, so that the gas stays trapped on the floor. Of course, someone in normal health would react, would rise to his feet when he started to have difficulty breathing. But for someone who was lying there in a drunken stupor...' The Detective Inspector shook his head '...I'm afraid it's going to be very bad news indeed.'

'And that's what you think happened?' asked Charles.

'Seems a reasonable assumption. Subject to confirmation, as I say. See what comes out at the inquest. But yes, that's the way it looks at the moment.'

'So you think it was an accident?'

Detective Inspector Dowling's eyes narrowed. 'The only alternative to it being an accident, Mr Paris, would be murder.'

'Yes.'

The policeman sighed. 'I know actors make their living by dramatising things, but I don't think it's really necessary in this case. Looks like a straightforward accident to me. I don't think we need set in motion all the paraphernalia of a murder enquiry.'

'Then why are you telling me all this?' Charles was, in part, relieved that the threat of his being a murder suspect had lifted, but he was also intrigued about the reasons for his interrogation.

'You were on the spot, Mr Paris. You may have seen something that invalidates my theory.'

'Well, yes, I did, actually.' Charles leapt in without thinking of the implication of his words.

'Oh yes?' The Detective Inspector was suddenly alert. Once again he had snapped from casual courtesy to incisive interrogation. 'And what was that?'

'The brandy bottle.'

'What about it?'

'Did you find a second brandy bottle?'

'No. Just the one.'

'And you know it came from the store-cupboard?'

'We assume that.'

'Because when I saw Warnock, before the store-room had been broken into, he already had a bottle of Courvoisier.'

'Are you sure of that, Mr Paris?'

'Well, yes, I...' But suddenly he wasn't sure of anything. The night before was disappearing into a jumble of alcoholic images. 'I'm fairly sure.'

'Fairly, eh?' Detective Inspector Dowling grimaced. 'We in the police force prefer things to be a bit firmer than "fairly", you know. But let's say for a moment you're right...What you're suggesting is that someone set up the whole thing, got Mr Belvedere drunk, broke into the store-room, laid him on the floor, fractured the beer- and gas-lines...all getting pretty elaborate, isn't it, Mr Paris?'

'Yes, I agree, but –'

'And then of course if you are talking in those terms, it raises the question of who, doesn't it? Who are you suggesting set up this complicated scenario?'

'Well...'

'Mr Paris, if you'll pardon my saying it, you are not what the police regard as an ideal witness. During the period of what you like to think of as the murder, you were, not to put too fine a point on it, incapable with drink. I've spoken to other people who were in the bar with you last night...apparently you couldn't even stand up when you left. So I think anything you say about your encounter with the late Mr Belvedere must be a little suspect, don't you...?

'I'm sure he had a bottle then. He said that a generous friend had given it –'

'There is another point, too, Mr Paris, which I'm sure you will in time work out for yourself...'

'What's that?'

'If we are talking about a murder, so far as we know there was only one other person in the theatre at the time that Mr Belvedere died. Wasn't there, Mr Paris?'

The implications of Detective Inspector Dowling's words sunk in, as Charles went down to join the rehearsal.

He just didn't know. The policeman's manner was so deceptive. Maybe he genuinely did think that the death had been accidental. Or maybe that was just a ploy to disorient Charles, to put him off his guard.

One thing was clear, though. If the police were thinking in terms of murder, they had only one suspect.

And that was Charles Paris.

Chapter Ten

'YOU'RE NO fun any more, Charles Paris,' said John B. Murgatroyd, slurping a lunchtime pint in the bar. Charles squinted down at his Perrier water.

'No.'

'I mean, what you need is a hair of the dog.'

'That's what I had yesterday. I had so many hairs of the dog I could have knitted myself my own St. Bernard. And it didn't do me any good.'

'No. But that was yesterday. Today's today.'

'I know. I'm still laying off.'

'But, after the shock of discovering old Warnock's body, you need something.'

'That's true.'

'What'll it be?'

'I'll stick with this.' He looked again at the Perrier water. It didn't get any less pallid and uninspiring. Had he been a vodka drinker, or a gin drinker, perhaps it wouldn't have looked so strange. But to a man whose familiar spectrum of beverages ranged only from the gold of Bell's whisky to the russet of bitter, there was a mental jolt each time he looked at it.

John B. shook his head in mixed pity and disbelief. 'Sad to see a good man go.'

'Sad to see Warnock go...?' Charles ventured.

'Well, yes. Sad to see anyone go, obviously. But I don't think the old bastard's going to be mourned that much.'

'No.'

'Couldn't be a more appropriate end, though, could it? Drowned in alcohol.'

'That isn't quite what happened.'

'Well, to all intents and purposes. I mean, it was the booze that got him...or at least, the desire for the booze.'

'Yes.'

Something in Charles's tone made John B. look at him sharply. 'Oh, I understand. That's it. Seeing him lying there's put you off.'

'I suppose so. I mean, I've heard the expression "old soak" enough times, but I never thought I'd see it so literally demonstrated. The beer was just dribbling over him. His suit was like a wet dishcloth.'

'Yuk. Still, a few people round the theatre won't be sorry.'

'Who were you thinking of in particular?' asked Charles, suddenly alert.

'You name them. Little Ms. R.S.C., certainly. Now perhaps she'll get a Duncan who will allow her to...' John B. dropped into a parody of her thrilling intensity '...concentrate on the subtext of her part.'

'Hmm.'

'I've come to the conclusion that what would sort her out is a really thorough screwing. By an expert.'

'Are you volunteering or just giving your considered medical opinion?'

'Bit of each.'

'Well, good luck. I'll know when you've succeeded by your bent ears. Incidentally, Doctor, could I just ask why it is that you always recommend the same treatment for every female complaint?'

John B. dropped instantly into a cod Viennese accent. 'In my experience, Herr Paris, it seems to work wiz most of them.'

'You are a sexist pig and I shouldn't be listening to you.'

'Please yourself.'

'Who else, though?'

'Who else what?'

'Who else do you think will be glad to see the back of Warnock?'

'Well, everything Felicia does and thinks, someone else does and thinks, doesn't he?'

'Yes,' said Charles ruminatively, remembering the embarrassments of the first evening when Warnock Belvedere had made a pass at Russ Lavery.

'And dear old Gavin was having enough disciplinary problems without Warnock constantly undermining his authority.'

'True.'

'But, as I said, basically anyone in the company. One of the most popular deaths in the annals of the theatre, I'd say. A blessed accident.'

Charles didn't question this. No one in the company seemed to have thought of any possibility other than accident. Again he wondered how much Detective Inspector Dowling believed that conclusion, or how much he was playing his chief suspect along. Giving him enough rope .

'Come on, let me get you another drink, Charles. What's it to be? You can't pretend you're enjoying that Perrier.'

'No.'

'Go on, have a pint.'

'No, I won't.'

'A Bell's?'

'No. I am really on the wagon.'

'Dear oh dear. Well, what then – Coke, grapefruit juice, lemonade, cherryade, Tizer...?' John B. pronounced each name with mounting distaste.

'All of those are so bloody sweet, that's the trouble.'

'I know the solution,' said John B. triumphantly. 'I bet Norman's got one of those alcohol-free lagers tucked away somewhere.'

Charles raised a hand of restraint. 'No. I may have few principles, but the idea of alcohol-free lager offends one of my deepest. It's like...yuk, I don't know...like the idea of making love to an inflatable woman.'

John B. chuckled. 'See, there's nothing else you like. You're going to have to have a proper drink.'

'No,' said Charles resolutely.

'If you don't, I am going to leave you on your own and start my campaign to winkle my way into Felicia Chatterton's knickers.'

'Off you go then. Good luck. I'm going to stick to my Perrier.'

'Sissy.' John B. started to move away.

'Just a minute.' Charles gestured his friend close and whispered, 'I think your best approach is to find a subtext that proves Lady Macbeth was having an affair with Lennox. Then she'll leap into bed with you, no problem...you know, Stanislavsky, "Method", all that...'

'Hey, thanks. That's a brilliant idea. You can't think of any particular lines of Lennox's that'd be suitable, can you?'

''Fraid not. There doesn't seem to be a moment where he suddenly says, "How about it then, Lady Macbeth? Get 'em off".'

'No.' For a moment John B. looked downcast. Then inspiration struck. He raised a finger in triumph. 'I've got it. I'll tell her those lines were in the original text, but they got cut from the First Folio. Can't fail. See you, Charles.'

When John B. Murgatroyd had sauntered off, Charles was left once again with his own thoughts. And they weren't very comforting ones.

Also he did very desperately miss having a drink. Usually the worst effects of a hangover could be temporarily suspended by a lunchtime top-up, but his vow had forbidden that option. He thought back to the old joke about a drunkard having the advantage over a teetotaller that he knew from the moment he woke up, his day could only get better. What faced Charles was a long plateau of boredom.

But he was determined to stick with it. Enough people had told him over the years to lay off the booze. How gratified they would all be to know that he was finally taking their advice.

Frances, in particular. She'd be glad. From the start of their marriage, she'd been on at him, subtly but inexorably, to cut down. And now he was doing it.

That might be a good way of making contact again...Ring her and tell her he was on the wagon. He could offer his great sacrifice as a peace-offering.

Good idea, yes. He could go straight away and ring her at school. She was usually free to take phone-calls at lunchtime.

But he curbed his enthusiasm. It remained a good idea, but it would probably be even better if he waited a few days. Frances might not think giving up drink for fourteen hours was really worth crowing about. But when it got to fourteen days, yes, then it could be a useful reopening gambit.

It didn't take long for his thoughts to move from his magnificent self-denial back to Warnock Belvedere's death.

He'd really got himself into a cleft stick over that. If he accepted Detective Inspector Dowling's view of the death as an accident, then he had to deny certain memories he had of the night before. He knew he had been pretty fuddled, but he was sure that Warnock had had a bottle of Courvoisier before the store-room was forced, and also that the old actor had said it was the gift of 'a generous friend'.

But if he continued to maintain that memory, the only effect would be to concentrate the Detective Inspector's suspicions on him. Better, in that sense, to let sleeping dogs – or asphyxiated old queens – lie.

On the other hand, if Dowling was simply trying to put him off his guard, then he was still in danger. Any allegation of murder immediately pointed the finger at him as the murderer. So far as the police knew, he was the only person who had had the opportunity. The means were easily organised and, as for motive, well, everyone hated Warnock. He was sure members of the company could recall insults directed at Charles Paris as much as at anyone else.

So, in a sense, the only way he could protect himself against a charge of murder was by proving that someone else had committed it.

Because, however much he fudged round the issue, Charles Paris kept coming back to the certainty that Warnock Belvedere had been murdered.

It wasn't just the brandy bottle which he was now certain he had seen in the old actor's hand while the store-room door was still intact. There were a couple of other details.

First, there was Warnock's mention of 'a generous friend'. That implied that someone had given him the bottle, secure in the knowledge that the actor was likely to swig away until it was empty.

But more significant was another fact, which Charles had omitted, by genuine oversight, to mention to the police. Now, not wishing to encourage them towards suspicions of murder, he was quite glad of that oversight.

The second important fact was that when he went into the store-room, the light had been off. If Warnock Belvedere had followed the course of action which Detective Sergeant Dowling described, there was no way that he would have done it in the dark.

Which meant that someone else had switched the light off.

The show, as theatrical cliché and the economic health of the Pinero Theatre, Warminster, demanded, had to go on. Warnock Belvedere had been quickly replaced. One phone-call from Gavin had procured an elderly actor of benign competence contracted to start rehearsal on the Wednesday morning. No extravagant, inventive casting this time. The director had gone for someone who lived locally and with whom he had worked many times before. Given only two weeks to the opening night, he opted for safety. And there was a general relieved feeling in the cast that the production would be more relaxed without the flamboyant malignancy of Warnock Belvedere.

As it had on Charles (though in his case more literally), the death had had a sobering effect on the whole company. They had all felt slightly guilty about the lack of discipline which had been creeping into rehearsals, and slightly schoolboyish over the way they had taken advantage of Gavin's weakness. Warnock's demise had been a well-timed slap on the wrist, and they all settled down with renewed concentration to make sure that *Macbeth* would be ready in time for the paying public to enjoy.

It was just as well that they were prepared to work hard, because there was a long way to go. Apart from the problems of integrating a new Duncan and a new Macduff's Son into the production, there was also the problem of George Birkitt. His sojourn in Paris seemed to have wiped from his mind all trace of the previous week's rehearsal, and certainly very few of Shakespeare's lines appeared to have taken any lasting hold on the slippery surface of his memory. For him, the Tuesday rehearsal was like starting again at Day One.

Felicia Chatterton's concentration, of course, could not be faulted, but at times Gavin Scholes wished it could have been differently channelled. Since her approach to acting required that every intonation and movement should 'feel right', rehearsal was frequently interrupted by long silences while she tried to make the mental adjustment that one of Gavin's instructions necessitated.

On the Tuesday afternoon, for example, they were working on the Sleepwalking Scene. Felicia' s neurotic trauma was very convincing; Charles could feel the power of her talent whenever he was on stage with her.

'To bed, to bed; there's knocking at the gate,' she intoned in a tinglingly agonised whisper. 'Come, come, come, come, give me your hand. What's done –'

'Erm, can I just stop you there...?'

Gavin, who was leaning against the front of the stage, interposed.

'Sorry?' She seemed to come out of a trance. 'Yes...?'

'I think we want to make that a bit sexier, Felicia.'

'Sexier?'

'Yes. It's a hark back to the strong physical thing between the Macbeths we got going in Act One.'

'Oh, do you think so?'

'Yes.' Gavin didn't sound quite so sure now, but hoped he might convince her with a textual argument. 'It's in the words, love. "To bed"..."come". It's definitely sexual imagery.'

'Hmm.' Felicia gave this studied consideration. 'I suppose it might be. Certainly "to bed" has a sexual resonance...'

'Yes,' Gavin agreed eagerly.

'But I'm not sure about "come". I've a feeling its sexual connotation is more recent. Nineteenth century, I think. I mean, we know that "die" meant "achieve orgasm" in Shakespeare's time, but I'm not sure about "come". Maybe we could look it up…?'

'Well, yes…' Gavin was beginning to regret having started up this particular avenue. 'I mean, I'm not so concerned about the actual words…'

'Aren't you?' asked Felicia, shocked.

'Well, yes, of course I *am*. I am. But I mean, it's more a *feeling* that I want to come across.'

'Ye-es?' She sounded uncertain.

'You see, we've established at the beginning of the play that the Macbeths have this strong sexual thing…'

'Yes.'

'And that a good part of her power over him is based on what she can do for him in bed…'

'Sure.'

'And then, when he starts to get real power – i.e. when he becomes king – her sexual power over him is weaker. He goes his own way, he starts to exclude her from his plans…'

She nodded her earnest blond head. 'Be innocent of the knowledge, dearest chuck.'

'Exactly. So really that signals the beginning of the breakdown of the marriage. He doesn't need her any more. He thinks he can manage on his own now he's got power. The balance of the relationship has shifted…'

'Yes. I accept that.'

'Probably the balance of the sexual relationship has shifted too. Maybe he is now the initiator. Unfortunately, we can't be sure…' Gavin lightened the atmosphere with a little joke. 'Shakespeare didn't write any bedroom scenes for the Macbeths.'

'No,' Felicia concurred with unfeigned regret. 'It's a pity, isn't it?'

'Yes, anyway, what I'm saying is that the sleepwalking scene expresses the breakdown of Lady Macbeth's personality under the stresses of what she's done, and I think it also expresses the breakdown of her marriage – i.e. her sexuality – and I think we want an echo of that, a reminder of what the sexual relationship used to be like – in this scene.'

'Hmm...'

'I mean, as well as everything else, as well as her revulsion for the monster she has unleashed in her husband…'

'Hmm…' Felicia Chatterton's pretty little brow wrinkled as she endeavoured to accommodate this new idea.

'You see,' Gavin went on, 'I think this scene's got to be sexy. We can help it with the cozzy. I mean, I think the nightgown's got to be really low-cut, show us a lot of…you know. In a way, I think that makes it more poignant. I mean, it's one of the reasons I wanted to cast a young Lady Macbeth…so that what we witness is not some menopausal breakdown but the crack-up of a woman at her physical peak.'

'Yes. And you think I can get all that into the "to bed" lines?'

'Well, I hoped so. But if you think it's too difficult…'

'No, no, no.' She brought her hand up to her face and held the bridge of her nose between thumb and finger as she focused her concentration on the problem. 'Just give me a minute to see how I can make it work.'

The minute of silence stretched to two minutes. Charles, in his role of the Scottish Doctor, shuffled his feet and tried to avoid the eye of the Waiting-Gentlewoman, in case he giggled. Felicia Chatterton remained immobile, shoehorning the new thought into her mind and seeing how it fitted.

'Erm…' said Gavin eventually. 'I think we'd better move on.'

'Yes, sure, I know, Gavin, but what you've just suggested is a kind of reinterpretation of the whole part…I mean, a shift in her relationship with everything around her.'

'Yes, I take that.'

'Going to take a bit of time to work out the ramifications…'

'Yes,' Gavin agreed, bitterly regretting that he'd ever given the note. 'Well, if you could possibly just, sort of, work out the ramifications later, you know, in your own time, and if you could just, for the minute, say the lines a bit sexier…'

'What, without working out why I'm saying them sexier?'

'Exactly.' The director looked jubilant. She had got his point at last.

'Well…' said Felicia Chatterton dubiously. 'I suppose I could *try*...'

All of this, inevitably, took time. And, unfortunately for Charles, he was not occupied during that time. He was standing on stage, true, but he didn't have a lot to do – just deliver the occasional line in the intervals between Lady Macbeth's agonizing over her motivations. As a result, his mind was free to wander. And it kept wandering back to the same predictable subject.

If Warnock Belvedere had been murdered, the main suspects for that murder were the people who had been in the bar at the end of the Monday evening, when Charles had made his ignominious exit. He strained his memory to recall the scene. It hurt his head to concentrate. His brain felt bruised and dry, unaided by the temporary assistance of a lunchtime drink.

Who had been there? Norman, behind the bar. His wife, Sandra, as ever ignoring him, on the other side of the counter. Felicia Chatterton and Russ Lavery, rapt over more open-heart surgery on the character of Lady Macbeth. Gavin Scholes, with Lady Macduff and two Witches.

Given Warnock Belvedere's propensity for putting everyone's back up, any one of them might have had a motive for wanting him out of the way.

Hmm, Charles thought without enthusiasm, I'm going to have to start checking on the movements of all of them, aren't I?

Chapter Eleven

LADY MACDUFF and the two Witches were quickly eliminated.

Charles didn't have to be over-elaborate in his enquiries. An apology for his drunkenness and the confession that he couldn't remember anything of the previous evening got Lady Macduff talking, with suitably theatrical emphases, about how *ghastly* it had been for Warnock to have died like that, and how *awful* to feel that if only they'd stayed in the theatre a little longer they might have been able to *help*.

'Why, what time did you leave?' Charles asked casually.

'Almost immediately after you did. Gavin gave us a lift. Our house is on his way home.'

The three actresses, it transpired, were sharing a rented house some four miles from the theatre. Gavin had deposited them there together at about half past eleven. So, unless he wanted to get into elaborate conspiracy theories or imagine them walking back and breaking into the theatre, Charles could rule Lady Macduff and the two Witches out of his investigations.

Mind you, he thought, if I open the enquiry up to people who could have broken into the theatre...or indeed people who might have hidden themselves in the theatre all evening and not gone up to the bar, the field becomes infinitely wide. At least I'll start with the obvious ones.

He didn't rule out Gavin Scholes along with the actresses whom he had driven home. The director stayed on the list. For a start, he had suffered publicly from Warnock Belvedere's attacks on his professional competence, which gave him a degree of motive. Also, he had a car, which made returning five miles to the theatre no problem. And, most significantly, he had keys which would let him into the theatre once he got there. What was more, he knew the building so well that he could easily have worked out the potential of the liquor store-room as a scene for a murder.

But there was another person on the theatre staff who knew that store-room even better.

Norman Phipps wasn't in the bar at the end of the Tuesday's rehearsals, so Charles prepared to give his order to a spotty youth in a bow-tie.

He had to bite back his instinctive 'Large Bell's, please'. He was really determined about this not drinking business. His body and his soul both needed the scouring of abstinence.

But actually thinking of what to order again presented a problem. Perrier still seemed too insipid; he wanted something with a bit of taste.

'Um, could I have a...'

'Yes?' prompted the spotty youth, aware of the increasing arrivals of actors at the end of rehearsal. Charles, even off the booze, had not lost his practised skill at being first to the bar.

'Um, a, er...'

'What? Come on, I've got lots of people to serve.'

'Yes. A...er...' He took the plunge. 'Tonic water.'

'Ice and lemon?' the barman asked as he turned to the shelf of bottles.

'What's the alternative?'

The spotty face looked back balefully. 'No ice and lemon.'

'That's all you can have with tonic water, is it?'

'Some people,' the spotty youth replied in a voice heavy with long-suffering, 'have gin or vodka with it.'

'No, I meant non-alcoholic.'

'Ice and lemon is the most usual. Angostura bitters some people ask for.' This was spoken with undisguised contempt.

'Oh, get on with it,' urged a thirsty Donalbain, pressing against the counter.

'I'll try the Angostura,' Charles concluded hastily.

It wasn't very nice. As he sipped it, he reflected that he'd never liked pink gin much. And pink tonic water excluded the only element that made pink gin even mildly tolerable.

Also it was bloody expensive. The prices of soft drinks were iniquitous. For the first time in his life he felt the righteous anger of the teetotaller against the discrimination of an alcohol-oriented world.

He looked across the bar-room to John B. Murgatroyd steering two fistfuls of pints to a seated group of actors. Oh dear, was giving up the booze going to lose him friends as well?

He wondered where Norman was. Obviously the Bar Manager couldn't be expected always to be on duty, but he had been behind the counter for most of the previous week. Saving money on staff, no doubt. After all, with just the cast rehearsing, business was fairly slack. He'd need to draft in extra help once the season really started with the opening of *Macbeth*.

But, even as he thought this, the next best thing to Norman entered the bar. Sandra Phipps was, as ever, dressed to emphasise her sexuality, this time in a tight flying-suit of shiny scarlet material. Perhaps a bit too tight. The constricting belt drew attention to the little roll of fat at her waist, a legacy presumably of bearing Stewart.

Charles waved to her and she came across to him readily enough. 'Get you a drink?' he asked.

'Ooh, you men,' she simpered. 'Always trying to get girls drunk, aren't you?'

He began to wonder if there was any question in the world to which Sandra Phipps would not give a sexually loaded answer.

Still, he played along. 'Of course,' he leered. 'You know we're only after one thing.'

She giggled and said thank you, yes, she'd like a Tia Maria. Somehow, that seemed to him to epitomise her character, cloyingly sweet and in some way synthetic.

He gave the spotty youth the order. 'And I'll have a...'

'What?'

'Um...'

'How was the tonic and Angostura?'

'Quite revolting.'

The spotty youth nodded. 'Could have told you that.'

'Well, is there anything you could tell me that is nice?'

'Lot of things. Bell's whisky's not bad.'

'I know that,' Charles said testily. 'I mean, non-alcoholic things.'

'No. You got me there.' He addressed his mind to the problem. 'I have seen people,' he offered cautiously, 'drinking alcohol-free lager...'

'Does it make them look happy?'

The spotty youth shook his head. 'Miserable as sin.'

Charles threw in the towel. 'Oh, I'll have a tomato juice.'

'Worcester sauce?'

'Yes. Salt. Pepper. Eggs. Ketchup. Everything you've got.'

'Vodka?'

Ooh, it was tempting. His head still felt as if it had been the match ball in a South American Cup Final. And surely a Bloody Mary was just medicinal...

But virtue triumphed. 'No, thank you.' After all, it was going to be his peace offering to Frances. A dried-out husband. Goodness, she'd think her birthday and Christmas had both come at once. Must ring Frances, he thought. Must ring Frances.

He took the drinks across to where Sandra perched on a bar-stool, stroking her scarlet thighs.

'Cheers.'

She raised her glass. 'May you always get enough.' Predictable again.

'Norman not about?' he asked casually, thinking how he could ease the conversation round to the questions he wanted to ask.

But her reply removed that necessity. 'He's with the police.'

'Oh?'

She giggled. He was aware that, beneath her customary brassiness, she was very nervous. 'Yes. Do you reckon they'll've arrested him yet?'

'What for?'

'The murder of Warnock Belvedere.'

'What? Goodness, it never occurred to me that the old queen might have been murdered,' Charles lied.

'No, of course he wasn't.' She giggled. 'Only joking.'

'So why do the police want to see Norman?'

'Check out about how he kept the store-room. He was quite worried going to see them.'

'Why?'

'Well, he's the licensee here, isn't he? If they can prove negligence, you know, if there was something wrong down in the store-room, he'd be liable. Big insurance claim is the last thing he needs.'

'Yes. I've had a couple of sessions with the police,' Charles confided, softening her up before he started on the important questions.

'Oh yes. Why?'

'Well, I found the body.'

'Of course. How did they treat you?'

'I think they're deeply suspicious of me.'

'Why?'

'My behaviour last night was a bit...well...'

'Yes, you were well gone.' She paused, then probed, 'What did the police seem to think?'

'About Warnock's death?'

'Yes.'

'That it was an accident.'

'That's a relief.' She relaxed for a moment before a new thought struck her. 'Unless, as I say, they reckon Norman's responsible for that accident.'

'They didn't imply that. They seem to reckon Warnock just broke into the storeroom and was so pissed he tore all the pipes down. I don't think any of the joints were loose or anything.'

'Good.' She looked at Charles as if he had somehow demanded an explanation. 'Like I say, big insurance claim we could really do without. Always bloody hard-up. Why I didn't pick a husband who was going to make a few bob I don't know. And now we've got Stewart's school fees to find...'

'How's Stewart taking it, being out of the play? Is he very upset?'

'He'll survive,' Sandra Phipps replied briskly, putting an end to the subject.

'Have you had to talk to the police...?' Charles ventured.

'Yes. I think they're working through everyone who was in the bar last night.'

Just as I am, he thought. Oh, the pointlessness of being an amateur sleuth, always limping a few steps behind the professionals. No doubt Detective Inspector Dowling and his acolytes already knew everything. They knew the death had been murder and they knew who had done it.

That made him feel uncomfortable. He still felt exposed as a potential suspect. He took a swig from his drink, but tomato juice didn't soothe him the way whisky would have done.

Once again, he came back to the conclusion that to clear his name he must pursue his own investigations. 'So did the police ask when you left the bar last night?'

'Oh yes.'

'And when Norman left?'

She looked at him suspiciously. 'You're as bad as they are. Everyone's so bloody suspicious.'

He tried to shift her mood with a platitude. 'I'm afraid that's what happens when something like a murder occurs.'

'Yes. Yes. Suppose you're right.'

'And I suppose you were able to put their minds at rest...?'

Again she looked up sharply. 'Yes, I was. Norman and I left together. Soon as he'd locked up the bar.'

'You drove home?'

'We walked. Only live the other side of the park. Always walk when we're both going to leave at the same time. If I'm going to be on my own I take the car. Nasty types around that park.'

'Yes. Oh well, at least you were able to put Detective Inspector Dowling's mind at rest.'

'Oh, sure. Mind you, he's a nosy bugger.'

'What do you mean?'

'Well, it wasn't just when did we leave. It was when did we get home, what did we do when we got home. Did we both stay at home all night?'

'I suppose that's because you live so near the theatre...'

'You mean they reckon one of us could have nipped back in the middle of the night?'

Charles shrugged. Even so far into his hangover, he was reminded that shrugging was a bad idea. 'Presumably they have to check everything.'

'Yes, well, fortunately...' Sandra Phipps leant close. Charles could smell the pungency of her musky perfume. 'I was able to give them chapter and verse. Embarrassing, isn't it, to have to describe your sex-life to the police?'

'Oh,' said Charles, mildly embarrassed himself.

'Thing is,' she went on coarsely, 'when Norman wants a bit, he really wants a bit. Amazing I ever get any sleep. At it till three o'clock last night he was.' There was a note of reluctant pride in her voice.

Charles felt a little shocked. He had got used to Sandra loading her every remark with sexual innuendo, but to hear her talking so glibly about the real thing was unsettling. It also put a whole new light on to her relationship with Norman. However much she diminished and dismissed him in public, it was clear from her words that he was the dominant partner in their sexual relationship. Once again, Charles was brought up against the immovable fact that it is impossible to see inside another couple's marriage.

'Ah,' he said. This didn't really seem an adequate reaction to what she had just said, but he couldn't think of anything else.

Sandra laughed raucously. 'As I say, dead embarrassing to have to tell that kind of thing to the police.' But she didn't sound embarrassed. She enjoyed talking about it, particularly, Charles realised, to strangers. He was being used, just as the police had been, to give her some kind of thrill.

'Anyway,' she concluded, 'at least that let us off the hook as far as any police enquiries go.'

As she spoke, she looked up and a flicker of anxiety crossed her face. Norman was walking towards her.

He nodded to Charles. 'No problem,' he said quietly to his wife.

'They're not worried about negligence?'

Norman Phipps paused almost imperceptibly, then shook his head. 'No, they reckon everything was secure. Anything that was done, Warnock Belvedere did to himself.'

Sandra looked relieved. She had been genuinely worried about the threat to their livelihood.

Without further words, Norman went across to the bar to relieve the spotty youth. Charles couldn't help his eyes from following the Bar Manager, fascinated by this new dimension, this new identity of Norman Phipps, Superstud.

But at least, he reflected, that rules out both of the Phippses. If they left the bar together at half-past eleven, and were then erotically engaged till three in the morning, there was no way that either of them could have arranged the death of Warnock Belvedere.

Chapter Twelve

ON THE WEDNESDAY of the second week's rehearsal, the new Duncan was quickly integrated into the production. It was a painless process. He was a quick-learning old pro and, though he lacked the stage presence of his late predecessor in the role, he also lacked Warnock's other, less endearing qualities, and no one in the company regretted the exchange.

The whole of the Thursday was spent on Act Five, which involved almost everyone. To swell the battle scenes, Gavin had enlisted even the three Witches and Lady Macduff, who he hoped, under sufficiently large helmets, would pass for members of Macbeth's or Malcolm's armies. Since the new Duncan did not share Warnock Belvedere's fastidiousness about doubling, he was also conscripted.

In fact, the only members of the company who would not be disguising themselves as Birnham Wood or dashing around the theatre with strange battle-cries were Macduff's Son and Lady Macbeth. This was just as well for the sake of the former's schooling and the sake of the latter's stamina.

The intensity which Felicia Chatterton put into her acting was beginning to take its toll. She looked exhausted when she came in to the Wednesday's rehearsal, her wonderful blue eyes smudged around with tiredness, and she kept stretching as if she were in pain from her back. Charles wondered whether the problem was one of pacing, if she was trying to cram into three-and-a-half weeks' rehearsal the mental processes of five or six weeks.

She also seemed to have distanced herself from her confidant, Russ Lavery. It had been noticeable on the Tuesday that they did not sit together in the auditorium during rehearsal, and that they did not eat together upstairs in the bar at lunchtime.

Charles wondered what had happened between them. The obvious cause of the estrangement – or the one that he would find most obvious – was that Russ had finally had enough of Felicia's wittering on and was taking a rest. But that didn't fit in with the doleful expression on his face or the way his eyes followed her every movement. There seemed to have been some actual rift, and Felicia seemed to have been its initiator.

Charles decided he must try to find out what had happened. After all, both Russ and Felicia had been in the bar on the Monday evening. Both were therefore potential suspects for Warnock Belvedere's murder.

So on the Thursday, while Felicia was, it was hoped, having a much-needed rest, Charles determined that he would get a private word with Russ Lavery.

It was easier to make the determination than to achieve it. The battle scenes proved to be very demanding, and the entire cast was kept rushing round the theatre, with little opportunity for casual conversation, let alone pertinent interrogation.

Gavin's approach to the battles was as traditional as his approach to the Apparition Scene and the rest of the play. Rather than recognising the numerical limitations of his cast and opting for some form of stylised action, he went determinedly for spectacle. He wanted to fill the stage with soldiers, to vie with the splendours of Hollywood in his presentation of warfare.

This, though an admirable intention, was difficult to achieve with two armies which, even allowing for the conscription of Lady Macduff and the Witches, not to mention sudden changes of allegiance by Charles Paris, still only totalled sixteen.

'Don't worry,' Gavin kept saying, 'we'll fill the stage with soldiers.'

The company, all trying to take up as much space as possible, looked at the large areas of emptiness around them, and could perhaps be forgiven for doubting their Director's word.

'It'll be all right,' Gavin went on. 'It's there in the text, after all. They cut down the branches of Birnham Wood to "shadow the numbers of their host", so that the enemy can't count precisely how many there are. They just give an impression of great numbers. That's exactly what we'll do.'

'But,' John B. Murgatroyd, who was holding up a mop (a rehearsal prop to represent a Birnham branch) objected, 'what happens when we our "leavy screens throw down, and show like those we are"? Isn't there a bit of a danger the audience might laugh?'

'I don't see why. I mean, we're not pretending you're the whole army. Just a sort of vanguard, you know, with the leaders up the front.'

'Well, how did we get cut off from the rest of the army?' John B. persisted. 'And aren't we going to be a bit exposed if Macbeth sends his army out after us?'

'Hmm...' Gavin looked pensive.

'Anyway, whoever heard of an army whose leaders were at the front?'

'Well, what are you suggesting as an alternative, John B.?' asked Gavin, seduced into the notion that the actor was raising serious points about his production.

'Suppose we kept on carrying our "leavy screens" right to the end...? Then the audience still wouldn't be able to count us.'

'Ye-es...but then we'd have to cut the lines about throwing down the "leavy screens". The Schools Matinées wouldn't like that.'

'But it'd help Macbeth's motivation if we kept the branches. Then it would seem as if Birnham Wood was still marching towards him.'

For a moment Gavin accepted the logic of this. Then he saw the objection. 'But how could you fight if you were still holding your bits of wood?'

'We could hit the enemy with them,' suggested John B., who was beginning to have difficulty controlling the tremor of laughter in his voice.

'Hmm...'

'And we could have a new battle cry.' The actor brandished his mop as he shouted, 'Join Malcolm's Army! It's the best! We have branches everywhere!'

This line, and the company laughter that attended it, finally made the director realise that he was being sent up. So he had a little tantrum and bawled John B. Murgatroyd out.

But it was the only breakdown of discipline in a hard-working day. And, whether the cast thought Gavin's method of presenting the battle-scenes was effective or not, by the end of rehearsal they all knew exactly the effects he wanted and how they were to be achieved.

By six o'clock Charles Paris felt physically very tired. For a man in his fifties, whose only gesture towards keeping fit was occasionally watching athletics on television, all that rushing up and down stairs, round the back of the stage and through the auditorium had taken its toll.

He felt in anguished need of a restorative pint or two. But he restrained himself. He was determined to stick with the new regime. Till...Till when...? He didn't know, but in a strange way his abstinence had become tied in with the murder. He wouldn't have a drink until he knew who had killed Warnock Belvedere.

Good heavens, now he really *did* have an incentive to solve the case.

Maybe, he thought, my brain will work better unfogged by alcohol. But there didn't seem much evidence of it. His mind still circled round the same handful of fixed facts, without making those intuitive leaps which he hoped for. Maybe, he thought cynically, it's all nonsense about such stimulants slowing you down. Perhaps I should go the whole hog, like Sherlock Holmes, and take up cocaine?

He ran through the possible advantages that not drinking gave him. His pledge was now sixty-seven hours old, and it was time for an assessment.

Well, for a start he hadn't got a hangover...

Second, he was sleeping better. On both the Tuesday and the Wednesday nights he had slept deeply, not even having to get up for his customary three-thirty pee.

And then...Well, presumably he was saving money.

And he was probably helping his long-term health prospects.

And, um...

No, that seemed to be all the advantages.

What was there to be said on the other side?

Well, he missed it desperately. Not in an agonised, physical way – he really didn't think he was chemically dependent – but he just missed the reassurance of a glass in his hand and the comforting warmth of whisky burning down his throat.

He also missed the punctuation of his day. For almost all his life he been attuned to the soothing diurnal rhythms of opening times and closing times.

Without them he felt disoriented and dispossessed.

He missed the conviviality of getting drunk at the same pace as other people. He missed the communal element of drinking. In fact, not drinking took away the central pivot of his social life.

Also, further experiments with grapefruit juice, cherryade, Tizer and other highly-priced and highly-sweetened fluids had reinforced his opinion that all other forms of beverage, except for tea and coffee, tasted absolutely vile.

It really was becoming very important that he found out quickly who had murdered Warnock Belvedere.

Russ Lavery had the advantage of one of the biggest of the Pinero's dressing rooms, which was set on the corner of the building and therefore had a splendid view out over towards Salisbury Plain.

He also had the disadvantage that the dressing room was rather full. As well as Fleance/Young Siward, it housed Malcolm, Donalbain/Seyton, Mentieth and Caithness/Second Murderer. Since all of these were doubling various messengers, attendants, apparitions and soldiers, the dressing room was going to be even fuller after the costumes had been issued.

When Charles slipped in at the end of the Thursday rehearsal, Russ was sitting somewhat gloomily over in a corner of the dressing room by the window. Mentieth and Caithness/Second Murderer were packing their day's belongings into shoulder bags and talking in that loud, flamboyant manner of young actors which could be gay or could be just theatrical.

They seemed to be ignoring Russ and, as they left the room, nodding at Charles, they pointedly did not say goodbye to the younger actor.

'Wonder if we could have a word...?' said Charles. He hadn't yet worked out how he was going to play the scene, so his opening gambit wasn't particularly original.

But at least Russ responded. 'Sure.' He moved a chair to make space for his visitor.

'You don't look your most cheery,' said Charles, stating no more than the truth. Close to, Russ looked like a vulnerable fourteen-year-old, his eyes moist as if on the verge of tears.

'No,' he concurred.

'What is it? Anything you can talk about?'

'Not really.'

'You didn't seem to be getting a lot of support from Mentieth and Caithness.'

'No.'

Charles felt a sudden insight. 'They being tough on you because you're new in the business?'

'You could say that.' The expression in the boy's eyes told Charles that his guess had been correct.

'I'm afraid that happens. A couple of years out of drama school and they think they know everything.'

'And that nobody else knows anything,' Russ said bitterly.

'They're getting at you?'

The boy nodded.

'What, saying that the stuff you've done in drama school doesn't count for anything? That you don't know a thing about professional theatre?'

'All that. And then when I tell them things, they think I'm showing off.'

'What sort of things?'

'Well, like about my agent...'

'Ah.'

'I mean, you know, I just mentioned that Robbie Patrick saw me in an end of term show and signed me up, and they think I'm bragging about it.'

'He's a very good agent.'

'I know.'

'I mean, it really is good that he signed you up.'

'Yes, I know it is. But they seem to think I go on about it too much. I don't mean to.'

'They're just jealous. Who are their agents?'

Russ mentioned a couple of names.

'Oh well, they certainly are jealous,' said Charles encouragingly. 'Those two are way down the league.'

'Yes, so I've heard.' Russ managed a weak smile. 'Almost as bad as being with Maurice Skellern.'

'Oh?' said Charles casually. 'Do you know any of Maurice Skellern's clients?'

'No. I've only heard the name.'

'In what context?'

'Oh, just as a joke, you know. He's proverbial as the worst agent in the business.'

'Ah.' Charles decided they might perhaps not pursue this topic further. 'So, basically, the others in the dressing room are making you aware of your junior status?'

Russ nodded his head, plunged back into gloom.

'Just saying unpleasant things, or are they doing things too?'

'What do you mean?'

'Practical jokes, anything of that sort...?'

By way of answer, Russ Lavery reached into his jacket pocket and held a folded letter towards Charles.

The notepaper was headed 'Robbie Patrick Associates' and Charles read:

'Dear Russ,
Hope you're knocking them dead in Warminster.
Wanted to pass on the great news that the producers want you to test for a part in the new Bond movie. Ring me for details of time, etc.
Yours ever,
Robbie.'

He looked up. Now the boy's tears were really flowing. Charles had forgotten just how cruel young actors could be to each other.

'Little sods,' he said. 'Where did they get the paper from?'

'Easy enough these days with photocopiers,' Russ sobbed. 'I think they nicked one of Robbie's real letters from my pocket and copied the letterhead.'

Yes, there was a faint line across the paper above the typewritten text.

'And you fell for it?'

Russ nodded glumly. 'Right in. Talked about it, too.'

'Oh dear. And rang Robbie?'

'Yes. He thought I was mad. So now I expect I've screwed things up with him as well.'

'No, of course you haven't. You've just been the victim of a practical joke. You're sure it was them who did it?'

Russ nodded. 'Can't prove anything. But they've been sniggering all day, the bastards.'

'Well, look, it's done now. You've given them the satisfaction of falling for it, now you've got to make sure you don't give them any more satisfaction.'

'What do you mean?'

'Just never mention it again.'

'I suppose you're right. But I'd really like to get my own back on them.'

'No. That won't help. Honestly. You'll soon forget all about it.'

But Charles's soothing words disguised his very real anger. It had been a vicious trick, and its crudeness simply reinforced the viciousness. Only someone as naive in the business as Russ would have fallen for it. To think that an unknown out of drama school should be screen-tested for a Bond movie.

And yet Charles could empathise. He knew that silly bubble of hope trapped inside all actors, which can burst to the surface through any amount of logic and common-sense. He knew that, if he had received that letter, his first reaction would have been to believe it. Then experience and a native cynicism would have dampened his enthusiasm and he would have recognised the cheat.

But poor Russ Lavery hadn't got that protective armour. All he had was the boundless enthusiasm and vulnerability of youth.

'And is that all that's wrong...?'

Charles asked tentatively, remembering the purpose of his visit.

The boy shook his head. 'Oh, I don't know. There's money...'

'There's always money...' But it must be hard for a boy trying for the first time to budget on the pittance of Equity minimum. Particularly hard if he's trying to squire around an actress ten years his senior. A couple of flamboyant gestures of buying meals for Felicia could have written off most of his week's pay-packet.

'Well, Russ, I haven't got much, but if you need a fiver to help you out till Friday...'

'No, it's all right. I'm okay. I don't want to get into debt.'

'Very wise.' Charles himself always tried to avoid the endless circle of borrowing from other actors. It so quickly got out of hand, and the reputation of being a sponger was easily acquired.

'No other problems, though?'

Russ looked up defiantly. 'Why, what should there be?'

Charles shrugged. Two-and-a-half days into his abstinence, he could now once again shrug with impunity. Maybe that was another of the advantages of not drinking...? On reflection, though, it did seem a pretty small advantage.

'Well, there's always sex...' he ventured in answer to Russ's question.

'What do you mean?'

'All the old clichés of sexual angst. Somebody you like rejecting your advances...? Someone you don't like making advances...?'

The boy turned abruptly to look out of the window. 'I don't know what you're talking about.'

'Listen, I saw the way Warnock was behaving to you that first night.'

Russ's eyes flashed back at Charles. 'I'm not gay!'

'I never said you were. In fact, just the reverse. I'm saying how embarrassing it must have been for you to have that old queen pawing at you.'

The boy shuddered. 'Yes, he was horrible. I think the most evil person I've ever come across.'

It was quite possible that, in Russ's limited experience, that was true.

'The only good thing that's happened in the last few days,' the boy continued, his eyes burning, 'is that old bastard's death. He certainly deserved it.' This last sentence was spoken in an intriguing tone of satisfaction.

But Charles decided not to probe in that direction for the moment. Instead, infinitely gently, he said, 'And then, of course, there's Felicia...'

Russ seemed about to flash further defiance at this intrusion, but then subsided into misery. 'Yes, there's Felicia. I love her,' he confessed abjectly.

'She's a very beautiful girl.'

'Yes, but I...I think I misunderstood her.'

'What do you mean?'

'Well, have you ever...I mean, with a woman, have you ever sort of thought you were getting signals from her, and thought you understood those signals, and thought she wanted you to do something...and then you've done it – and suddenly realised that wasn't what she meant at all?'

'Yes, I've known that happen. Is that...with Felicia...?'

The boy's tears were once again flowing. 'I did what I thought she wanted...and now she's turned against me...'

'Are you talking about Monday night?'

'Yes. Oh, it's just awful. I ruined everything.'

'What, you mean you went back to her digs and –'

'No,' Russ interrupted fiercely. 'No, I didn't.'

'Where did you go?'

'I didn't go anywhere. I stayed round the theatre. I don't know what I did.'

'Russ, you must tell me if –'

Abruptly Russ Lavery rose to his feet. 'I've said too much.'

'It's good to talk.'

'No. You can't trust people. They suddenly turn on you and then you...have to get your own back.'

Charles rose from his seat to bar the boy's access to the door. 'I'm not going to turn on you, Russ. You can trust me.'

'That's what Warnock said,' the boy snapped bitterly.

Then in an instant he turned and, reaching for the catch of the window, opened it and slipped out on to the path that skirted the theatre. He was running and out of sight almost before Charles had time to register the movement.

Charles went forward and looked at the window. At the bottom of the frame was an anti-theft device that should have locked down into the sill. But the screw had broken.

In other words, anyone who knew about that window could escape from the theatre when everything was supposedly locked.

Just as it had been on the night of Warnock Belvedere's murder.

So the problem of the murderer's getting out of the locked building had suddenly evaporated.

And, as he had just demonstrated, Russ Lavery clearly knew about the broken window-lock.

Chapter Thirteen

HE KNEW IT was silly to be influenced by *Macbeth*, and yet there was a kind of logic about it. A crime committed by a man, but instigated by a woman. The idea of Felicia Chatterton as an unwitting Lady Macbeth to Russ Lavery's callow Macbeth made an ugly kind of sense.

From the very start of rehearsal, she had found Warnock Belvedere difficult. He had been extremely rude to her in front of the entire company on more than one occasion. Even worse than that from Felicia's point of view, he had threatened the single-minded concentration which was so essential in her build-up to a part.

And she was so obsessive about her work that she would want all obstacles to its progress removed.

No doubt she had said as much to Russ. The poor boy, absolutely besotted with her, excited at the thought not only of embarking on his professional career but also of having an affair with a *real actress*, would have done anything to gain her favour. And, though she probably did no more than express a wish that Warnock might be got out of the way, Russ might have taken her too literally and seen the murder as the ultimate proof of his devotion.

That would tie in with what the boy had said about getting signals from Felicia and misinterpreting them.

'I did what I thought she wanted...and now she's turned against me...' Yes, it fitted horribly well. After he had committed the murder, Russ had gone to her, figuratively presenting his beautiful Salome with the head of Warnock Belvedere, anticipating presumably some sexual reward for realizing her desires. And she, when she understood what he had done, had recoiled in horror. That would explain the marked estrangement between them after the Monday night.

There were other uncomfortably appealing elements in the theory. Russ did not just have Felicia's promptings as motivation to kill Warnock. The old actor's advances had clearly upset the boy. The vehemence with which Russ had asserted his heterosexuality to Charles betrayed an insecurity about his sexual identity. He was emotionally immature, as his puppy-like courtship of Felicia revealed, and he must have been deeply unsettled by Warnock Belvedere's overt importuning. He needed to remove that disturbing challenge from his life.

Charles suddenly recalled Russ's appearance in the store-room during the Saturday morning run-through. So there was no doubt that the boy knew what the room was. And, with sickening logic, Charles also remembered

Russ saying he had supplemented his grant by working as a bar-man. He would therefore know all about changing beer barrels and be aware of the potentially lethal presence of carbon dioxide in the gas cylinders.

It was beginning to look painfully likely that Russ Lavery had murdered Warnock Belvedere. The way to check of course was to talk to the poor boy's Lady Macbeth.

'God, I'm just having such difficulty sleeping,' Felicia announced, producing yet another parallel for anyone wishing to compare her situation with that of the character she was playing. Charles found himself half-expecting her to continue, 'Yet who would have thought the old man to have had so much beer on him', or to sniff distractedly at her fingers and murmur, 'Here's the smell of beer still. All the perfumes of Arabia will not sweeten this little hand. Oh! Oh! Oh!'

'Yes, everyone's getting a bit tense. The thought that we open Tuesday week and there's so much to do.'

'You can say that again. It's just never going to happen. I mean, I knew it was insane to try and do such a complex piece in three-and-a-half weeks. We need three-and-a-half weeks just talking about it before we even start rehearsal.'

'It'll happen,' Charles reassured. 'It always does happen. Somehow.'

'Not always,' Felicia disagreed gloomily. 'Some productions don't open on time. Particularly of the Scottish Play.'

'Oh, come on, you don't believe all that rubbish, do you?'

Her reply came back in a tone of pious reproof. He had challenged one of the articles of her faith in the theatre. 'There must be something in it. That sort of rumour doesn't build up for no reason. You hear such terrible stories...'

'Like what?'

'Well, this is absolutely authentic, because I know the people involved. Girlfriend of mine was playing Second Witch in Glasgow, and she had a thing with the Banquo. She got pregnant and...' the voice dropped to an awestruck murmur '...she lost the baby.'

'That could be regarded as a coincidence.'

'Maybe, but I think there's something else behind it. The Witches' incantations are supposed to be real black magic, you know.'

'Yes, I've heard that.' Charles spoke dismissively.

'And then I heard of a production when, in the fight at the end, Macduff's sword got knocked out of his hand and flew into the auditorium...and impaled someone to their seat in the front row.'

'Yes, I've heard that story. Everyone's heard that story. But I've yet to come across anyone who can name the production in which it occurred. It's always something heard from a friend of a friend. I'm sure it never really happened.'

'Well, what about this production then?'

'You think this one's got a jinx on it?'

'Oh, come on, Charles. Look at the things that have gone wrong. First, a three-and-a-half week rehearsal period...'

'Ah, now I know you think that's hopelessly inadequate, but it's a bit extreme to see that as a manifestation of malign influences. You can blame Gavin's judgement, you can blame the hard economic facts of running a theatre, but to blame the Powers of Evil is really excessive.'

'It's not just that, though. Other things...'

'Like...?'

'That Macduff's Son not being allowed to continue with the part...George being delayed in Paris...'

'Those are inconveniences, yes, but they're the kind of things that happen in lots of productions. I don't think they're evidence of a curse on the play.'

'And then...' The wonderful voice swooped even lower '...there's Warnock Belvedere's death.'

'Yes,' Charles agreed, glad the conversation had moved to that subject of its own accord. 'There is something strange about that, certainly...'

They were sitting in the bar at the end of the Friday's rehearsal. They had worked hard and knew that they would have to work harder the next day. Gavin was insisting on another Saturday run-through to fix the shape of the whole play and consolidate what they had done during the week. Straight through the play in the morning, then notes and detailed repair work on bits that weren't right in the afternoon.

Russ Lavery was not in the bar. He had been at rehearsal and done his work, but made no social contact with anyone. Whenever Charles had come near, the boy had taken evasive action.

Charles and Felicia were both sipping chaste Perrier water. Felicia, in her nun-like devotion to her art, very rarely drank alcohol during a rehearsal period. And Charles, of course...well, he'd made his pledge, hadn't he?

On his fourth alcohol-free day, after excursions to various other sickly fluids, he had come back to Perrier. With a decent-sized chunk of lemon, it almost began to have a taste.

It wasn't the same, though. Nothing was the same. He looked wistfully across to the bar, where other actors swilled their carefree pints or sipped convivial scotches.

His resolution wavered. The disgusting image of Warnock Belvedere's beer-soaked body was fading. So was the memory of the Tuesday's hangover. One drink wouldn't hurt, surely...?

But no. He had made a vow. Not until he had solved the case. When he knew who the murderer was, then he'd have a drink.

'What were you thinking of doing about eating?'

Felicia' s voice brought him out of his alcohol nostalgia. 'I'm sorry?'

'Eating. I wondered if you had any plans.'

'Not particularly, no.'

'Would you like to come back to the cottage? I could rustle up something...'

'Oh, that's very kind.'

'I always find cooking takes my mind off work. If you don't mind something pretty basic...'

'I'd be delighted.'

'And I'd like to *talk*,' Felicia said earnestly.

Yes, thought Charles. I'd like you to *talk*, too.

It had to be a cottage. It was the R.S.C. background. The villages around Stratford-upon-Avon are full of rented cottages in which actors and actresses stay up late into night performing microsurgery on Shakespeare's plays and discussing their art, to them so infinitely various and to outsiders so infinitely the same.

So, when Felicia looked for digs for the Pinero job, she homed in on what she knew, and rented a cottage. Her London base was a tiny studio flat in Maida Vale, but she hadn't even gone back there on the free Sundays in the *Macbeth* rehearsal period. She did not want her attention distracted from her ascent of the North Face of Lady Macbeth.

It was a pretty, chintzy little cottage and on arrival she allowed herself the indulgence of a glass of white wine and Perrier. Charles, though sorely tempted, had one without the white wine. In a way, that was the most difficult moment he had encountered in his campaign of temperance. It just seemed so against nature not to have a drink while sitting down waiting to eat.

What Felicia rustled up was lasagne and salad. Very nice, too. Not shop-prepared. The pasta came from a packet, but she cooked it all herself.

Charles could see her through the open kitchen door as she prepared the meal, but she was too far away for continuous conversation. He looked around the room. Let furnished, of course, so she had had little opportunity to impose her personality on the environment.

But there were a few characteristic touches. On a low table in front of the sofa books were piled randomly, some opened, some not. There were at least three different editions of *Macbeth*. The Cambridge *A New Companion to Shakespeare Studies*, *Shakespeare's Macbeth*, *A Selection of Critical Essays*, Edited by John Wain, Terence Hawkes' *Twentieth Century Interpretations of Macbeth*. Felicia Chatterton certainly believed in doing her homework.

On a dresser there was a book on aerobics and another on how to deal with back pain. A couple of cards on the mantelpiece. Charles managed to read their messages without snooping too overtly. Both wishing her good luck for rehearsals. Both evidently from actors and, judging from the in-jokey tone, actors who had been her colleagues at Stratford.

In the otherwise empty fireplace stood a tall vase containing a dozen red roses. A gesture of affection from someone. But there was no sign of a card. A few red petals lay wrinkling on the hearth, so the gesture had probably been made the previous week. By whom? Russ? That would have made heavy inroads into his Equity minimum. But it would have been typical of his romantic naïveté.

As Felicia had said it would, the cooking seemed to relax her, and when she came in holding the two loaded plates and balancing a wooden salad bowl between them, she looked more human and accessible than Charles had ever seen her.

And astonishingly pretty. There must have been a bathroom off the kitchen, because she had clearly titivated herself a bit. For the first time in their acquaintance, she had released her blond hair from its severe knot and it swung, silky and just-brushed, a couple of inches above her shoulders. She had also touched up her lips with the palest of lipsticks, and a breath of expensively-fresh perfume preceded her.

Charles wondered whether she made these changes every evening when she returned from rehearsal, or if they were for his benefit.

She gestured to him to rescue the salad bowl, which he placed on the floor. She put the plates beside it and reached for the wine bottle. 'Sure you won't, Charles...?'

Ooh, it hurt. But he managed to refuse. Gosh, wouldn't Frances be proud of him. He must ring and tell her of this new miracle. When? Maybe when he'd done it for a week...Yes, a week had a good, solid feel to it.

The thought of Frances made him think of sex. Funny, he hardly had thought about it at all in the last week. The shock of Warnock's death, and the hard work of rehearsal seemed to have driven it, atypically, from his mind. At least, he hoped that was the reason. It could, of course, just be that he was getting old. Like many men before him, he suffered a momentary panic at the idea that something he'd so frequently cursed as a troublesome distraction might be about to cease troubling him.

Or maybe it was because he was off the booze...Now that really was a terrifying thought. He tried to recall whether previous bouts of abstinence had had this bromide effect on his libido. Trouble was, he couldn't recall any previous bouts of abstinence.

Felicia sat beside him on the sofa. She didn't suggest moving her *Macbeth* library from the low table and they ate off their knees.

The lasagne was good, creamy and spicy. They were both hungry after the day's hard work and ate in silence. Charles chased the last strip of lettuce round his plate and leaned back in satisfaction.

'That was really good. Thanks.'

'Would you like some fruit? I've got apples and kiwi-fruit. Or there's yoghourt...?'

'No, thanks. That was fine. Just right.'

'Coffee? You do drink coffee, don't you?'

'Yes. In a minute, if you're having some. But there's no hurry.'

She finished her last mouthful and put the plate down on the floor. She too leant back, grimacing as she stretched against the sofa.

'Back bad?'

She nodded. 'Hmm. I know it's just tension. Always happens through rehearsals. Every vertebra seems to lock into the next one. I do exercises, but it still seizes up.'

'Has it ever stopped you going on?'

She looked at him in amazement. 'Good heavens, no. As soon as I get on stage I don't feel a thing. I can do really elaborate movement stuff without a twinge.'

'Doctor Theatre strikes again.'

'That's right. Oh, I know it's psychosomatic, really. Doesn't make it any the less painful.'

'No.'

'What kind of symptoms do you get?'

'Sorry?'

'Anxiety symptoms. You know, running up to a first night.'

'Oh.' Charles would have liked to say he got none. His pose of world-weary cynicism should put him above such self-indulgent frailties. But he knew that it didn't. 'Tends to go to my stomach. Always think I'm about to throw up just before a first night.'

'Do you ever?'

'Have done. Not for a while.'

'Do you know any actors who don't get nervous?'

Charles shook his head. 'Nope. I always feel with the ones who keep insisting that they don't, it's just their own way of expressing the nervousness. They go on about it so much.'

'Yes.'

There was a companionable lull in the conversation. Their mutual confession of nerves seemed to have made a bridge between them. Charles wondered how he was going to steer the conversation round to Russ Lavery and Warnock Belvedere's death. But he didn't wonder with any great urgency.

He glanced across at Felicia's head, near his on the sofa. Her eyes were closed as she relaxed and the little furrows, which during rehearsal became a fixture on her brow, had been smoothed away. She looked very young. Such soft, smooth skin.

He realised, with ironical relief, that the anxiety he had had before the meal was groundless. He was quite capable of thinking about sex without alcoholic prompting.

In fact, he was thinking about it quite a lot.

To divert his thoughts from that particular track, he deliberately moved the conversation back to his murder investigation. He must behave himself. Perhaps his new image of abstinence should carry over into his sex-life, too. Mr. Clean. No vices. Proper little Sir Galahad, he thought. 'My strength is as the strength of ten, because my heart is pure.' Hmm. It had some appeal. Not much, though. Sir Galahad's life may have been jolly pure, but it never sounded as if it had been much *fun*. All very well, in principle, devoting all your time to one long-term Grail; Charles preferred the idea of picking up a few nice little lesser Grails on the way.

As if it couldn't have mattered less, he floated a new topic of conversation. 'Felicia, about Warnock Belvedere's death...'

Chapter Fourteen

THE CHANGE OF subject did not seem to upset her. She still lay back on the sofa with her eyes closed, and said nothing.

'I think very few people were sorry to hear about it,' Charles continued.

'I certainly wasn't,' Felicia agreed sleepily. 'He was making my life impossible.'

'Oh?'

'Not just the rudeness. I could ignore that. But his constant interruptions made concentration so difficult. And I am trying to get inside Lady Macbeth,' she said, confirming what Charles had thought earlier. 'In fact, it was just as well that he did die when he did.'

Charles rationed himself to just another 'Oh?'

'Well, I'd given Gavin an ultimatum. I said either Warnock would have to go or I would.'

'Yes, I heard you say that to him after last Saturday's run. I didn't know you'd meant it literally.'

'Oh, I meant it. I said it again on the Monday. Saw Gavin on his own and told him that if Warnock was at rehearsal the next morning, I was going to have to leave the company.'

'Really?'

'I know that sounds unprofessional, threatening to break a contract, but you can only be professional if other people around you are being professional. Warnock Belvedere was sabotaging any chance I had of building a performance.'

'Yes.' Charles allowed a cosy pause to develop before he continued diffidently. 'So Warnock's death was quite timely for you.'

'Couldn't have been more timely. I really meant what I said. If he had still been there on the Tuesday, I would have walked out. He was an obstructive, offensive old man, and death was the best thing that could have happened to him.'

This was spoken so openly that it seemed to Charles to absolve Felicia from suspicion of direct involvement in the murder. But the possibility still remained that she had, either knowingly or unknowingly, inspired someone else to commit the crime.

'Did anyone else know how strongly you felt about Warnock?'

'I didn't make a secret of it. Anyone could have worked it out for themselves.'

'Hmm. What about Russ?'

The mention of this name broke her serenity. The eyelids snapped open to reveal, unnervingly close to Charles, the concentrated blue of her eyes. The little furrows were once again etched between her eyebrows. 'What do you mean?'

Charles shrugged. 'I just meant, did Russ know how much you wanted Warnock out of the way?'

'Yes. Of course he did. We...we talked a lot about the production. I told Russ that I couldn't go on unless somehow Warnock was got out of the way.'

'You said that? You used those exact words?'

'Something like that, certainly.'

Again the ingenuousness of her reply seemed to rule her out as a suspect, and even as a deliberate prompter to murder. She had told Russ in all innocence that she wanted her tormentor 'got out of the way'. But how the blindly besotted youth might have interpreted her remark was another matter.

She arched her body and brought back her elbows behind her to alleviate the pain in her spine. 'Ooh, gosh, it's tense,' she said, as she did so.

'Bad luck,' Charles commiserated, trying to think of something other than the splendid way in which that posture accentuated her breasts.

Once again, he moved his thoughts away from sex by pressing on with the investigation. 'Russ is rather keen on you, isn't he?'

She diminished the idea with a gesture. 'Oh. Maybe a bit. I don't know. We certainly got on well, talking, you know. He's a very intelligent boy. He sees Lady Macbeth in very much the same way as I do.'

'Ah. You don't think it's possible, do you, Felicia, that he –?'

Abruptly she stood up. 'Ooh, Charles, sorry. This back's just so tight. And my shoulders. I say, would you mind just massaging it a bit?'

'No, I wouldn't mind,' he replied, very honestly.

'Thanks.'

She moved the table of *Macbeth* books and lay flat on the carpet in front of the sofa. 'If you don't mind just kneeling or...'

'No problem. Where, right down the spine itself? Like that?'

'Yes, and sort of easing off to either side. Yes, you can really press down on it. It needs a lot of pressure. Ooh, that's nice.'

Charles thought it was rather nice, too. Her spine was quite prominent through the soft cotton of her track suit, but there was no transverse ridge of a brassière. And the flesh was comfortingly soft.

He permanently revised his opinion about his interest in sex being dependent on the intake of alcohol.

But he wondered why she was behaving like this. It could be completely innocent, just the behaviour of someone with a bad back, or it could be one of the most blatant come-ons he had ever encountered. He was not yet quite sure which.

Of course, it had had the effect of breaking off the conversation about Russ, and Charles began to wonder whether maybe that had been its primary intention.

But he was determined not to be side-tracked. 'Felicia, about you and Russ...'

'I really don't want to talk about it.' Her voice was muffled by her arms on which she was lying, but he could feel its resonance with his kneading fingertips.

'I do want to talk about it.'

'Why?'

He decided there was no point in going the pretty way. 'Because I think it might have something to do with Warnock's death.'

She raised her head and squinted round at him. 'What on earth do you mean?'

'Felicia, most of last week you and Russ were as thick as thieves...'

'So...?'

'But nobody in the company could fail to notice that on Tuesday morning you didn't want to have anything to do with him.'

She coloured and turned her head back towards the floor. 'Surely that's my business.'

'Well, yes, it's your business, so long as it doesn't start involving other people.'

'It doesn't involve other people. Just Russ and me.'

'Listen. I've been asking myself – what happened between closing time in the bar on Monday and the start of rehearsals on Tuesday...'

'It's none of your business what –'

'...and the only thing that I know happened between those times,' Charles went on inexorably, 'was that Warnock Belvedere died.'

'But that's nothing to do with Russ and me.'

'By your own admission, you wanted Warnock out of the way...'

'Yes.'

'And wasn't the timing of his "getting out of the way" rather convenient?'

'Yes, it was, but ...' She rolled over and sat up, facing him. The eyes were disconcertingly beautiful. 'What are you on about, Charles?'

He had to play this carefully. He wanted to find out certain facts, but he didn't want Felicia to be frightened off by the direction of his questions. He opted for a straightforward lie. 'Listen, I was the one who found Warnock's body...'

'I know that.'

'...and, because I was presumably in the theatre when he died, the police have been asking me various questions.' All true so far. Time for the lie. 'In particular, they've asked me if I saw anyone else round the theatre at the relevant time.' He hoped she didn't remember that he had been out cold at the time he was supposed to be observing.

She appeared not to. 'I don't see how I can help you.'

'You can help me by telling me what you did after the bar closed that evening.'

'I came straight back here.'

'Yes, I thought you probably did. What is more pertinent, really, is: Do you know what Russ did?'

She hesitated. 'Why don't you ask him?'

'I have done.'

'Well, then you know the answer.' She had a moment of doubt. 'What did he tell you he did?'

'He said he stayed around the theatre for a while.'

The answer seemed somehow to please her. 'Then you know what he did, don't you?' She shuffled round so that she was sitting with her back to him. 'Charles, would you mind just doing a bit on the shoulders? The spine feels much better, but the shoulders are still really knotted.'

'Sure.' His fingers started to slide back and forth across the material of her track suit. As the sweeps grew broader, the fingers touched the soft perfumed flesh of her neck with each stroke. The sweeps grew broader still.

'Ooh, that's lovely,' she purred. She eased her neck luxuriantly round, and a few wisps of hair tickled across his chin.

'Thing is, though,' Charles continued gently, 'the police are going to question me closely about who I saw. Russ apparently was there, but I didn't see him.'

'Probably in his dressing room,' Felicia mumbled.

'The other thing is...if the police did know Russ was around the theatre, they might want to question him.'

'Why?'

No way round it. He'd have to be more direct. 'Has it ever occurred to you that Warnock's death might not have been an accident?'

'What – you mean that he might have been murdered?' The tone of incredulity sounded genuine. Either the idea never had occurred to her, or she was a very good actress. But then, of course, Charles reflected, she was a very good actress.

'It's a possibility that I'm sure the police must have considered.'

She turned her head round to look at him. 'And you mean, if they knew that Russ had been in the theatre at the time, they might suspect him of the murder?'

'Possible. Isn't it?'

The look of shock on her face seemed genuine, too. Maybe Russ had told her he had killed Warnock and she hadn't believed it, thought the boy was showing off, fantasising. But now she was having his story confirmed from another source, and that was frightening her.

There was a long silence. Then, in the deep voice which had so captivated Stratford theatregoers, she announced, 'Russ didn't stay around the theatre.'

'Oh.'

She knew she had to tell him more. 'He came back here, with me.'

'Straight after closing time?'

'Yes, I drove him here.'

'Oh well, that's fine. Lets him off the hook then, doesn't it?' Charles was surprised at the depth of his relief. He hadn't enjoyed casting Russ Lavery in the role of murderer. The boy was too young, too appealing, had too much ahead of him to do such a thing. Besides, Charles liked him, and he didn't enjoy unmasking murderers he liked.

So it had just been a secret lovers' assignation. Russ's devotion had paid off. He had achieved the prize which John B. Murgatroyd had jokingly set his sights on.

But, as well as relief, Charles couldn't help feeling a twinge of jealousy. Felicia was very lovely.

She turned her back towards him again. 'Do you mind going on? It really is working.'

'Knitting up the ravell'd sleave of care, am I?' he asked with a grin, as he fingered the sleeve of her tracksuit.

'That's it.' She let out a little contented sigh. She was comfortable with Shakespearean quotations. And they weren't in a theatre, so *Macbeth* could be quoted with impunity.

Charles's fingers worked round the neck and shoulders, sweeping in ever wider and wider arcs. She nuzzled back against him, though whether this was merely to make herself comfortable or with a view to making him comfortable too, he could still not decide.

'One thing's odd…' he murmured.

'What's that?'

'Why didn't Russ tell me he came back here with you?'

'Oh, I don't know...'

Obviously she did know, but it didn't seem too important to Charles, as the curves described by his fingertips moved lower and lower. Ho, ho, ho, John B. Murgatroyd, I may have something to tell you tomorrow that'll make you green with envy.

'Actually,' Felicia announced in a voice that was informative rather than admonitory, 'it's just the neck and shoulders that are tense. My breasts are fine.'

'You took the words right out of my mouth,' mumbled Charles as he moved his face forward to nestle in her soft hair.

She gently disengaged herself, and looked at him.

'Shall I tell you why Russ lied about what happened?'

'Sure. I'd be interested.'

'We were talking about *Macbeth* in the bar and I was telling him about one of the essays in this book.' She indicated *A New Companion to Shakespeare Studies*. 'He sounded interested, so I invited him to come back for a coffee and have a look at it.'

'Ah.'

'Unfortunately, he didn't understand what I meant.'

'Oh.' Another embarrassment arising from the fatal ambiguity of the word 'coffee'. Charles found he was now avoiding Felicia's eyes.

'Russ thought I was inviting him to come to bed with me.'

'Oh dear.'

'It was embarrassing. He's very young. He took it as a personal slight.'

'I'm afraid men often do,' Charles mumbled.

'I couldn't make him understand that it wasn't just him. It was any man.'

For a moment Charles wondered if he was about to receive a confession of lesbianism, but Felicia's next words fortunately cleared that up.

'Not while I'm in rehearsal,' she said, speaking of the mystery in an awed voice.

'You mean…' asked Charles, having difficulty piecing the idea together…you don't have sex while you're rehearsing?'

'No. I find it spoils my concentration.'

'Oh.'

'Don't you?'

'What – find it spoils my concentration?'

'Yes.'

'Well, no, I don't think I do, really. Seems to help it, actually…'

But she didn't pick up the hint and volunteer to experiment with this novel approach. 'No, I just can't do it,' she said.

Charles, whose recent edifice of plans for the rest of the evening had just crumbled in jerry-built chaos, was intrigued. 'What about when you're actually running…you know, when a show's on…do you find you can manage it then?'

She shook her head. 'Very rarely. I have tried, but it still does affect the concentration.'

Hmm. Charles hoped she wasn't very highly-sexed. If she was, and insisted on maintaining this Spartan discipline, she had certainly chosen the wrong profession. And all that time at Stratford…working in repertory, getting one show on and going straight into rehearsal for another…good heavens, it must have been years since she had had anything.

Poor Russ. Barking up the wrong tree.

Never mind. At least the boy wasn't a murderer.

'Actually, Charles, there was a reason why I invited you back here this evening…'

Oh well, that was nice to know. He wondered what it was. Not just the massage, surely. And definitely not sex. What? Maybe the odd light-bulb needed changing.

'No, it's because you're an educated man...'

That was different, at least.

'You read English at Oxford, didn't you?'

'Yes. Over thirty years ago, though.'

'Well, I wanted to ask you about the interpretation of some of Lady Macbeth's lines.' She eagerly pulled the table of books across towards them. 'I mean, particularly the "I have given suck" problem.'

'The "I have given suck" problem?'

'Yes, I mean it's a crux which has been discussed for centuries. Because of course it's at odds with Macduff's "He has no children".'

'Of course.' It dawned on Charles that, now Russ had blotted his copybook, Felicia was in need of someone else to discuss her work with. He groaned inwardly as he realised that he had drawn this particular short straw.

'So, you see, I think you have to get into Lady Macbeth this sense of bereavement, because clearly she has had a child which has died in infancy.'

'Ah.'

'But this raises particular problems in some of her scenes with Macbeth. And when we first see her and she speaks of "the milk of human-kindness", surely she must feel a pang, thinking of her own milk which was inadequate to sustain the life of her child. Incidentally, of course, there's quite a valid alternative reading of that as "the milk of humane kindness", which, I'm sure you agree, puts a rather different complexion on...

Felicia Chatterton continued for some time. Charles provided the occasional agreement or grunt, but she didn't seem to need them.

After a time, his chin sank on to his chest. His eyes closed and he slipped easily into a comfortable slumber.

Oblivious, Felicia Chatterton talked on.

Chapter Fifteen

CHARLES SPENT A restless weekend after the Saturday run-through. John B. Murgatroyd had offered another Sunday tour of the locals of the locality, but the idea of comparing the size of the lemon slices with which various pubs garnished their Perrier water did not appeal. So John B. went off with a couple of other actors from the company, leaving Charles feeling like the last child in the playground to be picked for either team.

He felt restless about Frances, too. He must make contact with her. But he'd promised himself a week of abstinence before he did, and he'd had his last drink at closing time on the previous Monday.

Even as he worked these sums out, though, he knew he was deceiving himself, and he came round reluctantly to the idea that he was actually afraid of contacting Frances. Her unwillingness to see him made him feel raw and adolescent again, fearing another rebuff. It was stupid to feel like that about his wife.

And yet he had to admit that Frances had put up with a lot. But always before, when he had suddenly turned up again in her life, she had been wryly welcoming. Now, for the first time, he wondered whether she actually meant what she said about their being better off permanently apart. Maybe she really could get on with her own life more effectively without the ever-present threat of her husband's reappearance.

It was a bleakly plausible possibility, and thinking about it did little to improve his mood. Her determination not to see him, combined with his own natural dilatoriness, could actually mean that they might never meet again.

Picking at the scab, he indulged this painful fantasy. Yes, it could easily happen. And then, finally, one of them would hear of the other's death through a third party. If Frances died, he would hear from his daughter, Juliet, from whom he now seemed to be equally estranged.

And if he died, how would Frances hear about it? His stature in the theatre would not warrant newspaper obituaries. Maurice Skellern would know, obviously, but Charles couldn't envisage his agent taking the trouble to contact Frances. (Actually, given the nature of their relationship, Charles could imagine some months elapsing before Maurice even realised his client was dead.)

He also wondered what their respective reactions would be to the news. Maybe, by the time it happened, Frances would have achieved the hermetic isolation from him that she seemed to crave, and be able to greet the event with a single philosophical tear.

If it were the other way round, he knew that hearing of Frances's death would tear him apart. She still meant so much to him.

'I must make contact with her,' he thought desperately. Even as he thought it, though, he added the automatic rider, 'but not quite yet.'

It wasn't just thoughts of Frances that dampened his spirits. There was also the unsolved murder at the Pinero to trouble him.

There hadn't been much evidence of the police round the theatre in the latter half of the previous week, but Charles didn't feel confident that they had completed their investigations. He still had the uncomfortable sense of being under suspicion. There was to be an inquest on Warnock Belvedere on the Monday morning, and he was anxious about the findings of that inquest.

Also, he didn't like the direction in which the compass of his own suspicions was pointing. Granted, the crime might have been the work of an outsider. Russ Lavery's revelation of the broken window-lock opened up all kinds of alternative possibilities; anyone in the company could have concealed himself (or herself) in the dressing room area, killed Warnock and escaped at will.

But the most likely suspects remained those who had been present in the bar when Norman called 'Time' the previous Monday evening. If one excluded elaborate conspiracy theories, Lady Macduff and the two Witches were out of the reckoning. The two couples, Norman and Sandra Phipps, and Felicia and Russ, both had mutual alibis, the one of sexual indulgence, the other of sexual abstinence.

Which left only Gavin Scholes.

He was uniquely positioned from the point of view of opportunity. He knew the Pinero inside out, he had his own keys. And, Charles kept remembering, he had been wide awake in the middle of the night when phoned with the news of Warnock's death.

With regard to motivation, the old actor had been a serious threat to the director's authority. By the Monday Gavin was beginning to lose control of the production, and Warnock Belvedere's constant sniping was fomenting disaffection within the company. Also, Charles now knew, Felicia Chatterton was actually threatening to walk out of rehearsals if Warnock were not removed. And, though replacing a Macduff's Son, or even a Duncan, was not an insurmountable problem, replacing a Lady Macbeth at that notice would have been nearly impossible.

After the disasters of that Monday's rehearsal, Gavin might well have contemplated desperate measures to regain control of his production.

Charles didn't like thinking ill of his old friend, but it was a matter of survival. If the inquest concluded that Warnock Belvedere had been murdered, the prime suspect for that crime was Charles Paris, and he might only be able to escape that charge by producing an alternative murderer.

He decided to watch Gavin Scholes very closely over the next few days.

The results of the inquest were good news and bad news. The good news was that the coroner did not reach a verdict of murder. The bad news was that he did not reach any verdict at all. The inquest was adjourned to give the police time to complete their investigations.

That was not very comforting for Charles, implying as it inevitably did that the police had further investigations to make. He wondered anxiously how long it would be before he was hauled out of rehearsal for another little chat with Detective Inspector Dowling.

But the Pinero Theatre's *Macbeth* was gaining momentum, and he had little time to brood. It was a long time since he had been so involved in a production. Charles was used to long lulls in rehearsal, while he sat vaguely watching the principals being coached, drinking too many cups of coffee, sharing whispered professional gossip with other lesser members of the company, whingeing about agents and the Inland Revenue, or toying with *The Times* crossword.

But there was very little chance for all that in *Macbeth*. Though none of his roles was a principal one, Charles had so many of them that he was rarely off the stage, and when he was, he was preoccupied trying to remember where the hell, and in what identity, he had to come on next.

The silly, optimistic fantasy grew that some sharp-eyed critic might recognise his prodigious work-rate. 'Charles Paris presented an amazing gallery of characters, each one so subtly distinguished from the others that I had to check my programme to assure myself they really all were the work of one actor.' Yes, that'd do. Or how about...'Charles Paris demonstrated a Protean ability which stands comparison with that of Olivier'? Or maybe – He curbed his galloping thoughts. No, be realistic, Charles. Remember the last time you played more than two parts in a production. What was it the *Lancashire Evening Post* had said?

'It's no secret that the theatre's hard up, but to have Charles Paris shambling on giving the same performance as three supposedly different characters seems to be a false economy.'

The mood of a company goes through many changes during a rehearsal period. There is the initial diffidence, frequently followed by a flood of confidence if the first few days rehearsal go well. This quickly gives way to total despair at the first set-back, which usually coincides with the cast 'getting off the book' and suddenly, in the desperate hunt for lines, forgetting all the subtleties they so easily performed with scripts in their hands.

This is frequently followed by a period of doldrums, when the progress of the production is so slow as to seem imperceptible. That may well give way to another nadir of despair after a run-through in which everything goes wrong.

Then, with a bit of luck, comes a sunny period of mounting confidence, as performances burgeon and the company begins to feel that really, after all, the show could be pretty bloody good. This mood will be bolstered by a good director, building the self-esteem of his cast, following that golden rule of all creative work that, even if part of you knows it's rubbish, for the period of most intense hard work you have to suppress that feeling and convince yourself that it's worth doing.

This fragile, but sometimes aggressively confident attitude is usually destroyed in the week before the opening by technical problems. The set, when actually erected on stage, bears no relation to the proportions of the furniture which has represented it for some weeks. Bulky costumes do not allow entrances which have been glibly rehearsed from Day One. Real props turn out to be the wrong shape for bits of business which worked perfectly well with rehearsal props. Doors will not open, swords will not come out of scabbards, helmets blindfold their wearers, cauldrons do not fit over the trap-doors for which they are designed. Anything that can go wrong goes wrong.

And that's before you get on to the problems raised by lighting.

Any pace that has been injected into the production goes, and with it the company confidence slinks away. It seems impossible that the show can ever open. No, never in a thousand years. And if it does manage to, then it shouldn't. It should be put out of its misery now, its sickly life terminated by a quick humane decision of the management. It's going to be the naffest, most incompetent, most amateur-looking production that has ever disgraced the boards of a theatre.

This mood shifts to a stoicism through the long torture of the first (and in many cases last) technical run, during which everything gets slower and slower as the company works deeper into the small hours, and the director, who's been up most of the night before plotting the lights, presses doggedly on, shutting his mind to what it's costing in overtime.

Then a dress rehearsal (or if they're lucky, more than one dress rehearsal), unsatisfactory for the actors however it goes. If it's good, they feel falsely reassured...first night bound to be a disappointment. If it's bad, they can comfort themselves with the old cliché about bad dress rehearsals. But that comfort is inadequate, too. Suppose the magic doesn't work this time. Suppose this time a bad dress rehearsal prefigures an even worse first night.

Then the seesawing from manic elation to nauseous panic of the opening day, the false bonhomie, the snapping nerves, the anticipated surprise of cards and presents. And the awful elasticity of time, moving too fast for the urgent things that still need doing, not moving at all for those of the company who have nothing to do but wait.

This is the day for private rituals, for walking to the theatre by special routes, for avoiding certain totems and seeking out others, for touching long-treasured mascots. For many, it is also the day of vowing to leave the profession, swearing that it's an inhuman strain, that it's ridiculous to put oneself under such intolerable emotional pressure.

And, finally, all of that is forgotten in the release of actual performance. Good or bad, however many reputations have been made or lost, however much work is still needed, at least the bloody thing has happened.

All of these changes, all of these swings of mood, all of these alternating images of triumph and disaster, were experienced by the Pinero company in the run-up to the opening of their production of *Macbeth*.

For Charles Paris, the most daunting moment of the third week of rehearsal came when his dressing room door was pushed open to admit a huge bundle of clothes, which advanced panting towards him.

'Um, can I help you?' he asked uncertain of the appropriate way to address a bundle of clothes.

He heard the muffled word, 'Wardrobe,' which suggested that the bundle of clothes had a voice. When he looked towards the floor, he saw that it also had feet wearing grubby tennis shoes.

'I'll just put them down on the table.'

The bundle of clothes heaved up in the air for a moment, then flopped down on to the dressing room table to reveal a gormless-looking girl with orange-streaked hair and a designer-torn black T-shirt.

'Those are all mine, are they?' asked Charles.

'Yes.' The girl picked up each of the garments as she itemised them in an impassively nasal voice. 'Right, Bleeding Sergeant.'

A leather jerkin, irregularly decorated with metal rings, and a pair of rough hopsack trousers. Those're going to tickle, thought Charles gloomily.

'What about the blood? Do you mind if this lot gets covered in Kensington Gore?' he asked.

'Kensington who?'

'Stage blood.'

'Oh, nobody said anything about that. I don't think they'll want blood on the costumes.'

'He is a Bleeding Sergeant. Shakespeare did specify that in the stage directions.'

'I don't care what anyone else said. I take my orders from the Wardrobe Mistress.'

Charles did not bother to argue. 'All right. I'll try to keep the blood just on my face and forearms. A few nice gashes, I think.' He relished the challenge of doing the gashes. Like being back in the old days of really elaborate make-up. That was the trouble with all this modern lighting, you hardly needed any slap, no matter what part you were doing. Still, a gash could be fun. Build up something gruesome with nose-putty. Even latex, yes. Then discolour the jagged edges with a touch of Lake, slap on the old Leichner's Arterial Blood and –

Oh no, sod it. That would only work for someone who wasn't about to enter in Act One Scene Seven as a Sewer. Shakespeare just didn't think ahead, did he? If only he'd written, 'Enter a Bleeding Sewer', as well. As it was, Charles would have to settle for less elaborate wounds.

The girl with the orange-streaked hair held up a long dark-blue velvet garment that looked like a mangy housecoat. 'For the Sewer.'

'Looks a bit grubby. The Macbeths aren't on the breadline, you know.'

'Be all right under the lights.'

'Oh yes?'

But she wasn't going to be diverted. 'I've checked with Gavin. Very low lighting for that scene.'

Before Charles could pursue his objection, she raised a stained crimson jerkin and a pair of stained crimson slashed breeches from the pile. 'That's the Porter.'

'But I'll never be able to do up that jacket.'

'You're not meant to. If you have it undone and stick your stomach out, you'll look fat and debauched.'

Charles flicked at his eyebrow in mock-affectation. 'Oh dear, love, another character part.'

But the girl from Wardrobe seemed to have been inoculated against jokes. She lifted up a full-length russet-coloured brocade gown. 'Old Man who talks to Ross in Act Two Scene Four.'

'What do I wear under it?'

'You can put it on over your Porter costume. It won't show.'

'But the shoes will.'

'Audience won't notice shoes.'

'I'm not thinking of the audience.' He dropped into his best theatrical knight voice. 'I'm thinking of me. You know, a lot of actors say, Get the shoes right and then you get the characterization right.'

Once again the attempt at humour was ignored. 'As the Third Murderer you wear this.'

It was a ragged garment of greenish net, like the sort of stuff used to camouflage aircraft in the jungle in B-movies.

'Just that?'

'Yes. Gavin says the lighting's very dim.'

Not just the lighting, thought Charles.

The girl held up an object which at a Fancy Dress party might have passed for a coal-scuttle.

'Um. Let me guess...' said Charles. 'Scottish Doctor carries that, in case Lady Macbeth's sick in the Sleepwalking Scene...'

'No, it's what you wear as an Apparition of an Armed Head.'

'Just that? But I'm going to be seen from the waist up.'

'It said 'Armed Head' in the notes Gavin gave me. Nothing about the rest of the body. Anyway, I thought you were in the cauldron.'

'The cauldron only comes up to my waist.'

'Then you'll have to crouch. This one...' she produced a long white nightshirt '...is what you wear as the English Doctor. And this...' She produced an identical garment in black '...is what you wear as the Scottish Doctor.'

Finally, she indicated a mass of silver-painted dishcloth chain-mail, a noisome sleeveless sheepskin jerkin and a horned helmet. 'And that lot's for when you're a soldier.'

'But I have to be two soldiers,' Charles objected.

'What?'

'I have to be on Malcolm's side, and then on Macbeth's side.'

'Oh.' The girl was momentarily stumped, but then saw a solution. 'You can turn the jerkin inside out.'

'Oh, what?' said Charles. 'You mean really be a turncoat?'

She didn't get that one either.

Oh, the pain of the first night party!

God alone knew how many first night parties he had attended, but Charles Paris was certain this was the first one he had attended without benefit of alcohol.

He felt sacrilegious, as if he were offending some basic tenet of his professional faith, sitting there in the bar watching the ice melt in his Perrier, while around him wine and beer glasses were tipped and emptied.

John B. Murgatroyd leant close over him, breathing out tantalising fumes of bitter. 'I felt, Charles Paris, that I had to say I thought your Drunken Porter this evening was masterly.'

'Thank you.'

'You had me remarkably convinced that you were smashed out of your skull.'

'Acting, mere acting,' Charles confessed modestly.

George Birkitt was sitting near by, knocking back the red wine. 'Of course,' he said, appropriating a line that had been said of Lee Marvin's drunken performance in *Cat Ballou*, 'it's the part you have been rehearsing for the last forty years.'

'But such a remarkable performance,' John B. continued in a tone of theatrical preciousness, 'from a teetotaller.'

'Oh, shut up,' said Charles.

'What I fail to understand...' John B. had now dropped into a surprisingly accurate pastiche of Felicia Chatterton's earnest huskiness, '...is how you could give a performance of such *truth* without being the role. I mean, in other words, how you could *appear* so pissed without actually *being* pissed.'

Charles took the opportunity to redirect the conversation. 'A propos of nothing, how is the get-Felicia-into-bed campaign going?'

John B. touched a finger against the side of his nose knowingly. 'Slowly, but surely. At my current rate of progress, I am not unhopeful of achieving my end – or should I say 'getting my end away' – within the next three millennia.'

Charles chuckled. 'Rather what I found.'

'Did you, you dirty devil?' John B. slipped back into Felicia' s voice for the next line. 'Of course, one could only do it if it were *right for the part*.'

'Of course. And that being the case, the only one who's in with any chance of scoring is dear old George.'

'Oh, really?' said George Birkitt, misunderstanding, and preening back his hair as if about to open another supermarket. 'Whole thing seemed to go rather damned well tonight, I thought. Never expected to get a round on my first entrance.'

This had been the work of a little claque of television sit com fans, who had greeted their hero's appearance with unruly ecstasy. Once he started speaking Shakespeare, they had grown noticeably quieter.

'No, went well for all of us,' said George, remembering the magnanimity which distinguishes great stars. 'Damned clever little actress, that Felicia, isn't she?'

Yes, way out of your league, Charles thought. He had been deeply impressed by Felicia that night. Given the stimulus of an audience, her performance had gone up several notches. Her talent was awesome. Felicia Chatterton would go far.

He looked across at her. Talking earnestly to Russ. Oh well, that was nice. No doubt, having been let down so badly by her substitute confidant's having gone to sleep, Felicia was returning to what she knew would be a ready audience. They could soon get over the embarrassment of their previous misunderstanding.

And, who could say, now the play had actually opened, maybe Russ would be in with a chance...? Charles doubted it, though. A role as demanding as Lady Macbeth was going to take all her concentration. He rather suspected that the only way to have an affair with Felicia Chatterton would be to book it with her agent six months in advance.

'Smashing, all of you. All the hard work's paid off. I can't thank you enough.' Gavin Scholes had joined them, full of relief and bonhomie.

Also more than a little drunk. A lot of quick alcohol, after two days of eating only the odd sandwich, combined with the relief of actually having opened the play, had left him cheerfully glazed and indiscreet.

'No, you all came up trumps. Terrific. Can't thank you enough. Because God knows I needed this show to be a success.'

'Oh?' asked Charles diffidently.

'Having a bit of trouble with the Board. Money, you know. Not getting enough bums on seats. To be quite frank, my job was on the line. If this show hadn't worked, I could have been out on my ear.'

If that were the case, thought Charles, Warnock Belvedere's disruptive presence must have been even more of a threat. His file of motivation for Gavin Scholes grew.

The mutual congratulation continued for a while, and then George Birkitt and John B. Murgatroyd drifted away to chat up the prettier two Witches.

When they were alone, Gavin looked at Charles and his eyes seemed slowly to find their focus. 'Charles, that policeman was round the office again today.'

'Detective Inspector Dowling?' The Director nodded. 'Wants to have another talk with you.'

'Oh yes?' was all he said, but the news gave Charles an unpleasant *frisson*. 'When?'

'He'll be around tomorrow afternoon. Four-thirty or so. Wondered if you'd mind having a chat between the Schools Matinée and the evening show.'

'No problem,' said Charles with an insouciance that didn't go very deep.

'I wonder what he wants...'

Charles shrugged.

'Presumably he's still investigating Warnock's death,' Gavin mused. 'I thought they'd had the inquest.'

'They have, but it was adjourned pending police enquiries.'

'What does that mean?'

'Well, I assume it means that the police haven't yet worked out what they think about the case.'

Gavin's fuddled mind was having difficulty grasping simple ideas. 'Why, what could they think?'

'Well, they could think it was an accident...'

'Yes.'

'Or they could think it was murder.'

Gavin's jaw sagged. 'You don't believe that they really think that, do you?'

'I don't know what they think. Presumably I will find that out tomorrow.'

'But why you? What can you tell them?'

'I was there, wasn't I? I'm their only possible witness.'

'Yes, but you were dead drunk all the time, weren't you?'

'Suppose the police thought I wasn't telling the truth...? Suppose they thought I just pretended to be out cold...'

The conclusion to Charles's unfinished sentences was, in his mind, that he might then become the police's number one murder suspect. But Gavin's shocked face suggested the director hadn't reached the same conclusion, and his words confirmed it. 'You mean you could have actually seen anything that did go on?'

'If I'd been awake, yes, I could have done,' said Charles, unnerved by the look in Gavin's eyes and trying to lighten the conversation. 'But I was dead to the world. Really.'

'Dead to the world,' the director echoed. His eyes narrowed as he said, 'I hope you really were. For your sake.'

Chapter Sixteen

HIS IMPERSONATION of Felicia Chatterton was now becoming one of John B. Murgatroyd's party pieces. 'But it's just so *difficult*,' he complained huskily in the dressing room on the Wednesday afternoon, 'to try and give a full performance at this time of day. I mean, one's *body-clock* is tuned to peak round eight in the evening, not straight after lunch.'

Charles chuckled, but he could see that Felicia, whom John B. was quoting verbatim, had a point. Matinées are welcomed by few actors. They make for a very long, hard day's work. And they always leave that awkward gap between afternoon and evening performance, not long enough to do anything properly, not long enough to wind down fully before winding oneself up again.

But of course on that particular day, Charles Paris had an engagement to bridge the gap. Detective Inspector Dowling. It was not an engagement he looked forward to.

'It does seem pretty callous scheduling,' he observed, 'to put in a Schools Matinée on the second day of the run.'

'Bums on seats, love.' John B. Murgatroyd's voice had now taken on Gavin Scholes' slightly ineffectual tone. 'Need the money, I'm afraid. Being a set text, you know, we can really cram them in for this show.'

None of the cast had thought much of the prospect of doing two shows on the Wednesday. Indeed, the Equity representative in the company had got quite heavy about it, citing any number of rules and regulations against the scheduling. But of course it had been billed for a long time, the seats had been sold to schools from a wide area, and there was very little that could be done about it.

Charles looked with dissatisfaction at the scar on his face and applied another trickle of blood. Not really very good. But the best he could do if he was going to have to whip it off and appear as an unwounded Sewer in Act One Scene Seven. Hmm, maybe if someone in the company was going up to London, they could buy him a stick-on rubber scar. Trouble with those is you have to match the make-up around them so carefully .

'Ping-ping-ping,' said John B. Murgatroyd suddenly.

'What's that for?'

Back into Felicia's voice for the reply. 'Sorry, just the alarm on the old body-clock. Telling me I need a little sustenance.' John B. reached into his shoulder bag which lay on the floor, and produced a pewter hip-flask. He unscrewed it and proffered the bottle to Charles.

The head was nobly shaken. A saint, not an ordinary man, thought Charles in wry self-congratulation.

'Well, please yourself,' said John B. in his own voice. 'I don't think I could get through a Schools Matinée without a few shots of this.'

Charles watched in a long pang of envy as his friend raised the bottle to his lips and swallowed.

'Sounds fairly rowdy already,' Charles observed, referring to the noise which came from the dressing room Tannoy. Actors all know the familiar buzz of a pre-performance audience, indistinguishable conversations and muffled movements from the stage microphones by the curtain. But the noise from a Schools Matinée is completely different in quality, much higher in pitch and with more giggling and movement. Most of the movement is caused by last-minute changes of seating arrangements, as boys jockey for positions next to the girls they would most like to sit in the dark with, and every child tries to avoid the awful ignominy of sitting next to the teacher.

The lot who were filling the Pinero auditorium that afternoon sounded louder than the average, and that did not augur well for the company.

'What lines do you reckon are going to get them going?' asked Charles.

'The giggles? Hmm.' John B. gave the question serious consideration. 'Well, the Witches'll certainly get a few titters. I'm still not sure Gavin's right to be playing them with lesbian overtones...And when George and Felicia kiss in Act One Scene Five, that'll start the usual whistles and catcalls. Individual lines...? Well, the obvious words'll trigger reactions. "Come to my woman's breasts..." Ooh, and if they're paying attention, George should get a boffo when he sees the line of kings in the Apparition Scene.'

Charles supplied the relevant quotation. '"And some I see

That two-fold balls and treble sceptres carry".'

'Exactly. They'll like "two-fold balls". And George should get a goody on "The devil damn thee black, thou cream-faced loon!"'

'Do you think I'm going to get anything on the Drunken Porter?'

John B. shook his head firmly. 'No chance. What, on a Shakespearean comic character, with school kids? Forget it. Well,' he then conceded generously, 'suppose you might get a tickle on the word "urine", but that's all. Mind you, could get something on your first entrance...'

'As the Porter?'

'No, Bleeding Sergeant. "What bloody man is that?" Should be good for a giggle.'

'Hmm. I think Felicia's going to get the biggest laugh. Wonder how she'll cope with it...?' Charles mused.

'Which line?'

'"I have given suck."'

'Ooh, yes.' John B. giggled with relish. 'Yes, particularly the way she delivers it. With that long pause afterwards, I don't think even the slowest schoolboy mind could miss the ambiguity.'

Charles felt a moment of conscience. 'Do you think we should tip her off? Then she could hurry the line through.'

'No way.' John B. looked professionally affronted. 'Don't be such a wet blanket.'

'Trouble is, John B., I know what I'm like. Once we start getting those sort of laughs, I begin to break up. Giggle through the whole show.'

'Of course. But that's what matinées are *for*, aren't they?'

'Later in the run, maybe.'

'No, right from the start.' John B. Murgatroyd shook his head like a parent whose son has just been caught smoking cannabis behind the school cycle-sheds. 'Honestly, Charles, since you've given up the booze, you've got really prissy.'

To reinforce his point, he took another infuriatingly slow swig from the hip-flask.

At that moment the dressing-room door opened to admit Gavin Scholes. As if by magic, the hip-flask disappeared into the folds of Lennox's brocaded gown.

'Oh, Charles,' said the director. 'Just a note I forgot to give you yesterday.'

Was it imagination, or did Gavin really seem to be avoiding his eye?

'Yes? Which character is this a note for?'

'Apparition of an Armed Head.'

'Right, I'm now thinking Apparition of an Armed Head.'

'Last night from out front it looked as if you had been waiting in the cauldron all evening.'

'What do you mean?'

'Well, your head sort of came up tentatively.'

'You try not being tentative on that trap-door platform. It's very unstable. Particularly when you're not allowed to show your torso, because that's still dressed as the Third Murderer.'

'But it looked as if you were holding on to the sides.'

'You bet I was holding on to the sides. Bloody dangerous with that thing if you don't.'

'Well, could you try it not holding on?'

Charles looked dubious.

'Oh, go on, just for this afternoon. Please. Must dash.'

As the director hurried out of the dressing room, Charles felt a little cold tremor run down his back.

It was a riotous performance, for the audience at least. Every line John B. Murgatroyd had predicted got its laugh, and a good few others did as well. The audience of schoolchildren, confident that their teachers could not identify them individually in the dark, settled down to have a good time. Having early on decided that the cause of that good time was not going to be Shakespeare's great drama, they enjoyed every ambiguity the text offered.

The company could not be immune to what was happening in the auditorium and, again as John B. had predicted, they became very giggly and undisciplined. George Birkitt seemed unworried by all this; perhaps all his years of television sit coms had led him to expect laughs in whatever role he played. But, for Felicia Chatterton, to judge from the tight scribble of lines between her brows, it was a very trying experience.

Charles Paris didn't enjoy the performance, either. Two anxieties preoccupied him as he ran through his repertoire of parts.

First, he was worried about the imminent interview with Detective Inspector Dowling.

And, second, he was worried that Gavin Scholes wanted to ensure that that interview did not take place.

Charles reasoned it thus. If, as he was coming increasingly to believe, the director had killed Warnock Belvedere, and if, as their conversation of the previous evening suggested, Gavin was afraid Charles had witnessed that crime, then the obvious course was to eliminate the witness before his follow-up interview with Detective Inspector Dowling. Which logic did nothing to put Charles at his ease.

So he was very wary throughout the Schools Matinée. He was uncomfortably aware of the number of potential murder methods a theatre offered. Scenery could fall on people. They could be 'assisted' down flights of stairs. And of course Macbeth demanded a whole armoury of swords and daggers. With so much lethal hardware around, and with much of the action played in half-light, it was no surprise that ugly stories of fatal accidents had built up around the play.

And then there was the trap-door. In rehearsal John B. Murgatroyd had demonstrated that the apparatus could at least give someone a nasty jolt. Charles wondered uneasily whether it could be doctored to cause more permanent damage.

There was no sign of Gavin as Charles, in his coal-scuttle helmet, moved cautiously towards the wooden framework under the stage. The usual Assistant Stage Manager stood by to operate the mechanism, and looked curious as Charles inspected the ropework.

'What's the matter?' the boy hissed.

'Just double-checking,' Charles hissed back.

'It's okay.'

'Did Gavin give you any notes on the trap-door?'

'Said I should bring you up faster.'

'Well, ignore the note. I'm quite happy with the speed I have been going.'

'Look, if Gavin said –'

But above them the three Witches were chanting,

'Come high or low, Thyself and office deftly show.' With a silent prayer, Charles mounted the platform. He took a firm hold on the sides of the cradle, and closed his eyes as he felt the platform surge beneath him.

There was a sudden sharp pain in his knuckles as he broke through the stage and they were barked against the edge of the trap's opening.

In the moment of pain he forgot to crouch.

The Apparition of an Armed Head burst through the bubbling dry ice vapour in the cauldron, with its helmet askew, and rose to reveal its Third Murderer costume underneath. One agonised hand was clutched in its armpit, and from its lips emerged the involuntary word 'Shit!'

The Schools Matinée audience were loud in their appreciation of the best bit of Shakespeare they'd ever seen.

He didn't know. Certainly he'd never held on so tight to the cradle before, so maybe that was why he had barked his knuckles. Alternatively, the apparatus might have been booby-trapped (though, fortunately, inadequately booby-trapped).

All he did know was that he was going to keep his eyes skinned for the rest of the performance.

And he would be very relieved when the fights were over.

Charles had more costumes than the other actors in his dressing room, and, since some of his changes were so quick they had to take place in the wings, it took him a little while to collect up all his belongings after the performance. This was a chore that should have been done by Wardrobe, but he didn't have much confidence in the girl with orange-streaked hair, and preferred to be responsible for his own stuff. Nothing worse for an actor than suddenly to find he hasn't got the right pair of trousers in the middle of a quick change.

So, by the time he got back to his dressing room after the Schools Matinée, its other residents had already doffed their armour and rushed to get out of the theatre for a break before the evening show.

Charles was hanging up his costumes on a long, wheeled rack, when he heard the door open behind him.

He turned sharply to see Gavin Scholes. The director was breathing heavily, and looked flustered and upset.

'Oh, Charles. Others all gone?'

'Yes.'

It was then that Charles noticed Gavin was carrying the sword used by Macbeth in his final fight.

Chapter Seventeen

STILL, GAVIN SCHOLES seemed to be avoiding Charles's eye. 'Charles, I have something to ask you...'

'Yes?' He spoke casually, but he was carefully assessing the distance between him and the sword which he had so recently seen carried in the service of both Malcolm and Macbeth.

'I don't like doing it, but I'm afraid I've made a ghastly cock-up...'

'Oh yes? What?'

The tension was great, but the bathos was greater.

'Look, I'd completely forgotten, but when I set up this matinée, I agreed with one of the teachers that I'd lead a discussion of the play afterwards. With the cast.'

'Oh.'

'And I've just bumped into the bloke and he's reminded me about it, and I've dashed back here and everyone else seems to have gone. So I'm sorry, Charles, but would you mind coming and talking to them?'

'No. No problem. Have I got time to get out of costume?'

Gavin grimaced. 'Sorry. I've kept them waiting some time already.'

'Okay. Don't worry. Just one thing, Gavin,' Charles asked, 'why have you got that sword?'

'Oh, give them something to look at. There's sure to be a question about whether or not the swords are real.'

Charles felt relieved. But he still kept his distance from Gavin as they left the dressing room.

In the passage outside, another shock awaited him. The door to the liquor storeroom, on which a new padlock had been fixed, was open. Inside, Norman Phipps could be seen, piling up crates of bottles.

Outside, watching him, stood Detective Inspector Dowling.

The policeman turned at the sound of the dressing-room door. 'Ah, Mr Paris. I was just having another look at the scene of the...er, accident. Are you ready for our little chat?'

Charles explained about the discussion. Gavin endorsed how important it was that Charles should participate.

'Fine,' said the Detective Inspector blandly. 'It'll keep for half an hour. May I use your office again, Mr Scholes?'

'Of course.'

'See you up there when you're ready, Mr Paris.'

The discussion was predictable. The boys of only one school had stayed to talk about the play, and clearly they had done so not of their own volition, but because their teacher had told them to.

The boys were also disappointed to see the Director accompanied on the stage by only one member of the cast. And, though the range of that member's performance had encompassed the Bleeding Sergeant, the Sewer, the Drunken Porter, the Old Man, the Third Murderer, the Apparition of an Armed Head, the English Doctor, the Scottish Doctor, and soldiers fighting on both sides in the final battle, they did not disguise the fact that they would rather have seen George Birkitt, whom they knew from the telly, or Felicia Chatterton, who was dead dishy.

Gavin gave a brief exposition of his view of the play, which seemed to engage his audience's attention no more than had the actual performance, and then invited questions.

The response was sluggish; only heavy prompting from their teacher, a small, enthusiastic man with gold-rimmed glasses and a wispy beard, elicited anything.

The first question was the one Gavin had anticipated about real swords, and, with a knowing look to Charles, he produced Macbeth's weapon from the wings. He then asked if any of them would like to look at it. This was unwise, because it precipitated a rush on to the stage. The sword was snatched from him and brandished dangerously by a series of small hands before order was re-imposed by the teacher.

'If you've got real weapons,' asked a grumpy voice from the front row, 'why didn't the fights look more realistic?'

'Oh, I thought they were quite realistic,' Gavin objected defensively.

This was greeted by a chorus of derision. 'No way', 'They were pathetic', 'I could do it tons better', 'No, they were missing each other by miles' and '*The A-Team*'s much better' came from various parts of the auditorium.

'Yeah.' The grumpy voice from the front row added a supplementary question. 'Why isn't *Macbeth* more like *The A-Team*?'

This enquiry was greeted with considerable enthusiasm and seemed to be the cue for a series of machine-gun noises and Mr T impressions.

'Well,' said Gavin as the hubbub subsided, 'I think this is one that perhaps Charles can answer better than I can.'

You bastard, thought Charles, as he scraped the bottom of his mind for something to say. He had at least heard of *The A-Team*, thank God. When he had last seen his grandsons, Juliet's boys (which, he realised with horror, had been nearly six months previously), they had talked of nothing else.

'Um, well, you see, what you have to remember is that, for the people of Shakespeare's time, there was no television. Plays were their television, if you like.'

'Cor, give me *Eastenders* any day,' came an opinion from the back of the auditorium.

Charles persevered. 'So for them, you see, the theatre provided everything. Tragedy, comedy...'

'Where's the comedy?' demanded an aggressive recently-broken voice.

'Well, even in *Macbeth*, there's comedy.'

'Where?'

'The Drunken Porter. He's a comic character.'

'But he's not *funny*.'

'No, I know he's not *funny*, but he is a comic character.' Dear, oh dear, this is uphill work, thought Charles. How on earth does Frances manage to be a teacher, doing this every day? 'You see, for people of Shakespeare's time, the Porter was making very good jokes.' He parroted this opinion because he had heard it so often stated, but he couldn't really bring himself to believe it. 'You see, you have the latest sit com, but in the same way the people of Shakespeare's time had the Drunken Porter. You have *The A-Team*, they had *Macbeth*.'

'Poor sods,' said a voice from the back.

The short bearded teacher leapt up in fury. 'Who said that? Come on, who said it? We are not leaving this theatre until the boy who said that word owns up.'

Oh God, thought Charles. We could be here all night.

'Now, come on, I don't care what language you use at home, but when you're in my charge, you don't use those kind of words. What will Mr Scholes and Mr .er...the other gentleman think of you?'

'I don't think they'll actually mind,' said an earnest owl-faced boy sitting near the teacher. 'I think they're probably used to it. I mean, when that one...' He pointed at Charles '...popped out of the pot, he said "Shit".'

This was greeted by choruses of 'Yes, he did', 'Protheroe's right, sir', 'He really did, he said "Shit"' and 'Did Shakespeare write that?' Once again it was a while before a relative calm was re-established.

'Any further questions?' asked the bearded teacher, glaring round the auditorium.

The owl-faced boy raised his hand. 'Yes, sir, please, sir,' he asked with the same unsmiling earnestness.

'Right, Protheroe, what's your question?'

'Well, sir, it's about that bit with the pot.'

'Cauldron, Protheroe.'

'What, sir?'

'It's called a cauldron.'

'What is, sir?'

'The pot, Protheroe.'

'Oh yes, sir, right, sir. Well...when all those people popped out of the pot...'

'Yes?' Gavin Scholes smiled encouragingly at the boy.

'Were the Witches going to eat them?'

'I'm sorry?'

'That's my question – were the Witches cannibals?'

'Don't be stupid, Protheroe.' The teacher's hand reached round to clip the boy's ear.

'But I wasn't being stupid, sir. I really meant it. It was a serious – ow!'

The teacher rode over a chorus of 'Ooh, you hit Protheroe's and turned to address the two figures on the stage.

'I must apologise for the stupidity of some of my pupils. But I would like to say…' At this point he reached into his pocket and produced a file card scribbled with notes. Oh no, Charles groaned inwardly, speeches. 'I would like to say how much we appreciate having had this opportunity of talking to you about the…er…' He heavily italicised the next words '…*nuts and bolts* of production. We realise that you are all…er, both…busy people, and we do appreciate you giving up your time to give us a *glimpse backstage*. As Head of English, I am aware that I can talk about a play until I'm blue in the face – and I'm sure some of my pupils present today reckon I do…' He waited for reaction, but his charges were too familiar with his jokes to bother to give him any. 'Be that as it may…' For a moment he lost his place in his notes. 'Be that as it may, yes…Yes, well, I can talk about a play till I'm blue in the face, but I'm sure the boys learn a hundred times more by actually seeing the play in production. I sometimes think the best way for them to get to know *Macbeth* is for us actually to mount a school production, but unfortunately, with Mr Palmer currently locked into rehearsal of *Joseph and his Amazing Technicolour Dreamcoat*, that is not logistically possible.' He lost his way. 'Be that as it may…And it is…I would like, finally…' Thank God, thought Charles. '…er, finally, to thank Mr Scholes and Mr…er…' The teacher glanced down at his programme '…Mr. Murgatroyd…' Huh, thought Charles, so much for all my finely-differentiated character work '…for giving up their time and leading such a stimulating discussion. So, boys…' He turned back towards the auditorium '…I would be grateful if you could show your appreciation in the usual way.'

With three rousing 'Hip hip's, he wrung three limp 'Hooray's from the boys, who immediately started to shuffle out of the auditorium, and the discussion was over.

Charles watched Gavin warily as they left the stage, but the director did not seem too interested in him. 'Thanks very much for your help, Charles. I must go and sort a few things out in the office.'

'Well, if Dowling's up there, tell him I'm on my way.'

'Oh, I'd forgotten about him,' said Gavin casually, as he set off up the auditorium.

Charles wondered if that could possibly be true.

He changed back into his ordinary clothes and left his dressing room.

Through the open door of the store-room, he could still see Norman reorganising his supplies of drink. It seemed months to Charles since he had discovered Warnock Belvedere's beer-sodden body there, but he knew grimly that he was about to relive that experience in an interview that could prove to be very uncomfortable.

He slipped through a pass-door into the theatre foyer and was about to start up the stairs towards Gavin's office when he caught sight of movement through the glass doors at the front of the theatre.

The bearded schoolmaster was tetchily herding his recalcitrant charges into a minibus.

But it was what was printed on the side of the minibus that caught Charles's attention.

And it brought instantly to his mind another possible solution to the mystery of Warnock Belvedere's death.

Chapter Eighteen

CHARLES RUSHED back into the theatre foyer as the school minibus drove away. At the foot of the stairs stood Detective Inspector Dowling. 'On my way up to Mr Scholes' office. Care to join me?'

'Just a sec. Must just sort out something at the Box Office.'

The detective cocked an ironical eyebrow at him. 'A more sensitive man, Mr Paris, might think you were trying to avoid him.'

'Only take a minute, I promise.'

Dowling glanced at his watch. 'Very well. See you up there.' And he started up the stairs.

Charles looked through the window of the Box Office to confirm who was on duty, but he went through the pass-door out of the foyer and entered the small room by its back door.

Sandra Phipps looked round in surprise. She sat there, queen of her domain, theatre plans spread over the telephones on the counter in front of her. Behind her were rows of wooden pigeon-holes, each with its stock of different-coloured tickets and its date neatly printed on the frame.

'Charles. What do you want? If it's about comps, you should come to the window, you know.'

She looked tired. The defiant brassiness was still there, but under their make-up, her eyes sagged. Her shoulders, under the tight satin of her blouse, drooped.

'I know,' said Charles. 'It's not about comps.'

'Oh?'

'It's about Stewart.'

Panic flashed in her eye. 'Is he all right?' Sandra asked.

'Yes, he's fine.' She slumped with relief. 'Or at least he's not fine, is he?'

'What do you mean?'

'Well, he's not gone to school today, has he?'

'No. Tonsillitis.'

'Stayed at home.'

'Yes. He often gets it. Look, Charles, what is this? What are you on about?'

Before he could answer, the phone rang. Sandra answered it. 'Pinero Theatre Box Office.'

She took the booking punctiliously, shuffling her plans to check availability, offering a range of prices, repeating the details of the caller's credit card.

When the call was over, she turned back to Charles. '*Macbeth*'s booking very well. Seems like Gavin's got a success on his hands. Of course, George is a good telly name...' Charles said nothing, as she reached round to the relevant pigeonhole and withdrew a book of tickets, from which she tore two, carefully checking the printed details. 'What I really need,' she continued, 'is to have this whole system computerised. But of course that's money, and...'

She seemed to realise that this babbling was not getting her anywhere. She looked straight at Charles. 'What is this about Stewart?'

'Just a pity he should be ill today. When St. Joseph's had a trip to *Macbeth*.'

Sandra shrugged. 'Yes, it's bad luck. But the run's only just started. Be plenty of other opportunities to see the show. I'm sure I can slip him in.'

'I don't think you will, though, Sandra. Will you?'

She flushed as she looked up at him.

'What do you mean?'

'I've just been talking to Stewart's form teacher.'

'Oh?'

'He's the Head of English at the school.'

'I know that,' she snapped.

'Which is why he led the school party to the play.'

'So...'

'He said in the after-show discussion that he thought his pupils would learn more by seeing the play than by any amount of talking about it.'

'Look, it's very good of you to take my son's education so much to heart. I will ensure that he sees the play at some point. Will that satisfy you or would you rather –?'

Charles cut through her heavy sarcasm. 'Stewart's form teacher also said how much he thought his pupils would learn by actually being in a production of the play...'

Sandra avoided his eye. 'Well, yes, I'm sure they would, but I don't see what –'

'And yet you say he stopped Stewart from taking part.'

'Yes. The understanding was, right from the start, that Stewart could do it, so long as his work didn't suffer. Unfortunately, because the rehearsal schedule got out of hand, he missed some homework and...' She gestured helplessly. '...that was it.'

'I see.' Charles let her relax for a moment before continuing, 'Except that Stewart's form teacher gives a completely different version of events.'

'What?'

'He says he never made any fuss about Stewart's work. He didn't care a great deal. He reckoned a boy who wasn't basically academic was going to learn more about *Macbeth* by being in the production as Macduff's Son than by writing any number of essays about it. He said he didn't care how much time Stewart needed to have off for rehearsals.'

'Well then, he's changed his tune. He told me –'

'No, he didn't. You told him. He didn't ring you over the weekend after the first run-through. You rang him, and said that the rehearsals were proving too much for Stewart, that he was getting overtired, and you thought it was your duty, as his mother, to pull him out of the show.'

'Well, all right, what if I did?'

A tap on the glass in front of her drew her attention. 'Excuse me. Do you have two tickets for this Saturday's matinée? They will be at Senior Citizen rates.'

She concentrated once again on her charts and dealt with the booking. Her voice retained its customary professional cheer, but from behind her, Charles could see the flush spreading to her neck.

When the Senior Citizens had departed with the tickets, she turned back to him. 'All right, so I thought the show was too much for Stewart. That was my judgement as his mother. What's wrong with that?'

'If that was the case, why did you tell Gavin it was the school that objected?'

'I thought it sounded better. If I said it was just me, Gavin would have tried to persuade me.'

Charles nodded. 'Good. But not, I'm afraid, good enough.'

'What are you suggesting?'

'I'm suggesting that tiredness wasn't the reason you wanted Stewart out of the production. I'm suggesting that there was something about this production of *Macbeth* that upset your son. That still upsets him, which is why he suddenly developed tonsillitis this morning, so that he didn't have to come and see it.'

'I don't know what you're talking about.'

'But I do.'

And he did. Suddenly, he saw what had happened with dazzling clarity. It was all in the play. Think about Gavin Scholes' production of *Macbeth* and it all became clear.

Charles had observed before that nearly everyone was involved in the battle scenes. Even Lady Macduff and the Witches had to change sex and don armour. So once the battle scenes started, almost all the company would be milling round the stage area, and the dressing room area would be virtually deserted.

As it had been at the end of the first Saturday run-through.

In fact, there would only have been three people in the dressing room area.

Felicia Chatterton, having given her all in the Sleepwalking Scene, would be lying on her dressing-room floor doing relaxation exercises.

That left two.

Warnock Belvedere, who had refused to double, had been there since the end of Act One Scene Six.

And Stewart Phipps, good-looking thirteen-year-old Stewart, had been there since Charles and the other Murderers had killed him in Act Four Scene Two.

'I think, Sandra, that what upset Stewart about this production of *Macbeth* was that Warnock Belvedere made a pass at him.'

The panic in her eyes told him that his guess had been right.

'And I think that that is the reason why Warnock Belvedere was murdered.'

All of the colour drained from Sandra Phipps' face.

Chapter Nineteen

NORMAN PHIPPS was still reorganising his store-room when Charles Paris found him. The actor looked at the tubes from the beer kegs and gas cylinders. All had been replaced and looked as good as new. There was no sign that this was the place where one elderly actor had met his untimely, but universally welcomed, demise.

Norman looked up and nodded a greeting. He avoided words whenever they weren't strictly necessary.

'Norman, I've just been talking to Sandra...'

'Oh yes?'

'About Stewart and what happened.'

Norman deliberately placed another crate on top of a pile. 'How do you mean – what happened?' he asked evenly.

'About Warnock Belvedere.'

The Bar Manager froze for a split second before asking, 'What about Warnock Belvedere?'

'About how he died.'

'I thought we knew that. Asphyxiation from the carbon dioxide.'

'Yes, but what caused it?'

Norman gave a little shrug. 'He was drunk, wasn't he?'

'On a bottle of Courvoisier.'

'On top of what he'd had in the bar, yes. Surprising the drink alone didn't kill him.'

'Hmm. The question is – where did he get that Courvoisier from?'

Norman looked Charles straight in the eye. 'Police seem to reckon he got it out of this cupboard. After he'd broken in here.'

'I think he had it before he broke in here.'

'Seems unlikely.' Still there was no change in the man's even intonation.

'I know he had it before he broke in here,' said Charles.

'Oh. How's that?'

'I saw him when I came down from the bar at closing time.'

Norman Phipps again saved words, but said it all with a sceptically raised eyebrow.

'Yes, I know I was pissed, but not that pissed. He was definitely holding a bottle, and he said it had been given him by a "generous friend".'

'Afraid I didn't know any of his friends,' said Norman, turning back to his pile of crates.

'There was another suspicious thing about the death.' Charles waited for a reaction, but didn't get it. 'When I found Warnock's body in here, the light was switched off.'

Again, the momentary freeze before Norman said, 'So what?'

'It seems unlikely that he switched the light out before conveniently passing out on the floor.'

'Possible.'

'But, as I say, unlikely.'

A non-committal shrug.

'Norman, Sandra says she gave Warnock that bottle of brandy.'

This, at last, did produce a reaction. Norman's body went rigid; then he turned slowly to face Charles. To the latter's surprise, on the Bar Manager's face was a smile of pleasure. 'Did she?' he asked softly.

'Yes. She did. Which would suggest very strongly that she was responsible for Warnock's death.'

Norman Phipps shook his head slowly. 'No,' he said. 'She's lying.'

But he didn't say the words as if they were important. The feeling of pleasure still meant more to him. As a casual afterthought, he added, 'Sandra didn't kill him. I did.'

'Because of what he did to Stewart?'

A slow nod of the head. 'Yes. I wouldn't have done it. I thought Stewart would just get over the experience, in time. I mean, I agreed he should come out of the production, but that was all. Not enough for Sandra, though. I suppose she was feeling guilty. She should have been keeping an eye on him. That's what a chaperone in the theatre's for, isn't it?'

Charles nodded. 'Yes, to protect children from people like Warnock... amongst other things.'

'Hmm. Norman spoke as if in a dream. 'Anyway, Sandra went on so, I had to do something...'

So Charles had been right. It was like *Macbeth*, the woman urging the man to murder. But he had got the personnel wrong. Not Felicia Chatterton and Russ Lavery, but Sandra and Norman Phipps.

It all fitted. Even, he thought, ironically, down to Duncan being murdered by his host. Hadn't Warnock always insisted on addressing Norman as 'Mine Host'?

'So what you mean is that Sandra told you to kill him?'

'No. It wasn't like that.'

'How was it then?' asked Charles Paris gently.

The Bar Manager came out of his reverie and focused on his interrogator. 'Not a great marriage, Sandra and me. Doesn't look that good from the outside, does it? Afraid it's not that much better from the inside. Fact is, we're...different. Sandra's more...what's the word? Passionate? Physical?'

'I see.'

'Yes, I bet you do. What I mean is, in crude terms, she likes sex more than I do. I don't mind it once in a while, but…'

He shrugged.

'So the alibi she gave the police…'

He let out a short bark of laughter. 'Just getting at me. Again.'

'Like she got at you over Stewart?'

Norman Phipps nodded. 'She went on and on about it. Said that an experience like that, at that age, would make a boy homosexual for life…'

Now it was Charles's turn to be quiet. He didn't want to break the intimacy of the confessional.

'I said I thought he'd get over it, and then she said…she said…' His voice did not break, but he seemed to be having physical difficulty in getting the words out. 'She said that he'd grow up like his father. She implied that the reason I didn't like sex as much as she did was that I was…that I wasn't a real man…'

His voice stopped again, but still his manner remained unemotional.

'She said a real man wouldn't let someone like Warnock get away with doing something like that to his son.'

'So you thought you'd show her?' Charles prompted gently. 'Show her that Warnock hadn't got away with it?'

A slow 'Yes' and a nod. 'It wasn't difficult. I'd thought about the carbon dioxide many times before. I once nearly passed out down here when I was fixing that electrical socket.' He pointed to the bottom of the wall. 'There was a leak from one of the cylinders. I knew what was happening, so I just got out. But, even at the time, I remember wondering what it would be like for someone who was already unconscious.

'You're right, of course, I had got the bottle out earlier. Just left it on the table in his dressing room.'

'But how did you know he'd stay in the theatre? He might have taken the bottle back to his digs.'

'I went down just after closing time. I…' For the first time, the voice was choked with emotion. 'I told him that…that Stewart had liked what he'd done. I said Stewart wanted to see him again. I said, if he waited in the dressing room, I'd…bring Stewart to him.' That fitted. Charles remembered Warnock's unwholesome desire for a 'nice little bumboy'. He also remembered with distaste that the old actor had even propositioned *him*. So, with Norman's offer of his son, and a bottle of brandy to while away the time, Warnock would happily wait in his dressing room.

'I went home with Sandra usual time. I waited an hour, then came back to the theatre. I've got keys, you know.'

'Was Sandra asleep?'

'Just about. She doesn't sleep well.' Lady Macbeth again, thought Charles. 'As I had hoped, the old bastard was out cold. I took his stick and used it to break the locks. Then I dragged him in, laid him on his face and put the empty bottle in his hand.'

'Did you wear gloves?'

Norman shook his head. 'I've handled everything in this room. Nothing odd to find my prints on the bottle. And there would be plenty of his.

'Then I broke the beer tubes and the gas lines. I closed the door, to make doubly sure the CO_2 wouldn't escape, and waited.'

'How long?'

'Twenty minutes. When I opened the door, the job was done.'

'So then you made your one mistake by switching off the light, and went back home?'

'That's it. Sandra was awake when I got back, worried where I'd been. I told her what I'd done, but she...she...' Once again emotion threatened. '...she didn't react like I'd hoped...'

The murderer turned away, and rubbed the back of his hand noisily against his nose. When he turned back, he asked pathetically, 'But she really did say she'd given him the bottle of brandy?'

'Yes, she did.'

Norman Phipps let out a sigh. Again, the information seemed to comfort him. Perhaps it proved that, beneath the jagged surface of their marriage, his wife really did feel some love for him.

'Mr Paris...'

Charles turned guiltily at the sound of the voice behind him.

Detective Inspector Dowling stood framed in the doorway. There was no longer any diffidence in his manner; on his face was an expression of uncompromising anger. 'You're not going to be able to hide from me, Mr Paris.'

'Oh, I wasn't trying to. I just...' Charles felt himself blushing. Why did he always revert to a guilty adolescent when faced by an authority figure?

'I've had enough faffing around, Mr Paris,' the Detective Inspector continued. 'I want to ask you some serious questions about the murder of Warnock Belvedere.'

Oh, thought Charles in panic, so the police know it was murder. Oh God, and I'm still their main suspect and they're bound to –'

But his illogical ramblings were interrupted by a voice from the other side of the room.

'I think, Detective Inspector,' said Norman Phipps quietly, 'that I'm the one you want to talk to.'

Chapter Twenty

IT WAS THE following Wednesday's Schools Matinée, and the buzz from the auditorium on the dressing-room Tannoy sounded even more hectic than the week before.

'This lot's going to be trouble,' said John B. Murgatroyd, his voice strangely muffled inside his helmet.

'Why are you wearing that bloody thing?' asked Charles.

'Protection, laddie, protection. Filter the beer fumes emanating from your gob, me old chum.'

Charles giggled weakly. Shouldn't have gone into the bar at lunchtime. Fatal. He knew that, really. And shouldn't have had three pints. Would have a desperate urge to pee in the middle of the Apparition Scene. Oh dear, wouldn't do to pee in the Witches' cauldron.

Still, it was only a Schools Matinée.

His pledge had lasted till after the previous Wednesday's second show, but no longer. Well, he had promised himself a drink once he'd worked out who'd killed Warnock Belvedere. In fact, in all the relief of ceasing to be a murder suspect, it'd been a good few drinks.

And the familiar dry ache of a hangover had greeted him on the Thursday morning. It hurt, but it certainly felt more normal. Felicia Chatterton might go on about her body-clock, but Charles Paris had one too, and his had been thrown seriously out of kilter by those eight days without the regular imperatives of licensing hours.

Eight days. Not bad. Damned nearly nine days. At least, he could prove he could do it. Drink? Well, I can take it or leave it, he would now be able to say with confidence. But he wouldn't leave it again for a while.

Well over a week, though. Pretty good. Well over the week that he'd promised himself he would announce to Frances as a proof of his reformed character.

The trouble was, he hadn't got round to ringing her during the period of actual abstinence, and to ring her and speak of it retrospectively wouldn't have quite the same dramatic effect.

No, he'd have to think of another approach. He would ring her soon. Really.

'Saw some of the kids coming in.' John B. Murgatroyd's muffled voice brought him back to reality. 'Looked a right load of scruffs. Yes, I think they're going to be trouble. Still, Gavin's away,' he added innocently.

There wasn't much comfort for Charles in the director's absence. Gavin was in London auditioning for his production after next, Alan Ayckbourn's *Ten Times Table*. He was already into rehearsal for *Deathtrap*, the second show of the season. And he hadn't drawn Charles aside for a little chat about either play. So it looked as if Maurice Skellern's optimism about 'other parts' had been misplaced. Once *Macbeth* finished its run, it was going to be back to London, with all the delights of his bedsitter and the Lisson Grove Unemployment Office, for Charles Paris.

Oh well, wouldn't be the first time.

And at least Russ Lavery had been kept on to play the young man in *Deathtrap*. Good part for someone so new to the business. That boy will go far, thought Charles, with only a twinge of jealousy.

John B. Murgatroyd reached into the folds of his Lennox gown and produced the hip-flask. This time Charles accepted his offer.

'Settle the beer,' he said, somehow making the whisky sound like a medical necessity.

'Five minutes, please,' called the Stage Manager's voice over the Tannoy, facing Charles with a dilemma of the bladder. He felt he should have a pee before the show started, but it was more a logical thought than an urgent necessity. And he knew, with that amount of beer inside him, if he had one pee, he'd be peeing all afternoon. Better to keep his nerve and hold it. Sometimes go for hours like that.

On the other hand...It would be dreadful to be taken short on stage. He didn't want to add a new legend to the apocrypha of stories of actors peeing into pot-plants, bottles and armour during performances.

Hmm. Tricky one.

He succumbed and had a pee.

As soon as the play started, it was evident that John B. Murgatroyd's assessment of the audience had erred on the side of charity. They were an awful load of little buggers.

They greeted the Witches' first appearance with raucous catcalls, which drowned most of their words. And, predictably enough, Duncan's opening line, 'What bloody man is that?' got a huge belter.

The bloody man in question, waiting at the back of the auditorium, felt a tremor pass through Lennox, who was supporting him. 'Come on, love,' murmured John B. Murgatroyd, and began to steer the Bleeding Sergeant down the aisle.

They would never be absolutely certain, but they both remained convinced to the end of their days that the leg outstretched across the gangway had been deliberately placed. Certainly no planning could have made it more effective. Charles lost his footing and stumbled forward, dragging John B. in his wake.

Their tumbled arrival at the foot of the stage was rewarded by a huge laugh. The audience of schoolchildren settled back. They were going to enjoy this.

Charles was still supported by Lennox, as per rehearsal, when he went through the Bleeding Sergeant's somewhat wordy account of Macbeth and Banquo's battle against 'the merciless Macdonwald'. At one point he looked full into Lennox's face, and at that moment John B. Murgatroyd closed his eyes.

Charles realised instantly why his friend had kept his helmet on in the dressing room. This joke had taken preparation. Neatly written on the pale make-up of the right eyelid was the word 'Fuck'; and on the left eyelid the word 'Off'.

Charles, who was maundering on about 'shipwracking storms and direful thunders', felt his voice begin to tremble as the giggle caught up with him. John B., making it look as if he were helping out his ailing comrade, slapped him on the back and took his hand in a comforting, manly grasp.

Charles felt something hard and round thrust into his hand. Squinting as he tried to continue his lines, he looked down.

There, nestling in his palm, was a walnut.

While being dragged off to have his gashes attended to (moving rather faster than usual because he was desperate for another pee), Charles managed to fall against Donalbain, and as the other actor reached to help him, shoved the walnut into his unsuspecting hand.

From there on, throughout the play it did the rounds, provoking a whole lot of giggling backstage, and a whole lot of new moves onstage, as actors desperately tried to avoid the fate of being the one who had to take the walnut off.

And the audience continued to chatter, whistle and devise other diversionary tactics.

They rustled crisp packets. Then one of them, no doubt a future captain of industry, had the bright idea of blowing them up and bursting them.

In a more planned campaign, a group of them set the alarms of their digital watches to go off at one-minute intervals.

And, meanwhile, the barracking also continued. Many lines took on new and filthy meanings. All the play's dramatic climaxes were defused by heckling.

'I have done the deed,' Macbeth announced.

'Ooh, you dirty beast!' came a cry from the audience.

In the Banquet Scene Lady Macbeth's line, 'When all's done, You look but on a stool' was capped by a call of 'Well, you should have flushed it, shouldn't you?'

As the Witches loaded their ingredients into the cauldron there were demands for more ketchup.

And so on and so on.

Once that kind of thing starts in a performance, it's difficult to stop, and the cast, relaxed into the second week of their run and secure in the knowledge that Gavin Scholes was in London for the day, made little attempt to stop it.

Mounting hysteria ran through the company. They knew it was unprofessional, they knew they shouldn't. But they did.

Felicia Chatterton alone seemed immune to the general mood. She was incapable of levity and continued, against all the odds, to give her Lady Macbeth.

And it was good. As ever, Charles had to admit that. But he really would like to see her break up on stage. Just once.

He watched her as she drifted about the stage in her low-cut nightgown for the Sleepwalking Scene. Oblivious to the catcalls from the audience, her concentration on the role remained total.

He moved his legs uneasily. Oh God, he couldn't need yet *another* pee, could he? He tried to think of something else.

The Gentlewoman in the scene seemed to be acting closer to him than usual, and as she said the line, 'I would not have such a heart in my bosom for the dignity of the whole body', she suddenly tapped Charles on the shoulder.

He started at the unexpected action, and as he turned, felt a familiar object thrust into his hand. The Gentlewoman, backing away downstage, stuck her tongue out at him.

Charles Paris knew he shouldn't, but he couldn't resist it.

He walked across to the sleepwalking Lady Macbeth, and neatly dropped the walnut down her delicious cleavage.

He was rewarded by a look of amazement, and then a sweet, sweet moment as Felicia Chatterton dissolved into uncontrollable giggles.